W9-BTB-803

# PRAISE FOR LINDA JONES, WINNER OF THE COLORADO ROMANCE WRITERS 1997 AWARD OF EXCELLENCE!

### *DESPERADO'S GOLD*
". . . a heartwarming time-travel romance, portraying that true love can exist in any world."
—*Rawhide & Lace*

". . . a tale of trust, courage and a passion that transcends time. Readers will be hooked from page one."
—*Romantic Times*

### *SOMEONE'S BEEN SLEEPING IN MY BED*
"This brightly written romantic allegory sparkles with humor and shines with fairytale joy."
—*Romantic Times*

### *LET ME COME IN*
". . . a book to reread again and again—a definite keeper!"
—*Rendezvous*

Paperback Heaven
Book Exchange
Rt. 45 & Alliance Avenue
Heights Liquor Plaza
Woodbury Heights, NJ 08097

# RAGING DESIRE

If Rafael held any grudge for last night's refusal, he didn't show it. His smile was easy as his eyes flickered pleasantly over her from head to toe.

"I trust you slept well after the storm passed," he said blandly.

Sabrina hadn't been able to close her eyes even for five minutes after he'd left the cabin. "Very well, thank you. And you?" Her answer, her lie, was so polite, so distant.

"I slept not at all," he said nonchalantly, and with a wicked grin. "One storm passed, but another raged on."

Surely she turned eight different shades of red. She could feel the heat in her cheeks. All she could manage was a weak, "Oh."

Rafael lowered his voice, and moving very slowly he placed his face close to hers. "How many times must I tell you not to lie to me? You slept no better than I, for the same storm raged within you, *sirena mia*. Do not deny it."

She couldn't. At the moment she couldn't find any words at all.

Paperback Heaven
Book Exchange
Rt. 45 & Alliance Avenue
Heights Liquor Plaza
Woodbury Heights, NJ 08097

Other *Love Spell* and *Leisure* books
by Linda Jones:
**LET ME COME IN**
**BIG BAD WOLF**
**DESPERADO'S GOLD**
**SOMEONE'S BEEN SLEEPING IN MY BED**

Writing as Linda Winstead:
**NO ANGEL'S GRACE**
**IN ENEMY HANDS**
**WEST WIND**
**GUARDIAN ANGEL**
**CHASE THE LIGHTNING**

# On A Wicked Wind

## Linda Jones

LOVE SPELL BOOKS  NEW YORK CITY

*To Joanna Cagan*
*For seaweed and piglets, faxes and chocolate—*
*not necessarily in that order.*

LOVE SPELL®

March 1998

Published by

Dorchester Publishing Co., Inc.
276 Fifth Avenue
New York, NY 10001

If you purchased this book without a cover you should be aware that this book is stolen property. It was reported as "unsold and destroyed" to the publisher and neither the author nor the publisher has received any payment for this "stripped book."

Copyright © 1998 by Linda Winstead Jones

All rights reserved. No part of this book may be reproduced or transmitted in any form or by any electronic or mechanical means, including photocopying, recording or by any information storage and retrieval system, without the written permission of the Publisher, except where permitted by law.

ISBN 0-505-52251-9

The name "Love Spell" and its logo are trademarks of Dorchester Publishing Co., Inc.

Printed in the United States of America.

# On A Wicked Wind

# Chapter One

"Sabrina, don't."

Patrick's voice followed her along the board-walk from the restaurant to the fishing pier, exasperation breaking through his normally cool facade. She didn't turn to watch him, didn't have to. She knew he was following. His determined footsteps echoed on the long pier, a weathered wooden structure that was deserted but for Sabrina, her irate fiancé, and a single fisherman.

The white-haired fisherman leaned over the railing and ignored Sabrina as she passed, his gaze following the fishing line into a moonlit ocean.

Why hadn't she turned right instead of left as she'd left Annalina's? A simple change of direction and she'd be fleeing from Patrick on the sturdy concrete of the parking lot.

9

Beneath her feet, far below the weathered boards, the Atlantic danced, gentle waves swirled and crashed. Sabrina kept her eyes on the waves in the distance, far beyond the end of the pier. A full moon touched the water, made it sparkle as if the waves were sprinkled with diamonds and silver. It was so enchanting she could almost forget that she hated the water. All water. Lakes, rivers, and especially oceans.

"Dammit, Sabrina!" Patrick yelled.

At the end of the pier, Sabrina stopped and turned to face the man who had asked her—a hundred times or more, it seemed—to marry him. Tonight, after an unpleasant late dinner in the newest of her chain of seafood restaurants, he had demanded that she set the date.

"I'm too busy to think about a wedding right now. You know that." She lifted her chin, decided too late that it was a childish move, and as Patrick reached her she lowered her gaze to his chest. "With the new restaurants and all the changes . . ."

"Your father's been gone nearly eight months." Patrick whispered, his voice taking on a tested patience. "This opening went fairly well, and we've got four months before the Wilmington opening."

Sabrina smoothed her sensible navy skirt. It was a transparently apprehensive gesture, and unlike her. She didn't allow anyone to make her nervous.

"There's so much to do."

"And Sabrina Steele has to do it all herself," Patrick snapped. "The chef almost quit tonight, you know. It took me nearly an hour to calm the man down. You don't tell a chef of Paolo's caliber that there's too much red pepper in his signature dish." His patience was fading quickly. "Are you ever going to learn that you can't do everything alone?"

Patrick put light pressure on Sabrina's chin, forcing her eyes to meet his. It had been coming to this for months, but she'd tried to convince herself that her growing doubts about Patrick were the result of the stress of her father's death and the sudden responsibilities that came with her new position as head of his company. Steele Corporation owned and operated twenty-eight Annalina's restaurants, and there were four more slated to be opened in the next eight months. Stress.

But it was more than that. Or less. In her heart, Sabrina knew the answer was much less complicated.

She didn't love Patrick. There had been a time when she'd felt something more than this . . . not true love, not passion, but a kinship. Their unofficial engagement was three years old, and in that time they'd settled into their relationship like a pair of old shoes. Broken in, comfortable.

This wasn't the way she wanted to spend the rest of her life, and she knew there had to be more than this to a relationship. It wasn't as if she asked for the moon. Sabrina Steele was nothing if not reasonable. She didn't expect her life to be exciting. It never had been, and she didn't expect that to change. She wasn't the kind of woman anyone would call wild. Or beautiful. Or irresistible.

Sabrina Steele was competent and unfailingly practical. In a crisis she could keep her head when everyone else was frantic.

And Paolo's dish had been entirely too spicy for this Florida crowd.

Her fingers twittered at her side. Even if she wasn't the most exciting woman in the world, there had to be more to life than *this*.

She and Patrick hadn't made love in months. First, there had been her father's sudden death to deal with, and after that there was always something . . . a business trip for her or for Patrick, an out-of-town emergency, a headache. Sometimes hers and sometimes his. They didn't live together, and when they were traveling out of town, as now, they didn't even share a hotel room.

Appearances were important, they agreed. She was his boss, after all, and had been long before her father's passing.

Something had to happen.

"I don't want to get married," she whispered.

Patrick's eyes softened in the moonlight, and the pressure at Sabrina's chin lessened. "Bree," he cooed. "I'm sorry. I didn't mean to pressure you." He smiled, a patented Patrick Windham grin, charming and disarming. "We'll wait, as long as you need."

It would be easiest to nod her head in assent and go on, but Sabrina knew she couldn't put this off any longer. Unpleasant as it was bound to be, there would never be a more appropriate opportunity. There was no one around to overhear, or to interrupt.

She was only vaguely aware of the smell and sounds of the ocean beneath her feet and behind her.

"Time won't make a difference. I can't marry you."

Patrick's smile died, and he let his hand fall as he stepped away from her. "You mean not now."

Sabrina shook her head. "I mean not ever. I . . . I'm not happy, Patrick."

Spoken aloud, it sounded childish, petty.

"Not happy," he repeated.

"I've devoted my life to this business, to the exclusion of everything else." She delivered this truth calmly, without flinching or looking away like a coward. "You can't tell me that what we have is anything special, or ever was. It was just . . . convenient."

How could she explain to him the doubts that had plagued her lately? She didn't think it was as simple as the passing of her thirtieth birthday, but that, combined with her father's death, might have been the trigger. Life was passing her by.

Sabrina had a growing feeling that somewhere along the way she'd missed something. Something important. It wasn't money, wasn't anything money could buy. Lately that certainty had been keeping her up at night, long after she'd turned off the light and crawled into bed.

Her first job had been at sixteen, as hostess at her father's original Annalina's. She'd never worked anywhere else. Her degree was in business, her job just out of college that of vice-president. And Patrick? Patrick had always been there. Indispensable to her father . . . willing to make himself indispensable to her as well.

"You can't just change your mind after three years." She saw the disbelief on Patrick's face, the anger.

"I'm sorry . . ."

"Sorry? Dammit, I put up with your moods, your demands, your insatiable need to control everything and everyone around you . . . and now that the old man's gone, you want me to walk away?"

"It's best for both of us."

"No," Patrick shook his head, reached out and grabbed her wrist. "You're not going to stand there and tell me that I've just wasted the last six years of my life, courting you, finally getting you to agree to marry me, putting up with your spoiled-brat attitude. Now that it's all yours you want me to back off?"

Patrick pushed her against the railing, pressed himself close . . . too close for comfort. He towered over her, and she could see the anger in his eyes. *Naive* . . . she thought, afraid to speak. All these years, and it had never occurred to her that Patrick was using their relationship to secure and advance his place in the company.

"Let me go," she demanded, her voice a hoarse whisper.

She heard the crack of dry and splintering wood, felt the railing at her spine give way just slightly. It was the only warning she had before the support at her back disappeared and Sabrina dropped, falling back and away from the pier and pulling Patrick with her.

Her descent stopped with a jerk, and she looked up into Patrick's face. His anger was gone, and she could see that he was scared. Truly scared. He gripped her wrist tightly, his hold alone keeping her from plunging into the ocean below.

Beneath her feet the waves crashed, as if they'd suddenly become angrier, fiercer, and one shoe slipped off her foot and fell into the water. For a moment she was unreasonably disturbed at the loss of one half of her most comfortable pair of pumps.

"Hang on." Patrick was chest down on the pier, his head hanging over the edge. One arm was wrapped around a post that didn't appear to be any more substantial than the railing that had given way beneath her weight, and the arm that held her was obviously straining. "Everything will be all right, Bree."

She wished she could believe him, but she didn't. Her irrational fear of water had prohibited her from learning to swim. Even her father, a man who detested weakness in anyone—and most particularly in his only child—had relented after several disastrous attempts at swimming lessons.

He had finally decided to give in to her one fear, and when he quit demanding that she learn to swim—Sabrina had been nearly fourteen at the time—the nightmares had stopped.

Vivid nightmares of drowning, of being unable to breathe, of being pulled deeper and deeper into the darkness.

"Hey!" Patrick turned his head, calling to the lone fisherman she had forgotten about. "Help us!"

She heard running footsteps on the pier, and everything shook lightly. The wooden slats, Patrick's arm, her entire body. The remaining shoe fell into the water.

Patrick's grip on her wrist was slipping. His hand had begun to sweat, and damp fingers slid over Sabrina's thin wrist.

When the fisherman took hold of Patrick's feet, Patrick released his hold on the bracing post and lowered that hand to her. Sabrina reached for it, but she was shaking, and her hand brushed past his.

And that was when the wind shifted, whipping as it changed direction. It was a cold gust, much too cold for July in Florida. It grabbed her, literally seized her and tried to wrench her from Patrick's grasp.

"Bree!" Patrick closed his eyes tight. "There's something in my eye! God, I can't see!" His hand slipped, until only his fingers held hers. There was nothing more to keep her from falling.

Sabrina hung on, knowing she wouldn't last much longer, seeing with bittersweet clarity the mistakes she'd made. She'd missed so much, trading it all for the chance to be head of her father's company, to have the power he'd had. But there wasn't a single friend who wasn't somehow related to business, and she knew now that Patrick didn't love her, had never loved her. It was a poor trade.

The wind lifted her hair, buffeted her all around and attacked Patrick, as well, and when Patrick's fingers slipped away from hers and she fell, it seemed the wind cradled her, carrying her into the black waves.

The moon lit Rafael's path along the sand, a path that carried him away from the blazing fire and his raucous crew. They were jubilant tonight, so soon after the division of a rich treasure wrested from English buccaneers.

Their pockets were filled with gold, and when they returned to Tortuga for a well deserved rest, there would be women and rum and feasting long into the night.

For now, they waited as Franco and Esteban saw to minor repairs to the ship. They were safe here, some leagues south of St. Augustine. Safe for the night, at least. By tomorrow morning the repairs would be completed, and they would sail for home. In truth, it would have been safe to continue on, to make the repairs in Tortuga, but some instinct had cautioned Rafael to beach here and see the repairs done.

Perhaps he was not as anxious to return home as was his crew.

The home that awaited him on a smaller island not far from the refuge of Tortuga was a thousand times finer than the captain's cabin in his fast and lucky ship. Elena was there to see to the running of his household, and close by, on Tortuga, there were women . . . women available at a single word. There were men from around the world who called themselves his friends, who drank and sang and gambled long into the night.

In truth, he completely trusted none of them. There was not a single person on Tortuga, the island that was home to pirates from around the world, upon whom Rafael would turn his back. Man or woman. Child or curved-back ancient. They were greedy, and he knew that any one of them would gladly kill him for the gold and gems he harbored.

If that were to happen, if he were killed by an enemy or a friend, the world would go on. His crew would mourn him for the length of time it took to elect another captain. The women of Tortuga would cry for him until another man entranced them with sweet words and shining coin.

The sand was giving beneath his feet, and the water lapped just a few feet away.

Rafael had everything a man could possibly want. His own ship. A fierce reputation as a merciless cutthroat. The women, of course. His comfortable home, the only place he felt safe. Treasures hidden near and far, on his island, on other islands, even close by their primitive camp for this night.

He had everything, and yet he was more and more discontent as the days flew by. He had lost his zest for life . . . Impossible. He was questioning his chosen profession . . . Ridiculous.

He was restless. Perhaps it was time to once again visit Falconer.

The wind that rose was cold, too cold for this time of year. Rafael turned his eyes to the sea, searching for signs of a storm, but there was only soft and brilliant moonlight on the waves that rolled in the distance and crashed near his feet.

And it did not die, but swirled swiftly, touching him with chilled fingers, forcing him to turn his head from the blast that stung his eyes.

With that simple turn of his head, he saw the pile of pale flesh along a curve in the beach. Moonlight shone bright on what Rafael was certain was a body. Some poor soul, washed overboard and then onto the white sand.

The surf crashed over the body, trying to drag it back into the sea. Water rolled over flesh, trying to reclaim its victim, but an arm moved, grasped at the insubstantial sand, and clawed away from the relentless waves.

As Rafael drew near he saw the tempting curve of a well-shaped hip, a nicely rounded bottom, a magnificently contoured back wet and glistening in the moonlight.

The woman was face down in the sand, conscious, but barely so, and she wore not a stitch of clothing. Her hair was cut rather short, barely covering her ears, and it was plastered to her skull and the bit of cheek he saw nestled in the sand.

As the sea tried to claim the woman again, Rafael lifted her, moving her to safety so that the waves crashed only at her feet. He knelt beside her and rolled her onto her back so that he could see her face.

She breathed, but did not open her eyes, and Rafael studied the vision before him. Grains of sand were pressed into her flesh, and he tried to brush some of them away, his hands gentle on her delicate skin.

What a shame, that she probably would not live. It was hard to tell, with the sand and the oddly cut hair, but she appeared to be quite lovely. Her shape was certainly enticing. It distressed him that he would never know her name. Where she came from. How she had come to be tossing about in the ocean completely and wondrously naked.

Perhaps she would not die. Perhaps she was a gift from the god of the sea, a gift for him. In spite of the uncertainty of the situation, Rafael smiled. He had done nothing in his life to warrant a prize such as this.

She opened her eyes, his gift, to lock a brilliant gaze on his face. After a moment's hesitation she tried feebly to push away his hands, hands that continued to brush sand from her skin.

He spoke to her, first in his native Spanish. A greeting, an introduction of sorts. She merely closed her eyes as if she were very tired and shook her head. He tried French. There were still French settlers along the coast, though they were few, and fewer every day.

No response.

He hesitated. She was probably English. Too bad. He positively *hated* the English.

"Beautiful lady," he began. "You have been delivered to me." She tensed, tried to draw away from him. "And I want only to assist you. Are you injured? What can I do to take away the fear in your eyes?"

She took a deep breath. Beneath his fingers her chest expanded and fell. "For starters, you can take your hands off my tits."

He did as she asked and she sat up, looking around, looking down. "Where am I? What have you done with my clothes?" The fear was back, in her eyes and in her voice.

"I cannot answer your questions," Rafael answered calmly, "but to tell you that you are as I found you."

She crossed her arms over her breasts and quickly drew up her legs in a way that shielded her lower belly and the junction of her thighs from him. As if he had not already seen every inch of that beautiful body.

"If you were a gentleman you'd give me something to wear."

"I am not a gentleman," Rafael informed her gently. "I am many things, but never that."

His words frightened her, and she drew into herself even further, tightening the arms she clutched herself with. Her helplessness touched him. That realization was alarming, but true.

"Here," he said, resignation in his voice as he slipped off his vest and offered it to her.

She took the leather vest and donned it, but it did little to protect her from his gaze. The openings for her arms fell nearly to her waist, and the vest was cut too deeply to cover anything more than her dark nipples.

He could not stop the grin that spread across his face.

"You think this is funny?" she asked, incredulous.

"Of course not, *querida*." He knew his smile told her he lied, but he did not care. The telling smile had taken away her fear.

"How about the shirt?" She motioned with one hand, while the other held the vest closed.

"I do not know." Rafael turned his face thoughtfully to the ocean. "There was a cold wind a moment ago, and it might return. I would not wish to be caught as you are now. Unprotected. Bared to the chill."

"That was a freaky wind," she whispered.

Rafael did not ask her what she meant. The tone of her voice told him all he needed to know.

He removed his shirt and handed it to her, watched as she waited in vain for him to turn away. She finally turned her back to him and slipped on his shirt, trying so hard to show him nothing but her most elegant bare back.

All too soon she turned to face him. "Thank you," she whispered, tossing him the vest. Her thanks were not particularly gracious. "I couldn't very well go back to the hotel in the altogether."

"The hotel?" He slipped the vest over his bare torso.

She turned toward the massive growth, the

unwelcoming darkness inland that made up so much of this country.

"I didn't think there was any undeveloped land . . . I *know* there isn't any."

She turned to him again, and he saw with dismay that her fear had returned. "Where am I?"

"We are some leagues south of St. Augustine, *querida*." Her eyes widened, great, mesmerizing pools in the moonlight. A shapely lower lip trembled. He had thought her afraid before, but now . . . "Do not look at me this way."

She jumped up and set out along the shoreline headed away from the camp. Her feet kept to the hard sand, where the water occasionally lapped at her feet. With a muffled curse Rafael followed her, knowing that alone she would not survive.

"There is nothing . . ."

She ignored him and broke into a run. The long tail of the white linen shirt she wore reflected the moonlight as he followed her, first at a walk and then at an easy run.

When he caught up with her he grabbed her arm and forced her to spin around and face him.

She was more than afraid. She was near panic.

"For tonight, you can stay in my camp." He wanted to reassure her. He wanted the shoulders beneath his hands to relax. "Tomorrow, we sail for Tortuga, and I will gladly take you there."

"Tortuga?"

"*Sí*. Do not be afraid. I will not allow anyone to hurt you."

She allowed him to turn her back toward the camp, and even to walk beside her. His gift took small steps across the sand, hugging herself as if the night was cold. She did not seem to be embarrassed by her bare legs and feet—and such lovely legs and feet they were.

Rafael placed an arm around her shoulders, seeking to comfort her, to warm her if she needed it. How she trembled, down to her bones.

But she was strong, stronger than he had thought. The trembling soon subsided, and she stepped away from him, preferring to stand alone.

"I shouldn't be here," she whispered when they saw the light of the blazing fire. "One minute I'm falling off a pier, and the next I'm . . . washed ashore as naked as the day I was born and being fondled by Ricky Ricardo."

"Rafael," he corrected her. "Antonio Rafael de Zamora."

She halted suddenly, and cocked her head to look at him in a way that was oddly enchanting. If he had believed in mermaids or nereids or sirens, he would have wondered . . . but Rafael no longer believed in myths. Whatever she was, whoever she was, she was a woman.

Strands of damp hair brushed her cheek, plastered against skin that he knew to be flawless. Flawless not only on her face, but everywhere. That back, her shapely thighs, the breasts he had touched all too briefly.

"Sabrina Steele," she said after a moment's pause, and she offered him her hand, stiff fingers, rigid wrist.

Rafael took Sabrina's hand and drew it to his mouth, apparently surprising her. What had she expected? He barely had time to kiss her knuckles properly before she snatched her hand away.

"What am I doing here, Rafael?" she asked, as if he should know.

He shrugged his shoulders slightly and turned away from Sabrina Steele and those wide eyes that looked at him as if he should have answers to all her questions.

# Chapter Two

Hell.

She'd drowned, and this was hell.

What had she done to deserve this? Sabrina stopped well short of the campfire, so that she remained in the shadows, and the man she'd awakened to find leisurely dusting grains of sand from her naked body stopped beside her to lay his hand lightly on her arm.

"Do not be afraid," he whispered. "No one will hurt you. I promise you that. No one would dare to touch what Rafael claims as his own."

"I beg your pardon?" Sabrina stepped away from the man who *claimed* her with that mesmerizing accented voice. How dare he?

"I said, do not be afraid." He raised his voice, as if she were hard of hearing.

"I heard you fine, Ricky," Sabrina snapped.

Hell or not, she wasn't going to roll over and play dead.

"Rafael," he corrected gently. "Who is this Ricky you speak of?"

"Never mind."

She dismissed the idea that this was any sort of afterlife, her own heaven or hell. It felt too real, too earthly. Besides, Rafael was no demon, and he was certainly no angel.

In all her overly protected life she'd never seen a man quite like this one. Dark hair waved and curled wildly well past his shoulders, and gold hoops, one in each ear, sparkled in the light of the fire. Every move he made was slow, sensuous, like some sort of powerful animal. At his waist he wore a knife with a nasty-looking curved blade at least twelve inches in length.

Since she wore his shirt and he wore only the inadequate vest he had thought she'd be content to clothe herself in, she had a moonlit view of his chest. There were swirls of dark hair over lean muscle, a tight stomach that hadn't been earned through sit-ups or some machine in a gym, and arms that were obviously strong without being overly large. That strength was evident not only in the lean muscles but in the cautious ease with which he moved. Like a snake, or a tiger.

When he turned toward the campfire, she got a better view of Antonio Rafael de Zamora. The dancing firelight illuminated an angular face, with high cheekbones and a strong chin. Lean, but not thin. Hard, but not severe. It was a fascinating face, handsome to a fault, every feature distinct, but it was Rafael's mouth upon which Sabrina fastened her eyes. The upper lip was just a little bit fuller than the bottom one, an imperfection that was undeniably sensual.

And, of course, he claimed her, as if she were a mangy stray dog.

"*Sirena mia*," he whispered. "Do not be afraid."

"I'm not afraid." Her voice didn't tremble as she delivered the lie. Of course she was afraid. Any sane human being would be afraid upon waking and finding that the world had somehow changed.

Rafael said they were some *leagues* south of St. Augustine. Who measured in leagues anymore? Sailors, maybe, but still . . . it didn't sound right. The timeless ocean was unchanged, but before her there was nothing but wilderness where there should be hotels and restaurants and condos, complete darkness where there should be the illumination of city lights. Again, she reminded herself that there was no undeveloped land south of St. Augustine, and there hadn't been for a very long time.

She should be looking at streetlamps and headlights and maybe the brightly colored lights of a small amusement park or a miniature golf course. There was nothing.

Her musings brought her back to the same questions she was afraid to ask aloud. What had carried her here? Where the hell . . . when the hell . . . *was* she?

Wherever she was, she didn't belong. She was

lost. Out of time and out of place. How would she survive here? She was a businesswoman, a strong woman. In her element she was confident; fearless, even. She'd fired men twice her size without a qualm, could do every job that was required of her employees, from cook to bartender to advertising. Her father had demanded it.

Men and women worked for her, at the home office in Atlanta and in restaurants across the Southeast, and she had, more than once, bought out failing restaurants and turned them into moneymakers. Her father had always said she had a gift for finding the good ones, that she knew when to smile sweetly and when to dig in, that she was a natural when it came to business.

She had a feeling that here, in this world where everything had changed, her business skills would be useless.

The only other time in her life when she'd felt this defenseless had been at one of the very few disastrous swimming lessons her father had insisted on. And even then, she hadn't felt distanced from reality, as she did now. She hadn't felt so completely disoriented.

It was almost as if she'd been reborn. The thought gave Sabrina a chill. Reborn, bringing into this world nothing of the other one. Not even the clothes on her back. Just moments before the fall, she'd questioned her life. Had she devoted herself to the business just to please her father? Why had her life felt so achingly empty in those last months?

Was this her chance to do things differently?

The men who gathered around the fire had not noticed her yet, and as she studied them a chill crept down her spine. They were a rough-looking bunch, so much so that even the tamest of them made Rafael look like a Boy Scout. Together, they laughed at one man's joke, hearty and coarse laughter that rang through a night that was still but for the lively camp and the roar of the ocean.

No cars, no planes, no faraway city lights.

Out of time. Out of place.

Sabrina prided herself on being—if nothing else—practical. Some instinct told her she was safe with the man at her side, while a purely feminine instinct warned her that she would not survive in this place alone. Not with that rough bunch around.

For now, until she found herself in a situation she could better control, Rafael seemed to be the logical solution to her immediate problems.

"You're sure," she whispered, "that they'll listen to you, that they'll respect your . . ." She swallowed hard. Her dignity didn't go down easily. "Claim?"

He grinned, an easy and thoroughly wicked grin that lit up his face. "Of course, *querida*. They follow me as any loyal crew follows their captain."

"You're their captain?"

Why had she not seen it before? Rafael raised his hand and gestured to a ship that had been anchored close to shore. The sails were down, but the mast stood tall, and at the fore of the ship a flag fluttered. A gust of wind caught the flag and straightened it for a split second, just long enough for Sabrina to get a good look at the skull and crossbones.

"Pirates?"

"*Sí,*" Rafael whispered, and when she turned to him he gifted her with a brilliant smile, wide and wicked and anything but charmingly boyish. That sensuous mouth was curved into a confident and inviting smile that would make any self-respecting female run for her life. Surely this was the way a wolf grinned at his prey before taking the first big bite.

Sabrina studied the men who were gathered around the fire, viewing them in a new and more frightening light. Pirates. Lawless and violent men. For the first time she noted the weapons each and every man had at hand. Knives, like the one Rafael wore, and sabers of every length and breadth hung at their waists, blades curved and straight. Pistols were tucked into waistbands, nothing but polished handles and steel hammers visible above colorful silk sashes.

One of them, a broad man who had until this moment had his back to Sabrina, twisted his head around, saw her, and stood. The pirates around him, the men who circled the fire, followed his gaze and rose as well. They appeared to be stunned, at first. Then the smiles began to bloom, one after another, and Sabrina's blood ran cold.

Rafael began to speak, rapid Spanish that had none of the unexpected charm of his careful and accented English. She couldn't understand

31

his words, not a single one, but the smiles of his men faded, one at a time.

Rafael stopped speaking abruptly, then crossed his arms over his chest in a gesture that spoke of finality and required no interpretation.

"What did you say?" Sabrina hissed.

"I told them that you are mine," he whispered, his eyes never straying from the immobile pirates.

Sabrina opened her mouth to protest, but decided against it. For the moment . . .

The marauder who had seen her first spoke. He was taller than Rafael, wider in the shoulders, and completely bald, and in the flickering firelight he looked like some sort of evil Mr. Clean. His words were deep, slow, and even though she couldn't understand a single word, Sabrina felt threatened.

"What did he say?" she whispered.

"He is only reminding me that we share everything. The captain's share is half, with the remaining treasure being divided among the crew." He sounded as if he didn't have a care in the world.

"I'm no treasure."

Rafael finally turned his gaze to her, allowed his mouth to transform once again into that lazy and somehow depraved grin. "I would beg to differ, *sirena mia*."

"My name is Sabrina, not Serena," she snapped. "And I may not speak Spanish, but I do know that *mia* means 'my,' or 'mine,' or something like that. Cut it out!"

"Pablo is awaiting his answer, *sirena mia*,"

Rafael said calmly. "Perhaps we can finish this discussion later.

"In English, Pablo," Rafael said as he returned his attention to the still standing crew. "*Señorita* Sabrina becomes anxious when she cannot understand. As I said, I found her, she is mine. As she was not taken at sea, I do not believe it violates our agreement to . . ." Rafael paused, raised a hand palm upward, as if he were grasping for something. "To keep her for myself," he finished.

A few heads were turned as translations were made for those who did not speak English . . . but most of the crew understood quite well.

"Over here, *querida*," Rafael said gently, ignoring the men who stared at them as he led her to a small pile of folded blankets, bending to snatch up one without stopping as he walked away from the fire.

Out of the corner of her eye, Sabrina watched the pirates reclaim their seats around the fire, one by one, until only Pablo remained standing. Finally, he turned away and lowered his large body to the sand.

Rafael placed a thin blanket on the ground a distance from the fire. The light barely touched the sand here, and none of the heat of the fire reached them. No added heat was needed, not tonight. The air was mild, calm, without a hint of the cold wind that had come up so suddenly earlier. The memory of that wind gave her a chill.

"Lie down," Rafael whispered.

"I'm not tired," Sabrina insisted. "Really." She

hugged her arms, more for comfort than for warmth. The linen of Rafael's shirt was fine, soft against her skin, and the wide ruffles at the wrists fell over her hands. The tail end came almost to her knees, and still she felt naked.

"Lie down," he insisted, leaning forward slightly. His eyes narrowed.

Sabrina had never felt helpless in her life. Her father hadn't allowed it in his child, and she'd never been at a loss as an adult. There wasn't a situation she couldn't handle, a crisis she couldn't endure with her spine straight and her head held high.

Until now.

What was she supposed to do now? She felt as if she should *do* something, but all she really wanted was to sink into the sand and cover her head and hope this was all a crazy dream.

Rafael must have seen the confusion on her face because he pulled away from her slowly. "I will not touch you. If that is your wish," he added, as though it was possible he was mistaken about her hesitation.

"It is."

He shrugged his shoulders, appearing to be disappointed but far from heartbroken. "Lie down, *sirena mia,*" he insisted.

"I told you, my name is Sabrina," she said as she lowered herself carefully to the blanket. "SaBREEna," she said slowly.

Rafael laughed lightly as he lowered himself to sit behind her. They both faced the fire and the men who pointedly did not look their way.

"I have not forgotten your name. *Sirena mia* means my . . . mermaid."

"Mermaid," Sabrina scoffed as she lowered herself until she was lying on her side. "There's no such thing as mermaids."

"Of course not," Rafael agreed easily.

Of course not. There was also no such thing as falling off a pier and ending up in another time. No such thing as rebirth into the past. No second chances. No pirates. Not any more.

"Rafael?" she whispered.

"*Sí?*"

"What year is this?"

He didn't answer immediately. Was he trying to remember himself? Or was he wondering why she didn't know?

"The year is 1665, *sirena mia.*"

She started to tell him *not* to call her his mermaid, but she decided against it. It was rather soothing, and his voice was really much more pleasant than Ricky Ricardo's. More mesmerizing. Sexier. The kind of voice that could make a woman melt.

"1665," she repeated.

"Go to sleep," he ordered softly.

"I'm not tired." It was an out-and-out lie. She was exhausted, more completely drained than she'd ever been.

"Go to sleep anyway. Ah, you are like a naughty child," Rafael whispered, and then he launched into a litany of soft and rapid Spanish, his voice a soft caress that washed over her so wonderfully.

"In English, Rafael," Sabrina insisted as she closed her eyes.

"I think not."

The sand beneath the thin blanket was warm, had retained the day's heat and was releasing it slowly. The warm sand yielded as Sabrina settled herself more comfortably, making herself surprisingly cozy.

"I'm not tired," she insisted again, weakly. "I'll never get to sleep, not after everything that's happened tonight."

But Sabrina felt drained, as if her strange journey had sapped her strength. Rafael tucked the blanket around her legs with a light touch.

"Sweet dreams, *sirena mia*."

"Good night, Rafael," Sabrina whispered as the lush darkness took her.

There were grains of sand in her hair and on her neck, and Rafael passed the time removing them with great care, one grain at a time.

She did not stir, not even when he let his fingers lie against her neck, there beneath a delicate ear. He spoke to her softly, in Spanish, of course, so that if she did awaken she would not understand.

It would not do for her to know that he found her most beautiful, that he wanted her more than he dared to reveal. If she knew . . . if she understood, it would give her power over him, and that he could not allow.

A man in his position should not have any weaknesses, and if perchance he discovered one he most certainly should not share it.

He reclined behind her, his chest almost touching her back, his head propped in one hand.

Sabrina was most definitely a weakness. Why did he insist on protecting her when she refused to allow him even the simplest touch? He knew, deep in his heart, that if Pablo had been more insistent, there would have been bloodshed. What would make him challenge a man who had sailed with him for many years? A woman who appeared—impossibly—out of nowhere, not knowing even the year. Why?

It was possible that she had been held prisoner for some years, an indentured servant, perhaps. Anger rose within him and he squelched it quickly. After watching her for such a short time, he was convinced that was not the case. Sabrina Steele did not have a subservient bone in her lovely and tempting body. He was certain she had escaped from a cheerless place, but not an altogether unpleasant one.

If that were true, he could show her what it was like to be truly cheerful. To smile and dance and fall into a soft bed with peals of laughter. To allow those peals of laughter to fade into shared and deep breaths of passion and pleasure.

He fingered the linen of the shirt she wore, and yet she did not stir. It was not until he placed his hand on the swell of her hip that she moved, rocking slowly back until her bottom rested against him, nestled against his own hips provocatively before she became still again.

Rafael smiled as he moved forward to close

the narrow gap between them, to place his chest against her back. He could feel her shallow and easy breathing, the brush of her thigh against his, the easy fit of her nicely rounded bottom against his own aching body.

And he was achingly hard.

Rafael's smile faded quickly, and he comforted himself with planting several small kisses, so feathery the sleeping Sabrina would certainly not be disturbed, against the back of her neck. He traced the outline of her hip with an indolent finger, using great restraint. Very great restraint.

He was not so desperate that he would stoop to taking advantage of a woman so distraught and exhausted as his gift from the sea. But she could tempt a saint.

When she woke she would not remember that he had held her so close, but her body would know. Her body would remember.

His earlier uncharacteristic melancholy had disappeared. Sabrina Steele's appearance in the surf had cured him, quickly and completely. She intrigued him, she tempted him, she tormented him, even now.

It would not be easy, but she would be his. Sabrina would come to him, share his bed, and they would be together for a time. He knew that already, though he doubted she would accept that truth so easily. She would come to him, and she would stay until he tired of her. Until she no longer intrigued him. Until it was no longer enjoyable to wake to her face.

But first, before he made her his lover, he

wanted to see her smile. He wanted to dance with her, to hear her laugh, to see passion and trust in her eyes instead of fear.

Perhaps he would even come to trust her, a little.

Already this woman was becoming a weakness. You would think he had never seen a comely woman before, never held a sleeping woman in his arms.

His smile crept back, and he placed a small and almost innocent kiss at Sabrina's spine, his lips brushing not skin but the linen of his own shirt with which she had covered her nakedness. She shuddered, so faintly he felt rather than saw it,

Yes. Her body would most certainly remember.

The unlikely concept of love entered his thoughts and was brushed quickly aside.

Love was the greatest weakness of all.


She woke often at night, particularly since her father's death. Worries about the business, regrets for words unsaid, indecision about her own life, all these kept her awake or woke her in the middle of the night.

For some reason she couldn't move, but there was no resulting panic. This wasn't a complete wakefulness tonight, but a heavy half-sleep. She felt wonderfully weighted down. Safe. A fragrant sea breeze brushed her face, and Sabrina halfway opened her eyes.

The surf crashed, rhythmic and soothing. The moon lit the sand before her, and she recognized the weight that warmed her and kept her from being able to move.

Rafael.

No restaurants, no worries, no Patrick. And she felt so wonderfully sheltered. So deliciously warm.

She smiled as she closed her eyes.

What an odd and wonderful dream this was.

# Chapter Three

"Awake, *sirena mia*," the enchantingly accented voice demanded with an added and unnecessary sharp slap to her backside.

Sabrina opened her eyes to be blinded by the sun. For a moment, just a split second, she wondered where she was, and then it all came back with a flash that was as blinding as the sun. 1665. Pirates. Rafael.

He towered over her, his stance impatient, his charming smile missing. Sabrina looked past his black-clad legs to the commotion on the shore, as his crew prepared to sail. This was no dream.

"Perhaps you should just leave me here," she suggested.

"I will take you to Tortuga, as I promised last night."

"I don't know . . ."

LINDA JONES

"It is not safe for you here," Rafael said impatiently.

"Sailing with a band of pirates is?" Sabrina muttered as she sat up. She straightened the loose shirt, covering herself as best she could. "How much worse could it be just to stay here?"

Rafael grinned as he squatted beside her. "Indians," he whispered. "They will not bother us. We are too many, and well armed, and not afraid to fight. But you . . ." He touched her chin with a single long, brown finger. "There is nothing that can happen to you on board my ship, with or without my protection, to compare to the horrors that await a captive of the natives of this region."

"All right, all right." Sabrina snapped her head back and away from the annoying finger. "Can I at least get some clothes? Something besides this shirt?"

"That can be arranged."

"I don't suppose there's a shower on board. Or a bathtub?"

"We must go." Rafael was clearly restless as he took Sabrina's hand and stood swiftly. She had no choice but to rise with him, to follow as he took long steps toward the shore and his anchored ship.

A ship that was, she decided, much too small for all these people.

She stumbled only once in the warm sand, but was able to regain secure footing quickly. It was a good thing, since Rafael didn't slow his long step at all.

The ship was close to shore, and the pirates

42

waded through gently lapping water to a rope ladder that hung from the side. Sabrina stopped well short, so that the waves only tickled her toes. Rafael continued to hold her hand, and her sudden halt caught him by surprise. He turned to her, standing solidly where the waves crashed over his ankles and calves.

"What is wrong?" he asked impatiently.

What's wrong? Where to begin? A bathroom would be nice, underwear would be nice, coffee . . . shoes . . . a pier.

"I can't swim," she said, rejecting her other objections, for the moment.

Rafael sighed. "There is no need for you to swim, *querida*. You need only to step a little farther into the water. It will barely come to your knees."

"The waves . . ."

"Are small and harmless this morning. Come." He tugged gently on her hand. "I have rarely seen the sea so tame."

Given his nature, Sabrina half expected Rafael to lift her and carry her quickly and impatiently to the ladder. Humiliating as that would be, she almost wished he would. She could protest with indignation, while he saved her from her own irrational fear.

But he didn't. He pulled her close, continued to hold her hand, and steadied her with his other hand, so that he was practically backing his way to the ladder. He guided her slowly through the warm ocean, and gentle waves brushed the backs of his knees as he reached the ship.

Sabrina held on to Rafael's hand for dear life, gripped his fingers so tightly she expected him to protest. He remained silent, patient as Sabrina accustomed herself to the caress of the soft warm waves that broke against her legs.

"See?" he said as Sabrina took her first step onto the rope ladder. "All is well."

"So far," she mumbled. Sabrina lifted her head and paused there on the ladder as she read the name that was painted in scrolling letters on the weathered wood. *Venganza*.

"Rafael." Sabrina hung on to the rope, and turned to look down at the pirate who waited impatiently at the end of the ladder. It wasn't really important, but she was fairly certain she knew what *venganza* was. "What does that mean?"

She freed one hand from the rope and pointed up to the ship's name.

In spite of his impatience, Rafael grinned. By the light of day that grin was even more devastating than she remembered. His smile was bright, but his words chilled her. "*Venganza*. Vengeance. Revenge."

"That's what I thought," Sabrina mumbled as she resumed her ascent.

Okay. So she was not only in the company of pirates, for the moment, she was in the company of a pirate bent on revenge. For what? Or for whom?

It would be best not to stick around to find out.

Once they reached Tortuga she would make her way ... somewhere. Safely settled, she

44

could try to find her way home, or else accept the fact that she had undertaken an impossible journey and was here to stay. Even in 1665 there were cities, civilized countries, places where she would not have to constantly fear for her life.

Weren't there?

Rafael climbed the ladder in half the time it had taken her, launching himself over the rail with pantherlike grace. He locked his eyes on her immediately, and Sabrina shivered. Not so that anyone would notice, of course, just a little tremor she disguised quite well by hugging her arms to her chest.

When Rafael turned away from her, Sabrina loosened the hold on herself and clutched the rail. In a matter of minutes the anchor was hoisted and the *Venganza* got underway.

The deck was crowded, every one of the pirates engaged in one activity or another. Securing the anchor, setting the sails. There were, counting her, seventeen people on a boat that couldn't *possibly* have been meant for more than ten.

Sabrina stayed close to the edge and out of the way, her toes trying to grip the smooth deck that wasn't flat at all, but curved so that any water splashed on deck would roll back into the ocean.

Soon Rafael was at her side. He stared silently at the hands with which she desperately clutched the rails, but Sabrina didn't loosen her hold.

"You need a bigger boat," she said, unable to hide the tenseness in her voice.

Rafael just smiled and leaned forward to watch the beach where they had camped. "*Sirena mia*, my gift from the sea who is, it seems, afraid of the water."

In the sunlight, she could see that his hair was not black, but a warm, coffee brown. Soft curls touched his shoulders, partially hiding the gold loops in his ears.

"I am not afraid," she protested.

Rafael turned to her, and for a moment Sabrina couldn't breathe. He was staring at her with such intensity, staring at her with piercing pale brown eyes the color of brandy in a fine crystal glass, with the sun shining through. It was a light she could swear came from inside.

"Do not lie to me, *sirena mia*. Ever." His voice was low, a rumble no one would hear but her. "You do not lie well, and I will always . . . always know."

They were underway, a vast and empty ocean before them. Sabrina held on to the rail tightly and tried to enjoy the beauty.

She couldn't.

"I still say you need a bigger boat."

"If I had a bigger boat, I would not be able to pull so close to shore. I would not be able to outrun the *flota*, or my old friend Falconer."

Sabrina pulled her gaze from the ocean. "Falconer?"

Rafael's grin widened, and his eyes narrowed until he appeared to be more animal than man.

46

It was a look that made Sabrina's heart skip a beat.

"*Venganza*," he whispered.

The entrance to the captain's quarters was a square hole in the deck, just beneath the aft bridge. There was a grate covering the hole, and beyond that—darkness.

Rafael lifted the grate and, at her insistence, he went down first. Until she saw the light of a lamp in the dark hole, Sabrina waited.

The stairs, if you could call them that, were tiny wedges built into the corners of a narrow passage, and Sabrina lowered herself carefully, finding the notches in the walls for her hands to grip. By the time she'd lowered herself to the cabin, Rafael had laid a suit of clothes on a narrow cot, and had filled a wide, deep bowl with fresh water. There was even a small linen towel, neatly folded and placed at its side.

"No bathing tub, as you can see," he said, his back to her. "I hope this will suit for the moment."

It would more than suit. Cleaning the sand from her skin was a heavenly prospect.

A single lantern lit the small windowless room, and already Sabrina was feeling claustrophobic. "This is your cabin?" she asked, wondering if he'd been lying and had relegated her to a closet of some sort.

"*Sí*," he said with a shrug of his shoulders. "Yours for the duration of this short voyage."

"Are there sleeping quarters for the others at the front? I saw the grate over a big square

LINDA JONES

opening toward the front of the boat."

He grinned at her, amused it seemed. "That is the hold, where we store food, water, whatever treasure we may have on board. The crew sleeps on deck."

"You're kidding."

"Excuse me?" He turned a puzzled face to her.

Sabrina almost smiled. He couldn't quite manage his *x*s. "That can't be true."

"Of course it is true."

"Don't they ever . . . roll overboard?"

He laughed, but it was a pleasant and warm sound. "My crew are men of the sea, *sirena mia*. They do not roll overboard in their sleep."

Sabrina glanced at the narrow cot that took up a good portion of the cabin. "Is that what you'll do for the rest of the trip? Sleep on deck?"

Rafael grabbed a shirt from the bed, a replacement for the one she had taken and still wore. "That, *sirena mia*, is up to you." He tossed the shirt over his shoulder.

She busied herself inspecting the clothing he had chosen for her. His own, no doubt, another linen shirt much like the one she wore, a pair of pants, black and well-worn but clean and free of sand. A black vest. A red silk sash, she supposed to keep up the too-large pants. "I do hope you don't roll overboard," she said dryly.

He was close, too close, but there was nothing to be done for it in the small space he called a cabin.

"How kind of you to be concerned for my welfare," he growled, his voice low, his mouth much too close to her ear.

Before she could respond, Rafael was climbing from the cabin, leaving her in privacy to clean the sand from her tender skin. She waited until she could no longer see his feet, and then she stripped off the shirt.

He didn't climb back down, but dropped gracefully into the cabin.

"One more detail," he began.

Sabrina spun around, holding the shirt before her like a shield. "Rafael!"

He seemed unconcerned, shrugging his shoulders. "I have seen it all, *querida*. Every magnificent inch of that body. There is no need to be prudish."

No one had ever called her magnificent. Patrick had often told her that she looked "nice," or that she looked particularly "striking" in a dress he liked. His way, she'd decided, of telling her that she cleaned up nice but was no raving beauty.

"What do you want?" she snapped, trying to hide yet another deep tremor.

"Ah, yes. You will have a choice to make, in a few days' time. Many of my men have homes on Tortuga, and if you would like I will leave you there. If you would prefer . . ." He paused, and his eyes narrowed, as if he were hiding something from her. "You may come with me to my island. You are welcome there, for as long as you wish. As my guest, of course. As you were my gift from the sea, I do feel some obligation to care for you. But of course . . ."

"I'm not your gift, and I'm not your mermaid." Why did he insist on claiming her this way? It was degrading, that he thought of her as an object; a gift from the sea, for God's sake. "I'm not your anything, Rafael. Tortuga sounds just fine."

"You do not have to decide now." He sounded almost disappointed.

"Is there a town on Tortuga? People? Other ships?"

"Of course."

"And on your island?"

Rafael grinned. "On my island there is only my house, my very small plantation, my servants and crew, and my ship."

"Sounds like *my* idea of a nightmare," Sabrina snapped. "Do you mind?"

He disappeared again, and Sabrina waited a moment before she dropped the shirt.

"My, my, my," she muttered.

"Will you sell her in Tortuga?"

Pablo had approached silently, and Rafael turned away from the sea, which stretched endlessly before them, to face a man who was undoubtedly the best sailor on this ship.

"No." That short, low answer should have been enough, but Pablo did not depart.

"Why not? She would bring a good price, even with her hair shorn as it is."

"She is no slave, no indentured servant," Rafael said patiently. "She is simply a lady who has had some misfortune."

Pablo was not satisfied. "She is English."

50

Pablo's hatred for the English was as strong as Rafael's. Their reasons for such hatred were much the same, though they never spoke of it. Not any more.

"This is true, but she is unlike any English lady I have ever met. I will not sell her, and I will not hesitate to challenge any man who takes it in his head to do so." Rafael glanced without care to the cuff of the fresh shirt he had donned, straightened the bit of lace there. Out of the corner of his eye, he watched Pablo back away.

"As you wish, Captain," Pablo conceded.

Rafael controlled his temper, so that Pablo never knew that a nerve was struck. He told himself that his strong reaction to Pablo's suggestion stemmed from his aversion to trading in flesh, that there was nothing more involved in his revulsion.

He did not have long to ponder. As Pablo moved away, Sabrina climbed from the cabin. He had known she would not stay below decks for long. His quarters were too dark, too small, fit for nothing but sleeping.

She had rolled up the black trousers, so that her small pale feet peeked out, and she had wrapped the red sash around her waist to hold up the trousers. The linen shirt she wore was as big on her as the one she had donned the night before, but it was tucked in so that it did not appear so large. The vest helped, somewhat, hiding the billowing fabric. But the lacy cuffs fell over her hands, and the neck was cut too deeply.

51

Her hair was dampened and tucked behind her ears, her face freshly scrubbed. Such skin she had, glowing and beautifully alive.

She came more alive when she stepped into the sun, out of the shadows the aft deck cast over the entrance to his quarters. In the sun he could see the red highlights in her brown hair, the touch of green in her blue eyes.

*"Sirena mia."* He offered her his hand and she ignored it, stepping to stand beside him at the rail. "You are lovely, as always."

She cast him a suspicious sideways glance.

"How long?" she asked.

"Excuse me?"

"Tortuga. How long before we reach Tortuga?"

Rafael shrugged and faced the sea once again. "A few days. It depends, of course, on the wind." He lifted a hand to indicate the sails that were presently filled with the pleasant brisk breeze.

"Of course," she sighed. "A few days."

*"Sí."* He reached out to her, placed his finger against a grain of sand just beneath her ear. She evidently did not expect the sudden movement and jumped back as he touched her. "Just another grain of sand," he explained, attempting to show her the particle on the tip of his finger. "See?"

She was a suspicious woman, and laid her hand against her neck, there where he had touched her. "I thought I got it all."

"Should I check for more contrary grains of sand?" he offered casually. "I would be happy to give you a thorough inspection."

"No, thank you," she said, a most ungracious tone in her voice.

Rafael smiled. English or not, he rather liked his stubborn mermaid who was afraid of the sea.

"I do not recognize your accent, *sirena mia*. Where do you come from?"

"Atlanta," she said softly.

"Atlantis?"

"No." She actually smiled, but she did not look directly at him. She kept her eyes on the sea, looking ahead, looking to Tortuga. "Atlanta. It's . . ." Her smile faded. "It's difficult to explain."

"We have nothing but time, *querida*."

"I came from a place where everything is different from what you know. Everything."

Her face paled as she delivered this statement.

"What are you escaping from?" He did not need to know. No matter her circumstance, he would care for her, for a while. He would pamper her and make her laugh and hold her close at night. He did not *need* to know, but he found he wanted to very badly.

"I'm not running away," she insisted. "At least . . . I don't know."

"Family?"

She shook her head. "There was just my father, and he died late last year."

"Mother? Sisters? Brothers?" he prodded.

"No," she said softly, and he decided not to pry. "I was engaged to be married, but . . ."

She did not continue, and appeared to be

53

somewhat distressed. If he touched her now, would her body remember how easily it had come to him in the night?

"But what, *sirena mia*?"

She faced him then, eyes wide and clear and confused. "I broke it off."

"Excuse me?"

"The engagement. It wasn't right. It had never been right. Patrick got angry, and he pushed me. He didn't mean for the railing to break, I'm certain of it." Rafael could tell by the tone of her voice that she was trying to convince herself, and not him, that this Patrick had meant her no harm.

"That is why you were in the sea?"

"Yes."

"If you would like, I will hunt this Patrick down and cut out his heart for you."

The offer made her smile.

"As tempting as that suggestion is, I think I'll have to pass."

"Excuse me?"

"No. No, thank you."

"It would be my pleasure."

"I'm not into revenge, Rafael."

She was so innocent. So forgiving. Forgiveness was not a trait with which Rafael was familiar. He neither gave nor asked for such a boon. Perhaps Sabrina was not *into* revenge, as she put it, but at this moment he wanted to hunt down this Patrick and take revenge for her.

She turned her head, so that he was presented with a sun-drenched profile. Sabrina was as perfect in harsh sunlight as she was in soft moonlight.

"What *are* you into?" he asked softly.

She hesitated, and the smile on her face went on and on. "I'm into second chances. New choices. New beginnings."

When he did not speak, she turned to him, her fresh face expectant. He shook his head slightly. "You don't agree?" she asked.

Ah, she was naive to speak so clearly and hopefully of such dreams. "Your past has made you who you are, good or bad," he said. "You can try to deny your life, but it will always find you."

"I didn't think you were a cynic."

Rafael brushed his finger beneath her chin, and this time she did not move away. "I do not lie, not even to myself."

She took a short breath and held it for a long moment before she spoke. "Looking for more sand?"

"No," he breathed.

"What are you looking for?"

Rafael stroked her soft chin. It was like satin beneath his fingers. "Fun. Adventure. Excitement. No more."

Her lips parted slightly, her eyes danced, and he was totally captivated.

"I've never . . . our lives are very different," she said softly. "Fun was always at the bottom of my list. Adventure? Excitement? The most exciting thing I ever did was go shopping the day after Christmas."

Rafael raised his eyebrows and stroked the

back of his hand down her neck. "Sometimes you make no sense, *sirena mia*."

"I know." She backed away from him, slowly, almost as if she did not want to move, and then she faced the sea again, silent, her bright smile gone.

For a moment, just for a moment, she had wanted him. Just a little, perhaps, but there had been a spark in her eyes as he had stroked her neck. He could have kissed her, then, and she would not have drawn away. At least, not quickly. She would have allowed his mouth a twinkling against hers, a taste, a lingering brush . . . and then she would have withdrawn from him.

When he did finally take her, there would be no question of her pulling away, no doubts in her mind. There would be nothing but her body and his, the way of a man and a woman.

He would see that spark in her eyes again.

# *Chapter Four*

It was just the old rebound, Sabrina tried to convince herself as she stared up and into a completely black ceiling. And Rafael was, after all, a fascinating character. Charming, handsome, a pirate, for God's sake.

And those eyes . . .

Any brief attraction she felt for the man shouldn't be totally unexpected, but it shouldn't be taken seriously, either. If her fading affection for Patrick had been inadequate, then her occasional salacious thoughts about Rafael were . . . insane.

She hated this cabin. It was small and dark and musty, but she didn't dare show herself on deck. Rafael's men would be stretched out here and there, and he would be . . . no matter how she tried, she couldn't see him sleeping there with the other men. It would be much too ordinary for a man like Rafael.

When the ship lurched, Sabrina gripped the sides of the narrow cot. The wind howled, and she could hear heavy drops of rain pounding the deck above her head, and dashing against the side of the ship, as well.

The pitch increased, and she rolled onto her stomach to better grip the sides of the cot and to bury her face in the thin mattress. It didn't help much. The world was hurled this way and that, and the howl of the wind above her head whistled through the grate that covered the opening.

She lifted her head just once, and the sound that filled the cabin was somewhere between a scream and a plea. Without a second thought she dropped her head back to the mattress, to muffle any unwanted protests that might escape from her mouth.

Her stomach rolled with the ship, but that wasn't the worst of it. The worst, the very worst, was the certainty that any moment the ocean was going to pour through the opening in the ceiling and she was going to drown in salty water, just as in those old but too-well-remembered nightmares.

She considered leaving the cabin, escaping to the deck, but she knew that would be no comfort at all. The deck would be crowded with men, and she didn't fool herself into thinking that she could keep her footing on that convex surface when it was slick with rain and pitching as violently as the little cabin.

When she heard booted feet dropping onto the floor, she knew it was Rafael, and all she felt was relief.

"We're going to die," she said, very calmly.

"Ah, *sirena mia*," he crooned. "We are not going to die, not tonight."

"This boat is too small for all these people, and it's going to pitch over and we're all going to drown."

"Is this why you are down here screaming?" he asked, his voice near. He stood beside the cot.

"I didn't scream."

"You are right," he said soothingly. "It was more of a squeal, like a wild boar who has just been speared."

Oddly enough, with Rafael kneeling at her side, she was no longer so certain of her own watery death. He was too calm, and surely he knew the ocean and its storms better than she did.

Just as she was beginning to calm down, a gust of wind rocked the boat violently, and Sabrina bit her lip to keep from squealing again.

It almost worked.

"It is a small storm, *querida*," Rafael whispered. "We will all survive."

Her eyes adjusted to the darkness, and she could almost make out his face near hers. He had to be sitting on the floor to be so close, but it was too dark to tell if he was smiling, or serious, or annoyed. All she could see was the shape of his face and his damp, curling hair.

When he took her hand, prying her fingers

from the edge of the cot, she didn't object, but gripped his hand tightly. There was nothing so comforting as a warm, strong hand in a storm, she decided. Her heart rate returned to somewhere near normal, and after a few quiet minutes, she relaxed her grip. But she didn't let go.

"Talk to me," she whispered.

"About what, *sirena mia?*" His voice was a balm, and he rocked his thumb against her wrist.

"Anything. Wait. Anything not to do with the ocean. I used to have nightmares about this, about drowning in the ocean."

"I will not allow you to drown," Rafael promised, and against all reason, his assurance made her feel better. Calmer.

Where on earth did this guy come from? "Your childhood," she suggested. "Where did you grow up?"

He hesitated, and Sabrina wondered for a moment if he might decide not to answer. Maybe her question was too personal.

The ship lurched again, and she clutched his hand tighter.

"I was the youngest of twelve children," he began. "Raised on a farm in northern Spain. We did not have much, and we worked very hard, but we were never hungry."

"How does the youngest son of a farmer get to be a pirate?"

Sabrina relaxed her hold on Rafael's hand, but not too much. For the moment she would depend on Rafael for this comfort. She would forget that he called her a gift, that he was a seventeenth-century pirate and she was a twentieth-century businesswoman. For now, there was just his hand in hers and the storm that threatened to destroy them all.

"My father wanted me to be a farmer, like him. There was never any doubt in his mind that I would stay there, work with my brothers, marry a girl from the village, and have twelve babies of my own."

"But you had other ideas." She actually smiled at the thought of Rafael as a farmer, it was so ridiculous.

"I had never seen the sea, but I had heard such stories." There was a touch of wonder in his voice, and she could almost see him, a young man holding on to a dream. "When I told my father that I wanted to be a sailor, he laughed at me, called that wish nonsense, and reminded me that I would never leave our village."

"And your mother?"

Rafael laughed, lightly, warmly. "My mother wanted me to be a priest, a vocation I knew, even then, I was less well suited for than farmer."

Even then. "How old were you?"

"I was twelve when I left the farm."

"Twelve!" Sabrina lifted her head from the safety of the cot.

"*Sí. Doce.*" He mumbled, as if thinking out his interpretation in Spanish. "Twelve."

She tried to picture a pre-teen Rafael packing

up his belongings and leaving home, but it was impossible.

"I made my way to the sea. . . ."

"How?" Sabrina interrupted. "You were a child."

"I walked, I worked here and there, I stole, but only food and only when I could not find work and I was very hungry."

Sabrina couldn't remember a time in her life when she'd been truly hungry. "And you made your way to the ocean."

"*Sí*. I will end the tedious tale there, since you do not wish to hear of the sea."

"Did you ever go back? Back to the farm?"

There was a long pause, and Sabrina was afraid, once again, that she had asked a question that was too personal. She didn't want to scare Rafael away. Not now. She didn't want to sit alone in this dark and roiling cabin without a hand to hold.

"Six years ago," he answered softly. "I went with jewels for my mother, silver and gold for my father. I wanted them to know . . . I wanted them to know that I had fared well. But I was too late." His voice was casual, cool, but Sabrina could hear the strain there. "My father was gone, many years dead, and my mother was ill. Pearls and rubies mean little to a woman who is dying, when she has not seen her youngest child in ten years."

"I'm sorry."

"Do not be. I stayed until the end, saw her buried properly, and left the small treasure I had taken with my brothers who were still

62

working the farm." For a long moment, he didn't speak, but rocked his thumb rhythmically against her hand. "They looked so old, so old and unhappy. I knew then that I had not made a mistake in leaving."

"Do you ever think about going back to see them?"

"No," he said quickly. "And now you must answer my questions. Why did you cut off all your hair? It is so beautiful, but there is so little of it."

"It's easy to take care of. . . ."

"If that is the only reason, you could shave your head like Pablo." There was a trace of disgust in his voice.

"Where I come from, it's . . . the style. A style. Some women wear their hair long, some cut it short, like mine. And it's not all that short. It's almost chin length."

"You should let it grow."

She'd always worn her too-straight, too-fine hair short. It was a sensible style, after all. "I might," she answered.

Rafael reached out and took a strand of the hair in question between his fingers. He held it, rested that hand against her neck while with the other he continued to hold hers.

He was so close, and she was agonizingly aware of his every breath, his every move. She'd never in her entire life let a man affect her this way. Her heart was beating much too hard, and it seemed as if every inch of her skin was only waiting for the stroke of those strong fingers. All she wore was Rafael's own thin linen shirt.

There was nothing else between them.

It would be so easy, and dammit, she wanted it.

She could see and feel him coming closer, lowering his face to hers, and she parted her lips as he laid his mouth against hers, a mouth so soft and warm and inviting. There was comfort in his kiss, and more. Passion and longing, heat and certainty.

Rafael moved his lips against hers, and Sabrina answered him. Nothing had ever tasted so sweet, so tempting.

She could feel her own heartbeat, in her ears, in her head, she could feel it pounding against her chest. It wasn't fear of the storm that increased the thudding of her heart. It was Rafael, and the way he kissed her, slow and sweet and hard.

He made her forget everything. Where she was, when she was, who she was. And she wanted to forget.

But it was Sabrina who moved away, who slipped her mouth from his. "I can't," she whispered.

"Of course you can." Rafael strengthened his assertion with the pressure of his lips against her throat.

"I can't. It's too soon."

"It is not too soon." His voice rumbled against her neck. "It is destiny, *sirena mia*. You know that as well as I do."

Destiny? It was such a simple answer. Too simple for Sabrina to accept.

"I want to do everything right, this time," Sabrina insisted. "I'm on the rebound. Everything's changed. I don't want to make the same mistakes I made before. I don't want to make new mistakes, either."

"Shhh. You think too much." He slipped his head downward, kissed the sensitive valley between her breasts.

"No," Sabrina whispered, and Rafael drew his mouth away from her skin.

"No?" he echoed, as if he hadn't understood.

"No," she repeated, trying to sound stronger than before.

He sighed and drew away from her—except for the hand that continued to hold hers.

"You test my patience, *sirena mia.*"

Suddenly, Sabrina was aware that the ship no longer pitched and swayed. Outside the cabin, all was calm.

"The storm has passed," she said, and Rafael murmured his agreement, and then he added a few soft words in his native language. Sabrina almost asked for a translation, but decided she didn't want to know.

The deck was wet and slippery, and the sails were filled with a chilling wind that carried them toward Tortuga. Sabrina's sudden storm was long past, and the stars sparkled bright in a black sky.

Rafael gripped the rail and turned his face into a cool wind that was not nearly cool enough.

What if she decided to stay in Tortuga? What if they never finished what had begun in his cabin as the mild storm lashed them about? Un-thinkable.

Antonio Rafael de Zamora had never wanted a woman he did not get.

It was more than lust that made him hunger for her. She had washed ashore at his feet. Not north, not south, where she would have been lost in darkness, but *at his feet*. He jokingly called her *sirena mia,* my mermaid, and he had halfheartedly referred to her as his gift from the sea.

But he did not doubt that destiny had placed her there. His mother would have given God the credit. A few of his men would have praised Neptune. Rafael did not venture to guess what force had brought her to him, but he did know one undeniable truth.

She belonged to him.

It was a rather frightening certainty. He claimed nothing for himself in this life. Gold, certainly, taken from those who did not need and had not earned it. His island refuge and the house he had built there. Jewels, silver, the finest objects of art from around the world. These were things he took, but if he awoke in the morning and they were all gone, he would not grieve their loss.

But if he woke in the morning and Sabrina was gone he would be devastated.

He swore, low curses spoken in his own language, just as he had sworn at Sabrina's side in the darkness of his quarters. He silenced himself only when he heard the slap of wet bare feet behind him.

Rafael turned just as Pablo reached his side, and the big man looked out over the sea as Rafael had.

Pablo was a simple man, a man of few words, one of the few crewmen who preferred the peace and quiet of Rafael's island to the excitement in Tortuga.

Neither of them spoke for a long while. It was not unusual for Pablo to join Rafael for a few quiet moments on a night like this one. He loved the sea as much as Sabrina hated it.

Pablo leaned against the rail. The moonlight shone on his bald head, on a battered face that had frightened more than one of the *Venganza*'s victims. All he had to do was smile, and an otherwise brave man would run.

Rafael knew the man behind the face. Those brave men had been wise to run.

They did not speak for a long time. Their clash over Sabrina was unusual, but Pablo did not seem to be taking the defeat too badly.

Rafael cursed himself for the fool he was. She was only a woman. His fascination was surely an illness brought on by the moon, or the wind, or the fact that he had been too long at sea.

When Pablo finally spoke, as he turned and walked away from the railing, his words were simple.

"I still say you should sell her."

Leaving the cabin was like escaping from prison. Fresh air, sunlight, no walls closing in. Her price for this freedom was facing Rafael.

How could she have gotten so carried away

last night that she'd actually considered . . . that she'd actually *wanted* him to make love to her? She'd never been what anyone could call a loose woman. Patrick was the only man she'd ever shared intimacies with, and even then not until several months after their engagement.

She'd barely known Rafael a day.

It was the storm, the shock of all that had happened. She didn't really want Rafael, she'd just been searching for comfort. Assurance. Someone to hold during a storm.

As soon as she saw him, standing on the aft bridge above her, she knew she was kidding herself. She was attracted to this pirate in a most troubling way. Of course he was handsome, but she'd never been so silly as to be affected by a man's physical appearance. Before.

That didn't mean she would allow anything to happen. Everything she'd said to him in the darkness of the cabin was true. It was too soon, and she didn't want to make any mistakes.

Somehow, miraculously she'd been reborn into another time. This was her chance to live life differently, to claim what had escaped her in a sorry existence of ambition and cold calculation. She didn't want to blow her second chance by falling for, literally, the first guy she'd seen here.

In a way, that had happened with Patrick. He was the first man who'd ever truly pursued her. Every other man who'd expressed any interest in her had been easily discouraged. But not Patrick. He'd persisted, even after she coolly rebuffed him.

Eventually, she had convinced herself that it was romantic. That his pursuit of her was sweet, his refusal to give up a sign of something that might even be love. She'd been flattered, but now she knew he'd been using her all along. That knowledge hurt, even though she didn't love Patrick and never had.

So why should she fall head over heels for the first man she ran across now? The first man she'd seen after falling from that pier? Maybe, deep down, she was afraid of facing life in this time alone. 1665. Reminding herself of where she was, when she was, gave Sabrina a chill. From what little she knew of history, women didn't go it alone in the seventeenth century. They were wives, and mothers, and perhaps occasionally lovers. There were no other options.

She would find an option. Somewhere. Somehow. Surely she wouldn't have been given this second chance just so she could latch herself to a pirate with a charming smile and killer eyes.

When he saw her he left the bridge, swiftly descending the ladder that brought him to her side.

"Good morning, *sirena mia*."

If he held any grudge for last night's refusal, he didn't show it. His smile was easy as his eyes flickered pleasantly over her from head to toe.

"I trust you slept well after the storm passed," he said blandly.

She hadn't been able to close her eyes even for five minutes after he'd left the cabin. "Very well, thank you. And you?" Her answer, her lie, was so polite, so distant.

"I slept not at all," he said nonchalantly, and with a wicked grin. "One storm passed, but another raged on."

Surely she turned eight different shades of red. She could feel the heat in her cheeks. All she could manage was a weak, "Oh."

Rafael lowered his voice and, moving very slowly, he placed his face close to hers. "How many times must I tell you not to lie to me. You slept no better than I, for the same storm raged within you, *sirena mia*. Do not deny it."

She couldn't. At the moment she couldn't find any words at all.

"Pablo!" Sabrina started when Rafael shouted to the very large, very bald man who stood near the hold. "Food for *Señorita* Sabrina."

Sabrina was prepared for the same simple meal they always seemed to eat. Dried meat— she was afraid to ask what kind—and rum. She wasn't disappointed. She chewed on the meat and sipped at the rum, and Rafael returned to his duties on the bridge.

Sabrina leaned against the rail, lifting her eyes to the bridge when she thought Rafael might not notice, keeping her attention there when it became clear he had completely forgotten she was on board.

He didn't glance down at her, not once.

Her insides churned. It was the strange meat, the rum, the sway of the *Venganza*.

It was Rafael.

70

# *Chapter Five*

Tortuga. It was not what Sabrina had expected, when Rafael had first mentioned the island. She'd imagined sand, palm trees, a flat base.

But the island was mountainous, lushly green, and from the right angle resembled a tortoise in shape. Rafael told her, in a calm voice that indicated that he didn't care that she'd ignored him for three days, that only the southern portion of the island was populated. In the north, he said, there was no access to the shore, and the land was too harsh for habitation.

He leaned casually against the rail as he played tour guide. His hand waved indolently, on occasion, toward the island, and he kept his eyes on Tortuga.

Rafael hadn't come to the cabin in the dead of night again, but then, there had been no more storms. He hadn't whispered to her any nonsense about destiny, and when he touched her it was accidental or brief and innocent. The brush of an arm, perhaps, or a steadying hand as the ship rocked. Nothing more.

They arrived at the port of Cayona, and the *Venganza* became one of many ships. It was one of the smaller vessels, but not the smallest.

Next to some of the larger ships, the *Venganza* was dwarfed.

"You have made your decision, *sirena mia*?" Rafael asked nonchalantly as he followed her down the plank to a sturdy and motionless pier.

"I've told you all along, Tortuga is fine."

She was cursed. Just as she said the words two drunken sailors, no doubt pirates but dirtier and more odoriferous than any man on Rafael's ship, appeared on the pier, and moving forward without care they almost bowled Sabrina over. They gave her a startled glance as they became suddenly aware of her presence, taking in her hair and her baggy masculine clothing, and then they looked at Rafael.

They moved on.

"You need me to protect you, *sirena mia*," Rafael insisted, and she could hear the strain in his voice. He might appear to be indifferent, but right now he was losing his cool.

"I don't need anyone to protect me," Sabrina insisted. "I have a plan."

"A plan," he repeated. He said the words so coldly, so incredulously, as if he was shocked a woman could come up with a plan of her own.

"Yes. I'll make my way to the colonies." She kept her voice clear and free of the uncertainty she couldn't deny. "Is it even called America yet? I'm not sure. If I'd known I was coming here, I could have brushed up on my history."

The land far ahead was lusciously green, but before her lay a dry and dusty street. People. Shops.

"Boston, New York, Charleston. I don't even know what's been founded yet, but I'll find a way."

"At times you make no sense," Rafael said, staying diligently at her heels. "Come with me to my island for a short while, and then, when the time comes, I will take you anywhere you want to go."

"No."

"Why not?" He grabbed her arm and spun her around. He had such an expressive face. Rafael said he didn't lie, and in truth, with a face like that it would have been impossible. She could read all his emotions there. Anger, frustration, lust.

She had given this a lot of thought in the past three days. Why she was here, what came next. "You're a pirate, for God's sake."

"And if I were a planter, or a hunter, you would come with me?"

"I don't know."

He stared down at her for a moment, eyes narrowed, curls falling over much of his face. Someone brushed against his back, jostling him into awareness, and he began to speak, low menacing words in Spanish.

The person who had bumped into him was gone, and still he muttered those words she couldn't understand, staring at her, leaning close, so that she couldn't inhale without taking in Rafael's scent. He smelled like the sea, like sunshine and salt water. She had always been terrified of the sea.

"I can't understand a word you're saying." She tried to sound calm, but her voice shook.

Abruptly, Rafael was silent. She would never know, but it seemed he halted in midsentence.

"You make me forget my English," he said, releasing her arm and backing away. "I will be in Tortuga until morning. If you change your mind . . ."

"I won't."

Rafael turned his back on her, throwing a hand into the air as he surrendered. And he was muttering in Spanish again.

The woman was a fool. She walked through the town of Cayona unescorted, making inquiries into passage when she found sailors who spoke English. Turning away in disgust when their interest turned personal.

What did she expect? She was dressed in loose clothing, his own, but she looked not at all like a man. Sabrina Steele's shape was entirely female, and her face lovely and pale, still, even though her days in the sun had given her cheeks a touch of color. Even more telling, she moved with a natural grace that made her stand out in a street rife with drunken pirates who spent so much time at sea they never quite found their land legs.

She would have been in serious trouble by

noon if Rafael had not followed her. If he had not dissuaded those Dutch pirates who tried to pursue Sabrina even after she turned so naively away. If he had not explained, so very carefully and with the tip of his knife at that Frenchman's throat, that she was not to be molested.

And like the unsuspecting innocent Sabrina was, she never knew that he was there, that her ridiculous inquiries put her life and her virtue in danger.

He had expected she would be discouraged when faced with the reality of Cayona. Sabrina was a woman obviously not accustomed to such a common and rough way of life. Since that one kiss, that one maddening kiss, he had distanced himself from Sabrina as she seemed to wish. Surely she would see that his island was a safer and more pleasurable place than any other.

He stayed out of sight, lurking around corners and behind the crowds, and he watched as Sabrina's enthusiasm faded. She was tired, and she was undoubtedly hungry, and when she finally wilted onto a rock just past the inn at the edge of town, sitting down and placing her head in her hands, Rafael smiled.

How could she refuse him now?

*"Sirena mia,"* he said cheerfully as he stepped around the corner. "Have you secured your passage?"

Sabrina lifted tired eyes. She did not even appear to be surprised to see him. "Not yet."

So stubborn, she was. "Would you like some fruit?" He sat beside her, his thigh barely brushing hers, and offered her a yanna and a paquay.

LINDA JONES

She eyed the fruits suspiciously and hungrily before taking the yanna.

"Thank you."

She begrudged him even that, thanking him sullenly. It was all he could do not to smile. "Are you still eager to sail to your Boston or one of those other ports?"

"Yes."

She sounded so tired, not certain at all.

"Why? There is much suffering there. Hunger and bitter cold in the winter. Do you have friends there?"

"No."

She devoured the yanna, and he handed her the paquay. "Why would anyone prefer such a harsh place to an island where it is never cold, where the fruit grows so large and abundant the inhabitants can never eat it all? I do not believe yanna or paquay grow in your Boston. Or magniot or bacones."

Sabrina looked down at her bare feet. When she hung her head that way she had the look of defeat. It made him angry, that she should allow herself to suffer so. A woman like this should have slippers on her feet, and silk gowns against her skin rather than his own rough clothing. She should wear pearls and emeralds. The emeralds would surely bring out the spark of green in her eyes.

"*Sirena mia,*" he said, lifting her chin so that she was forced to look at him. "Why do you fight me so?"

"I told you why," she whispered.

"Because I am a pirate."

"Yes."

"Every man you have spoken to today is a pirate as well."

"You've been watching me?" Anger flashed in her eyes.

Rafael smiled. "Every man on the island is a hunter, a planter, or a pirate. I do not think any hunter or planter can transport you to your Boston. And if I did keep an eye on you today, it was for your own welfare that I did so."

She had her doubts, his gift from the sea. The day had not gone as she had planned, and perhaps traveling on to his island was not such a distasteful idea, at the moment. Just a little more persuasion and she would relent.

"Stay with me a while longer," he whispered, lowering his face so that it came near to hers. He remembered what it was like to kiss her, how she melted against him. How she quivered when he placed his hand against her back or on her arm. "You know it is destiny, *sirena mia*. We are meant to be. For today, for tomorrow." Her lips parted slightly. "Until this fire is out."

Sabrina inhaled sharply and drew away from him. "You degenerate."

"I do not know this word." That was the truth, but he did grasp, quite well, the meaning of the word she snapped at him. She was angry.

"Pig. Do you know that word?"

"*Sí.*" Rafael sighed.

"The fact that I'm here is incredible. Momentous. I don't know why I'm here or how this happened." She looked around him, beyond him, amazement in her lovely eyes. "But I do know I wasn't given a second chance just to become some pirate's mistress until he tires of me."

The color was back in her face, and her exhaustion was no longer evident. What fire she had. What passion. "Perhaps I would never tire of you, *querida*."

"Perhaps I'm the queen of England," she said softly, bitter sarcasm dripping from each word.

Rafael trailed the back of his hand across her throat, lightly, carelessly, and he sighed as he studied the soft skin there. "You need me, *sirena mia*."

It was, evidently, the wrong statement to make. "I *do not* need you," she snapped, standing so that his hand fell away from her satin skin. "So back off."

"Back off?" he repeated.

"Go away, Antonio Rafael de Zamora. Find another beached mermaid to harass."

He allowed her to walk away. "But you are the only one," he said softly, when no ears but his own could hear.

It took the rest of the afternoon, but she finally found an English-speaking sailor who took her inquiries seriously. He was sailing for Portsmouth, north of Boston, in a matter of days.

Twice that afternoon, she'd caught Rafael following her. A glimpse of that unmistakable head of hair rounding a corner. That soothing, menacing voice, directed at a pair of lascivious pirates who had no interest in helping her find her way home. Or, rather, as close to home as she was going to get.

Did he think she was a child? She would prove him wrong, and make her way to America on her own.

"And it's acceptable to work off my passage on the other end?" she asked again.

"Of course." The sailor smiled. Sabrina preferred to think of him as a sailor, even though Rafael had said they were all pirates here. His name was John Clarke, and English was his first language, though it was an English so accented she had almost as much trouble following it as she did Rafael's. "You will work for a merchant or a planter until your passage is paid. It's often done."

"Splendid."

She was as good as on her way. This was what she wanted, right? The knot in her stomach was normal trepidation, and she couldn't fool herself into thinking this was over. What awaited her in America? Everything there would be as strange to her as Rafael's ship and this island.

But she had done it, even though Rafael had been sure she would fail.

"More rum?" Clarke offered, lifting his own nearly empty tankard.

They sat in the public room of an inn, at a small table near the center of the room. Sabrina wasn't the only female in the room, but the other women were obviously . . . professionals. They hung all over the pirates who filled the room, and one even bared her breasts when a thin little man in tattered pants and a red vest offered her a gold coin to do so.

Sabrina kept her head turned, but Clarke enjoyed the show, as did every other man in her line of vision.

"I've had enough," she said, eyeing her half-filled tankard. Didn't anyone here ever drink water?

The door opened, and Sabrina automatically turned her head to the door. She immediately wished she hadn't.

Rafael stood there, the setting sun behind him, one of his men at his side. Esteban; she remembered the name as the toady little man stepped aside to allow Rafael to enter the room. Esteban darted his eyes all around the room. Everywhere but at her.

Not Rafael. He stared directly and boldly at her, annoyed, restless, and when he entered the room he stalked straight to the table. Esteban closed the door quietly and planted himself before it, a stern and imposing guard.

"*Sirena mia,*" Rafael said harshly. "What are you doing?"

"Arranging passage, as I said I would."

Clarke slowly lowered a hand into his lap, and Sabrina wondered what sort of weapon waited there. She didn't want to see the man lunge for Rafael, didn't want this to go any further.

"Not with this English scum, I trust."

Rafael didn't even spare a glance for the man he insulted.

"John Clarke," she said calmly, trying to avert

disaster. "Really, Rafael, it doesn't matter how I get there . . ."

"It does not matter." There was utter disbelief written on Rafael's face as he repeated her assertion. "How will you pay your passage, *querida*?"

"I'm going to work it off at the other end." She would have said more, but Rafael's face went white. Even in the dim light of the public room, the change was evident.

"You will not," he said, his voice low.

"I don't have to get your permission. . . ."

"I forbid it."

"You *what*?"

"I forbid it," he shouted.

There was not a sound to be heard in the room. Tankards were not lifted. There were no whispers, no laughter. Clarke drew a short-bladed knife from beneath the table as he stood to face Rafael.

"No!" Sabrina shot to her feet. "Put that away," she demanded.

The English pirate looked at her briefly, and as if she were off her rocker.

Rafael drew his knife, brandishing the curved blade that was three times as long as Clarke's weapon.

"Esteban," Rafael said calmly as Clarke backed away. He delivered his instructions in rapid Spanish, one eye on Clarke and one on her, it seemed, as the little man disappeared.

"I have been very patient with you, *sirena mia*," he muttered darkly. "But this time you have gone too far."

81

Too far? *She'd* gone too far?

"It's none of your concern. . . ."

"There are some . . . some outrages I will not allow."

"You can't . . ."

The door crashed open and Esteban stepped in, with Pablo and four more of Rafael's crew behind him.

"We leave tonight," Rafael said. Pablo, Esteban, and the rest of Rafael's men entered the room quickly, forming a half circle of protection around them. Only then did Sabrina notice the number of men in the room who had drawn their weapons. John Clarke's crew?

"Rafael, this is not necessary. . . ."

She stopped protesting when he turned his full attention to her. No one had ever looked at her like that before. Angry. Hostile. Gold-brown eyes that seemed to be on fire locked with hers and wouldn't let go. The face of a man-eating tiger about to strike couldn't have been more menacing.

He didn't take her arm, didn't say a word in English *or* Spanish, but simply lifted her with one arm and tossed her over his shoulder.

"Put me down," she muttered through clenched teeth.

*"Sirena mia,"* Rafael cooed in a low voice meant only for her, "be quiet."

They ran, Rafael in the lead with her dangling uncomfortably over his shoulder, six of his men behind them. Sabrina lifted her head to watch the mob that followed them down the street.

Behind Rafael's men were at least twenty

other armed pirates. They swung swords and knifes, for the most part, but she had seen one firearm brandished.

She waited for the roar of that weapon, but all she heard were angry and occasionally excited shouts in at least three different languages.

Rafael ran up the plank to the deck of the *Venganza* and deposited her roughly beneath the aft bridge. Carrying her as he ran down the street had evidently been no effort for him. He wasn't even breathing hard.

Sabrina opened her mouth to blast him, but she didn't get the chance.

"Stay," he barked, and then he returned to the plank and disappeared from view.

One by one his men appeared, panting and sometimes bloody, but no one seemed to be seriously injured. Sabrina didn't move from the spot where Rafael had deposited her, but watched silently as they got underway. Not the entire crew, but Rafael, Pablo, Esteban, and the others who had come to the inn to abduct her.

Rafael was the last on board, and as they pulled away from the pier he tossed one persistent English pirate over the side, watching until the man splashed into the water.

And then he turned to Sabrina. With a smile.

Sabrina stormed across the deck. "You idiot! What the hell do you think you're doing?"

"I am rescuing you."

"You're *abducting* me!"

Rafael shrugged his shoulders, unconcerned.

Perhaps in his mind they were one and the same.

"I will not allow you to sell yourself into slavery for passage to a miserable place. Even for passage to paradise, I would not allow such an indignity."

"You will not allow?" He continued to grin down at her, and that smile only infuriated her more. "I was hardly selling myself into slavery."

"An indentured servant is no different from a slave, to most." His smile faded. "And yes, there are some atrocities I will not allow."

How dare he? He looked at her as if she were an errant child who needed to be protected from herself. As if he had no qualms about what he'd just done.

And of course he hadn't a one.

"If I could swim, I'd jump off this boat right this minute."

"Then it is my good fortune that you cannot swim, for I would only follow and bring you back, and it will soon be dark."

Sabrina stamped a bare foot.

"Do not worry, *sirena mia*," Rafael said softly. "You are safe now."

# *Chapter Six*

Rafael's island was a smaller version of Tortuga, with green hills and water an impossibly blue-green color. At dawn it was a sight to behold, a realm where certainly fantasies reigned and dreams came true.

Sabrina watched from the rail of the *Venganza* with a silent Rafael at her side, steeling herself against the fanciful notions that filled her head. No way would she allow him to see how enchanted she was.

She had finally decided, last night as they'd sailed away from Tortuga, that the silent treatment was the way to go. No matter what she said to him, how angry she got, her insults only seemed to delight him.

As they docked and the plank was lowered, she saw it: a roofline in the distance. Rafael certainly didn't live in a hut. The tiled roof was broad, tall, and she had no doubt but that a veritable palace waited there. She should have expected nothing less.

"My home," he said quietly, no doubt noting her interest. "Your home, for the moment," he added.

"Bite me," Sabrina muttered.

"It would be my great pleasure."

As she walked sullenly down the plank, Rafael close behind, the people came, appearing from the thick growth of trees. There was an older man, gray and hobbling, who supported himself on the arm of a much younger woman who was round and short.

Directly behind them were other dark-haired women who stayed close together and watched the *Venganza* with wide eyes. Children appeared, not toddlers, but adolescents. All were smiling and shouted greetings to the pirates.

It soon became clear, as the crowd grew, that some of these pirates had families. Pablo was greeted by a surprisingly good-looking and fairly young woman who was very pregnant, and Sabrina saw the big man in another light when he lifted the woman with great care and spun her around twice before he set her easily on her feet.

"That is Aqualina," Rafael whispered, following her gaze. "She is Pablo's wife. You will like her, *sirena mia*, except . . ."

"Except what?" Sabrina prodded with little patience.

"Well, she has no English, and you have no Spanish." He sounded not at all concerned.

"Figures. Does anyone on this island besides you speak English?"

"Pablo, a little, as you know. Cristóbal, but he only knows a few words to impress the women. Bernardo . . ."

"Anyone besides your crew?"

Sabrina cut her eyes to Rafael as he pondered her question. Already, there was something different about him. A touch of serenity in his animal eyes. He was home.

"No," he finally answered with a casual air.

"Great. Stuck on an island in the middle of nowhere, and I won't even be able to communicate. I think I was right the first time I saw you and your crew," she muttered. "I'm in hell."

"Oh, no, *sirena mia*," Rafael assured her with a smile. "This island is more heaven than hell. I will convince you of that, with time."

They followed a footpath through abundant, junglelike growth that was as primitive as Rafael. The women chattered, excited, musical words that meant nothing to Sabrina. They gave her suspicious sidelong glances, as the pirates from the *Venganza* whispered to them. Like she could have understood if they'd shouted.

Sabrina got tired of avoiding curious glances, and so she kept her eyes on the beauty around her. She'd never seen anything so lush and green, never seen flowers so bright. They grew everywhere, those flowers, on the ground and in the trees, vivid flashes of color amongst the dark green.

Throughout the short walk, Rafael stayed

close to her, but he wisely decided against trying to convince her again that this was any sort of heaven.

They left the path, and before them was a large white house. It was no palace, but neither was it the sort of home you would expect to find on a small island.

The architecture was definitely Spanish, with arched doorways and windows, and a rust-colored tile roof. Plants grew at the edge of the structure, brushing the walls with large, glistening leaves of deep green and flowering vines that climbed well past the second-story windows.

The others, the pirates and their families, continued on, following a path around the house and leaving Rafael and Sabrina alone. She stared at the building, impressed, awed, determined not to show her surprise.

"It is beautiful?" Rafael asked.

"It'll do, I suppose." She glanced at him out of the corner of her eye, and saw that her cool response hadn't dampened his enthusiasm.

"It took me five years to build this house. Clearing the land, bringing in the materials, watching it grow so slowly. And then there came the storm that destroyed it all, just after the first walls went up, and I had to begin anew."

Sabrina saw it once again, the hint of peace on Rafael's face she'd noticed as he'd left the ship.

"All right," she conceded with just a hint of ungraciousness. "It is beautiful."

His smile widened, and Sabrina decided it was worth the small concession to see his face glow like that.

The door burst open, and a short, thin woman greeted Rafael with a reserved smile and a brief curtsey. She was an older woman, perhaps fifty, and wore an apron that was dusted with what could have been flour or some sort of meal.

After the greeting, the woman turned her eyes boldly to Sabrina.

"Elena," Rafael said as he took Sabrina's arm and led her to the door, "*esta es Señorita Sabrina.*"

Sabrina gave the woman a small hello.

Elena stared, stone-faced, and replied in rapid Spanish. Sabrina could only make out one bitter word. *Ingles.*

With a brief instruction from Rafael, Elena turned and left, shaking her head with what could only be disapproval.

"She hates me," Sabrina said as they stepped into the house.

"No, no, *sirena mia,*" Rafael assured her. "She is surprised, that is all. I have never brought a lady to my home before."

"You don't make a habit of kidnapping women and imprisoning them on your own personal island?"

"No. Only you, *sirena mia.*"

"I feel so much better," she drawled.

As she stepped into Rafael's home, her irritation faded. They were in a large main room, and the beamed ceiling was the full two stories high. At the far end of the room were matching curved staircases, and the upstairs hallway was visible through gilded railings on three sides.

Beneath her bare feet was a rug that was almost certainly Persian. Scattered around the room was a collection of mismatched but obviously expensive furniture. Delicate chairs, a long polished table. A still-life, rich colored oils on canvas in an elaborate gold frame. The colors in the room were as sumptuous as the blooms that grew untended in the jungle, as strong and alluring as Rafael himself. Deep reds, royal blues, a profusion of gold.

On the floor near the fireplace there was a massive collection of pillows, large and small, brocade and satin, tassled and plain.

It was something out of a fairy tale, rich and forbidden, opulent and exciting.

And all of it was most certainly stolen.

"Elena is preparing your room, *querida*." Rafael's voice was low, but it almost echoed through the great room. "And then we will see to that bath you so badly wanted when I found you, and some clothing befitting such a *señorita bella*."

"When do I get out of here?"

Rafael's smile faded, and the sparkle left his eyes. "When the time comes for you to leave, I will take you anywhere in the world you wish to go. That time has not yet come."

His carefree words sparked her anger. Okay, maybe this *was* paradise, but he'd kidnapped her to get her here, and she wouldn't let him play the gracious host.

"Oh, yeah? Says who? What am I, a two-year-old? Who decides when it's time for me to leave?"

"I do." Rafael's voice was perfectly calm, perfectly reasonable, and it only infuriated her more.

"I don't need some two-bit pirate making my decisions for me, thank you very much. I've done just fine on my own, up until now. . . ."

"*Sí*, you've done so very fine," Rafael snapped, taking a handful of the vest she wore. "You've done so fine that you wear my clothes on your back and have my food in your belly. You've done so fine that if I had not watched over you you would be some diseased English buccaneer's strumpet by now, and in no more than a few days you would be another man's slave."

He lowered his face, bringing those narrowed eyes close to hers. "What do you think a man does with a slave such as you, *sirena mia?* Do you think you would pass your days in some rich man's fields, or cleaning his house, or caring for his children? No, my stubborn mermaid. You would pass the days and nights on your back, until your heart and your soul grew weary. And then? And then that master would sell you to another."

"Don't be ridiculous," Sabrina said calmly, but her heart beat wildly. "I wouldn't allow . . ."

"You would not allow," he interrupted with slowly spoken, soft words. "You would run, they would catch you. The first beating would not be too bad, perhaps. You would recover, and you would try again. They would catch you again, and the second time is always worse than the first. Harder. Perhaps, even, you would die." He took a deep breath, almost as if to temper his anger. "You would most certainly wish to die."

There was a darkness in his eyes she had not seen before. Was this the man sailors saw when Rafael boarded their ship intent on piracy?

"You can't know . . ."

"I know," he whispered. "The next time you tell me how you do not need me, think of where you would be if I had not saved . . . kidnapped you, *sirena mia*."

He had never uttered that endearment so darkly. Sabrina shivered uncontrollably, and Rafael released her. "Elena will arrange for your bath and anything else you need."

Spinning away from her, Rafael left the house, slamming the wide door he had, moments earlier, entered with a smile on his face.

He was impossible, insane, domineering, and beneath her anger there was a kernel of regret that she had ruined his homecoming.

Rafael followed the path past the cottages where those of his crew who chose to reside on the island with their families lived, without sparing a glance for those who gathered together to celebrate their return.

His path carried him over a rocky hill, to the other side of the island and a secluded cove. This was his territory, and no one else on the island came here. There were other stretches of beach that were longer, clearer, more beautiful. But this cove was his.

This place was wild, and dense growth extended to a narrow strip of sand. Beyond the white sand was a pool of blue-green water that was warm, almost motionless.

He stripped off his shirt and tossed it aside, left his trousers and boots in the sand as he walked into the water, diving forward when the sea touched his thighs.

The water flowing against his body calmed him, so that he could think clearly once again. He pushed, fought the water and worked with its forces, became a part of the powerful sea that surrounded his home.

She was such a fool, his gift. She enraged him with a word, a look, frustrated him completely with her refusal to accept what he offered. Any reasonable woman would be grateful for his assistance, but not Sabrina Steele. She acted as if he had wronged her somehow.

Was she truly so naive that she had no idea of the dangers awaiting an unprotected woman in this world?

Rafael relaxed, rolled onto his back and drifted with the tide, closed his eyes and allowed the warm sun to bathe his face.

Somehow, it was true. She did not know how close she had come to being destroyed. In her heart, she viewed him as an abductor, not as a savior. This island was, to her, a prison, not a refuge.

Why was he so enamoured of her? She was English, and stubborn, and ungrateful, and hot-tempered, and . . . and she kissed with all of her stubborn heart, smiled with the warmth of the sun, called him the most ridiculous names when she was angry.

In his bed, she would be as wild as the sea from which she had come, as fiery as her temper. As sweet as her mouth against his.

He had told Sabrina he would decide when it was time for her to go, and on that decision he would not waver.

She would not leave his island until he had seduced her. Until she came to his bed of her own free will. Until the anger in her eyes was replaced with passion. Before he released her they would dance, and laugh, and make love until dawn.

Only then would he let his gift go.

The bedroom to which Elena escorted her was much like the grand room below. A luxurious, deep green satin coverlet was draped over a wide, soft bed. Heavy drapes hung over a balcony door, and there were pillows everywhere, pillows in the bright colors of jewels. Ruby, emerald, sapphire, topaz. There was a single chair in the room, a delicate piece of furniture that appeared much too fragile to actually sit in.

The room was large, like the others she'd seen. It was, in fact, opulently spacious, with high ceilings and wide windows and plenty of airy space. It suited Rafael, a man who was larger than life, and who was accustomed to the open sea. He would surely not be comfortable in a tiny house with tiny rooms.

For the first time since the fall—she didn't know what else to call the incident—there was no sand in her hair or on her skin. She'd sat in the tub until the water had cooled and Elena, crotchety, sour-faced Elena, had lost patience.

It was impossible to tell the woman, who apparently understood not a word of English, that she was perfectly capable of drying and dressing herself, thank you.

Completely alone at last, behind the closed door of the room in Rafael's house, Sabrina covered her face with her hands. Hiding, as best she could. Denying, for a moment, all that had happened.

She'd gone from a world where she had control over every aspect of her life to a time when she had none.

It was more than her lack of control that distressed Sabrina. There was a part of her, a very tiny part, that wanted to believe there was no other reason for her journey than to be here. With Rafael. Still, that was impossible for her to accept.

Her moment of meditation was much too short. Elena was back, a pile of clothing in her hands. The little woman spoke constantly, under her breath and with apparent displeasure. Sabrina had to shoo the muttering woman from the room, relying on gestures that required no translation, and Elena left most ungraciously.

The clothes Elena had provided were comfortable and plain. There was a white blouse that was cut too loosely at the scooped neck and a full cornflower blue skirt that just covered the soft black slippers Sabrina slipped gratefully onto her feet.

Apparently Elena didn't understand the concept of underwear.

It felt so good just to be clean, Sabrina decided she could live without underwear if she had to.

She threw open the drapes and stepped onto the balcony. The small railed terrace was at the side of the house and faced the junglelike growth that surrounded Rafael's home. Sunlight slanted comfortingly to the balcony, warming Sabrina and reminding her that this was all very real. The island was alive with the harmonious sounds of life. A bird, the chirp of insects, the rustle of something unidentified. Paradise could be deadly, she imagined.

Beneath her was the path the others, the pirates and their families, had taken. An unexpected smile crossed Sabrina's face as she remembered the way the frightening Pablo had so tenderly greeted his beautiful wife. She never would have thought . . .

She heard him coming, booted footsteps on the path, muttered soft Spanish words. Sabrina leaned over the balcony and watched Rafael stalk down the path. Dark, wet hair curled around his face and danced gently with each long stride.

There was certainly nothing wrong with watching, just for a moment. What red-blooded American woman wouldn't? She held her breath as Rafael passed beneath her balcony, never bothering to look up. He was too intent on his tirade.

The front door slammed, and Sabrina returned to her room. She held her breath as she listened to Rafael's footsteps pounding on the stairway, as he stalked down the hall. She licked her lips. This was it. He was going to burst into her room and demand . . .

The door of the room next to hers opened and then was slammed forcefully, and Sabrina released the breath she'd been holding. Of course, his room was next to hers.

She sank down on the bed, reminding herself more than once that she was not disappointed.

There were no other noises from the room next to hers, no stomping around or muttered Spanish that she could hear. She listened closely anyway, just in case.

When Rafael left his room a short while later, he closed the door quietly behind him. No more slamming, no more stomping around. In fact, she had to strain to hear him at all.

Because she was listening so closely, she heard the soft footsteps in the hallway. A moment later Elena threw open the door, without a knock or a single word of greeting.

Elena's instructions that Sabrina was to leave the comfort of the bedroom were very clear. She motioned with her bony hands, gesturing sternly into the hallway and then pointing down.

Of course, Rafael was waiting.

Sabrina held her head high as she followed Elena down the hallway. The spry woman hurried down the staircase, but Sabrina hesitated.

Rafael stood at the foot of the stairs, hair curling and damp, the clothes in which he'd sailed the ocean replaced by a finer suit, gray trousers and shiny boots, an unruffled shirt that was open at the collar, a waistcoat of yellow and silver.

She paused in the middle of the curved stairway. He had been so angry when she'd watched him coming down the path, but that anger was gone. In fact, he managed to appear quite pleased with himself.

"Lovely, *sirena mia*," he said softly.

He didn't look so bad himself, but she wasn't about to tell him so.

"Come." He lifted a hand to her. "We have much to do."

"We do?" Sabrina resumed her descent.

"*Sí.*"

As she reached the last step, Rafael took her hand and drew her to the long table. It had been bare when they'd arrived, but now there were several bolts of fabric piled haphazardly there. Luxurious fabrics, brocades and silks and satins. Colors bright and dull.

"For your wardrobe," Rafael said, pausing to study the fabrics carefully. "Which do you fancy?"

Sabrina slowly slipped her hand from his, and she studied the bolts silently for a moment, the ruby red and the emerald green. A white shot with gold. Silver gray, deep blue, black satin. All so very beautiful. All certainly stolen.

"None of them," she said shortly. "I won't be here long enough to need a wardrobe, in any case."

"One gown," Rafael pressed. "One fine gown

befitting *sirena mia*. Perhaps while you are my guest you can forget that I am a pirate. If you like, you can pretend that I am nothing more than a planter, and in this very room we will dine and drink wine and have a proper dance, you and I."

It was so tempting. She could see it, dancing in this room with Rafael, gliding across the empty floor as he spun her around and around and around. . . .

"I can't dance," she revealed. "I was going to take lessons, but . . ."

"Lessons?" Rafael whispered, and only then did Sabrina realize that he stood so close behind her. His breath touched her bare shoulder. "Where you come from do they give lessons on how to dance, how to breathe, how to make love?"

"I sometimes think that wouldn't be such a bad idea," she muttered as Rafael lowered his lips to her shoulder. Taking a deep breath of resolve, she stepped away from him. "All right. The black, I suppose."

Rafael said nothing, and she turned to note the displeased expression on his face. "You are in mourning?"

"No."

Rafael literally turned up his nose.

"All right, the blue."

Rafael shook his head. "It is almost as dark as the black. I do not like the blue."

Sabrina lifted her hand in supplication. "What do you need me for? Why bother to ask what I want?"

"You are right, of course," he replied, signaling for Elena to join them.

Rafael ran his hands over the fabrics, talking swiftly to Elena while Sabrina fumed. It took him only a moment to choose the red.

"Going for the bimbo effect, are we?" Sabrina muttered. Rafael glanced at her and smiled. A moment later, he placed the white shot with gold with the red, and handed them both to Elena, adding instructions Sabrina couldn't understand. The sour woman nodded her head several times, and glanced at Sabrina only once.

When Elena left, taking the two selected bolts with her, Rafael turned his attention to Sabrina again. "You will see that I have chosen wisely."

"You are impossibly arrogant, pigheaded and egotistical and presumptuous . . ."

"*Sirena mia,*" Rafael interrupted softly. "Arrogant I know. Pigheaded I know. The others . . . I can only assume that they are insults."

"You bet your ass they are."

Rafael grinned, and in spite of it all Sabrina's heart took a quick spin.

"Indulge me, *querida.*" His voice caressed her, washed over her as warmly as the sun she'd basked in on the private balcony. "Allow me to take care of you, for a short while. I have never before found anything on the seaside but a shell or two, and I fear I shall never again stumble across a gift such as you."

He was good. Actually, he was *very* good. It would be disgustingly easy to melt at those sweet words spoken in that musically accented voice, to look into those brandy eyes and surrender completely. To allow Rafael to treat her as if she were truly a gift. His gift. His mermaid.

It was tempting.

But Sabrina knew that if she relaxed, if she allowed Rafael to take over her life, to care for her, to kiss her, to love her . . . she would never leave this island.

# *Chapter Seven*

The island was too tempting, and Sabrina found she couldn't confine herself to Rafael's house, no matter how much she wanted to avoid the pirate.

Whenever she left the house he was there, either at her heels or watching from a safe distance as she explored the coast or walked the paths.

This morning she decided to follow the path that crossed beneath her balcony. Before she'd rounded the house, Rafael was with her.

"Good morning," he said brightly.

She glanced at him just long enough to see that he looked particularly content. Smug, almost. He placed his hand familiarly at the small of her back to guide her along the path. It was nothing. A brush of his fingers, pressure so insignificant she could barely feel it. She wanted to dart away from that light touch, but it would have revealed too much.

"Would you like a tour of my very small and insignificant plantation today?" He ignored the fact that she hadn't returned his greeting, and smiled warmly.

"Why not?" she conceded.

Rafael led her down the path, over a small rise, and there it was. The old man Sabrina had seen upon her arrival was working on Rafael's plantation, with the help of the woman who had been on his arm that day.

"That is Domingo," Rafael said softly, and the pressure at her back increased slightly. "The woman working beside him is his wife, Nelia."

The fingers at her back began to rock back and forth, slowly and nonchalantly. Sabrina stood very still, but it wasn't easy. "This is not a plantation," she said calmly. "This is a big garden."

Rafael shrugged his shoulders. "You are right, of course. Domingo grows vegetables and some tobacco, all that we need here."

About that time Domingo lifted his head and grinned, and waved energetically before he returned his full attention to the garden.

"Why did you tell me you had a plantation?" she asked, her eyes on the old man and his young wife.

" 'I have a garden' does not sound so impressive." There was too much humor in his voice for Sabrina not to smile.

The hand at her spine inched higher, brushing against her back casually. It was too much.

**103**

It was not enough. Sabrina stepped forward so that Rafael's hand fell away.

"Was Domingo . . . did he used to . . ."

"Was he a pirate?" Rafael read her thoughts and spoke the question for her. "Once, Domingo was a very fine pirate. He taught me much about the sea before the injury to his leg. It did not heal well, and he was dispirited."

Rafael stepped forward and placed an arm around her shoulder. He leaned in close, whispering even though Domingo and Nelia were much too far away to hear. "So he came here, to protect the island while I am away. To run my little plantation. To make babies with his wife."

Could he feel her shiver? "You took him in."

"No, *sirena mia*," he whispered. "That would be charity, and there is no charity in my heart."

That she could believe.

Sabrina had to stop to remind herself that Rafael was a pirate, a merciless and selfish man. No matter what a charming smile he had, no matter what an intriguing face he had . . . no matter that he had been trying to seduce her from the moment he'd found her on the beach. Blatant one moment, like the kiss in the cabin, and sly the next. Like now, with his hand on her shoulder and his breath against her ear and neck.

"I think I'm ready to go back to the house," she said, turning away quickly so that once again Rafael's arm fell away.

"So," he said, falling into step behind her, "what do you think?"

Sabrina started. God, she couldn't possibly tell him what she thought.

"About my little plantation," he clarified when she didn't answer right away.

"About your garden," she mumbled.

He didn't respond, so Sabrina glanced over her shoulder. It was a mistake. She tripped, most likely over her own clumsy feet, and started to fly forward.

Rafael snagged her around the waist, caught her before she could fall, and pulled her up against his chest. Her heart pounded too fast— a result of the scare, she told herself—and she trembled. Just a little.

Sabrina waited for Rafael to release her, but he didn't. He kept that arm tight around her waist, holding her so closely against his chest that she could feel his body against hers from shoulder to thigh.

She stared at his shoulder. "Put me down," she whispered.

"You are afraid?" His voice was low and soft and his breath brushed her hair.

"No."

He held her tight. Tightly enough to feel her trembling? Was that why he thought she was afraid?

Sabrina lifted her head slowly, to find those gold eyes staring down at her. Rafael's easy smile was gone, and the normally bright sparkle in his eyes had been replaced with something that smoldered.

"I am going to kiss you now," he said, moving his mouth slowly to hers.

"I know," she whispered as Rafael carried out his threat, covered her lips with his and kissed her. There was nothing demanding about his mouth. Instead it was a caress, sweet and tender and arousing.

Sabrina closed her eyes. He had been right all along. There was more heaven here than hell.

The change came slowly, as the kiss transformed from tender to demanding. Rafael parted her lips with his tongue, explored and stroked the inside of her mouth until she was aching for him, and his arms tightened around her.

A kiss had never made her feel boneless, as if she had no will of her own, as if the world was spinning out of control beneath her feet. But Rafael's kiss did all that and more. Warm, sensual, this was a joining of more than their mouths.

It was the low moan in Rafael's throat that broke the spell. She couldn't do this.

He wasn't expecting her to break away, so there was no resistance when she backed out of his arms and turned toward the house. He called her name just once, but she didn't stop or glance over her shoulder.

After a few faltering steps, she ran.

The woman was in his blood, curse her. He woke in the morning wondering where she was, if she was awake or still slumbering in her room next door. He fell asleep at night listening for her footstep in the hall, straining to hear her movements in the chamber in which she ensconced herself.

Rafael lay in his own bed, hands behind his head, listening in vain. Tonight all was silent. The doors to his balcony were open, allowing fresh, cool air to wash through the room and over his body.

He could close his eyes and feel her mouth on his, that wonderfully responsive mouth that had seemed so willing just that morning. For a while. In his arms she melted, and then she broke away. Just when he thought that she was his at last, she ran.

Never had a woman resisted him so.

He should leave her here, take to the sea where he belonged. Perhaps a few months with no one but Elena for company would help Sabrina change her mind.

But he knew that would never happen. When it was time to leave, Sabrina would be with him, and their time together would be over.

The sound was so faint he would not have heard it had he not been so intent. It was only a whisper, the creak of a door. And then he heard a single scuffling step on the balcony next to his own.

Sabrina.

Rafael rose from his bed with a smile. Did Sabrina find herself restless? He stepped into a pair of gray trousers and slipped on a short vest. There was no time to tarry with a proper shirt.

The moment he stepped onto the balcony he saw her. Sabrina stood with her hands gripping the rail, her moonlit face turned toward the lush growth that surrounded his haven. For a moment, he said nothing, only studied her pensive and desolate expression. She looked so defeated, so vulnerable. This was not the face she presented to him, when he approached her. The face she presented to him was invariably defiant, determined. Contrary.

But now she looked lost, staring away from the house where she was his guest. Her prison, she called it. Elena had grudgingly provided a plain nightgown, until others could be made. Sabrina wore a proper muslin nightdress that was worn quite thin. Even in the dark of night, he could see the silhouette of the body he had first seen lying on the sand, washed by the sea, pale and perfect in moonlight such as this.

She turned her head, and while she did not seem surprised to see him watching her, that desolate expression hardened.

"You cannot sleep, *sirena mia?*" Rafael asked softly.

"No." Her answer was sharp, but there was a gentle wavering of the single word.

"What distresses you?"

"I want to go home," she whispered.

She said the words as if she suffered, and Rafael might have felt a twinge of guilt if he had not been so certain she was safer on this island than anywhere else in the world. Still, she would not, could not, stay forever.

"I have said I will take you . . ."

"You can't. No one can."

Rafael stepped to the railing. No more than four feet separated her balcony from his. It would be so easy to leap across that short distance, to comfort her as she needed to be comforted.

He did not leap, but leaned over the railing. "What is it that you miss so terribly?"

Sabrina trailed her fingers against the rail of her own balcony as she turned to face him, and took a few short steps so that she stood before him, face-to-face. "I don't know. I only know that I don't belong here."

"You could, you know," he whispered. "Easily."

She shook her head, sending that oddly short hair into an undulating dance.

"You do not know yourself why you want to return to your home. What awaits you there that this island does not offer? Is there a man who will care for you more completely than I? A home finer and more warm than this one?"

Sabrina closed her eyes and shook her head again. "You don't understand. I have no control here, and I hate that. I've always had command of my own life, and now I find that I'm trapped in a time and a place where everything is determined by someone else."

"By me."

"By you, Rafael." She opened her eyes to stare boldly at him. "Why won't you let me go?"

"I will," he promised.

"When?"

"When the time is right."

She evidently found no comfort in his answer. The sharp retort he expected did not come.

"Until the time comes," he continued, "accept what is. Bask in the sun. Bathe in the calm waters. Let Elena pamper you."

Her face did not soften, did not yield at all.

"Allow me to adore you."

He expected a barrage of nonsensical insults, but Sabrina was silent. When she finally spoke, she managed to surprise him.

"Why?"

"Excuse me?"

"Why me?"

"Ah." Rafael allowed the smile that came so easily to creep across his face. "Why is the sky blue? Why does the sea pound against the sand one day and caress it as a whisper the next? Why do flowers bloom and birds sing?"

"Rafael," she chastised.

He shrugged slightly. "It just is, and unlike you I have learned to accept what each day brings, without question. At times, *sirena mia*, you think too much."

"I can't accept this."

She denied him, but her anger had faded. Soon she would see that he was right to keep her here, for a time. Soon she would allow him to adore her.

"Fate does not care what you accept, *querida*."

"Fate is the stuff fantasies are made of. Fantasy and excuses. If something doesn't work out, blame it on fate. If everything fails, shrug and complain that success just wasn't in the cards. What about free will? Control?"

"Ah, you are fond of your control, are you not?"

"Yes." She was becoming agitated. "I've been called a control freak on occasion. I took it as a compliment."

Rafael shook his head. "When you get angry you make no sense."

"I'm not angry," she seethed.

Rafael stepped away from the railing. She would not come to him tonight. He wanted her badly, but she was not ready, and he would never ask more of Sabrina than she was willing to give. "There are forces on this earth more powerful than the control of any one man . . . or woman. Perhaps you do not believe in fate. In destiny. As you lay in your bed tonight ask yourself this."

She waited silently, as if she were expecting some explanation for the forces that had brought her here.

"What carried you to my feet, *sirena mia*? An aimless wave? Chance? It was certainly not your choice, your control. There are leagues of deserted coastline where you could have washed ashore, away from my sight, but you did not. I might have chosen to sail straight to Tortuga and wait for repairs there, but I did not. You may call this chance, misfortune perhaps, but I believe there is something more."

Sabrina took a step back, but she listened, still. Her lips parted slightly, quivered, it seemed. Perhaps at last his argument was swaying her.

"Destiny," he whispered. "Fate. I do not believe the mysterious forces that surround us care if you believe or not."

Rafael smiled at Sabrina, hoping to ease her disquiet but doubting that was possible. "Good night, *sirena mia*. I will dream of you."

He turned away, his smile remaining even as he stepped into his darkened chamber. There was a crack in the shield his gift hid behind, a doubt where there had been none, a vulnerability as she questioned her determination.

He would not have long to wait.

Destiny. It would be so easy to accept Rafael as her fate. Easy and . . . impossible.

She was not a seventeenth-century woman dependant on a man for her survival. No matter what Rafael thought, she *did not* need him. She couldn't.

But she'd never before felt her heart race at the sight of a man, had never before craved the sound of a man's voice. A laugh, a ridiculous endearment. Control? Not much left, and it was fading fast.

Rafael wanted a sexual relationship with her. He'd made that more than clear. With a touch, with a kiss, with his soft assurances that destiny had brought them together. He was just biding his time until she caved.

Unable to sleep, she listened to the soft breeze that wafted through and atop dense foliage to perfume her room with sea air and tropical flowers, and she remembered all the mistakes she'd made. Patrick. Her obsessive work. The realization that came—too late—that she'd made terrible choices in her life. Work had always come first, and in her personal life she'd settled for convenience, safety.

She'd never known real love, and in her last moments in that world, she'd realized the folly of living life without it.

And she knew without a doubt that no matter how much Rafael wanted her, no matter how often he spoke of destiny, he would never love her. He wasn't the kind of man to give his love to one woman . . . not for an extended period of time, at least. His type hadn't changed in three hundred years.

Women were to be protected, perhaps even loved for as long as it suited. But never forever. Rafael was the kind of man who would use her, make her love him, and then break her heart.

God help her, she was falling in love with him already, and that would never do.

For the first time in her life, her heart was ruling her head. She fought, a silent battle no one could share, and every day it grew a little harder.

Perhaps if he hadn't kissed her, as that storm had raged and tossed the boat, and again on the path. Perhaps if he didn't smile at her, or speak to her or *look* at her. . . .

Sabrina hugged a satin pillow to her chest, smothering her pounding heart. Perhaps if he was bald, or had beady, squinty eyes, or didn't look so damn good in nothing but tight pants and a vest. . . .

Perhaps this attraction had nothing to do with her heart, after all.

She was forced to consider his argument.

Why had she washed ashore at that exact spot? Coincidence? Or Rafael's destiny?

Was she here only so Rafael could *adore* her for as long as he pleased? Would destiny bring her to him for a cause so insignificant?

Sabrina moved the pillow from her heart to her face as she stiffled a scream.

Maybe Rafael was right. Maybe she did think too much.

Elena had placed three pieces of clothing that could only be nightdresses across the foot of Sabrina's bed.

She'd be better off sleeping naked.

One was white, one was lavender, and one was a pale green. All were sheer enough for her to see the bedcover clearly through two thicknesses of the material, and the front and the back were cut so low the neckline would surely fall to her waist.

"No," she said, gathering the offensive articles of clothing and trying to hand them to a sour-faced Elena. "I don't want these."

Elena took the offered nightgowns from Sabrina, and with a sigh placed them across the foot of the bed once again.

"No," Sabrina said, her patience wearing thin. She shook her head and gathered the nightgowns once again to present them to Elena. "I will not wear these. They're insulting."

Elena could not, Sabrina knew, understand a word she said, but the housekeeper answered anyway, in rapid and angry Spanish. They managed to argue this way for several minutes before Elena held one of the nightgowns in front of Sabrina, and uttered one sharp sentence. There was one word Sabrina had no trouble interpreting.

*Capitán.*

"Rafael," Sabrina said calmly, holding up the lavender gown.

*"Sí."* Elena sighed.

"Rafael instructed you to make these for me?" Sabrina pointed to the gown, and then to herself, and Elena nodded.

"And where is Rafael?"

Sabrina wracked her brain for the little Spanish she knew. *"Dónde está Rafael?"* Her accent was terrible, but Elena understood. "That degenerate," Sabrina added as she followed the spry little woman down the curving staircase.

Clutching the nightgowns, Sabrina followed Elena through the kitchen and out a narrow door. Without looking back, Elena led Sabrina down the path to Rafael's garden and beyond to a row of quaint cottages. Children played and worked, and women who stood in a tight little group to chat stopped to watch Sabrina and Elena pass.

They were well past the pirate community when Elena halted at the base of a small hill, turning to Sabrina as she pointed, wagging a scrawny finger and scowling.

"Rafael?" Sabrina asked, pointing at the hill.

*"Sí,"* Elena said as she turned to walk away.

Sabrina climbed the small hill, expecting to find Rafael and perhaps another garden on the other side. Maybe he worked a plot of land himself, more farmer in his blood than he cared to admit.

Would she embarrass him, showing up with these disgraceful nightgowns to throw in his face? Of course not. Rafael? Embarrassed? Never.

There was a clear path, and she followed it, pushing aside the dark green growth that occasionally got in her way. The pathway sloped downward slightly, and Sabrina watched her feet, taking cautious steps in spite of her anger. This looked too much like a jungle, and God only knew what creatures waited alongside the path. The foliage thinned just before she stepped onto the sand and lifted her head to see the water lapping at the shore, the quiet and peaceful cove where Rafael swam.

All she could see was his head, dark hair slicked back, sun glinting on rivulets of salty water that ran down his face. Spying her, he grinned and stood, so that the water hit him at mid-chest.

"Ah," he said, lifting one hand to her. "You have come to thank me."

"Thank you?" Sabrina shook the disgraceful nightgowns in his direction.

"You are most welcome."

The sun hit Rafael full in the face, while Sabrina remained in the shade.

"You pig."

"Again with *el cochino*," he muttered. "You do not like my gift?"

"No, I do not like it." Sabrina took a deep breath. It seemed Rafael had no idea that she was offended. "This is not a proper gift for you to give to me."

"Why not?"

Sabrina tried to remind herself that this was 1665. "This would be a proper gift for a wife, or a . . ." The word *lover* stuck in her throat. "A fiancée, perhaps."

"So your Patrick gave you gifts such as this?" What an innocent face he presented, the dog.

"No."

"What sort of gifts did your Patrick give you?"

"Let's leave him out of this."

"How am I to know what is proper and what is not if you will not teach me?"

His easy manner took the wind out of her sails. "Patrick gave me practical gifts. A toaster, a coffee maker, a yearly planner."

"No pearls and emeralds? No gold? No silks?"

Sabrina looked down at her bare left hand. "A small diamond, once." A very small diamond. "Patrick was very sensible."

It was the sad truth.

Rafael snorted. "Sensible. Practical. It is no wonder you could not marry him."

"We're straying from the point," Sabrina insisted. "This . . ." she swung the filmy nightgowns before her, "is insulting."

"Wearing them, you will look most beautiful. The white is my favorite, I think, but I will not know until you wear them for me."

"You still don't get it." Sabrina left the shade and walked to the edge of the water. "It will be a cold day in hell when I wear one of these." She tossed the frothy creations into the water.

Rafael lifted both hands in supplication. "I did not mean to insult you, *sirena mia*. I only meant to surround you with things as beautiful as you are, to pamper you."

He sighed, and began to walk toward her, shaking the water from his hair, bringing the weighted curls to life once again.

"I will instruct Elena to make new nightclothes for you. What do you wish?" he asked lightly. "Wool? Velvet, perhaps?"

Sabrina opened her mouth to answer, just as his step revealed to her the curve of his hip, a flat bare belly. She spun around to face the foliage.

"You're naked," she muttered.

"Of course. What do you wear to swim in, *querida*?"

"I don't swim, but if I did I would wear a bathing suit."

"A bathing suit," he repeated calmly. "Why am I not surprised?"

Sabrina stepped away from the shoreline as Rafael neared. "I've said all I have to say," she mumbled as she headed for the path.

"Wait," Rafael called. "You can turn around now."

She did. He had not dressed quickly, but held the three wet nightgowns strategically before him. Sabrina stared at his forehead. There wasn't another portion of his body she could look at without risking her heart bursting through her chest. Certainly not his eyes, or a bare, wet chest that had just a sprinkling of dark hair, and he really did have great legs, and the wet nightgowns didn't completely cover his sleek hips. . . .

"I gotta go," she said, spinning around.

"Wait," Rafael called again. "If I clothe myself will you stay? Sit on the sand with me for a while? The ocean, she is more beautiful here than anywhere else in the world."

"I don't think . . ."

"We can talk," he interrupted. "You can tell me why you want so badly to go home."

"All right." Sabrina told herself that she only stayed because there was a slim chance she could convince Rafael to take her home . . . to what would one day become her home, at least.

"You can turn around now," he said a few minutes later. "I am properly clothed."

Sabrina turned around slowly, half expecting Rafael to be standing at the edge of the ocean wearing nothing but a smile. But he was dressed, as he'd said, in a pair of black pants and a matching vest that hung open, exposing his chest.

"See?" He spread his arms wide and grinned. He knew her too well, knew that she didn't trust his word.

He had tossed the soggy nightgowns aside, and as Sabrina stepped forward he took her hand—her fingers, really—and together they sat on the sand and faced the water.

"It is beautiful, is it not?"

"Yes, it is." Serenity was a feeling almost foreign to Sabrina, but it was impossible to view the scene before her and experience anything else. "I'm sorry if I overreacted about the nightgowns. I'm not usually an overly emotional woman, but . . ."

"Your life has changed," Rafael finished for her. "Very much, from what I understand. And you are a woman who, I think, does not like change."

Sabrina almost laughed. She did smile at Rafael's correct assessment. "I suppose I don't."

Rafael sat a short distance from her, a foot or more, and he leaned back on his elbows to offer his face to the sun. "Life is change, *sirena mia*. Winds shift, waves swell, storms come from nowhere. A wise man accepts what life offers him, makes the best of it, and awaits the next transformation."

"A philosopher, as well as a pirate."

How quickly her anger had faded. Was it Rafael himself, or the fact that he was the only English-speaking resident of this island and she was desperate for companionship?

"That is your one fault, *querida*, that you refuse to accept what life offers."

"My one fault."

Rafael grinned. "Look around you. If there is a more peaceful setting on this earth, I have never found it or heard tales of it. Soft breezes, long growing season, fish in abundance . . . the sea, the flowers. All this surrounds you, and still you long for a home where you were unhappy."

A chill crept over Sabrina. She had told Patrick, not long before the fall, that she was not happy, and he had looked at her as if she'd lost her mind. But Rafael saw it, even now. "How do you know?"

"I know you, *sirena mia*, better than you realize. I see determination when you ask to go home, fear, perhaps, at the prospect of facing the unknown. But I have never seen longing in your eyes, as you speak of your home and your sensible Patrick."

Rafael seemed not to have a care in the world. He smiled so easily.

"Are you happy?"

He hesitated, the span of a heartbeat or two, before answering, "There have been a few happy times in my life," he revealed. "They come, and I accept."

"Are you happy now?"

Rafael rolled onto his side, fastened those brandy eyes on her. "I could be."

His vest fell open, and there, just under his heart, was a long thin scar, pale and old.

"What happened?" She pointed, careful not to move her hand too close as she attempted to change the direction of their conversation.

Rafael followed her gaze, and touched the scar with a long, dark finger. "This? A Scot by the name of MacDowall. We boarded his ship off the coast of Africa. I was just a boy, and not as skilled with a sword as I am now."

"A sword? A sword did this?"

"*Sí*," he said nonchalantly. "And this." He lifted the other side of his vest to reveal an even more wicked scar, short, but puckered and white.

"MacDowall?" she asked.

"No. An Englishman."

*Venganza*. "Falconer?" she asked.

**121**

Rafael's smile faded, and his eyes grew cold. There was no more hint of happiness on his face. "No."

Wishing she hadn't asked, Sabrina chattered on. "I heard somewhere that you can tell the kind of life a person's led by their scars. You know, accidents, surgery. I don't have any. Not one."

"I know," Rafael divulged in a low voice.

She ignored the comment. "I guess my life has been dull, particularly compared to yours."

"That is good. Your life should be dull, safe. A woman like you should have no enemies, no danger, no harsh memories."

"Still," Sabrina motioned from a safe distance to the scars Rafael had revealed, "they're . . . interesting."

"Interesting?" he said, as if he couldn't quite believe what he'd heard. "You find scars interesting?"

She didn't get a chance to answer. Rafael sat up quickly, shrugging off the sandy vest to toss it aside. He stared at her intently for a long moment. How could eyes so warm a brown turn so cold?

Without a word of warning, he turned his back to her, and Sabrina stifled a surprised cry.

His back was crisscrossed with scars, old, puckered, so many she didn't dare to count. Unable to help herself, Sabrina reached out and gently touched Rafael's damaged skin. She could not bring herself to do more than lightly brush the tips of her fingers across the leathery skin as she wondered how he had survived such injuries.

She didn't want to cry, but tears stung her eyes as she took a deep breath and placed the palm of her hand against Rafael's back.

And then he looked over his shoulder. "Falconer," he whispered.

*Venganza.*

# Chapter Eight

He had never seen her cry. There had been no tears during the sudden storm that had frightened her so, none as she pleaded with him to take her home.

But Sabrina cried silently as she touched his scarred back. She cried for him.

"How . . . why?" She whispered her question.

Did she know nothing of the harsh world in which she lived? She must have lived a sheltered life before she came to him on the moonlit waves. Where had she come from?

"When I made my way to the coast of my country, I had no money. I had nothing, *sirena mia,* but the ragged clothing on my back."

"You were twelve," she breathed.

"*Sí.*" Rafael turned to face her, and her hand fell away. "There was a ship sailing for the Spanish Main, the treasure house of the world, and I was determined to be on it, even though it meant promising five years of my life to some unknown master."

He saw the dawning realization on her face, the pale surprise, as he revealed more of himself to Sabrina than he had to anyone in a very long time.

"I loved the sea, even the storms that rocked us. Such power, such beauty. I followed the captain when he allowed it, staying at his heels, watching, learning everything I could. And he promised to try to sell me to another captain, so that I could go to sea and learn the ways of a sailor."

All Sabrina's anger had vanished, washed away so easily. The tears that had shone in her blue-green eyes were gone, and he made no mention of them. Did she understand now why he had been forced to rescue her from John Clarke and years with an unknown master?

"Did he?" She swallowed. "Sell you to another captain?"

"*Sí,*" he said grudgingly. "To Hadley Falconer. An English pirate who prefers to call himself a buccaneer."

"Did he . . ." Sabrina lifted her hand in a helpless gesture. "He did that to you?"

Her voice broke with softhearted outrage. There was a softness in Sabrina's eyes, a yielding, a hint of the tender woman she was and tried, so very hard, to deny. With a few words, he could break down what remained of her icy shield, then take her in his arms and comfort her . . . allow her to comfort him.

But he had already revealed too much. He did not want Sabrina's pity, he wanted her passion. Nothing else would satisfy him.

"*Sí,*" he said shortly, lying in the sand and closing his eyes.

"Why?"

He ignored her question.

"Dammit, Rafael," she persisted, "why?"

"It does not matter now, *sirena mia,*" he said with a yawn to convey his boredom with the current topic of conversation. "It was long ago."

Sabrina would not relent. "That's why you named your ship *Venganza*. It's not revenge, though. It's justice. A man who would do something like that should be shot." There was such anguish in her voice, such outrage over an injustice.

"*Sí, sirena mia,*" Rafael said tiredly. The sun bathed his face, Sabrina was at his side, the water lapped just a few feet away. But the perfection of the moment was ruined by memories he did not want to share. "One day I will send Falconer to hell where he belongs, but I decided long ago that death was not enough."

"What do you mean?"

"Before I kill him, I will take everything away. His gold, his ship, his home. Everything and everyone he loves. Slowly, so that when I strike he does not expect me. He has a plantation on Jamaica." The plantation where Falconer had put his young Spanish indentured servant to work, taking away the dream of a life at sea. "Earlier this year I burned his fields."

In his mind he saw the rising smoke over

damned fields that still brought back strong and terrible memories that almost paralyzed him, and he heard the shouts of Falconer's men as the fire was discovered.

"How can you feel safe while you're at . . . at war with that man? Doesn't he retaliate?"

"He has tried." Rafael's voice was low, even. He wondered if Sabrina would ask him to elaborate, wondered how much he would tell this mystic woman with the angelic face. "There is nothing he can take from me that I cannot recapture. No way for him to hurt me the way I can hurt him. Falconer delights in all his treasures, possesses them with great relish. Gold, land, the people he owns."

A man who loved anything made himself vulnerable, offered himself up to his enemies for pain and even death. And Falconer had a weakness for becoming attached to beautiful things.

"That's why . . . that's why you kidnapped me."

"Rescued you," Rafael corrected.

"Rescued me," Sabrina conceded softly. "So I wouldn't end up an indentured servant."

It was an incomplete truth, Rafael rationalized. Not a lie. "*Sí*. There are others who are as evil as Falconer. Where do you come from that you are not aware of that danger?"

Sabrina did not answer, and Rafael opened his eyes to look up at her. She sat beside him, silent, pensive.

"You wouldn't believe me," she whispered after a long pause.

"Certainly I would," he assured her.

The smile that crossed her face was small, not a happy smile at all. "No. It's too fantastic. I can hardly believe it myself."

"You must have traveled far, for you come from a world I cannot imagine. A world where the word *justice* can be spoken with a grain of belief in such a concept. Where even women have control." Only a gentle world could have produced someone like Sabrina. "You speak at times words I have never heard, and my English is quite good."

"You have no idea how far I have traveled, Rafael." Sabrina pulled her eyes from his and stared at the sea before her, a sea that obviously fascinated and terrified her. "I don't think I can ever go back, don't know if it's even possible." She drew her knees to her chest and rested her chin on the blue linen of her skirt. "I don't even know if I want to go back."

It was a hesitant confession, and the first time Sabrina had admitted that perhaps her home was not the place to be. Perhaps she finally realized, as he did, that she was meant to be here.

"Then stay," he whispered. "Here. With me."

She was silent for a long moment. Rafael wanted to believe that she was giving his invitation serious consideration.

"I can't," she answered finally, and he took little comfort from the fact that the refusal seemed to be painful for her. "This is not . . . It can't be . . ." Sabrina took a deep, calming breath. "Do you believe in second chances, Rafael? Fresh starts?"

"Not really. Your past makes you what you

are. Your scars, your memories, your nightmares. They cannot be wiped away."

"This is my second chance." A strand of reddish brown hair caressed her cheek, and Rafael reached out to brush it away. Sabrina did not flinch, did not draw away from his touch. "My chance to live life differently. Do you know what I want this time? Not power, not riches, not even control. I've had all that, and it isn't enough."

"What do you want, *sirena mia*?" he whispered. "I will gladly give you anything. Everything. Whatever your heart desires."

She glanced down at him, a spark of uncertainty in her eyes. "Love," she whispered. "Not just affection, but forever love. Children. A home. I want happiness this time."

He might have told her that he could offer her that, but it would be a lie. Their time together, when it came, would not be tainted by deceit. "What you want does not exist any more than the justice you speak of with such passion. Ask for the riches of the world and I will lay them at your feet. I can drape you in silk and jewels, and in my home you will never go hungry. I will adore you, and I promise . . . I can make you happy." He traced the line of her jaw with his finger, stared at the path of his skin against hers rather than meeting her questioning gaze. "Maybe it will last for only a moment, a day, a year. I offer you all that I can."

She did not turn away from the hand that lazily stroked her face, but instead seemed to lean forward just slightly so that his touch was firmer.

"Do you love . . . anyone? Anything?" she asked.

Rafael allowed his hand to fall and tore his eyes away from her. She asked questions that shredded his heart and reminded him of a time best forgotten. "No," he finally answered.

Sabrina did not stand and run from him, as he expected she might, but turned her eyes to the sea again, and together they stared silently at the force that had somehow carried her to his feet.

She was soaking in the short tub when Elena walked into the room, without bothering to knock, of course.

"Do you mind?" Sabrina sank lower into the cooling water. Elena ignored her, depositing a pile of clothing on the end of the bed before scooping up Sabrina's white blouse and blue skirt with an air of disdain.

"Hold it, hold it," Sabrina ordered, one wet hand in the air. "You're not taking my clothes."

With a sigh, Elena tossed the skirt and blouse to the floor by the closed door. Then she lifted the first gown from the pile and held it before her.

It was a gown made with the white silk shot with gold, a truly magnificent dress with a full skirt and scooped bodice. Before Sabrina had time to examine the gown fully, Elena laid it aside and lifted the red.

It was not as classy as the white, but was just

as impressive. The red was dark, but not a burgundy. The silk was the color of rubies, rich and deep. The neckline plunged in a deep *V*, and the skirt, while full, was not as voluminous as the white.

Elena placed the red gown carefully on the bed before lifting the last of the stack she'd carried in.

The three nightgowns, frothy confections she'd tossed into the sea just a day earlier. They had been cleaned and pressed and neatly folded. Elena scolded Sabrina, in unintelligible Spanish, as she placed the nightgowns in the trunk at the foot of the bed.

Silently, Elena stored the white gown as well, and then she straightened the red across the bed, searching closely as if for imperfections, and finding none.

As the sour housekeeper gathered the soiled and discarded clothing from the floor, Sabrina tried to stop her.

"Elena?"

The woman turned slowly, firm lips set, eyes narrowed. Ready for battle.

"Did you make that gown?" Sabrina pointed to the red dress that covered most of her bed.

Poor Elena, she was so accustomed to Sabrina's outbursts that she began to defend herself, pointing to the gown and speaking sharply, finally pointing to Sabrina and to the gown, emphasizing the word *capitán*.

"Rafael wants me to wear the red?" Sabrina asked, pointing, and Elena nodded her head.

Figures.

Sabrina pointed to Elena. "Did you . . ." she tried to mimic sewing, using two dripping wet hands, and then pointed to the gown once again.

Elena narrowed her eyes and nodded.

There were few Spanish words Sabrina knew, but she was picking them up one at a time. *"Bonita,"* she said. *"Gracías."*

Evidently she surprised the grouchy housekeeper, because the woman almost smiled.

Sabrina stepped from the tub and dried herself after Elena had left the room, closing the door behind her. Finally, with gestures and the few Spanish words she dredged up from movies and television, she had been able to communicate to the woman that she did not need or want help getting bathed, or dressed.

For a moment, Sabrina studied the gown that was spread across the bed. Evidently, Rafael expected her to wear it down to supper. It was outrageous, presumptuous, and she really shouldn't cater to his whims. She certainly shouldn't care what he expected of her.

Last night at supper, he had been so quiet. Sabrina had wondered, over the uncomfortable meal and later as she stared at the ceiling, if he regretted sharing a bit of his past with her. Antonio Rafael de Zamora, who wanted so badly to appear a heartless and bloodthirsty pirate, had suffered in a way she could not imagine.

Today, she hadn't seen him at all. Perhaps he had spent the day at his secluded cove, swimming. She had even, once, considered seeking him out.

But she hadn't, of course.

Finally, relenting in a way that Sabrina Steele *never* relented, she slipped the dress over her head. The material was luxurious, heavy, satiny against her skin. The neckline was cut much too deep, showing what little bit of cleavage she had. The back was cut even deeper.

She could almost reach the tiny buttons at her back. Straining, she was able to fasten the two at the bottom, but no matter how she contorted herself she couldn't reach the rest.

Sabrina stepped into the hall and to the railing to look down into the great room below. She had to wait a moment, and then Elena appeared from the kitchen, bearing a tray of fruit for the dining table.

"Elena?" Sabrina called. It would serve her right if the woman ignored her. So far, every time Elena had tried to help her dress, Sabrina had ordered the woman from the room. Now, she crooked her finger at the woman.

Elena placed her hands on her hips in evident exasperation and stared up at Sabrina.

With a grimace on her face, Sabrina resorted to pantomime again, trying to reach the buttons, throwing her hands into the air when she was unsuccessful.

Elena climbed the stairs impatiently, and Sabrina slipped into her room to wait.

In seconds, Elena had the tiny buttons fastened. The gown was a perfect fit, a carefully crafted masterpiece, and as Elena left the room Sabrina tried to thank her again.

It wasn't like she hadn't owned nice dresses

before, gowns nice enough for any occasion.
Black, mostly, though there had been that one
navy gown she'd worn for New Year's Eve a couple of years back. Her clothes were invariably
nice, but sensible. Expensive, and of a style that
would last for years. Never daring. Never eye-
popping.

Never red.

Sabrina smoothed back her hair, tucking it
behind her ears. What she wouldn't give for her
makeup case, her hair dryer, hot curlers, that
expensive perfume her father had given her for
her birthday last year. It seemed a shame to
wear a gown like this without all the trimmings.

"Who are you trying to impress?" she whispered to herself.

Not Rafael, certainly. He hid the truth behind
warm smiles, but his pirate's heart was as cold
and hard as his Falconer's.

Sabrina shivered at that thought, knowing instinctively that it wasn't true. He had his faults,
but she couldn't imagine Rafael hurting anyone
with cruelty, the way Falconer had hurt him.
She saw the real Rafael in his warm eyes and
easy smile.

"Idiot," she whispered. "He's a pirate."

He hadn't harmed her, and had always
touched her gently and easily. Too gently, sometimes, so tenderly his touch made her skin
scream for him. His hands had never been
rough, had never demanded more than she was
willing to give. Those were marks of a gentleman.

But what of his vow to destroy everything and

*everyone* Falconer cared about? Would he really . . .

"Stop it."

At least he was honest with her. If he had told her yesterday that he could love her, she would have fallen into his arms like an infatuated teenager. Dammit, she *wanted* Rafael to love her, but he never would.

He was more than willing to adore her, for a while. To make her happy, for a moment. For a day. For a year.

By the time Sabrina left her room, Rafael was waiting for her in the great room. He stood when she stepped onto the staircase, walked toward her as she neared the last steps. His bright smile was absent, but still her heart skipped a beat.

His hair was gathered in a ponytail that restrained his curls and allowed them to fall in a softly curling mass down his back. He was dressed, as he often was, in black, with only the gold hoops in his ears and the bright white of his shirt for contrast.

"*Sirena mia*, would you be insulted if I told you that you look magnificent?"

"No."

A hint of a smile, perhaps, but yesterday's confession hung between them, dimming his brightness.

"It's just the dress," she said, breaking the awkward silence. "It's very beautiful."

"It is not the dress," he insisted, taking her hand and leading her to the table. "It is the woman wearing it who brings it to life."

Rafael took her arm and led her to the table. There were candles and flowers there, as always, but tonight the candles blazed more brightly than before, and the flowers seemed more vivid. More alive.

Sabrina stared at her plate, recognizing the slice of roasted wild boar she had—amazingly—become accustomed to, the thick and crudely sliced bread, the arrangement of native fruits.

A moment, a day, a year. What if that was all she could ever have? There was no guarantee that she would find any happiness at all in this new world, much less a lifetime of it.

She lifted her head and studied Rafael as intently as she'd studied her evening meal. He had dragged her from the ocean where she certainly would have drowned, kidnapped or rescued her, depending upon your point of view, and he'd bared his soul to her on the beach . . . but could she trust her heart to a man who claimed that he loved nothing and no one?

He lifted a fine crystal goblet filled with red wine, toasted her, locked his brandy eyes to hers . . . and Sabrina realized that it was too late.

Rafael already had her heart.

# *Chapter Nine*

In the candlelight, Sabrina's face looked quite serene, and for a moment Rafael could almost make himself believe that she was content, that she had at last accepted the inevitability of destiny.

But he knew what he saw was nothing more than an illusion. Sabrina's appearance of serenity was false, a combination of the perfection of her face and the gown she wore, the soft candlelight and his own impossible desire to possess her.

Elena cleared away the dishes, and before Sabrina could rise and leave the table, Cristóbal entered through the kitchen door, his guitar in hand.

"What's this?" she asked, her eyes following Cristóbal's steps as he crossed to the far end of the room and settled into a comfortable chair.

"Tonight, we dance," Rafael said, ready to argue if necessary, prepared to coax and cajole, even to beg. . . .

"I told you I can't dance," Sabrina said in a low voice.

Rafael left his seat and walked the length of the table that was much too long for two solitary diners. When he reached Sabrina he offered her his hand, and after a moment's hesitation, she took it.

It was a hand so soft and small, with fingers so delicate Rafael wondered that she had ever labored with them. Against such softness his own hand appeared crude, too rough and too large.

Perhaps Sabrina did not think so, as she folded her delicate fingers over his.

She stood, and Cristóbal began to play. The notes were slow, clear, rhythmic, and Rafael led Sabrina to the center of the room.

"I really can't dance," she protested hesitantly. "I don't know what to do. I don't think . . ."

She lifted her face to him, and there was no defiance there, no rebellion. Just a softness that called to him, an inviting spark in her eyes.

"Do not think, *sirena mia*. Listen, for tonight, to your body. Look into my eyes and allow me to guide you. Let the music wash over us, and forget what you know and do not know."

Surely a woman such as this one had danced before, courtly dances in elegant ballrooms crowded with lords and ladies dressed in finery to put their own simple costumes to shame. A minuet, a gavotte, perhaps the chaconne.

He took a step and Sabrina mirrored it, her eyes on his face, her hand light against his. They moved slowly, coming together and then, too quickly, moving apart, their movements a marriage of harmony and motion.

At first Sabrina's steps were hesitant, but it did not take her long to relax, to smile up at him so brightly his heart leapt in his chest. By the time the minuet was over, and Cristóbal increased the tempo for the gavotte, Sabrina's every move was near flawless.

"We're dancing, Rafael," she whispered as they came together for a moment that was much too fleeting.

"*Sí, sirena mia.*" After a few moments, Cristóbal changed the rhythm again, his fingers quick on well-used guitar strings, and Rafael spun Sabrina around the room so that her skirt whipped around her legs and her face became flushed. Once, she closed her eyes and laughed, a clear peal as musical as the notes that drifted to them from Cristóbal's guitar. It was just as he had imagined, to hold her hand in his and hear her laugh, and he savored it, spinning her again and again, until her laughter faded to a satisfied smile and her cheeks were aglow.

The music became slow again, but instead of returning to the genteel minuet, Sabrina melted against him, rested her head against his shoulder. She did not stop moving altogether, but placed the hand she did not grasp at his shoulder.

"Where I come from," she said breathlessly, "this is a dance."

It was like no dance he had ever seen. He held Sabrina so close he could feel her breasts pressing against his chest, could feel the movement of her legs against his. Her head rested easily against his shoulder, and he could feel her warm breath against his neck.

Gradually, their steps slowed until they did not tread across the floor at all, but merely swayed in the middle of the room. Heart to heart, thigh to thigh. Rafael placed his hand high on Sabrina's back, so that his fingers brushed bared skin. Skin so warm and smooth, so perfect. She did not object when he trailed his fingers along her spine, but quivered in his arms.

"*Sirena mia*," he whispered, and the gentle sway that was dance and not dance stopped.

She stayed in his arms, did not move away. Rafael lifted a hand in a silent signal, and the music came abruptly to an end. Cristóbal left the room quietly, swiftly, guitar in hand as he passed into the kitchen.

Rafael lowered his lips to Sabrina's shoulder, tasted her sweet, soft skin, trailed his mouth to her throat, where he felt her throbbing pulse against his lips. Never had he wanted anything as badly as he wanted this woman.

When he moved his lips to hers she met him eagerly, ardently, with the passion she tried to deny but had never been able to hide from him.

She was his. His mermaid, his prize, his gift. His only gift.

"Rafael," she whispered, taking her mouth from his. "I can't. . . ."

"Listen to your body." He slipped a bit of red silk aside so he could taste skin that had been hidden from him. "Forget everything else. Your doubts, your dreams, your nightmares." The flesh against his lips was enticing enough to make him forget everything, himself. "They mean nothing now. There is only this."

He slipped his hand into the bodice of her gown, caressed a hardened nipple with rough fingers. Sabrina did not move away, but swayed toward him so slightly he did not think she realized what a telling movement she had made as her body came to him.

His lips found and claimed hers, in a rush of hunger so intoxicating it swept him away. The kiss was soft, and then suddenly stormy. Sabrina opened herself to him, offered her sweet mouth and the warm, silky body she pressed against his hand.

*Destiny.*

Without warning there was a distinct faltering in her response, in her lips against his, and when she backed away from him he allowed his hands to fall away from her without protest.

Sabrina turned her back to him, gathered her skirt in her hands and stepped to the stairway so quickly she almost ran. When she was halfway up the curved staircase, Rafael stopped her with a single whispered word.

*"Querida."*

Sabrina turned slowly, gripped the balustrade as if it alone kept her standing. And she waited, without a word, without a hint of protest, until he spoke again.

"I need you."

Perhaps she did not expect such simple honesty from him. Perhaps she had expected a demand she could rail against. An edict she could refuse. Even now, though she looked down at him with passion still in her eyes, she could deny him. She could flee.

She did not. "I am a fool."

Rafael stepped toward her, placed himself at the foot of the staircase. "So are we all, *sirena mia.*"

Her surrender came with the lifting of a hand, an offered palm, and Rafael climbed the stairs to take that hand in his own. To hold it, to caress it. He kissed her there, with her back against the balustrade, and he felt the submission in her lips, in her body that trembled against his.

"I need you," he repeated, breathing the confession against her mouth.

"Yes," she whispered. "And I . . . I . . ."

"Tell me," he demanded.

"I need you."

Rafael lifted Sabrina in his arms and climbed the stairs with her head against his neck, her hands in his hair, her reluctant confession exciting him more than he had imagined it would.

*I need you.*

Rafael's bedroom was much like her own, square and lushly furnished, and the balcony doors were opened to allow the ocean breeze to wash over them as he worked the tiny buttons at her back.

When that was done, he lavished attention on her back, touching and then kissing slowly, as if they had all the time in the world, as if this night would last forever.

Maybe it would.

He removed the gown from her with such ease, such tender deliberation, allowing his hands to touch her only lightly as he worked the clothing from her body, allowing his mouth only the lightest of kisses against the skin he exposed. A shoulder, an arm, the base of her spine.

When she stood before Rafael as naked as he'd found her, he began to stroke, her shoulders and arms, her back and her breasts, with hands large and tender, loving and sure. It was as if he studied her with affection and wonder, with his hands as well as his eyes.

His mouth joined his hands in their leisurely exploration, warm lips lingering on her flesh as he tasted sensitive areas she'd never known would react to a touch so light.

Rafael trailed his mouth along the side of her neck, kissed her shoulder and then lifted her arm to flick his tongue against the flesh at the crook of her elbow. She felt it to her toes. He kissed her wrist, the palm of her hand, the valley between her breasts. That tender mouth trailed lower, and Rafael grasped her tightly as he made a path with an adoring mouth down her torso to her navel.

When Rafael raised himself up slowly, never

quite taking his mouth from her flesh, and placed his lips against hers, she was starved for them, aching for his mouth on her own, for that now familiar connection that made the doubts and the fears and the whole world stop.

She reached beneath his jacket and slipped it from his shoulders so it dropped silently to the floor. She never took her mouth from his, not as the vest followed, not as she loosened the leather strap that held back his hair, not as she fumbled with his belt and then the drawstring that was tied at his waist.

He lifted her, dragging her body across his slowly, allowing her to feel his arousal against her belly, holding her close, but not close enough. They could never be close enough.

His bed was soft, and she sank into the mattress as he lowered her slowly.

She no longer felt as if they had all the time in the world. The urgency was building, growing at an alarming rate. She thrived on his touch, his mouth and his hands, and she wanted more.

With her help Rafael removed his shirt, and in a flash he discarded his boots and trousers.

He covered her, pressed his warm skin against hers, kissed her lips long and slow before he lowered his head to caress her neck and then her breasts, sucking lightly on responsive nipples. Dark curls fell across her skin, and Sabrina threaded her fingers through the silky tresses that teased her flesh.

With an impatient hand he spread her thighs and positioned his body between them, so that she cradled him gently. She wanted him so much she could barely take in a full breath.

The curtains at his balcony door wafted with a fresh and vigorous breeze, as if the island breathed for her.

When Rafael brought his face back to hers, kissed her soft and deep, he pressed the tip of his erection against her wetness, teasing her with a promise of what was to come. Sabrina lifted her hips and he plunged deep, filling her, stroking her hard and long, driving his tongue deep into her mouth as he moved within her.

*Listen to your body.*

Sabrina rocked against him, and for a while there was nothing but the stroking of their flesh, nothing but the primal rhythm that ruled her body and the beat of her heart.

Nothing else mattered, but that he was a part of her, but that she loved him, but that he needed her.

The climax that erupted within her was like nothing she had ever imagined, unrelenting and explosive, all consuming and powerful. Did she cry out Rafael's name, or was it nonsense that escaped her mouth?

Once more, he thrust hard and deep, and she felt his own completion, the tremble that wracked his body, the heat of his fulfillment inside her. And then he was still, motionless atop her, his harsh breathing against her neck.

Sabrina trailed her fingers through his hair, unable to speak, unable to move. A soft breeze wafted through the open balcony doors, washed over their joined bodies like a gentle wave, and

145

as if the wind had energized him, Rafael lifted his head and smiled down at her.

*"Sirena mia,"* he whispered. "My mermaid, my siren. How completely you have entranced me."

She could not speak, still, so Sabrina lifted her mouth to Rafael's throat, tasted the salt of his sweat and the warmth of his flesh on her lips.

Surrender was glorious.

By the light of the moon, Rafael loved her again, whispered soft Spanish words that needed no translation. He cursed her, lavished his desire and his need upon her, breathed into her ear and into her mouth words that could only be assertions of love.

Rafael adored her, and she fell asleep in his cradling arms.

The morning sunlight touched the foot of the bed, and still Sabrina slept on. Rafael smoothed the hair away from her face so he could see more clearly the peace that was etched there.

When she yielded, she gave herself over completely, held nothing back. There had been not a single moment of doubt once Sabrina had admitted that she needed him. Not a hint of uncertainty. She was a generous lover, artless and passionate, and in her giving she had taken more than he had ever intended to offer.

In one evening, all his desires had been fulfilled. He had danced with Sabrina in his arms, she had laughed with abandon, and she had come to him with all the passion he had known her to possess.

She had even admitted, in a weak moment, that she needed him. Had proved to him, with her body, that it was true.

But she had claimed too much. Reached too deeply into his heart. Made him admit that he needed her more than she needed him.

Impossible.

Even now, hours after she had drifted into a deep sleep, she twined her legs through his, rested her head against his shoulder and a hand over his belly.

Even now, he wanted her beyond all reason, as he had wanted and needed her last night, so hard and so completely that he had once again lost his English.

It would not last, of course. Passion burned brightly for a while, and then it faded, slowly or in a moment of cold realization, but as surely as the rising and setting of the sun.

The bright sunlight crossed the middle of the bed now, touching Sabrina's pale and shapely hip, warming her skin with its bright caress.

He watched the play of slanting rays across her body, as the light came closer to her face, watched with fascination the illumination of skin so perfect and creamy, untouched by all but the gentlest kiss of the sun. It would not do for the light to touch her eyes and wake her, so he woke her in his own way before the sunlight reached so far.

A kiss first, light and lingering. A brush of his hand against a tender breast. His fingers explored her sun-warmed skin, danced over her flesh lightly and then with a hint of the need with which she filled him.

"Good morning." She greeted him with a low growl, a contented purr, and then she touched him. Her fingers across his chest, her palm against his belly. Everything in him tightened, his heart and his guts, his very lungs.

Before the sunbeam reached her face, Rafael towered over her, blocked the harsh light with his face over hers. He made love to her without pause, without words, without tenderness, and she reached for him with her body and her heart, arched and moaned beneath him.

He whispered then, low and deep, into her ear, until even that was impossible. And then he lost his soul in Sabrina's welcoming body.

When he rolled away from her, breathless and drained, she came with him, a content smile on her face.

"Did you mean it when you said you'd give me anything?" she whispered into his ear, kissed his neck.

"*Sí, sirena mía,* all that I can." What would she ask for? he wondered. More fabulous gowns? Jewels? Night after night like the one that had just passed?

"Teach me Spanish."

It was not what he had expected. "Excuse me?"

For some reason, his response made her laugh, a sweet, soft laugh that touched his cold heart. "Spanish. So I can talk to Elena, so I can understand what you're saying to your men."

She placed her lips against his throat, trailed them across his chin and finally to his mouth. "So when you make love to me I will know what you're whispering into my ear."

"Of course I will teach you." He didn't tell her that there were some words he would never explain. Some secrets he would keep for himself. "But you must allow me to teach you to swim as well."

"No way," she protested. "I've lived this long without knowing how to swim, and I don't need . . ."

He silenced her with a kiss. "I will teach you in my cove, and no harm will come to you. You have my word. Do you trust me, *sirena mia*?"

"Yes."

It was true. He saw that faith in bright eyes that could hide nothing from him.

Rafael kissed her, silently bemoaning the fact that she gave her trust so easily. It was a mistake born of ignorance, a failing he himself could not afford.

# *Chapter Ten*

She wasn't afraid. Saltwater surrounded her, caressed her, and there was no dread. There was only warmth, and pleasure, and Rafael.

Sabrina floated in Rafael's cove, the sun on her face and her pirate's sure hands at her bare back. He whispered assurances when she tensed, soft words in English and again in Spanish.

This was surely paradise. "I can't believe I was ever terrified of the water."

"You did not have Rafael to hold you in your past life, to keep you from sinking. You are learning to listen to your body rather than your head, and your body knows I would not allow any harm to come to you, even when your head does not."

His voice was lightly teasing and wonderfully seductive, but there was truth in what he said.

Sabrina had never trusted herself completely to another, not even her own father, and certainly not Patrick.

It was more than trust. She'd never loved anyone so much, had never even known such a strong emotion was possible. Her head told her that her love for Rafael made no sense, no sense at all, but her body and her heart accepted it easily.

She didn't dare to tell him how she felt. Rafael understood passion, and need, and perhaps even trust, but love—at least at this point—would scare him witless. For Rafael there was only pleasure that might last a moment, a day, a year.

He leaned forward and kissed her, lightly brushing his mouth against hers, and Sabrina stood. Her feet sank in the soft sand at the bottom of the cove, and she wrapped her arms around Rafael's waist, pressing her wet body to his, holding on tight in the water that was not much more than waist high.

"Where I come from this would be considered scandalous." She planted a small kiss in the center of his chest, near his heart.

"What is that, *sirena mia*?" he growled.

"Skinny-dipping. And it's not even noon yet."

"Ah, yes, you told me of your . . . bathing suits. Ridiculous." He placed his lips on her shoulder, trailed them to her neck, and then he stepped toward the shore, propelling Sabrina slowly backward.

"Lesson over?"

"For the moment. You need to rest."

"Rest? I've been floating." She laughed, but her laughter died when Rafael lifted her easily to carry her to the shore. "I have a feeling I'm not going to get any rest at all."

Rafael placed her in the center of a blanket that was half in and half out of the sunshine, and as he lay on his side beside her his hands stroked her wet skin lightly, lazily.

He would make love to her again, she knew, touching her and kissing her until she wanted to scream for him, or else taking her quickly as he had that morning. It seemed they were making up for lost time, trying to take as much as they could in the short time they might have together.

It wouldn't last. Rafael was a pirate, and he had no plans for anything more than a moment's pleasure. She was lost in a time that was not her own, and she wondered sometimes, as the breeze wafted over her, if another gust of wind would carry her away.

She wouldn't have forever with Rafael.

That knowledge should make her miserable, but as Rafael lowered his mouth to her, Sabrina knew that she had never been this happy, might never be this happy again. She had the sun on her body and Rafael beside her—adoring her the only way he knew how.

Sabrina threaded her fingers through his dark, damp curls, drew his mouth to hers, and wrapped her legs possessively around his.

He made love to her slowly, whispering in English his need for her, and then he loved her hard, falling into growling, reluctant Spanish as he proved that need.

Paradise.

When they were both spent and breathless, Rafael remained atop her, inside her, seemingly as reluctant to leave her as she was to have him go. Waves lapped with leisure a few sandy feet away, and a balmy breeze washed over them and sung through the trees and vines that sheltered this cove. Rafael lifted his head, and that breeze caught a few drying curls.

"What do you want, *sirena mia*?" he whispered hoarsely. "What can I give you? You should live like a queen, with silks and jewels and servants and whatever your heart desires. If you ask for the stars I will capture them and string them on a golden chain for you to wear around your neck."

Rafael stared down at her intently. Those dark curls shadowed his face, hiding too much from her. Sabrina wanted to see his eyes, brandy gold and warm and savage, and she wanted, more than anything, to see love mingled with his desire.

"I don't want the stars. I don't want to live like a queen." She pushed his hair back so she could see his eyes. She saw fire there, fascination, satisfaction. "All I want is you."

Her confession made him smile. "I would give you the world, and you ask for Spanish and a man who is already entranced by your charms."

"I don't need the world." Sabrina considered telling Rafael that she was happy for the first time in years, that it was all because of him, but she didn't. Surely he saw her happiness as easily as she saw his fire.

Their swimming lesson continued, and not once was Sabrina afraid. Rafael held her constantly, hands at her back or around her waist, fingers entwined through hers, and there was nothing else. Nothing but the sun and the sea, a warm breeze, and the man she loved with all her heart.

When the rain began to fall, a gentle, caressing rain, Sabrina closed her eyes and lifted her face to the sky, allowing the drops to pelt gingerly against her skin. Not even as a child had she welcomed the rain this way. There were always umbrellas and raincoats and quick dashes to a door and the waiting safety within.

Rafael muttered something softly—in Spanish, of course—and she opened her eyes to find him watching her intently. The same soft rain that she welcomed drenched his already wet skin and hair and splattered on the surface of the cove.

For her, time stood still. She had denied the truth for a long time, but it was no longer a ridiculous notion: Rafael's destiny that had brought her to him.

Once, in a land and a time that was now less real to her than this one, she had wished for happiness, and now it was hers. She had longed for something more than she had, and now she had everything. Who or what had been listening as she wished for a chance to live her life differently?

She didn't know, realized that she never

would know, and for the first time in her life Sabrina simply accepted what life had handed her.

"We have been on this island for a month," Pablo spat.

"Restless?" Rafael stared past the pirate and to the house where Sabrina waited.

"Yes!" Pablo shouted.

"Our last trip was profitable. You do not have enough?"

Pablo gritted his teeth. "Never. It is the Englishwoman. She has you walking around in a daze like some lovesick idiot."

Rafael gave Pablo his full attention. The man was older, taller, wider, undeniably stronger. "You forget yourself. I am captain. We will go when I say we go. No woman, no crewman makes that decision for me."

In spite of his obvious anger, Pablo took a step back. "And when might you make that decision?"

"Soon," Rafael growled.

In truth, he was in no hurry to leave the island and Sabrina. They had been lovers for many days, passionate, tireless lovers. He should be ready to let her go, but he was not. Her passion was strong, and he still, after all this time, felt a powerful need for her.

Even now, she asked for nothing. Twice he had gifted her with jewels that other women would swoon for, and yet they seemed to mean nothing to her. Emeralds, to bring out the green fire in her eyes, given to her as she lay in his bed. Pearls, which were no match for her perfect skin, placed upon a flat belly that was damp with mingled sweat and sand, as she reclined by the cove.

She had thanked him with sweet words, both times, and then put the jewels aside as if they were nothing to come to him again.

Sabrina had learned some Spanish, picking up the phrases he chose to teach her with ease. She learned quickly, but he kept from her the words of love that poured from his mouth when he became one with her.

He was bewitched.

Not since that day at the cove, before they became lovers, before her surrender, had Sabrina mentioned the love she desired. She did not speak of it, but he saw it on her face in unguarded moments, and he felt it in the gentle caresses she bestowed upon him when she thought he was sleeping in her arms.

Sabrina was his passion, the passion of his life, but love was impossible. He would have to let her go, in time.

Anything a man loved could be taken away.

Anything he cherished could be used against him.

"Soon," he promised Pablo.

Sabrina was not waiting for him in the main chamber, and there was no evening meal laid at table. Elena was curiously absent, the hall much too quiet.

He climbed the stairs slowly, his feet leaden in a way they had not been for a long time. How would he send Sabrina away? She could not stay here, could not make him love her. Everything Rafael believed, every truth that ruled his life, told him that to allow this liaison to continue was insanity.

He needed her more now than ever, and that was disaster.

She was waiting for him in her chamber. A silver tray of fruits and bread was laid at the foot of the bed, and Sabrina stood in front of the open balcony doors, the last sun of the day lighting the island beyond.

"The devil must be chilled," he said as he closed the door behind him.

Sabrina glanced down at the revealing white gown she wore, fingering the sheer material. "I did say it would be a cold day in hell before I wore this, didn't I?"

"You did."

How could he think to send her away when she smiled at him that way? When she greeted him in a seductive gown that hid nothing from him? Sabrina gave him everything a man could ask for. Her body and her heart, her very soul.

"Until now, I haven't had much of a chance to wear anything to bed."

"Nor will you."

Sabrina crossed the room on silent bare feet to unbutton and then slip off his waistcoat. She lifted the knife from his waist with a disdainful grimace and set it aside. When he tried to kiss her she moved coyly away, and when he reached out to touch her she skirted quickly just out of reach.

157

He might have been insulted had she not worn such a bright smile.

Sabrina reached out slowly to take his arm, and then she led him to the single chair in the room. Her body, a body that was all too apparent, brushed against his as she walked at his side. Obediently, he sat, and then she knelt between his thighs and began to feed him.

With a hand high on his thigh she placed a piece of yanna into his mouth. Her fingers trailed softly over his lips, and returned a moment later to repeat the ritual. Between bites of sweet fruit, he questioned her. "What are you doing, *sirena mia*?"

"I'm seducing you."

"Ah."

"You couldn't tell?"

He smiled at her feigned chagrin. "You have only to look at me and I am seduced."

After a few more bites of yanna and magniot, some delivered with those delicate fingers, others delivered to his lips between her own, Sabrina set the silver tray aside and pulled him to his feet. With slow hands she undressed him, fingering the scars on his chest, kissing them. She ignored the marks on his back, the scars that made her cry as if his pain were her own.

When all his clothes had been cast aside, Sabrina shoved him gently onto the bed, and she fell after him, covering his body and fastening her mouth on his.

Her kiss was enough to drive the sanest man wild, she yielded so completely.

She straddled him and took his straining

manhood within her swiftly. White froth pooled over him, fell from her shoulder so that one breast was free.

When she loved him, she had the face of an angel, so pure and bright, so full of wonder. As she rose and fell the wonder grew. He could feel it, Sabrina's love. Within himself, as if in joining his body with hers he had joined their hearts and minds.

He could not accept it. He could not fight it.

Sabrina trembled, she tightened above and around him. With trembling lips she whispered his name, and only then did Rafael allow himself the release he sought in her arms.

His gift, his destiny.

She tumbled, melted and fell until she rested her head beside his to whisper in his ear, to breathe against him words so soft they had no meaning.

Perhaps she whispered of the love he saw and denied. He did not ask. Would not ask.


"Elena!" Pablo's voice shattered the quiet of the great room below. Rafael left the bedroom, stepping into the hallway to look beyond the banister to the frantic man below. Sabrina stood in the doorway and watched his scarred back as he slipped into a shirt.

"What is wrong?" Rafael asked.

"Aqualina," Pablo said, his voice lowered but still strong. "The baby, it comes."

Rafael relaxed. Sabrina could see it in his shoulders, in the hands he placed on the banister. "The sun is just up. Elena is most likely gathering fruit or crabs for the day. She will not be far."

"I can go sit with Aqualina while you find Elena," Sabrina offered, already stepping into her blue skirt.

Rafael turned to her and gave her that devastating smile. "You would do that? You do not even know her."

She was already stepping past him, hurrying for the stairs. "Don't argue with me, and don't look at me like that or Pablo will end up delivering that baby himself. Go find Elena. All I know how to do is hold a hand, and that will only help for so long."

Pablo was distraught enough to accept her assistance, and while Rafael left to search for Elena, the father-to-be led Sabrina to his home.

The cottages were much smaller than Rafael's house, but very nice compared to what she'd seen in Cayona. Pablo's cottage consisted of one large square room, with a kitchen area in one corner and an occupied bed in the other.

There were three other women crowded around the bed, and Sabrina cringed when she saw them.

An older, heavyset woman Sabrina had seen upon her arrival stood at the side of Aqualina's bed. All Sabrina could see was the ugly rash that covered the woman's hands and forearms. Nelia was there, along with another young woman. They were rash-free, but far from clean. There was dirt from Rafael's *plantation* on their hands and under their fingernails.

"They're going to have to leave," Sabrina said curtly.

"Why?" Pablo asked, cutting suspicious eyes to her.

Sabrina lowered her voice. "I don't know what sort of disease that woman has, but I don't think you want your baby to get it. Likewise with the dirty hands on the girls."

Pablo frowned at her.

"Trust me," she whispered.

Pablo must have seen something on her face he didn't like, or else she hadn't lost her knack at ordering people around, because he did as Sabrina asked immediately, sending the other women from the cottage with a great shout in Spanish. Words Rafael had not yet taught her. He followed at their heels, shouting as he saw them out the door.

Aqualina didn't seem to mind. She was in great pain, sweating profusely, muttering words Sabrina couldn't understand.

*"Está bien,"* Sabrina said as she took Aqualina's hand, trying to assure the young woman that all would be well. Pablo's wife grasped Sabrina's hand tightly, squeezing with amazing strength as a contraction seized her.

Pablo reentered the room silently, and Sabrina cast a quick glance over her shoulder.

The big bald man was pale, almost green as he found himself helpless, perhaps for the first time in his life.

"What should I do?" he asked, looking to Sabrina for direction.

"Boil water." She nodded to the fire on the other side of the room.

"Why?"

Sabrina shrugged. "I don't know. It's what fathers do, isn't it?"

If nothing else they'd have some germ-free water for washing hands and to bathe the new baby.

She placed a cool cloth on Aqualina's forehead, as the mother-to-be closed her eyes and took a deep breath, preparing herself for the next contraction.

"It's going to be all right," Sabrina whispered, smiling down at the young woman who was in such pain. "Soon you'll be a mommy, and you'll have a sweet little baby all your own."

The next contraction came soon, much sooner than Sabrina had expected. Aqualina grasped her hand, a viselike grip, and screamed at the top of her lungs. Pablo cursed silently, but remained on the opposite side of the room.

What if Elena didn't arrive in time?

Sabrina moved to the foot of the bed and lifted the sheet.

"It's coming," she muttered, glancing at Pablo. "Hell. What do I do now?"

"You do not know?" he bellowed, just as Aqualina tilted back her head and screamed again.

"No, dammit, I don't know!"

Pablo's eyes were wide and more frightened than angry. "You are a woman! You should know what to do!"

Sabrina calmed herself and tried to give

Pablo a small and hopefully reassuring smile. "I'm about to learn, because it doesn't look as if this baby intends to wait for Elena to get here."

The baby was delivered into Sabrina's hands moments later, just as the door burst open and Elena rushed into the room. A girl, tiny and perfect. Sabrina wiped the blood from Pablo's daughter, and wrapped her in a length of clean muslin to keep her warm.

The baby cried, while Elena saw to Aqualina and Pablo flattened himself against the fireplace. He'd never looked like such a coward. Sabrina held the newborn close and gently, and crossed the room to present the child to Pablo.

"A girl. Congratulations."

He made no move to take the child from her. "You hold her. She is too small."

"She is not too small, she's absolutely perfect, see?" Sabrina presented the baby girl to Pablo, and he peered down at the tiny face.

"You keep her for a while. She seems to like you well enough." He sidled past her, heading for the door.

"Chicken," she whispered.

Pablo threw open the door and Rafael was there. Waiting. The new father disappeared, but Rafael held the door open, stared at her with a gradually paling face and narrowed eyes that hid his thoughts from her. Sabrina cuddled the now silent baby, rocked it in her arms, and the smile that spread across her face was wide.

She mouthed the words to him. *I want one.*

Rafael didn't respond, didn't move at all. He stared at her and the new baby for a long moment, and then he slammed the door shut.

# *Chapter Eleven*

Sabrina knew where to find Rafael, when she discovered that he was not waiting in the house. She followed the familiar path that cut through dense foliage, making her way to Rafael's cove. Their cove now.

What a high. Her heart was beating fast, and there was a wide smile on her face, and she felt absolutely exhilarated. There was a new baby girl on this island, tiny and perfect, and Sabrina had helped to deliver her into this world.

The smile on her face softened. If there was any sort of birth control practiced in the seventeenth century, she knew nothing of it. And even if there was, there had certainly never been anything between her and Rafael.

It was bound to happen, sooner or later, that she would have Rafael's child. The thought should have frightened her. Bearing a child in this time was dangerous. There were no hospitals, no obstetricians, no drugs to dull the pain . . . and still she smiled.

It was part of what she'd missed in what she'd come to think of as her last life. Warmth, love, a family of her own. Rafael never spoke of forever, and she wouldn't ask it of him, but when she left this magical island she could take his child with her . . . a baby to remind her of everything she'd found here. A child she would love with all her heart, and who would love her in return.

Rafael was far out today, swimming furiously where the water was too deep for Sabrina. The sun glistened on wet skin when he broke the surface, and then he disappeared beneath the water once again. She could swim, a little, but she never ventured where the water was over her head.

Leaving the skirt and blouse on the sand Sabrina stepped into the water, and Rafael swam toward her, his pace slowing. Sabrina fell into the sea, pushing herself forward and toward Rafael.

"How are they?" he asked as he neared her, soft waves touching his chin, curls floating.

"They're both fine." Rafael reached her, wrapped his arms around her beneath the water. "Aqualina's doing great, and the baby is healthy and beautiful."

His eyes were hooded, and dark curls fell across his cheeks, as if he meant to hide. Rafael couldn't conceal his emotions from her, no matter how he tried. She knew every nuance of those features too well to be deceived, and she couldn't ignore his displeasure. There was such thunder on his face, in his eyes, such unnatural tension in the body he pressed against hers.

"I need you." It was a hoarsely whispered demand, a plea Sabrina couldn't refuse.

"Yes."

Cool water surrounded her, and Rafael's hands were warm against her breasts and her thighs, demanding fingers on her skin and inside her as he propelled her toward the beach.

Once she tried to speak, and Rafael silenced her with a deep kiss.

He pressed her into the wet sand at the edge of the cove, half in and half out of the water, and he plunged deep while waves lapped against their legs. The sand was coarse against her back, a contradiction to the smoothness of Rafael's flesh on and inside her. Waves washed gently over their legs, and the sun glared, bright and hot.

The words that tumbled from Rafael's mouth were beautiful, harsh, guttural Spanish. She still knew so little of his language, and when he spoke quickly there were few words she could identify. There was one she knew well. *Mia.* Mine.

She held Rafael tight as the climax grew and finally shattered her, as he lost himself in her as completely as she lost herself in him, so freely, so naturally.

With a soft touch of her fingers she pushed dark, damp curls away from his face. "Rafael."

She breathed his name. "Wouldn't it be wonderful if . . ."

He silenced her with a kiss that was anything but gentle. "No talking," he ordered gruffly, breathlessly, as he pulled his mouth away from hers.

Rafael didn't leave her, but rested his head on her shoulder and his body over hers. When she placed her hands on his back she could feel the scars there, the horrible reminders of what Falconer had done to him. That touch reminded her of who Rafael was.

Was he becoming restless? Tiring of her? It didn't seem that was possible, not at a moment like this.

For a while they lay there, in the sun and the surf and the sand, bodies entwined, only silence between them.

When Rafael left her, he returned without a word to the water, turned his back on her and after a few long steps dove into the sea he adored more than anything or anyone.

Sabrina followed, but kept her distance as Rafael swam. What was bothering him? She had attributed his reaction at Pablo's cottage to the same male aversion to childbirth that had frightened the new father. Surely something so simple and natural wouldn't have Rafael in such a state.

He swam on top of the water, dove beneath the calm surface for too long, it seemed, reappearing at a distance from the spot where he'd plunged into the sea. There was such power in his strokes, such determination in an activity that took him nowhere.

He never seemed to tire, and eventually Sabrina returned to the shore to dress in her simple outfit. She sat on the sand and waited for Rafael to work off whatever had him in this near frenzy.

When he did leave the cove he was exhausted. She could see it in the set of his shoulders, the narrowing of his eyes. He dressed without speaking to her, keeping his gaze on the blue-green water that lapped before him.

"Rafael?" she called to him, after he had finished dressing.

"*Sí, sirena mia?*" He hesitated, but eventually turned to look down at her.

"You've said more than once that I can have anything I want."

"*Sí.*" Was there reluctance in his answer?

"I want a baby."

His face paled, as it had at Pablo's cottage, and he slowly turned his back on her. "No."

No? And in a voice that left no room for argument. "I might already be pregnant. How can you tell me no?"

Sabrina stood as Rafael spun slowly to face her. "Are you?"

What was that look on his face? The expression was easy to identify, though she tried to deny it for a moment. He was repulsed, thoroughly disgusted.

"I don't know," she said honestly. "It's possible."

"I have reached twenty-eight years and have

not fathered a child. There will be no baby."

It sounded like an edict. An incontestable law.

"What if it just happens?" She was too confused to be angry. She'd never seen Rafael like this. This man was Rafael the pirate, ruthless, demanding. Her Rafael was a lover, a gentle man.

"There will be no baby," he repeated darkly.

"How can you . . ."

"Elena will see to it," he snapped.

The full understanding of his statement came over her slowly, that gradual recognition touched with disbelief and outrage. The man who loved her and laughed with her and made her forget that she shouldn't be here could not be so cruel.

"I'm not asking you to marry me, or to take responsibility," she said, trying hard to maintain her composure. "I just want a baby. A child of my own."

"And how would you care for this child, *querida*?" Rafael spat, his anger rising. "In the cold of the English colonies, how would you survive?"

Sabrina couldn't contain her own anger any longer. "I could sell that ugly-ass emerald necklace you gave me and live off the proceeds for a few years."

His eyes narrowed.

"As a matter of fact, I think I've worn out my welcome here. I'm ready to leave."

"I will say when the time . . ."

"The time is now."

Rafael tried to stare her down, giving her his darkest, most threatening glare. He'd never looked at her that way before, not before they'd become lovers and certainly not since. No matter how he threatened her, she wasn't going to budge. Not this time.

"As you wish, *sirena mia,*" he whispered.

Sabrina spun away from that dark face, from the threat there. How could this man be her Rafael? The man who loved her and laughed as he lay in her arms and made her love as she never had before? How could she love a man so cruel?

She ran, taking the path and never looking back, pushing aside the lush island growth without a thought to what creatures might lurk there. Nothing could be hiding there that could hurt her the way Rafael just had. Eventually she slowed her pace, but she listened for footsteps behind her. She heard nothing. If Rafael was following, he was keeping his distance.

He offered the stars but refused her the simple gift of a child. Why? Was he afraid she would somehow use that child against him? She would never stoop to such a trick to keep a man. She'd never kidded herself that she and Rafael had anything more than a moment.

There was always the possibility that she was already pregnant. If that was true, Rafael could never know. Sabrina wouldn't allow Elena to put her hands on her, or to slip some poisonous witches' brew into her wine.

If only she had kept better track of time since her fall. On this island, in Rafael's arms, time had no meaning. One day faded sweetly into the next. No calendars, no appointments, no schedules to keep.

Only one thing was certain: She couldn't stay here. Her moment with Rafael was over.

He had known everything was changed as the door swung open and he had seen her in Pablo's home, holding the new baby so easily and tenderly in her arms. Sabrina with a brilliant smile on her face, a glow on her cheeks, a rapture in her heart. He had known, even before she had mouthed those damning words to him, what she wanted more than anything else he could give her.

Sending Sabrina away was going to be difficult enough without wondering if she carried his child. They would delay, for a short time, until they were certain.

Anything a man loves can be used against him.

What would Falconer do if he knew of a child? If he knew of Sabrina? Few thoughts had the power to chill Rafael's heart, but he felt now as if it was pure ice that beat in his breast.

He could send Sabrina away, because he had no choice. They could never have more than this, a brief encounter to remember when the days were not so warm. Rafael knew, had always known, that the years stretching before him were not endless. His luck had been too good. He had cheated death too many times.

Love was not a priority. It was a fancy meant for enchanted tales, not for real hearts.

Sabrina would surely hate him now, for the

sacrifices he was prepared to make, for the child he would refuse her. Perhaps that was best. She would never understand why he refused himself the love she offered so freely, the child she wanted to bear for him. Perhaps she could cling to that hate when she needed strength.

She likely did not know yet that hate was much stronger than love.

Sabrina did not appear for supper, and Rafael ate alone.

He had eaten many meals alone, in this house, at this table, but it had never felt this desolate. When Elena appeared to refill his glass, he ordered her to take Sabrina's empty plate and untouched wine away, hoping that if he was not reminded of her absence the loneliness would not be so intense.

The solitude of his island had always pleased him. There were women to be had for a night on Tortuga, when he wished it, women who never spoke of the days to come or wished for something so simple and impossible as a child. They knew how to prevent such disasters.

He sat at the table far too long, drank too much wine as he reminded himself of who he was—and of what was important in his life.

When he climbed the stairs it was late, and he was drained, and it seemed his entire body ached with his decision. Passing the place there on the stairs where Sabrina had stood and surrendered to him, where she had lifted her hand and confessed that she needed him, he clenched his fists with frustration.

There was no need to soften his steps in the

172

hallway, and he did not knock at Sabrina's door, but entered as he always did. As if the room were his own, as if she would welcome him.

He had not expected her to be asleep, and she was not.

She sat up in the bed, the covers to her waist, that muslin nightgown he had not seen for weeks covering her to her chin. A candle burned at her bedside, and he ignored her red-rimmed eyes, the desolation there, and concentrated instead on the stubborn tilt to her chin, the hard set of her mouth.

If he had known it would be this painful to send Sabrina away, he would have left her on the seaside.

"The time is near," he said, not moving from the doorway. "Soon, I will take you to the English colonies."

"How soon?" she whispered.

Rafael hesitated. "When we know."

She was silent for a long moment, and then he saw the light of understanding on her face. "When we know I'm not pregnant?"

"*Sí.*"

"You bastard," she whispered, as if even now she could not believe this of him.

"*Sí.*"

"Get out," she ordered. So strong, so angry. "You won't have long to wait."

He backed out of the room, closing the door behind him. It was for the best, even though she would hate him, even though that anger would overshadow everything wonderful that had come before.

In the quiet of his own room, Rafael sought the sleep he knew would not come. Perhaps he would never sleep again. There was no wind tonight, not even a whisper of a breeze through the balcony doors to tease his sweating body. It was a warm night, but his bed was cold and his arms were empty. He ached for Sabrina.

It was his punishment, that he would always ache for her. His arms would always be empty, his bed forever cold.

And still, he knew that he was right. That to allow the birth of his child would mean disaster for them all.

He could not love Sabrina, could not love a child.

God save him, he would not.

"Good morning." Sabrina walked down the stairs with a smile pasted on her face. She would not hide from Rafael, not again. Last night she had been stunned, hurt, but life would go on. Somehow.

Rafael was evidently surprised, and he glanced up from his morning meal to stare at her as she descended the staircase. His face was cold, and he did not return her greeting.

Elena appeared as Sabrina sat, and placed a full plate before her.

"Elena," Sabrina called, stopping the woman before she could retreat into the kitchen. *"Como están Aqualina y la bebé?"*

The housekeeper turned slowly. *"Bien."* Her tone was suspicious.

*"Y Pablo?"* Sabrina continued.

Elena laughed lightly, and then she launched into rapid Spanish.

"Whoa, whoa." Sabrina held up one hand. "I'm still learning."

"She said Pablo is fine, but still afraid he will break the baby," Rafael snapped. "And she says you did well." It was a bitterly delivered translation.

Sabrina ignored Rafael and thanked Elena before the woman returned to the kitchen.

There was a long moment of awkward stillness. She'd endured her share of strained silences in the past, but none like this.

She couldn't stand it.

"Elena does everything, it seems. Cook, housekeeper, midwife, seamstress. Where did you find her?" She phrased the question as a purely conversational one, calmly.

"She is Pablo's mother."

Sabrina was genuinely surprised. Pablo had a mother? "That tiny woman is Pablo's mother?"

"*Sí.*" Rafael returned his attention to the plate before him.

"Amazing."

They ate in silence, and in spite of the awkwardness Sabrina didn't dare to speak again until Rafael stood to leave the table.

"You can start with the preparations to leave this place," she said coolly. "I'm already packing. Do you mind if I take the clothes Elena made? I hate to start fresh in a new place with nothing to wear."

"They are yours."

175

"I'm thinking no more than a few days." She looked down at the tabletop, but only for a moment. "I'm feeling pretty irritable, a little puffy, you know, all the usual PMS symptoms."

Rafael remained standing at the far end of the table. "PMS?"

"Yes." She raised her eyes to his innocently. "I guess you don't know about that. Let's just say that in a few days I'll know without a doubt that I'm not pregnant. You can relax, and I can get myself back to the real world, such as it is."

*"Sirena mia,"* Rafael began, and she could almost believe that there was a touch of regret in his voice.

But he said nothing more. He offered no apology, no explanation for the sudden change in his attitude toward her.

Of course, he'd never promised her anything more than a moment, had never offered her more than a few glorious days. Just like that, the interlude was over.

She couldn't let him see how much this hurt. "As long as you stay the hell away from me, we won't have a problem, will we?"

Rafael spun away from her and stalked from the house muttering a string of Spanish curses.

# *Chapter Twelve*

The rasping scrape of steel against stone was comforting, as was the feel of the knife's handle in his hand. It was familiar, the sound, the feel, the smell, and Rafael needed familiar right now.

At his feet were half a dozen knives, and they rested on the leather pouch in which they were normally stored. This was the last, the final blade to be sharpened, as Rafael prepared to go to sea once again.

A few feet away the sea danced, calling to him, it seemed, with every wave, with every soft break against the sand. The sun glistened brightly on blue-green water, but Rafael remained in the shade, cool beneath the tall palm trees.

This was a nice place to spend the afternoon. Not as pleasant as his cove, of course, but he could not make himself return there. Not alone. Not yet.

He tested the weight of the knife in his hand, flipping it easily into the air and catching the smoothly polished handle. He tossed the knife into the air again, kept his eyes on the deadly blade as it twisted in the air before his face, and caught the weapon smoothly.

This was his life.

He caught the blade between his fingers, took aim, and hurled the knife at an invisible target on a tree trunk that partially blocked his view of the sea. The rotating knife was a blur, until it found the target and came to a sudden stop, the blade embedded deeply in the tree trunk.

"You were always a master of the knives."

Rafael turned to watch Pablo as the big man approached, uncannily silent for one so large. He should be concerned that he had heard nothing but oddly enough was not.

"Thanks to you." Rafael bent, scooped up another of the weapons, and without hesitation threw it forcefully. There was an oddly reassuring pleasure in the simple act. The blade of that knife landed, as intended, just below the first. How many hours had he and Pablo practiced just this way? Competing, for pleasure or for gold. Laughing, after weeks or months at sea when there had been nothing to laugh about.

Pablo selected a knife from those that remained at Rafael's feet, tested it in the palm of his hand, and then tossed it skillfully. His aim was as accurate as Rafael's.

"We will be leaving soon," Rafael said. He

looked not at Pablo, but at the knife he had plucked from the ground. "A matter of days, if all goes well."

"Good." There was no emotion in Pablo's voice, but Rafael detected a touch of approval. Perhaps relief.

Rafael let the knife fly, putting all of his strength into the smooth motion. "We have been here too long." It was a statement as much for his own ears as for Pablo's, but the big man nodded in agreement.

"I had begun to think that the woman had ruined you." It was a casual statement, delivered as Pablo hurled another knife into the tree trunk.

They reached down together to collect the last two knives from the ground at their feet. Rafael kept to himself the knowledge that he still was not convinced that Sabrina had *not* ruined him.

"A knife," Pablo said darkly, "is the best of weapons. With bloody steel in your fist you know your enemy is dead. You can feel his last heartbeat, the heat of his warm blood on your hands. You can look into his eyes and see death coming."

Pablo lifted his head and stared at Rafael with eyes so deep a brown they appeared to be black. Especially now.

"I am glad that we are going back to sea soon."

Rafael wondered just how restless his crew had become. Would they kill him and elect Pablo as their captain if the wait became too

LINDA JONES

long? Of course they would. He had always known that was true.

He tested the weight of the knife in his hand. The deadliest weapon? No. The deadliest weapon known to man was the soft and welcoming body of a woman. A body that could make a man forget who he was, *why* he was.

Rafael let the knife soar, putting all that he had into his final toss. "She is just a woman," he grumbled.

Pablo tossed the last of the knives so that it landed beside a still quivering handle.

A week had passed, and it was surely the longest week of Sabrina's life. She refused to avoid Rafael, but she just as strongly refused to allow him to touch her. Not just as a lover, but in any way. She avoided the brush of his hand or simply passing by him too closely.

It was torture, horrible and humiliating, but she smiled through it, each and every long, miserable day.

With every day that passed her anxiety grew, feeding on itself and the fears and hopes that became more real with every rising sun. Was it possible . . .

So she'd missed a period. She'd also traveled back in time more than three hundred years, and that was bound to play havoc with a girl's system. She wasn't ready to admit that she was pregnant, not even to herself.

If she waited any longer, Rafael would become suspicious. There was only one way to go.

Bluff.

"We can leave now," she said curtly, standing on the staircase. Rafael stood before the fire, head down, long hair gathered at the nape of his neck in a curling ponytail, and he lifted his head slowly, perhaps reluctantly, as she spoke.

"You are . . ." Poor Rafael. Was he embarrassed? Contrite? Did he regret . . .

"Not pregnant," she finished curtly, unwilling to allow her thoughts to explore the possibility of Rafael's regret.

He nodded his head, pleased, she was sure, and then he returned his stare to a fire that was not necessary on such a mild night.

Sabrina turned and began the short trek up the stairs, but she was halted by Rafael's shout, as he called abruptly for Elena.

She froze on the stairs, and listened closely to the brief conversation between Rafael and Elena. Even though she understood only a few words, she knew what was being said. She knew it with her heart, and she wasn't surprised, not surprised at all, when Elena joined her on the staircase.

"You don't trust me?" she asked calmly, not bothering to turn around. She didn't want to see Rafael's cold face, couldn't endure it at that moment.

"*Querida*," he muttered, "I trust no one."

Sabrina climbed the stairs, listening with dread to Elena's soft footsteps behind her. What would she do now? Elena would tell Rafael that she had lied, and if there was a baby it wouldn't have a chance.

Inside the room Elena lit a lamp, and she ordered Sabrina, in a soft voice and with a wave of her hand, to the bed.

Sabrina faced the tiny woman, clutched her fists at her sides, and stood at the foot of the bed with her feet planted firmly on the ground. She would do battle if she had to.

The face Sabrina stared at was not so harsh, and it appeared to soften before her eyes. Perhaps Elena knew more than she'd been letting on, of the crisis that was driving Sabrina from the island.

Elena whispered quiet words and waited for a response.

Sabrina shook her head, unable to understand the simple question.

They resorted to pantomime again, Elena locking her fingers and motioning before her, drawing an invisible pregnant belly. *"Bebé?"*

"I don't know." Sabrina shrugged and lifted her hands into the air. "But if I am . . ." How could she make the woman understand? "It's my baby." There was no way to know if it was true, or if Elena would understand what she was trying to say. Sabrina placed a trembling hand over her heart. *"My* baby."

Elena was unsure how to proceed, that much was clear. Rafael was her employer, the captain of his ship and king of this castle. She mumbled to herself, and more than once Sabrina made out the word *capitán*.

"Don't let him take my baby," Sabrina begged, unable to struggle for the words in Spanish, praying that the woman would understand.

She was suddenly and inexplicably certain

that there was a child, that her missed cycle had nothing to do with the fall or what came after. It was instinct, a phenomenon she'd never given much credence to in the past.

There was a relaxing of Elena's stern face, an evident acceptance that came with a nod of her graying head and low words Sabrina could not decipher.

Finally, the older woman sat on the edge of the bed. An obviously confused Elena stared away from Sabrina and whispered softly in Spanish.

"Please," Sabrina whispered. *"Por favor."*

After a few strained moments Elena stood, nodded curtly, and left the room. Sabrina followed, not sure what the woman would do, but feeling that perhaps in this one crucial matter, Elena was an ally.

Rafael waited at the foot of the stairs, and Elena began to deliver her report as soon as she stepped onto the staircase.

Sabrina held her breath. The curt words Elena delivered gave her no hint. Perhaps she told the lie Sabrina asked of her, but she could just as well be telling Rafael of the pregnancy of which Sabrina was now certain.

Elena brushed past Rafael at the foot of the stairs, and he didn't look up until she had passed through the room and into the kitchen. Sabrina held her chin high and said nothing.

"So," Rafael breathed softly, "the time has come. We will sail in three days, first to Tortuga, and then to the English colonies."

Sabrina released the breath she'd been holding. "I'm ready whenever you are."

"Are you, *sirena mia*?"

She had thought she knew Rafael, better than she'd ever known anyone, but the man at the bottom of the steps was a stranger to her. Cold. Cruel. He'd never promised love, had even disputed the concept of that emotion . . . but she had been so certain that there was a measure of love in his heart, that he had cared for her, that he adored her not only with his body but with a portion of his soul.

The man who stared up at her was not her Rafael, not her lover. He was a pirate who trusted no one, loved nothing, lived only for revenge.

She didn't answer, but turned from him and climbed the stairs slowly. Three days. It would be simple to stay in her room and avoid Rafael for that length of time. She could plead cramps and take to her bed, and ask that all meals be delivered to her room.

There was no need to face Rafael again until it was time to board the *Venganza* and set sail for Tortuga.

"Open it," Rafael ordered, motioning impatiently for Cristóbal to place Sabrina's trunk on the floor.

The red gown she had worn for him was on top of the stack of clothing in the half-empty trunk, and in spite of himself Rafael smiled. She had given him many nights to remember, treasured days to carry in his heart. Priceless mem-

ories, more so because no one else would ever
know how he cherished them.

With a wave of his hand, Rafael sent Cristóbal
away. Sabrina was waiting on the ship, and all
of his crew but Cristóbal was aboard and ready
to sail.

In a velvet packet beneath the red dress was
the emerald choker he had given her, a brilliant
and heavy piece that sparkled gold and green.
It was fit for a queen, but Sabrina had declared
it gaudy. With the emeralds were the pearls that
had suited Sabrina so well. They were flawless
and elegant, like the woman who was meant to
wear them. Those treasures would help her in
her new home, but they were not enough.

He withdrew the leather pouch from his vest
and tossed it atop the red gown. Pieces of eight
swirled inside the pouch with a deep and muted
ring, weighing down the ruby silk. What would
Sabrina say when she found the gold?

Rafael moved the pouch to the bottom of the
trunk, hoping that it would not be discovered
until Sabrina reached her destination. From another pocket, he withdrew a large pin, an ornate
piece of gold grapes and a twining vine and
leaves the size of his thumb. He tucked it into
the folds of the white gown. An emerald bracelet to match the choker Sabrina had disdained
followed, and another pin, and a sapphire pendant.

Last, he placed a ring atop the red silk, tucking it into a fold in the bodice. He should have
given it to her sooner, but now it was certainly
too late. She would throw it in his face, or

laugh, or refuse him with a lift of that stubborn chin.

It was plainer than the other gifts he had given Sabrina, but he thought it would suit her as well as the pearls. More, perhaps. The gold band was wide, the scroll that was etched into the metal delicate. No stone was set into the gold, no emerald or ruby or diamond. The ring was elegant, simple, the sort of jewelry a woman might wear every day, if she chose. Perhaps Sabrina would keep this one gift to remember him by, rather than selling it, as she surely would the other pieces.

Rafael slammed the trunk closed and hefted it angrily. What a sentimental fool he had become.

A lifelong fear, gone. Sabrina watched the ocean that stretched before the *Venganza* and could actually appreciate its beauty.

Not that she was any safer than she'd been before. Her swimming skills were negligible, at best. She could make her way across Rafael's cove, as long as he was beside her, and as long as she knew she could stand at any moment and the water would come no higher than her breasts, but here . . . the waves were powerful enough to draw her down and down and down, until . . .

It was a familiar nightmare, but right now it was no more than that—an irrational fear. A child's bogeyman.

What more could this sea do to her? It had sucked her into its waves and carried her here.

Propelled her to Rafael and an impossible new life. Was it possible that the vivid dreams had been a warning? A promise?

"*Señorita* Sabrina." Rafael stood several feet away, his hands clasped behind his back, his eyes on the ocean that stretched before him. He hadn't called her *sirena mia* since the day she'd turned from him on the stairs. It made perfect sense. She wasn't *his* anything anymore. "You travel well today."

"It's calm enough."

"We will stay for two nights on Tortuga. I would suggest that you stay on board. My cabin is yours."

"I don't know . . ."

"It would be safest for you here."

She knew they would be days sailing for the English colonies, and the idea of being confined to the ship for any longer than she had to was an unpleasant one.

But Rafael had used the magic word: *safe*. No matter what had happened, she still trusted Rafael with her life.

"All right," she conceded, and Rafael actually turned to her with a surprised lift of his brow.

She wished he'd left his hair down, so that coffee brown curls could hide a portion of his face from her. With it pulled back so severely his face appeared harsh, every line brutal and unforgiving.

"It pleases me to see that you have not lost all reason," he said, undoubtedly thinking his words a compliment of some sort.

When had she ever lost her reason? "You're

referring, no doubt, to my brief bout of insanity on your island. My lapse when I thought that you might be something more than a barbarous, vengeful thief."

"I never pretended to be anything other than what I am, but I am not a thief. I am a pirate."

"Semantics," Sabrina said with a wave of her hand. "You take things that don't belong to you. That makes you a thief in my book."

She knew it was her wish for a child that made Rafael question her sanity, but she refused to address that delicate subject.

"Most often I take from others like myself. The English pirates who befoul these waters, who carry gold and gems they take from the *flota*."

"Most often," Sabrina repeated. "And the rest of the time?"

Rafael shrugged his shoulders. "On occasion I have been forced to pursue the *flota* myself."

"Thief," she whispered.

"My men and their families must eat. This is . . ." Rafael paused, and waved his hand widely, as if to offer her the sea before him and the ship they sailed upon. "This is our world. A world unlike the one you come from, to be sure, but ours."

"There's no honor in being a thief," Sabrina goaded.

He turned to her with another disbelieving lift of his eyebrows. Brandy eyes twinkled beneath them. God, she'd missed this. A simple conversation, an argument, the sound of his voice.

"Honor? Are you so naive that you embrace such a concept as honor? I embrace survival, instead. It serves me well. Many an honorable man lies at the bottom of the sea. I wonder if, in their final moments, they wished to be less noble."

He didn't give her a chance to respond, but turned from her to climb the ladder to the aft bridge. Just as well. She had no answer to his assertions, no argument that would sway a man like Rafael.

He disdained honor, but there had been a time when she'd been so certain she'd seen it in his eyes. A sense of justice, a knowledge of what was right and what was not.

But an honorable man wouldn't insist that a child, his own or anyone else's, be destroyed before it had a chance to be born. He wouldn't deny a woman who only wanted a baby to love. He wouldn't . . . God, he couldn't.

Somewhere deep in her heart Sabrina held a kernel of belief that if Rafael knew about the child she carried he would relent. He would allow her this gift. But she wouldn't take a chance. Not with her child.

Pablo took Rafael's place, giving her a scowl that was much kinder than his usual expression.

"The new father," Sabrina said with a smile. "Elena tells me everyone is doing well."

"Yes. Aqualina asks me to thank you for your help." It was the most grudging thanks Sabrina had ever received.

"She is most welcome. I wanted to see her

189

and the baby again before I left, but . . . I haven't been feeling well."

He shrugged his shoulders, as if it didn't matter at all. Of course it didn't. They had a full and complete family. Pablo and Aqualina, Elena, the new baby. She envied them.

"How did you meet Aqualina?" Sabrina asked, as prepared for Pablo to turn his back on her as she was for an answer. She had wondered from the first moment she'd seen the young girl, adoration on her face as she'd met Pablo at the pier, what might have brought the two together.

"The captain save her."

"Rafael saved her? From what?"

"From Falconer." Pablo's face darkened. "Years ago. She was a child then. The captain released Aqualina and five others from Falconer's plantation. *Niñas.* They lived on the island until they were old enough to marry, and Aqualina . . ." He almost smiled. "She chose me. She asks me to be her husband."

"She loves you," Sabrina said softly.

The big man shrugged. *"Sí."*

"So Rafael, who claims to have no heart and no nobility, rescued a handful of girls from this Falconer. What was the creep doing? Working children on his plantation?"

Pablo turned away from her to stare at the ocean. "Falconer is a very bad man. If Rafael ever allows me to accompany him on an invasion of that man's home, I will kill the Englishman with my bare hands, and I will take great joy in the deed."

"He won't allow you to go with him?"

Pablo shook his head. "He goes alone, when the demons become too much for him to bear. I think that is why he does not kill the English bastard—because he is afraid the demons will come and there will be no way to be rid of them."

Sabrina lifted her head and watched Rafael on the bridge. Demons? The heartless pirate?

When she pulled her eyes away from Rafael, Pablo was gone.

# *Chapter Thirteen*

If anything, the docks of Tortuga were more crowded now than before, bustling and noisy. It was almost nightfall when the *Venganza* docked. For Sabrina, the beauty of the sunset was overshadowed by the coarseness of the town that lay before them. She didn't regret for a moment agreeing to sleep in Rafael's cabin rather than entering Cayona again.

Here, on this island of cutthroats, they would collect the rest of Rafael's crew, and when they sailed again the deck would be crowded with pirates.

Rafael had assured her in a maddeningly calm voice that they would deliver her with the utmost haste to the English colonies. After that, once she had been deposited in Boston or some other coastal town, she could only imagine that the *Venganza* would be menacing the seas again.

Sabrina wanted to ask Rafael about the girls he had rescued from Falconer—Aqualina and the others—but she hadn't had a chance. It didn't seem like the sort of subject that should be raised while there were others close by, and on this small vessel there were always others within earshot.

Rafael left the ship soon after docking, taking Pablo and Cristóbal with him. Sabrina watched the three of them stroll to town. Rafael never even glanced back.

He was done with her, had obviously considered their tenuous relationship severed since the moment she'd asked for more than he wanted to give. She should be relieved to see him go, even for a while, but Rafael's absence from the *Venganza* seemed to make Sabrina restless. That restlessness grew as the minutes passed. The pirates who remained on board ignored her—had probably been ordered to do just that—and the minutes dragged on.

Sabrina paced the deck as the sun set. Rafael's crew surrounded her, spoke in soft Spanish and occasionally even laughed out loud, and still she felt completely alone as darkness fell. Soon she was pacing by the light of a half moon.

Finally, she gave up and retired to Rafael's cabin. Below deck the darkness was complete. The night was still, quiet but for the gentle lapping of water against the ship, but the sleep Sabrina knew she needed eluded her.

Where was he? She remembered too well
every detail of Cayona. The inns, the noise, the
rough crowds. The women. Prostitutes, women
who would be more than happy to have Rafael
for a night.

She tried to relax on the uncomfortable cot,
but it was impossible. The linen blouse she
wore was serving as a nightgown, since she refused to wear the sheer nightwear she had
stored in the bottom of her trunk. Those gowns
were degrading, insulting, and they reminded
her too much of Rafael.

Her familiar blue skirt was folded neatly and
placed atop that trunk, and she'd be wearing it
again tomorrow. She'd always liked blue, but if
she had her way she'd never wear another hint
of that color as long as she lived.

Pablo's distinct voice drifted to her, and Sabrina slipped from her miserable bed and silently stepped upon the ladder that would take
her to the deck. She didn't leave the safety of
the dark cabin, but peeked from the shadows.
Just a glimpse, to know that he was here. That
was all she needed. If she knew Rafael was on
board where he belonged, that he rested somewhere above her head, perhaps she'd be able to
sleep.

Pablo and Cristóbal whispered loudly, their
heads close together. She didn't worry for long
that they would notice her spying on them.
They were obviously intoxicated, blindly
tanked, and Pablo even staggered a little as he
seemed to consider the best and most efficient
way to lower himself to the deck.

Cristóbal leaned forward and whispered to Pablo, coarse Spanish words that Sabrina would not have been able to understand even if she had heard them clearly, and then he laughed as he sank to the deck.

Sabrina stepped quietly down into the cabin, inexplicably heartsick. Rafael wasn't with them. He wasn't coming back, damn him, not tonight.

By the time Sabrina emerged on deck, long after sunrise, Pablo and Cristóbal were gone again. The remaining crewmen, who didn't speak English at all, cast sideways glances at her. One of them brought her wine and bread, handing it to her silently as he stared pointedly at her chin.

What did they think of her? She doubted that the *Venganza* had often served as a passenger ship, and certainly they had never delivered anyone or anything to the English colonies.

"Good morning."

The English greeting startled her, and Sabrina glanced down at the man who stood on the pier, his face turned upward.

"Good morning," she returned suspiciously.

"So you are English." He smiled, a bright smile on a handsome middle-aged face that was aristocratic, with fine features and pale blue eyes. Straight dark blond hair was gathered at the nape of his neck, and his clothing was as pale as his hair and face. Cream britches and white hose, a white shirt with ruffled cravat, a waistcoat in a slightly darker shade than the

195

britches. The sun shone on him, making him appear bright. Too bright.

"What are you doing in the company of these Spaniards?" he continued, apparently unperturbed when she did not respond. "Are you in need of assistance?"

"No," Sabrina answered quickly.

"I would be happy to rescue someone so fair as yourself." His voice was low, silky almost, with a sensual undertone.

Sabrina almost laughed bitterly, but she remained still and quiet. "I've been rescued quite enough lately, thank you."

The English stranger smiled as if he knew just what she meant, and then he raised a thin and finely shaped hand to her. "Then you must allow me to escort you through the town of Cayona, to buy you a meal more substantial than bread and drink. An hour in your company," he said. "That is all I ask."

Suddenly, Sabrina didn't like him. There was no reason for it, no reason she could name, but her instincts were strong. He was English, he was well dressed, he was polite . . . and still she felt safer in the company of Rafael's pirates.

"No, thank you." She turned away, but his quick response stopped her.

"This is a dangerous place for one so fair. What brings you here?"

"I don't know." Sabrina turned slowly to glance down again. "An unfortunate wind, I suppose."

The sun shone on a face that was lined subtly with wrinkles at the eyes and the mouth, wrinkles that increased with the smile he continued to present to her. "So, you are lost?"

"Sort of."

"And Rafael found you?"

Sabrina gripped the rail. How did he know about Rafael? Suddenly she realized that this was no chance encounter, no coincidence. He hadn't simply seen her there and wondered, as he'd first led her to believe, how she found herself in such company. "Yes," she whispered.

"Where is Rafael?"

The tone of his voice changed slightly, dropped subtly, and if she wasn't mistaken the Englishman on the dock below flexed his thin fingers. Behind her, one of Rafael's men began to hum softly. He was ignoring her even now, as they all did.

"I don't know." Even if she had, she wouldn't have shared that information with the man who continued to smile brightly at her.

He sighed deeply, as if he didn't believe her. "No matter. I will find him myself. We're . . . old friends, Rafael and I. I owe him a debt, and it's time to pay."

Rafael hated the English. No way was this man a *friend* of his.

"What's your name?" Sabrina tried to keep her voice level, calm, but her heart was beating much too hard, and her hands began to tremble just slightly. "If I see Rafael, I'll tell him you're looking for him."

The Englishman bowed curtly. "Hadley Falconer, dear lady, at your service. Are you most certain I cannot entice you to a morning walk through this exciting city?"

The monster had a face. A conventional, smiling face. There were no horns on his head, no telling scowl on his face. She couldn't answer him. As in a nightmare, she was unable to speak, and so she turned her back on Falconer and walked away, escaping to the only refuge she had in this world—Rafael's small cabin.

If there had been room she would have paced, but Sabrina could only stand and clench and unclench her fists. Falconer. The man who had scarred Rafael's back, who had somehow scarred his soul.

Where the hell *was* Rafael? Right this minute he was in terrible danger, and he didn't have a clue. Falconer could sneak up on him, surprise him from behind and . . . Sabrina left the cabin with as much speed as she'd entered it just moments before.

Falconer was gone, and Sabrina confronted the pirate nearest to her, a broad swarthy man she had heard the others call César.

*"¿Dónde está Rafael?"* she asked sharply. He pointed to town. "I have to find him, and I mean now. Do you understand?"

He didn't; that much was clear. His broad face was blank, his eyes suspiciously flat.

"Take me," Sabrina said, pointing to her chest, "to Rafael."

This he understood quite well. He shook his head furiously as he refused her in rapid Spanish. In his defense, he was only following orders, she supposed.

Sabrina took a deep breath, and evidently the pirate she faced took her calmness as surrender, because he smiled at her widely—just as she reached out and plucked his dagger from the sheath at his waist.

She wasn't going into Cayona alone *and* unarmed.

The poor duped César was right behind Sabrina as she ran down the plank and onto the pier, and he called sharp commands to her that she ignored. Her steps were quick, and she clutched the dagger in a death grip in her right hand. Perhaps that was what kept the pirate well behind her.

The protests stopped, but when Sabrina glanced over her shoulder the sullen pirate was still following her. César watched her progress from a short distance away, a darkly distressed expression on his swarthy face.

Eyes turned her way, but no one approached her. In fact, at times a crowd would part for her and her cheerless escort, as they threaded their way toward the opposite end of town and the bar where Rafael had found her on their last trip to Cayona. He had been familiar with the place. Maybe it was a regular hangout.

"*Señorita* Sabrina." The voice behind her was exasperated, tired. All she gave her escort was a short, impatient glance.

César called to her again, more urgently, and this time when she turned her head she saw that he had stopped in the middle of the road, and was pointing, was in fact jabbing thick fingers, at a two-story building.

199

"Rafael's in there?" Sabrina asked, spinning around.

"Rafael," the pirate answered, shaking his hand, that thick, dark finger wagging with great emphasis toward the door.

The building to which César had gestured so emphatically was an inn, and it took a moment for Sabrina's eyes to adjust to the low light in the main room, after her morning in the sun. A squat little man presented himself to Sabrina, and the pirate/guard César closed the door and placed himself before it like a sentinel.

"You take a room?" the man asked, his accented voice guttural.

At least he spoke English. "No. I'm looking for someone. Antonio Rafael de Zamora. Is he here?"

The man cast a sharp glance at the pirate who blocked the door, and then his suspicious gaze fell to the dagger in Sabrina's hand.

"I know no such person."

Sabrina glanced over her shoulder to César. He didn't move, even when the innkeeper repeated his insistence in Spanish. In fact, César nodded to Sabrina, a calm gesture that confirmed his assertion.

"He's here," Sabrina insisted, but the little man's face was stern.

With a sigh, Sabrina faced the stairs. She appreciated the fact that the innkeeper tried to guard his customers from angry pirates and women bearing knives, but there was no time for this. She had to find Rafael, and she had to find him now.

"Rafael!" she shouted at the top of her lungs, startling the innkeeper. She waited a moment, but nothing in the inn stirred. "Rafael!"

He appeared on the stairs, running, fastening his pants—the only piece of clothing he wore. "What is it? What is wrong?"

All she'd thought of since leaving the cabin was finding Rafael. Now that he stood before her, she didn't know what to do. If she told him that Falconer was here on Tortuga, he wouldn't leave. Unlike her, Rafael wouldn't run away. He would face Falconer, would probably relish facing his greatest enemy.

"Sabrina?" Rafael's voice was composed, serene, as he descended the stairs, and he no longer ran. He looked at her and waited.

Rafael didn't need anyone to protect him. He was capable of meeting Falconer, she was sure, of giving as good as he got. He could defend himself. All she had to do was warn him to be on the lookout.

God in heaven, Rafael needed someone to protect him more than anyone she'd ever known. He'd had no childhood, not in the sense that Sabrina could accept, and his life had been so harsh that he didn't even believe in love . . . much less embrace it. She didn't want to see Falconer challenge Rafael with a sword or a whip. Didn't want to see Rafael hurt, even now.

"Sabrina?" he whispered, standing directly before her. His hand covered hers, and with deft fingers he took the dagger from her.

He glanced over her shoulder to the pirate who continued to guard the door, and Sabrina calmed herself as she listened to their angry conversation. She didn't need to understand Spanish to know that Rafael was berating César for allowing her to leave the *Venganza*, and that the pirate defended himself.

"I want to leave," Sabrina said calmly, staring at Rafael's chest instead of his face. "This morning, instead of tomorrow. There's nothing to do on that damn boat, and I couldn't sleep last night, and I'm . . . I can't wait to get to the English colonies."

"Tomorrow," Rafael said calmly. "My full crew has not yet been assembled. Several of them live north of Cayona. Cristóbal has gone just today to fetch them. There remain supplies to purchase. Why do you do this?"

"Today," Sabrina answered. "What is it, you have a woman waiting in your room? Afraid you'll miss out on a little fun? I'm not going to sit in that tiny cabin while you get your jollies."

Sabrina lifted her gaze to see him smile wryly. "No woman waiting," he assured her. "No . . . jollies."

"Then why stay here?"

Rafael glanced at the innkeeper as he took Sabrina's arm and led her to the narrow stairway. "I will have many nights of sleeping on deck, *querida*. A quiet room for two nights does not seem too much to ask."

He held her arm as he walked with her up the stairs and took her to his room, and he finished dressing as she stood by the door.

This was not the sort of accommodation to which Rafael was accustomed, and was in fact not much bigger than the captain's quarters on the *Venganza*. The cot was narrow and looked to be hard. The floor was filthy. His clothing had been neatly folded over the only other furnishing in the room, a rickety-looking wooden chair with a straight back. There was nothing lush or fine here, not like there was on Rafael's island home.

If he'd had a woman in this room, no evidence of her visit had been left behind. What a relief. What a fool she was for feeling such relief.

"We will go tomorrow," Rafael said as he stepped into his boots. "Now, I will return you to the *Venganza*, and you will stay there."

"No," Sabrina said softly, "I won't stay there. I'll follow you, twenty-four hours a day."

"*Querida*, don't . . ." he crooned.

"Don't *querida* me, Rafael. I'm sick of sitting on that boat, day and night. I'm bored and I'm restless, and I want to go home."

"Tomorrow."

"I swear, Rafael, if we stay in this town one more day I'll go insane . . . and I'll take you with me. You won't have a moment's peace. I'll hound you; I'll stay at your heels every single minute."

"This is a threat?" Rafael raised his eyebrows just a bit.

"And can I have that dagger back?" she added, pointing to the knife he had laid aside. "Surely César has another."

With a swiftness that startled her, his face darkened, his eyes narrowed. "You need protection from my crew? I left you in the care of my most trusted men, *querida*. If they have harmed you . . ."

"No. They ignored me completely. I felt like the invisible man."

"Then why do you have need of a weapon?" Rafael was no longer completely calm. There was a touch of exasperation in his voice, a hint of fire in his eyes.

*So I can watch your back. Because I don't trust Falconer's pretty face.* "In case you get any ideas."

She knew good and well that Rafael wouldn't get any ideas. He was hiding here, in this tiny room. He wouldn't touch her, because that would mean he'd have to live with the horrible possibility that she'd bear his child.

"You are so anxious to leave?" There was a trace of surrender in his voice.

"Yes," she said insistently. "If a few of your men aren't on board, does it really make a difference?"

Rafael was on the verge of conceding, of giving in. She could see it on his face, and when he spoke she could hear the surrender in his voice. "Perhaps not. Cayona is filled with pirates anxious to sail. If we must, then we will sign on a few."

Sabrina smiled and held out her hand. "The dagger?"

"You will not need it."

"Just in case."

He placed the heavy grip in her hand. "You are so very beautiful when you win, *querida*."

"Let's get out of here."

# *Chapter Fourteen*

Sabrina didn't breathe normally until Tortuga was behind her, and all she could see was the ocean she had feared all her life. Rafael was indulging her, she knew, giving in to what he viewed as a whim. Cristóbal had not yet returned when they sailed, and Rafael had left one seaman behind to explain what had happened, and to assure the young pirate and the others he had collected that the *Venganza* would return as soon as possible.

Rafael had not, in the end, signed on any new crewmen. He trusted no one, it seemed, but perhaps Pablo. And that wasn't a certainty, just an unfounded assumption.

"You are happy now?"

Rafael startled Sabrina, joining her to watch over the waves that danced in their wake.

"Yes. Thank you." She would have to tell him,

before she left the *Venganza*, that Falconer had spoken to her, that he might still be in Cayona. Otherwise, Rafael might return to Tortuga unprepared. Vulnerable. Sabrina smiled at that thought. Rafael? Vulnerable?

"You are anxious to return to the English." Rafael leaned over the railing slightly, squinting as he lifted his face to the sun. "I suppose that is wise."

He was telling her, in his own way, that what had happened between them was a mistake, that they had nothing in common, no future, no past. That he didn't love her and he never would. Sabrina deciphered that and more from his quiet words.

But she still couldn't believe it. If she told Rafael what she suspected, would he really insist that she rid herself of their child? Maybe not. Surely not. It was a fleeting doubt that she didn't dare give much consideration. Still, now that they were away from the island where Rafael ruled like a king, there was nothing he could do.

She recognized that as a lie. As long as she was on this ship, Rafael was in control. Daring to hope that his threats were hollow was a risk she wouldn't take.

"I wish I had told Aqualina good-bye."

"I will tell her for you."

Sabrina sidled closer to Rafael, just a little. Her arm brushed his, and she leaned forward to catch a glimpse of his face. He was so harsh and still splendidly handsome. No matter what he did she would always feel his arms around

ON A WICKED WIND

her when she pictured that face on a balmy day,
or saw it in her dreams.

He hadn't meant to give her anything but cold
jewels and his own particular brand of adoration, but he had given her so much more. A
child, perhaps. And even if that hope was false,
Rafael had given her another gift.

She knew now that she could love, that her
heart was capable of the emotion she had lived
without all her adult life. If he hadn't threatened
to take away her child, she would have stayed
with him forever.

"Pablo says you took Aqualina and others
from Falconer," Sabrina said in a low voice.
"Why?"

Rafael twisted his head slightly and pinned a
darkening gaze on Sabrina's face. He always
squinted narrowly when he didn't want her to
see too much. Perhaps he knew how much he
gave away with those eyes. "It is not important,"
he growled. "Pablo talks too much. He rambles,
nonsense and jibberish." There followed a short
and seemingly threatening phrase in Spanish.
"He wanted to sell you, you know."

"Don't try to change the subject." She wasn't
distressed or surprised to hear that Pablo had
wanted to be rid of her and make a profit at the
same time. "I'm just curious. You told me once
that you wanted to take away everything Falconer treasured. What was Aqualina to him?"

The face Rafael pressed close to hers was that
of a devil. He presented her now with the same
dark and brutal face she had seen as he'd told

her she would not have his baby. "You go too far, *sirena mia*."

"I don't understand. . . ."

"No, you do not understand. You must come from a distant place, perhaps so distant that I cannot even imagine the journey you have undertaken, for you know nothing of evil, nothing of sacrifice." His voice was low, so that Sabrina knew no one could hear but her. Those soft-spoken words were eerily true.

"Maybe I just want to understand the man who hurt you so much that you won't let me love you."

She surprised him, even managed to surprise herself.

"You do not want to understand a man so evil as Falconer." Something in his expression softened perceptibly. His eyes were no longer quite so narrow, and his lips seemed to relax. Perhaps there was even less tension in his shoulders, as he leaned toward her. Could she look into Rafael's eyes and see his soul? There were times when she believed that to be true.

"Aqualina was twelve when I took her from Falconer's plantation. She was skinny, and frightened, and she had been hurt. She would allow no one to touch her for a very long time, not even to hold her hand. Pablo watched over her, and years later, when the time came, she asked him to be her husband."

"I still don't understand. . . ."

"There have been others, over the years," he interrupted, as if he hadn't heard her. "Some I have been able to free. Some I have not." He took her chin between his fingers and forced her to meet his stare. "Do you want me to tell you what Falconer did to Aqualina and the others, *sirena mia*?" he whispered. "Do you want all the sad, repulsive details, so that you will understand a man for whom pain is an amusement? So that you will *understand* a man who takes pleasure in the screams of little girls?"

"No," Sabrina whispered, surprised that any sound at all escaped her lips.

Rafael dropped his hand and turned from her, obviously anxious to escape the conversation that had turned hellish, and he climbed to the aft bridge without looking back.

There had been times, blessed hours and even days, when he did not think of Elisa. During his weeks with Sabrina that old pain had been completely lost. In her arms and in her heart he had found peace, and he had forgotten that old agony. Now it was back, sharper, closer than it had been in many years.

Rafael closed his eyes. The sun was warm, but it did nothing to ease the chill in his heart. Once, he had been almost as naive as Sabrina. He had known there was hardship and pain in the world, but he had never known that men like Falconer existed. Men for whom pain was pleasure. At fourteen, Rafael had still harbored so much impossible hope in his heart.

When Elisa had come to the plantation, sold to Falconer by her widowed father, Rafael had been there less than a month. The field work was hard, but he did not care. His mind was on the future, on the day when his commitment to Falconer would be over.

She was younger than he, by a little more than a year, and she was beautiful. So very beautiful. Hair thick and shining, eyes dark, lips full. He was besotted, and Elisa cast her eyes toward him on occasion, as well.

A single, chaste kiss, the kiss of children who think they know what love is, had sealed in his heart the knowledge that Elisa was his, and for a short time Rafael had been happy. When his time with Falconer was done, they would leave together. Even though he'd come to love the ocean, the idea of a life at sea was impossible when Elisa was with him, and Rafael began to think that perhaps farming was not such a terrible way to live, after all.

It did not last. He knew now that happiness did not endure, but then, so long ago . . . One night, Elisa did not appear at the evening meal. Rafael searched for her, even venturing silently into the big house, where he was forbidden to go, sneaking into fine, bright rooms that were uninhabited and eerily silent and unreal in their impossible elegance.

He did not find Elisa there, not that first night.

Almost a week passed, a week of heartache and worry, before he heard Elisa as he prowled outside the house. A window was open, and she cried softly. When Rafael located her, saw her leaning from a second-story window, she tried to send him away. She covered her face with trembling hands, but she did not leave the window, and Rafael would not be sent away. He wanted to know why she cried.

He went once again into Falconer's fine house, sneaking past a lazy house boy and up the stairs to rescue Elisa. They ran away that night, into the hills, away from Falconer and his damned plantation. Rafael swore to Elisa and to himself that Falconer would not hurt her again, that no one would hurt her again.

In the shelter of densely leaved trees, there in the safety of the hills, he held Elisa as she shook. She was unable to talk, afraid to sleep. There were bruises on her frail body, and scratches on her thin arms. Rafael had hated Falconer then, but he had not allowed Elisa to see his anger. Instead he held her, and he lulled her to sleep with promises that, in the end, he had been unable to keep.

If he had not fallen asleep, they would not have been caught. If he had pushed Elisa harder, that first night, they would not have been caught. There were a thousand *ifs*, and they had echoed through Rafael's mind and his nightmares for so many years. But nothing would ever change the fact that he had opened his eyes early the next morning to find Falconer's men surrounding them.

They ripped Elisa from him and carried her screaming to a waiting, smug Falconer.

Rafael never saw her again. By the next morning, Elisa was dead, and he himself certainly should have been.

Falconer flogged Rafael until he passed out, and when he came to, with a bucket of water thrown in his face or an angry hand pulling his hair and yanking his head back, the flogging continued. Unable to move, lashed to a tree just outside Falconer's fine home, Rafael endured not only the whip, but Falconer's constant chatter. He told Rafael and the men who watched what he had done to Elisa. How she had died beneath him with his hands around her throat. He told them again and again what he had done to Elisa before he had offered her death.

In the night, someone had cut Rafael down. He never knew if the one who had cut him down had believed him dead, or if his rescuer had simply felt pity for the half-dead boy who was lashed to the tree.

He crawled away on his belly. Away from the house where Falconer slept, and into the hills. He crawled, and he survived, and he grew strong. In a few months' time he returned to the plantation to kill Falconer. He had believed, for a while, that he had succeeded. Rafael had run from the house and Falconer's men while the tyrant lay in a pool of his own blood. It was months later before he heard that Falconer had survived and had returned to England.

Falconer should have stayed there, but in a few short years he was back in Jamaica, and Rafael began to torment the Englishman. Fire, theft, the freeing of slaves and indentured servants—especially the young girls. But Falconer was cautious, after his brush with death, and he surrounded himself with a dozen men. Rafael had never again been able to get close enough to cut the man who had ruined his life.

Falconer could not strike back. He could try to kill Rafael, but he could not hurt him. Rafael did not fear for his life, and there was nothing Falconer could take from him. Not anymore. Not again.

Not until now.

Sabrina said that he would not allow her to love him, and that was true. They had not spoken of love since that afternoon at the cove. He had discouraged her, laughed at her, offered her everything *but* love.

He could make certain that she did not carry any love in her heart for him, but he could not deny that what he felt for her was strong—too strong. It was love and passion and affection.

She could never know. No one could know.

The commotion started early. When Sabrina, curious, climbed the ladder and peeked out of the cabin, there was very little light in the sky. The world was gray, and should have been silent, but Rafael's men shouted. They grasped long knives and swords and loaded single-shot weapons.

Sabrina stepped into her skirt, grabbed César's dagger, and quickly left the cabin.

A larger ship was bearing down on them. Rafael's pirates waited, watching the buccaneers who clutched weapons of their own as they prepared to leap onto the *Venganza*.

"Get below!" Rafael shouted.

"No." Sabrina grasped the dagger that would be almost useless against the long swords and pistols the pirates of the other ship possessed.

"*Dios*, Sabrina, there is no time for this!"

"I don't want to get trapped down there!" she shouted. "Please!" It was too clear, the vision of waiting in the small cabin until some attacking pirate dropped down the hole. If that happened, there would be no place to go, no way to escape.

"Here." Rafael led her beneath the aft bridge, directed her into a cranny in the shadows where, if Rafael and his men were successful, the attackers would never reach. "Be silent. Do not move."

Sabrina reached up and grabbed Rafael's arm, clutching at the loose linen there. He held a knife in one hand and a sword in the other, but was he really prepared? What had she done? "It might be Falconer," she said quickly. "He was looking for you in Tortuga."

There was a horrible thudding sound, and Rafael turned away from her without responding. The attacking pirates had thrown huge hooks into the *Venganza* and were pulling the smaller ship against their own. They were landing on the deck one after another, to be met by Rafael's men.

Was it Falconer? The pirates were English, but she didn't see Rafael's enemy among them. These were coarse, vulgar, violent men who invaded the *Venganza* with a vengeance of their own.

Sabrina did as Rafael asked. She didn't move. She didn't make even the slightest sound. Rafael's men appeared to be more skilled than the Englishmen, and more confident, and in number they were evenly matched. Still, blood was spilled, English and Spanish.

Rafael had placed himself just beyond the aft bridge ladder. He was guarding her, keeping the intruders at bay, meeting any who dared to advance with unmatched fury and skill. To reach her hiding place, a man would have to get past Rafael's crew, and then get past Rafael.

One thin Englishman slipped through the melee and faced Rafael with a grin that revealed blackened teeth and wide, empty gaps where there had once been others. He looked like a bum, but he used his sword well. The encounter lasted much too long before the Englishman faltered and Rafael thrust the blade of his sword into the surprised buccaneer.

Rafael fought there at the edge of the melee, and no one passed him.

How long could this last? Metal met and sang, deafening dull and sharp tones. Men cursed in two languages or more, and cried out when blood was drawn.

Soon it became clear that Rafael's men had the advantage. The attackers retreated, climbing onto their own ship, and with swinging blades they cut the ropes that bound the two ships together.

Only a few remained, those stubborn English pirates who would not surrender easily. They fought, even as their ship pulled away. Sabrina slipped from her hiding place. Any noise she made was soft, a whisper, but Rafael turned to her. There was a stern look of disapproval on his face as he stared at her, allowing Pablo and

César to chase the last of the invaders off the *Venganza*.

The deck was littered with half a dozen bodies. Sabrina saw the rise and fall of a few chests, but two of Rafael's men were deathly still.

"I told you to stay," Rafael muttered.

Pablo shouted to his captain, and Rafael turned his back on Sabrina and walked away. She started to follow, afraid to be too far away from him, but she stepped into the sunlight and went no farther.

There was so much blood, on the deck and on the bodies that littered it. How long had the skirmish lasted? Fifteen minutes? Half an hour? Before her lay destruction, and it had happened so fast. . . .

When she was able to move again, Sabrina stepped over a motionless Englishman who was face down in his own blood, taking care not to look too closely. The English ship was pulling away.

Rafael had his back to her as he examined a wound to Pablo's arm. She wanted to touch him, to make absolutely certain that none of the blood she saw was his. No blade had touched him, she knew, but still . . .

She was almost there. If nothing else, she could offer to help with the wounded. To see to Pablo's arm and the other injuries that were evident.

The Englishman she had thought dead rushed past her with a grunt. There was a long bloodstained knife in one bloody hand, and the buccaneer was rushing toward Rafael's back.

"Rafael!"

He turned at the sound of her voice, and the Englishman's raised knife was now aimed at Rafael's heart.

Sabrina threw herself between them, planning to knock the unsteady Englishman aside. He was sturdier than she thought, though, and the knife that would have found Rafael's heart sliced into her shoulder.

It burned like fire at her back, and Rafael caught her as she began to fall. The dagger she had clasped rolled from her fingers and clattered to the deck as, somehow, Rafael swung her body to the side. He continued to hold her tight, and his right arm swung up to stop the attacking pirate with his curved blade.

The Englishman who had stabbed Sabrina fell to the deck again, and this time he was truly dead.

*"Vida mia,"* he whispered. "Why? What were you thinking?"

She tried to smile, but her body was shutting down. She could feel it, as if one circuit after another turned off. Her shoulder didn't hurt anymore; it was numb. She was numb all over. "I didn't think at all. I listened to my body."

Rafael muttered in Spanish as he lifted her and carried her into the shade beneath the aft bridge.

"Rafael?" she whispered.

"Hush." He slipped the sash from his waist, folded it into a thick square, and pressed it against her wound. The pain came back, and Sabrina wished for the numbness to return.

"Adrenaline sucks. You hear about this rush, you know, when there's danger, and it's supposed to be some sort of high . . . but it sucks. I don't like it." Her heart was still pounding, and she couldn't take a good deep breath.

"Hush," Rafael breathed softly.

"I want to go home."

"I know."

"You *don't* know." Rafael laid her gently on the deck, and Sabrina clutched at his sweat-dampened shirt. "Take me home, Rafael."

"I will, *vida mia*. I promise."

"*Vida mia*. What does that mean?"

Rafael leaned close, shielding her body with his own. "Darling."

"No. It's another of your *mia* words. Something mine. My something. You've done that since I first saw you, you know. My island, my boat, my garden." The world was going gray. There was nothing but Rafael and the pain that came and went like an angry tide. "You called me that once before, when we were . . . well, at the cove. That was a good day. We don't get many really good days, you know. I meant to ask then, but I forgot. You make me forget everything, Rafael."

"Shhh."

She was lying on the deck, but Rafael leaned over her, so closely his hair brushed her face. She almost wished that he would back away, just a little, so she could see his face in the sunlight. He reached out, almost as if he were afraid to touch her, and brushed the back of his hand across her cheek.

"Hold me," she whispered, and after a brief hesitation Rafael wrapped his arms too tenderly around her, as if she might break.

"Take me home," she demanded in a voice that was much too soft and unsteady to be demanding.

*"Sí, vida mia."*

The darkness came, until all Sabrina was aware of was Rafael's soothing voice and the hands that held her, and then even that was gone.

# Chapter Fifteen

"My life," Rafael whispered, but only after Sabrina had slipped away from him. *"Vida mia."*

Her breathing was shallow but steady. It was the intense pain that caused her to pass out, he was certain. Pain and the loss of so much blood.

After everything he had done and said, after the hurt he had intentionally placed upon her, Sabrina protected him. It made no sense. He denied her with furious displeasure what she wanted most in the world, and still she thrust her precious body between his and an English knife.

She had been trying to protect him earlier, also, rushing him from Cayona and the threat she could never completely understand. He had realized that truth the moment she had told him, as the English pirates boarded the *Venganza*, that Falconer had been on Tortuga.

The ship that had attacked them had not been Falconer's, but he might have had a hand in sending the English pirates after the *Venganza*, hoping to weaken Rafael. It was Falconer's way.

Sabrina's head rested on his lap, and he pressed his folded sash against the injury at her shoulder. There was much to do, wounded men to tend to, damage to assess, but he could not leave her here. Not like this. With an easy hand he brushed a strand of hair from her cheek.

"She is dead?"

Rafael lifted his gaze to a frowning Pablo. "No, she is not dead."

"Good," the big man rumbled. His own wound was serious, but not as deep as Sabrina's, and he ignored it. A kerchief had been tied tightly over the slash in a massive arm, and the bleeding had almost stopped. Pablo was tough, impervious to pain.

Beyond Pablo, the crew disposed of English bodies, tossing them into the ocean. Two of his own men were dead, but they would receive a proper burial at sea, with a prayer for their souls and gold in their pockets.

"She wants to go home."

"I know," Pablo said gruffly.

"Turn the ship about."

"But you said . . ."

"I said turn the ship about!" Rafael shouted. "We have dead and wounded and damage to the main sail. If we are attacked again, we will not stand a chance."

Pablo nodded his assent, and when he was gone Rafael returned all his attention to Sabrina. "Anything you want, *vida mia*, it is yours. I am taking you home, just as you wish."

She stirred in his arms, opening her eyes just slightly. "Did I pass out?" she whispered.

"*Sí.*"

"That's not good." Her words slurred slightly, as if she were drunk or half asleep. "Do you have any whiskey on board? Rum? I know you have rum."

Rafael ordered César to fetch a bottle, while Sabrina licked dry lips. "I think this will work."

"What is that, *sirena mia*?" Rafael took the bottle César had quickly delivered, and he lifted Sabrina's head as he put it to her lips.

"No," she began to protest, but took a small sip. She licked her lips again as he took the bottle away. "I want you to pour it over the wound."

"Hush. Sleep . . ."

"I will. It'll probably hurt so bad that I'll pass out again, but that's okay. It . . . it kills germs, so, you know, maybe the cut won't get infected."

"Germs?"

"I can't explain, not now. It would take too much energy, and I just don't have any right now. Make sure you pour some over Pablo's arm, too, and any other cuts your guys have." She was tiring quickly, and closed her eyes briefly.

"You are asking me to hurt you."

"You can do it."

Rafael shook his head. She was delirious already.

Sabrina refused to be still. She struggled in his arms until he had no choice but to lift her into a sitting position. With a breath of release, she fell against his chest.

"Do it," she ordered.

Rafael peeled away the bandage, wincing at the sight of Sabrina's wound.

"How does it look?" she whispered against his chest.

"Not very bad."

"Liar," she accused softly. "Just think," she whispered as Rafael lifted the bottle and prepared to douse her wound with the rum. "My first scar."

"Your last," he answered quickly, angrily, and he poured the rum over her laceration.

She stiffened in his arms, gripping his shoulders with strong fingers, and then she went limp.

"I hope you are right, *vida mia*. I hope there is magic in your cure."

She did not answer, but lay silent and limp against his chest as he replaced the bandage. The cut was deep, and Sabrina had lost a lot of blood, but the bleeding had slowed.

Rafael held Sabrina as they sailed for his island, reluctant to release her even for a moment. He wanted to be there, holding her, when she woke as she often did. Sometimes she stayed awake for a while; sometimes she just allowed her eyes to drift open to gaze at him, and then she slipped away again.

He could not move her into the cabin and to the bed. Getting her down the ladder would have been too risky, so he held her and kept her body warm and still, until at the end of a long day and well into the night, they arrived at his island.

He carried Sabrina from the *Venganza*, leaving Pablo to see to the ship. Down the long dark path to his house, through the front door and into a dark room, to the winding stairs he had no trouble finding in the dark. Finally, she opened her eyes.

"For goodness' sake, Rafael, you don't have to carry me. I'm perfectly capable of walking." Her voice was drowsy, weak, and she lounged against him as if she were boneless.

"I want to carry you," he said. "Indulge me." What would she say when she realized that he had brought her back to the island? She would no doubt be furious.

"That's very sweet." She sounded drunk, and when she opened her eyes it seemed to take her a moment to focus. The house was dark, but when he entered her room, lit by the moonlight that streamed through the balcony, she smiled in recognition. "We're home."

Elena tried to chase him from the room, but Rafael refused to go. His only concession was to move away from the bed while she tended Sabrina's wound.

He found himself pacing in front of the open balcony doors as Elena cleaned and stitched Sabrina's shoulder by the light of ten or more candles. Elena muttered soft, reassuring words to Sabrina, then a sharp reproach when she turned her head briefly toward the balcony doors where he stalked impatiently.

Of course she blamed him for this misery. Sabrina never should have been on board the *Venganza,* never should have been in danger. If he had protected her the way she should have been protected, she would never have known this kind of agony.

What she asked of him was so very little, and so very much. Love. Babies.

When Elena left the room to prepare a special tea for Sabrina, Rafael returned to her bedside. She was sleeping on her stomach, peacefully for the moment, and the leaves Elena had placed over her wound clung to a golden shoulder and curved down Sabrina's back.

When he had first seen that pale and perfectly shaped back, the night some powerful force had placed Sabrina at his feet, he had been entranced. Enchanted. Now it was damaged. For the rest of her life Sabrina would have a scar on that once-perfect back to remind her of her time with him.

"I wish I could give you everything you want." He knelt by the bed to place his face close to her ear. "You deserve to have your dreams come true."

He brushed a strand of fine hair away from her face, hair that was more red than brown in the candlelight that flickered over a sleeping Sabrina. "Weeks ago, I should have taken you to the English colonies, but I was greedy. I wanted you too much to let you go. If I had known that it would come to this, that you would be hurt because you stayed with me for a while, I never would have kept you here."

She did not hear him. There was no change in her shallow breathing, and not even a quiver of her eyelids.

"You will never know the truth, but you won this contest, *vida mia*. As constant as the tides, as sure as the sun that rises . . ." He recalled, with a chill that touched his bones, the unnatural cold wind that had carried Sabrina to him. "As Neptune breathes, I love you."

He remained at her side until Elena returned and chased him away with a wave of her tiny, gnarled hand. Nothing Elena could say or do would make him leave this room, and she finally turned her back to him and pretended he was not there.

Elena spooned a little bit of tea into Sabrina's mouth, and whispered to her soothing words in Spanish that Sabrina would not understand, even if she were to awaken.

But she did not awaken, and soon Elena was quiet.

It was near dawn and the sky had begun to lighten when Rafael finally sat on the floor and rested his back against the wall. When Elena left the room he had an unobstructed view of Sabrina's face. She was too pale, but Elena had assured him that she would recover, with nothing but a scar to remind her of her adventure.

It hurt. She didn't want to be a baby about this, but her shoulder really, really hurt. Of course, except for a sprained ankle and a paper cut here and there, she'd never been injured before. Twentieth-century business was a lot safer, she supposed, than seventeenth-century piracy, though the similarities between the two occupations became clearer to her every day.

She was on her stomach, her face half buried in a soft pillow. Sabrina opened her eyes slowly, reluctantly. It was morning. She could tell by the slant of the sun in her room. Last night was a blur to her. Vaguely, she recalled Rafael carrying her into this room and laying her on the bed, and she'd been so tired. . . .

Rafael stood in the sunlight, there by the balcony doors. What a thunderous expression there was on his face. Did he blame her for the attack? Of course he did. If she'd told him earlier that Falconer was in Cayona, he would have been better prepared for the attack.

"Don't be mad," she said. Her voice barely rose above a whisper.

He crossed the room and squatted beside the bed, placing his face on the same level as hers. "You ask the impossible of me, always." There was no anger in his voice, and Sabrina reached out to touch a dark curl that brushed past Rafael's cheek.

"I should have told you sooner, I know."

"About Falconer?" His eyebrows arched. "It would have made no difference. If I am angry it is because you risked yourself."

"That filthy pirate was going to kill you. And anyway, I just intended to push him away. It wasn't my plan to take a knife for you." It was a half truth, not exactly a lie. She was hurt, but Rafael would be dead now if that knife had found his heart. Sabrina would have thought herself a world-class idiot if she wasn't absolutely positive that Rafael would do the same for her.

"How do you feel?" Rafael ignored her assertion.

"I'm cold, and my shoulder hurts like hell."

Rafael placed his hand on her face, so that his fingers touched her forehead and his palm cradled her cheek. "You have a fever."

"Great."

"Elena will give you something."

"No." Her protest was brief but certain. She wouldn't take any potions or herbs, nothing that might harm the baby she was sure she carried. "I don't need . . ."

"She has cared for you for the past two days, *vida mia*. Cleaned and stitched your wound, forced liquids down your throat when you would not cooperate with me, bathed your body when the fever began. . . ."

"Back up. Two days?" She remembered none of it.

"*Sí*. Elena has been very worried about you. I think she likes you more than she cares to admit."

Rafael's thumb rocked gently against her cheek. It was such a comforting caress, Sabrina closed her eyes and savored it. He could swear up and down that he didn't care for her, but she knew he felt something. Maybe it wasn't love, but it was warm and tender, and Sabrina held on to that belief even though it didn't make sense.

"Sleep," Rafael whispered, drawing his hand

away from her face. "When you are strong again I will take you to the English colonies, as you wish."

"What if I don't wish?" Her strength was fading. Maybe it was the fever, but Sabrina was certain, at that moment, that if Rafael knew about the baby she carried he would be glad. At the very least he would accept the truth without anger. He wouldn't force her to do anything she didn't want to do.

"You will be safe there." It was a soft but certain refusal of her wish to stay.

She wouldn't beg, wouldn't risk rejection by telling Rafael outright that she didn't want to leave this island, that she trusted him to keep her safe. At least he was honest. Not once had he offered her forever, or declared his love, or made promises he wasn't prepared to keep. He had been, all along, an honest pirate.

"All right," she whispered, closing her eyes again.

Throughout the day Sabrina drifted in and out of consciousness, and Rafael was always there. Was it guilt that kept him at her side? Did he worry? She couldn't picture Rafael as a nursemaid, but if he left her at any time during the day she didn't know it.

He bathed her face, made her swallow sips of cool water, talked to her, in soothing Spanish she couldn't understand and didn't need to. She was aware of the passage of time by the light through the balcony doors that changed as the day went on, until she opened her eyes to candle and moonlight. Rafael sat on the floor by the opened doors, his back to the wall, his head down.

The fever was still with her. She was unbearably and deeply cold, in spite of the layer of blankets that covered her body, and she tried to curl into a ball against the chill. As if he heard that small movement, Rafael lifted his head.

Sabrina tried to smile, but she was so weak she knew it was a poor effort. That feeble smile disappeared quickly as the cramp hit her, a pang as sharp as the knife's blade that had been thrust into her back.

"What is wrong?" Rafael stood quickly, moving to the side of the bed where he looked down at her with a frown on his troubled face.

"Nothing," she breathed, praying that was true, trying to convince herself that she had imagined the cramp.

"Your shoulder will hurt for a while, *sirena mia*. You never should have . . ."

He stopped speaking when Sabrina winced. Another cramp hit without warning, harder, sharper, and no matter how hard she wished it, she couldn't convince herself that the pains in her abdomen were innocuous.

"No," she whispered, burying her face in the pillow. Tears of pain and frustration filled her eyes.

"Sabrina?"

Rafael so rarely called her by her name . . . he always referred to her with some possessive endearment. *Querida, sirena mia, vida mia* . . . There was anxiety in his voice, and the fingers that touched her neck trembled.

"Get Elena," Sabrina said into the pillow.

"What is wrong?" Rafael's face was close, his soft voice near her ear. "Sabrina, please . . ."

Sabrina lifted her head. Rafael was near, his face mere inches from hers. She reached up slowly and touched a cool, stubbled cheek. Rafael was usually so meticulous that she couldn't remember a single time she'd seen him unkempt, rumpled and unshaven as he was now. For a man who didn't believe in love he was awfully worried.

Perhaps it was the fever that convinced her for a moment that he did love her. Some sort of dementia that caused her to see love in his eyes.

"No matter what happens," she said, "remember that none of this is your fault. I knew what I was doing when I tried to push the English pirate away. I knew what I was risking." Another cramp twisted her insides, another stab of the knife deep in her belly. She closed her eyes against the pain and held her breath.

"Sabrina?" Rafael found her hand, held it, lowered his face until it was, perhaps, an inch from hers.

"Don't worry," Sabrina whispered when she could talk again. "Get Elena."

Rafael didn't move, didn't release her hand or move his face away from hers.

What if she died here? Not once since she'd been stabbed had that thought occurred to her. How could she die with so much undone, in this world as well as the old one? She'd made so many mistakes.

"Rafael." Sabrina tightened her grip on his hand, kept him close.

"What has gone wrong?"

Sabrina licked her lips, opened her eyes fully so she could see his face. "I love you. I'd never loved anyone in my entire, boring, cold life, until I came here and fell in love with you. It was worth it . . . leaving everything behind . . . to find you. No matter what happens, it's not your fault. I knew what I was doing."

"I could not protect you," Rafael answered. "The blame for this is mine."

"No," she whispered. If she could move she would wrap her arms around Rafael's neck and hold him tight, but she was afraid. Against all reason she was afraid any move would bring on another cramp. Somewhere in the back of her mind she thought that perhaps if she remained calm, if she didn't move again, whatever was happening would stop.

She was quiet and still, but too soon there came another cramp, an intense twinge. "I need Elena."

"Why?"

He wasn't going to leave her, not even for a moment, without an explanation.

Sabrina forced herself to look Rafael in the eye. She wouldn't apologize, not for loving him, not for lying in order to keep his baby safe. She'd do it all again, if she had the chance.

There was worry on his face, and guilt perhaps, and she wanted so badly to reach out to him.

But she couldn't move, and she wouldn't lie any more. "I'm losing my baby."

# *Chapter Sixteen*

"We sail tonight." Rafael strapped the curved knife at his waist, and with great care selected a weapon from the cache that was spread across the long dining table. He closed his fingers over the golden hilt of a rapier, lifting the blade to study the play of candlelight on steel.

"Our destination?"

Pablo's arm was bandaged, but the injury did not seem to hamper his movements. Elena had sewn his wound closed, cursing his clumsiness as she did so, but the stitches were not as fine as those at Sabrina's back. Elena had not taken the care with her own son that she had with the fragile woman the sea had given Rafael.

Elena had been upstairs with Sabrina all night and all day and into this night. Surely no single day had ever passed so slowly. It had been late afternoon when Pablo's irascible mother had told Rafael that Sabrina had survived the loss of her child, that she was sleeping, that he could resume his post at her bedside.

He could not face her.

"Tortuga," Rafael said softly, keeping his eye on the deadly blade of the rapier. "Cristóbal and the others are waiting." He lowered his voice. "Falconer is there, and it is time to end this."

"And then?" Pablo prompted.

And then? How could he explain to Pablo that he could not think past his anger? It was an impossible weakness. Rafael hesitated only a moment before answering. "Gaston Billaud has retired and is building a plantation on Hispaniola. Just last year he attacked the *flota* with twenty ships, and came away with enough treasure to last a hundred men a lifetime. Most of his crew is gone, dead or else signed on with others. On his plantation we will encounter only a handful of his men, Billaud, and his captain's share."

"He should be relieved of such a burden," Pablo said with a smile.

"*Sí.*"

"And what of *Señorita* Sabrina?"

Rafael turned away from Pablo and the question he was not ready to answer.

"When she is strong again we will take her to the English colonies." *If she survives.* That was a doubt he could not voice.

The answer was sufficient for Pablo. Rafael knew his first mate questioned the quiet weeks after Sabrina's coming, that all of his men were restless for adventure and danger and gold.

"She has been bad luck for you," Pablo said in a low voice. "Nothing has been as it should be since you found her."

"True."

"And still, I hope she does not die." Pablo's statement was casual, as though he were wishing for clear skies under which to sail, and not for Sabrina's life.

Rafael could not force such calmness into his voice or his heart. How would he survive if she did not? How could he live with himself knowing that he could never save the women he loved?

He had never once in his life wished for a child. Every word he had said to Sabrina as he denied her a child was true, every fear he had faced alone was a real one. So why was there pain? His heart ached, his eyes filled with tears without warning, and he wanted, with an almost uncontrollable passion, to destroy something, anything, with his bare hands.

Knowing that she would lose the child she wanted so badly, Sabrina had forgiven him, had told him that none of this was his fault. But Rafael knew that was a lie. He had driven her onto the *Venganza* by denying her the love and the child she wanted—needed. If she had been here, where she belonged, there would have been no danger. She would not have been hurt, and his child would be growing inside her still. Falconer knew nothing of this island . . . very few men did, and even fewer knew where it was located.

She would have been safe here . . . but he had driven her away.

And would again.

"Within the hour," he said, his back still to Pablo. All he could think of was escape. He could not bear to see Sabrina's pale face, to watch her die, to bury her. He could not endure hours of waiting, only to watch her open her eyes and fasten them on him in accusation.

Pablo was gone when Elena came down the stairs to tell Rafael that Sabrina was awake and asking for him. She could not promise him, when he asked it of her, that Sabrina would survive the night, that she would not die while he held her hand and listened to her forgive him for killing her and their child.

He would never forgive himself. It was another failing, another sin to join to the lengthy record of his transgressions.

He did not look back at Elena as he instructed her to tell Sabrina that he had already left. That he would return in a few days or a few weeks or a few months, when he was ready to return. Rafael expected the housekeeper to lambast him as he left his house, but she was oddly and eerily silent.

After that first night, she quit asking for Rafael. Elena's brusque pantomime had been clear enough. He was gone, had sailed away without a word, without a care.

Sabrina's life had never been full, emotionally, but without Rafael and the baby she felt painfully empty. She had nothing of her own, nothing to hold on to. Her existence was as meaningless here as it had been before—and what she had with Rafael was no more genuine that her relationship with Patrick had been.

She mourned her baby, the fleeting life that had never had a chance. The day would come, she knew, when she would have another child, but there wasn't much comfort in that certainty. She wanted a baby too badly to believe that the one she'd lost was the only one she'd ever carry, but at the same time she couldn't make herself see another child, not the way she still saw *this* one.

She was sure Rafael wouldn't touch her again, and she couldn't imagine letting another man touch her, couldn't even think about having another man's baby.

He obviously hadn't forgiven her for lying about the pregnancy. That was why he'd left her here alone, why he'd sailed away without a word. The next time she left this island she would have nothing of Rafael with her.

Her strength was finally returning, but there was no reason to leave her room, nothing to carry her beyond the balcony. Elena delivered her meals and usually spent the better part of the afternoon sitting near the balcony doors with a pile of sewing at her side.

It had been two weeks or so since Rafael had left the island; Sabrina couldn't be sure. The days were the same, blending from one beautiful sunrise to another. Communication with Elena was frustrating at times, but they had settled into a sort of truce, conversing in Spanish words Sabrina understood, English words Elena had picked up, and increasingly clever pantomime.

Sabrina watched the woman who was Rafael's housekeeper, Pablo's mother, Aqualina's mother-in-law, as the tiny woman's fingers flew through the material in her lap. Elena had probably saved her life, but whenever Sabrina tried to thank her, Elena brushed her off, as if she didn't understand.

"For you," Elena said in a heavily accented voice. She held up the material that had covered her lap, and displayed a brown-and-gold-striped skirt. From the pile of clothing on the floor at her side, Elena took a linen blouse with a wide ruffled collar.

Sabrina took the new clothes, thanked Elena in halting Spanish, and opened the trunk at the foot of the bed.

She hadn't ventured into the trunk since her return. Elena had provided plain nightdresses, and that was all Sabrina needed.

Elena left the room as Sabrina delved into the trunk. There was another white blouse beneath the red gown, and somewhere there was a gold sash that might match the skirt Elena had given her.

Sabrina was searching for that sash when her hand brushed against something that shouldn't be there . . . a small bag that clanked heavily when she wrapped her fingers around it and removed it from the trunk. She dumped the contents onto the bed, incredulous at the sight of gold coins against the coverlet.

Did he think she was a whore? A working girl like the woman in Cayona who had bared her breasts for a gold coin? For the first time in the course of her recovery, Sabrina felt anger. White-hot fury directed at the man who had ripped her life apart and apparently thought he could make amends with stolen gold.

Sabrina removed the red dress and tossed it aside, and discovered the velvet bag that held her emerald necklace—the jewels she had planned to use to support her child. The gold pin that had been placed with the emeralds was new, and there was a bracelet, a pendant. . . .

She gathered it all together, the gold coins and the jewelry—including the emerald necklace—and for the first time since Rafael had carried her, wounded and barely conscious, into this room, she left it.

His bed in the room next to hers was as he always kept it—neatly made and piled high with mismatched and brightly colored pillows. Sabrina dumped the treasure on the middle of the bed. She couldn't be bought, not for a chest full of gold and gems. What she wanted couldn't be purchased with any amount of gold.

Rafael could never give her what she desired most in the world. He was incapable of love.

That realization cooled her anger. She couldn't hate Rafael for who he was. She'd never lived in a world where survival was so difficult it overshadowed everything else. Where there was no time for thoughts of love and happiness that lasted more than a moment. A world where happy endings only came in magical stories.

She couldn't hate him, but she couldn't forgive him, either.

Back in her own room, Sabrina bathed quickly and dressed herself in the new skirt and blouse Elena had made. Maybe the gift had been more than a simple change of clothing. Maybe it had been Elena's way of telling her that it was time to be up and about.

It was definitely time for a change. She still felt weak, but she wasn't bedridden. A walk would do her good. There were miles of beautiful coastline, fragrant and bright flowers at every turn, trees heavy with fruit. Magnificent dusks and dawns.

There was one small cove she'd have to avoid, though. Too many memories waited there.

Sabrina was returning the red dress to the trunk when she saw the glitter of gold peeking out from a fold near the neckline. She slipped her finger into the crevice and hooked the ring.

This was, she knew immediately, different from the rest. It was plain, not particularly valuable compared to the gems she had left on Rafael's bed. There was an inscription on the band. *Autre ne veux.* French, she supposed. It was certainly not Spanish. It made little difference what language the inscription was in. Who would have thought, when she sensibly chose computer classes over a foreign language, that she'd end up in a time where even a nominal understanding of a language other than English would be more useful than her expertise with computers?

Did Rafael even know what the inscription said, or was it just another bit of gold to him? The words reverberated romantically when she sounded them out, her voice soft and hesitant, but they might mean nothing at all. Damn him, every time she began to accept that she and Rafael had nothing, he did something like this.

She slipped the band onto the ring finger of her left hand, and held it out for examination. It was a perfect fit, and sunlight glinted on the gold.

This one piece she would keep. For old times' sake, as a remembrance of her days on this island, the good and the bad. With a sigh she slipped the ring off and placed it on the ring finger of her right hand.

Rafael slashed his way through stumbling, drunken French pirates, his movements and his very survival instinctive, the room and the men in it unreal, hazy. Settled on the island of Hispaniola, the fools had thought themselves safe. There was not a musket in sight, and the knives and swords that were drawn were flailed inexpertly about.

This was much too easy.

If he had been able to locate Falconer, his fury would not be so great, but the man had eluded him again. The Englishman had left Tortuga and was not to be found on Jamaica . . . and so Rafael vented his anger on the French and his search for the treasure they had stolen from the *flota*.

He fought mindlessly, striking out at everything in his path, until soon he swung his sword through the air with no hindrance. His arms stung from shallow slices in his skin, from the wounds he had taken without flinching, and blood ran from one gash that was much more. Blood, his own and that of the Frenchmen who had refused to get out of his way, covered his arms and his once white shirt, but Rafael ignored the blood and the pain and faced the single man who remained before him.

Gaston Billaud dropped his own sword as he fastened his eyes on Rafael's face, surrendering in great fear. The man shook as he fell to his knees and dropped his head.

Rafael knew that Pablo was at his back. No one was before him but a kneeling, cowering Billaud.

"Do you yield?" Rafael asked, holding the point of his blade at Billaud's neck.

Billaud lifted his head slowly, so that he once again looked Rafael in the eye. There was such defeat there, but Rafael took no pleasure in it. "If you are going to take everything I own, kill me now, you Spanish bastard."

Rafael dragged the point of the sword from Billaud's neck to his heart, trailing the tip over pale skin and dirty linen. He considered doing just as the Frenchman asked, running the rapier through that heaving chest. He had killed before, many times, but he had never killed a man who knelt helpless at his feet. That would be murder. Another sin to pay for.

Billaud bowed his head again, and waited.

The hall of Billaud's house was silent. It was recently finished, devoid of furnishings or art or comforts of any kind. The large room was empty but for the press of sweating bodies. Behind him, Rafael knew, Billaud's men and his own crew waited.

"Why do you wish to die?"

Billaud shook his head. "You have taken everything, and I am finished. I have nothing." His voice broke, and he took a deep breath. "What a fool I was to think that I could start a new life."

"With gold stolen from the Spanish fleet?"

"Yes."

The tip of Rafael's sword wavered. "You will live to sail and steal another day, Billaud."

As Rafael's sword was lowered, the Frenchman stood. His face showed surprise, and then hatred, as he rushed blindly forward.

It would have been simplest to run the unarmed man through as he plunged ahead, but Rafael dropped his sword and lashed out with his fists. Two blows, and the Frenchman was on the floor. Unconscious but alive.

Rafael glanced behind him. Pablo and the rest of the crew held Billaud's men at bay with their own swords and muskets. Without their protection he would surely be dead now, shot or stabbed in the back.

"We burn this house?" Pablo asked.

"No," Rafael said as he lifted his sword from

the floor. "We take the gold; that is all."

Pablo snorted, and Rafael knew his first mate saw this pardon as a weakness.

Billaud had struck a nerve when he spoke of starting again, of claiming a new life. Sabrina had spoken of that impossibility often.

He had been away from the island for a month, and every night he dreamed of her. Alive and dancing in his arms, offering her body to him with outstretched arms, laughing. She had such a wonderful laugh, so bright. It was the most beautiful music he had ever heard.

Those nights were hard, because when he woke he knew that all those wonders were in the past. But accepting that was not as hard as when the nightmares came.

In his nightmares Sabrina was dead. Cold. White. Bleeding to death in the bed where he had made love to her. He had seen bloodshed all his life, had lived with violence and death, but it had never given him nightmares. Not like this.

Sometimes he woke feeling as if he were covered in it—covered in Sabrina's blood—only to discover that what he felt on his skin was his own sweat.

They left most of the French pirates alive and sailed from Hispaniola with enough gold for each man to live well for the rest of his life. No one thought for a moment that it would be enough for very long, but it was time to go home.

He was a coward. He did not want to return to the island and find that Sabrina was dead.

Even in his dreams, he tried to forget the other life that had been lost . . . but he could not. Her child. *Their* child.

Rafael did not condemn Sabrina for keeping the baby a secret. He had told her, quite clearly, that he would not allow her to give birth to his child. And she had wanted a child so much. He had known that truth from the moment he had seen her holding Pablo's daughter. He remembered that brief sight, that view of Sabrina with a newborn in her arms and a brilliant smile on her face, as one of the most frightening moments of his life.

Just two months ago he had been fearless, a warrior with nothing to lose.

And now he had lost everything.

If Sabrina had survived, she would surely hate him. There would be no more dancing, no more laughter, no more nights of losing himself in her body.

They sailed for Tortuga, the hold filled, the *Venganza* heavy with Billaud's gold. They would not stay long in Cayona. When the gold was divided and those who lived on that island had departed, the ship would sail for Rafael's island and whatever waited there.

245

# *Chapter Seventeen*

If she had known that sewing was going to be required, she would have paid more attention in Home-Ec in high school. Math had been a breeze, English hadn't been an effort at all, and she'd only struggled minimally in History, but Home Economics was another matter altogether. She could, at the age of seventeen, cook a gourmet meal that would put the Home-Ec teacher's efforts to shame, but she didn't give a fig for sewing. It was an archaic art she had no intention of ever practicing. Surely there was nothing more tedious.

And now, of course, here she was. The tiny stitches Elena insisted on had to be in just the right place, or else what Sabrina ended up with was useless.

Elena had been amazingly patient with her, Sabrina decided, even though that patience

didn't seem to come naturally. Her first as-
signed chores had been simple. Repairing a
hem, stitching a small tear here and there.
Some of the clothes mended were Rafael's, she
knew, some were her own, some were Elena's.

They had tried, for one very long day, to share
the kitchen, but that had been a disaster. Everything was so primitive, and when Sabrina had
tried to make a few suggestions, Elena had not
taken it well. She was responsible for a good
number of restaurants, after all, or at least she
had been in the past—or would be so far into
the future it was impossible to comprehend.

They had peaceably decided that the kitchen
would remain Elena's domain.

The natural light here by the balcony was sufficient, and the view was breathtaking. Huge
flowers, red and orange and pink, grew just beyond the balcony railing, and just beyond her
reach. She had tried unsuccessfully, more than
once, to snag one of the elusive blooms. Never
mind that the same sort of flowers grew everywhere . . . she wanted one of the flowers she
woke to.

Sabrina was separated from the rest of the
small island community by a short distance and
the language barrier she and Elena had managed to dent a little. There was no interaction
with the other women on the island. They were
suspicious of her, it seemed, because she was
English, and because she was the captain's
woman.

There was Aqualina, of course, who had tried
to visit twice. The first time Sabrina had been

standing near the window, and had seen the young mother walking along the path. Aqualina had an abundance of energy, a smile on her face, and a sleeping baby in her arms. When Elena and her daughter-in-law climbed the stairs a short time later, Sabrina slipped quietly into bed and pretended to be asleep.

The second time she'd been caught unaware, Aqualina bursting in as she and Elena argued lightly over some small detail in the kitchen. Sabrina had allowed Elena to win that argument, and she'd turned and all but run to the sanctuary of her room.

It wasn't Aqualina she was afraid of, it was that tiny and perfect baby girl Pablo's wife carried in her arms. Sabrina couldn't face the child, couldn't look at it and smile and pretend that her heart wasn't crushed.

After that day, Aqualina quit coming to the house.

Sabrina rarely felt lonely, even when she was alone. That feeling came only late at night, when she couldn't sleep.

She missed Rafael. His warmth in her bed, his seductive voice, his body against hers. She even missed his odd and infrequent sense of humor. That rare laugh of his. The sparkle in his eyes as he teased her.

There should be no tender remembrances of Rafael in her heart, she knew. She should concentrate on his harshness and complete inflexibility as he'd told her she *would not* have his child. She should remember that he had left her to die without so much as a word.

For a moment, Sabrina thought she had conjured up his voice, a faint echo from the main room below. She dropped the shirt she was in the process of mending and listened for a repeat of that vibration.

There was no mistaking that voice.

Every feminine instinct in her body, every ounce of self-respect, told her to stay put. She was not going to run to Rafael like a smitten schoolgirl, not after what he had done to her.

Still, Sabrina didn't bother to collect the mending she'd dropped to the floor. It shouldn't be so damn hard to put Rafael from her mind, but it was. The mending was left behind as she stepped through the door and into the hallway to look down into the room below.

Rafael and Pablo hefted weighty bags onto the table, and they spoke softly in their own language. All she could see of Rafael was his back. His shirt was filthy and torn, and a length of curling hair fell from a leather strap at the nape of his sun-darkened neck. Sabrina noticed after watching for a few minutes that he moved cautiously, and that he didn't use his left arm at all. He held it against his side, immobile.

She needed to see his face. Damn him, after all he'd done, she still needed to assure herself that he was all right.

"Rafael?" She hadn't intended to whisper so tentatively, and for a second she wondered if he had even heard her. But he stiffened, straightened his shoulders, and seemed to take a moment to prepare himself before he turned around and lifted his face to her.

*"Sirena mia."* His voice was no stronger than her own, and as she looked down at him her heart broke. God, he was so battered. One cheek was bruised and swollen, and his arms were covered with filthy bandages. Worst of all was the hollow-eyed look he gave her, the dark circles beneath those eyes. "You are . . . well?"

She couldn't feel sympathy for him, not after all that he'd done. "Obviously I survived, if that's what you mean. What have you done to yourself?"

Sabrina made her way to the staircase, and Rafael's eyes followed her every step. He didn't answer her, though. It was Pablo who enlightened her as she stepped onto the stairs.

"The captain, he try very hard to get himself killed, but he no do so good." There was more than a touch of humor in Pablo's unrefined voice, and a crooked grin to go along with it.

But Rafael didn't smile, and neither did Sabrina.

"What happened?" She wasn't sure how she made it down the stairs. Her whole body was numb, and her eyes never left Rafael's face.

"Nothing serious," he tried to assure her. "A few scratches, that is all."

One of those scratches was severe enough to keep his left arm idle and tucked against his side. "It won't be nothing serious for long if you keep those filthy bandages on." Sabrina wagged her fingers in the direction of the largest, bloodiest bandage. "Let's see."

"No. It is not necessary."

Rafael tried to turn away from her, and without thinking Sabrina reached out and snagged his wrist. She wasn't going to let him run, not this time. One look into his eyes told her that was exactly what he'd done when he'd taken to the sea and left her behind. Running. Leaving behind everything he was afraid to face.

She wrapped her fingers tightly around his wrist, knowing that her strength alone was not enough to hold him there. Physically, she was no match for him. She waited, but Rafael didn't break away, didn't move at all.

"The cuts need to be cleaned and rebandaged," Sabrina said calmly. "If you won't let me do it, then call Elena. Pablo says you tried to get yourself killed, but it seems to me that blood poisoning would be a nasty way to go."

Without another word of protest Rafael slipped his hand from hers and took a chair near the cold fireplace. With apparent bored resignation, he offered his right arm to Sabrina. She ignored his offer and lifted the more severely injured left.

The bandage was stiff with dried blood, and Sabrina cursed under her breath as she slowly unwrapped it, vile words she'd never thought to use in the company of another human being, forbidden curses normally reserved for the incompetent drivers ahead of or beside her on a busy road.

She stared at the arm, the wound, the dried blood, so she wasn't sure when the change came over Rafael. When she glanced at his face again it seemed he had relaxed, just a little. His eyes were wider, his mouth softer.

"You are speaking to me or to the Frenchman who did this?"

Sabrina lifted her eyes to his briefly. "Both of you, I suppose. A Frenchman, huh?"

The cut was deep, nasty, jagged, and Sabrina took a deep breath to still the nausea that rose within her.

"Pablo?" She spoke curtly to the man who stood silently behind her. "Fetch me a bottle of rum or whiskey, an ewer of water, and all the clean rags Elena can spare."

Rafael actually grinned, a flash of white teeth against his sun-darkened skin, and Sabrina turned to see that the big bald man had not moved. He crossed his arms over a massive chest. "Fetch, did you say?" Pablo asked softly.

"Fetch," she repeated. "Pronto."

Still, he didn't move.

"Dammit, Pablo," Sabrina seethed, turning and taking a single step. "Move!"

He did, a single step backwards and then another.

It took a soft command from Rafael before the big man left the room.

"Pig," Sabrina muttered as she returned her attention to Rafael's injured arm.

"Pablo is not accustomed to taking orders from anyone but me," he explained.

"What you really mean is that he won't take orders from a woman."

Rafael shrugged, a small movement as he favored his wounds. "This is true, too."

When Pablo returned he placed all that she had asked for at her side, and Sabrina began to clean the worst of Rafael's injuries. "I should let this arm rot and fall off," she muttered under her breath.

"You should," Rafael agreed.

She said nothing else as she finished the unpleasant chore, and then poised the bottle above Rafael's arm.

"This is going to hurt," she said as she tipped the bottle and allowed a healthy portion of rum to pour over the gash.

Rafael stiffened, but he didn't move and he didn't cry out. She wrapped the cleaned and sterilized wound with strips of linen, making the bandage as tight as she dared.

She heard Pablo leave the room as she turned her attention to Rafael's right arm. The cuts she revealed here were nasty, but compared to the wound on the left they were, as he'd claimed, just scratches. These she could clean and bandage without a twinge of misgiving.

When she was done, she stood quickly, drawing away from Rafael. "You should change those bandages often, you know. Keep the cuts clean."

"Why?" His voice was little more than a whisper, a dark and silky question.

"So they won't get infect . . ."

"Why do you do this?"

Sabrina took a deep breath. She couldn't help loving him, but she wouldn't allow him to see it. "If you get sick and die, I'll never get off of this fu . . . this *lovely* island." She went for sarcasm, trying to distance herself from the man who watched so calmly from his chair.

It wasn't easy, but Sabrina turned her back on Rafael and headed for the staircase that would take her to her room. There was no way to remain neutral with Rafael, so she was going to have to hide from him again, keeping her distance until it was time to leave this place.

How was she going to manage? All her life she'd been in control, a reasonable person who didn't waste her time on pursuits that weren't going to pay off. Right now, against all reason, she wanted to scream at Rafael for leaving her, for risking his life, for walking back into this house so calmly, as if nothing had happened. More than that, she wanted to kiss him. Against all reason, against every shred of common sense . . .

*"Sirena mia."*

The soft words stopped her, halfway up the stairs, and she turned to face him. He remained seated, composed, his newly bandaged arms crossed casually across his chest.

"I am . . ." He faltered, hesitated, and Sabrina didn't help him out by attempting to finish the statement for him. "I am glad to find you well," he finally said, quickly, in a low voice.

Sabrina didn't answer immediately, wasn't sure what a proper response would be. *So am I. You don't say? I don't believe you.* Nothing seemed right.

"Thank you," she finally muttered as she turned away. Thank you? Had she lost her mind? The man had left her to die and she was *thanking* him?

At the top of the stairs she gathered all her

strength to turn and face him. He watched her without a hint of remorse on his tired and battered face, had probably had his eyes on her the entire time. "I'll never forgive you," she said.

"I know."

"Leaving was a cowardly thing to do."

"*Si.*" He didn't hesitate, didn't take his eyes from her.

Sabrina took yet another deep breath, stiffened her spine. "I would have done anything for you."

"I know."

Damn him, he was going to sit there and agree with everything she said. It was a waste of time to lash out at a man who wouldn't even argue with her, so Sabrina turned her back on Rafael once again and stalked to her room.

The door slammed with a force that shook the house, and Rafael released the breath he had been holding.

Sabrina wore the ring he had given her, the gold band he had hidden in the folds of her red dress. It was on her right hand, and not on the left where it belonged, but still he was pleased. She likely did not know what the phrase inscribed on the band meant, and he would not tell her. If he did she would likely rip it from her hand and toss it into the sea.

He could not describe the relief he had felt upon seeing Sabrina. His nightmares had been proved false with the whisper of his name from the gallery above. She had come to him, healthy, roses in her cheeks, strength in the fingers she wrapped around his wrist.

She was right in her assessment of his character. He was a coward. When had he begun to run? At twelve, when he had left the farm. At fourteen, when he had run from Falconer and Elisa's death. In all the years since then he had never thought himself a coward. He would face swords and muskets without a qualm. He would risk his life without fear, in the name of revenge or in a quest for treasure. But he could not face what Sabrina wanted. What she *had* wanted.

Forgiveness was not expected. Not deserved. He knew Sabrina did not blame him for his part in the injury that had led to the loss of their child. Perhaps she did not even blame him for denying her that child.

But he had deserted Sabrina in her weakest moment . . . in his weakest moment. He had left her to lose the child she had wanted so badly, alone but for Elena. He had left her to die, knowing there was nothing he could do to help her, no way for him to save her. He had allowed his own pain and frustration to drive him from this house when Sabrina needed him most.

He sat for a long time. Elena did not come. Sabrina did not reappear. Finally, he headed for the stairs and his own chamber. He had not had a decent night's sleep since leaving this place, and he was suddenly very tired.

There was no guarantee that he would sleep any better with Sabrina so close at hand. Perhaps she would continue to haunt him.

He saw the pile of glittering treasure on his bed even before he quietly closed the door behind him. The afternoon sun lit the room and glinted on Sabrina's jewels and the gold coins he had placed in her trunk.

If she did not have his child, she wanted nothing of him. She would go hungry before she would lower herself to take this stolen treasure he offered. Rafael almost smiled as he fell to the bed beside the returned gifts, favoring his left arm as he dropped crosswise atop the pillows. He had come to know Sabrina so well, better than he knew anyone.

Sabrina was a proud woman, prouder than was wise. With contempt she returned all of his gifts. With anger in her eyes she told him he was a coward. And no matter how he wanted to deny it, he knew Sabrina well enough to know that she told the truth when she said she would never forgive him. In all his life, he had never asked for or expected forgiveness.

But she also still loved him. It was in the eyes that could never lie to him. In her soft hands on his wounded arms. There was frustration, also. Perhaps Sabrina wondered, as Rafael certainly did, how a love so tenuous could survive a betrayal such as this.

A tired smile crept across his face. She was alive. Warm, vibrant, angry, and alive. He had wanted so badly to take her into his arms, to feel her body against his, even if just for a moment. As she had bandaged his arms, he had wanted so badly to lean forward and kiss her that he had hurt with it.

He finally slept there, lying across the bed fully dressed, soft pillows cushioning his back, Sabrina's emerald necklace clutched in his hand, and for the first time since he had left her, Rafael did not dream of Sabrina.

She sat on the balcony, her legs folded beneath her, and watched the light fade from the sky. Rafael hadn't made a sound since he'd entered his room hours earlier, but she kept glancing toward the balcony next to hers, expecting him to appear there with a smile and a whispered *sirena mia*.

She had wished to live her life differently, and here she was. She'd decided that living life without love was foolish, that devoting herself to business had been a poor choice.

No one had ever told her that love was so painful. Could you have love without misery?

She'd lived all her life behind a shield, and now that it was gone she knew what it was like to be truly vulnerable. It wasn't a feeling she cared for. When emotion took over, control was gone, impossible.

Love. Hate. Passion. Loss. Fear. She'd never truly known even one of those emotions, but now they were all a part of her—and they battled constantly for dominance.

She loved Rafael and she hated him and, God help her, she still wanted him. There were moments when the loss of her child overpowered all those feelings, and at times it was a tangled part of the loss of what she and Rafael had found and savored for a short while.

And at times like this, as the sky grew dark, it was fear that overshadowed everything.

In this world she had nothing. She was completely alone, and the weeks and months and years to come were a dark mystery. Once she left this island behind, once she left Rafael behind, she would be facing a complete unknown.

Maybe some would consider this an adventure. Another time, a fresh start; a chance, perhaps, to change history.

Sabrina didn't see this as an adventure. She saw what was to come as a penance. Her price for loving Rafael, and hating him, and losing him.

Even after it was dark, she found herself looking at Rafael's balcony, and waiting for him to appear with a smile and a whispered *"sirena mia."*

# *Chapter Eighteen*

There had been nothing life-threatening about the wounds she'd bandaged on the previous afternoon, so there was no reason for her to be so frantic that she stalked outside Rafael's door. No reason for her stomach to be tied in knots. And still Sabrina paced.

Twenty hours had passed since she'd left Rafael sitting in the great hall below. She was so angry with him, for leaving her, for coming back battered and bruised and bleeding. Almost an entire day had passed since she'd heard him climb the stairs and quietly enter his own room next door. She'd listened closely, but there hadn't been a sound from his room since.

She'd never known Rafael to sleep for more than a few hours at a time. Even when the nights were long and calm, he was restless, a light sleeper, always alert. So where the hell was he?

Elena had claimed not to understand Sabrina's request that the housekeeper peek in on Rafael, placing her bony fingers to her lips and ordering silence. She wasn't yet worried enough to search for Pablo to order him, in English, to check on his captain. Besides, he needed to be with Aqualina and the baby. He would never appreciate or understand her concern.

Sabrina stopped at Rafael's door, laid her hand on the door handle, and held her breath, steeling herself to take a quick peek. Logically, she knew that she was being silly, worrying like this, but for the first time since she'd met him she wished that Rafael would snore like a normal man.

She was being ridiculous. There was surely nothing wrong with Rafael. Her fingers dragged reluctantly across the handle and she stepped away from the door.

Doubts welled up again. What if her pathetic attempts at doctoring had been too little and come too late? So much could go wrong. Blood poisoning, fever, infection. Rafael could be dead or dying.

This time she didn't hesitate, but opened the door slowly and quietly.

Rafael was laying sideways on the bed, as if he'd collapsed there and been unable to move. One hand was beneath a red brocade pillow and the other clasped the emerald necklace she'd deposited on the bed days ago.

His chest rose and fell steadily, and Sabrina felt a rush of relief. He wasn't dead, at least. She took a step forward, taking care not to make a sound. Like it or not, there was no way to tell if he'd come down with a fever unless she touched him.

The horrid-looking bruise on his cheek was days' old, and fading already. Why did he do this to himself?

She didn't notice the littered floor until she stepped on a gold coin. There were many scattered on the floor around the bed, along with a couple of pieces of jewelry. The rejected treasure she had left on Rafael's bed.

Sabrina lowered her hand slowly. Just a brief touch, and she would know. And then she could forget him again, for a while.

Her fingers had barely brushed his cheek when he sat up with a jolt. The hand that had been beneath the red pillow flew up, clutching a knife, and before Sabrina knew what was happening she was flat on her back, there on a bed that was warm and soft, and Rafael held his body over hers and the knife at her throat.

She couldn't make a sound. He had knocked the wind from her, and the knife didn't waver as he stared down at her with narrowed eyes.

"It is you," he said, still half asleep. The knife came away from her skin, and he blinked hard several times.

"Dammit! You're sleeping with a knife under your pillow?" She pushed at Rafael, and he rolled slowly away from her.

"Always, *sirena mia*." He returned to his back and closed his eyes.

"Always?" She told herself to calm down, told her heart to be still. "Even when I was . . ."

"Always," he whispered. "What are you doing here?"

Sabrina left the bed. "I was worried. You've been here for a whole day. Almost twenty hours."

"No wonder I am so hungry," Rafael murmured contentedly.

Sabrina leaned forward. "I'm going to touch your face now," she warned, "to see if you have a fever."

He was silent and still as she brushed her fingers across his cool cheek and then laid her palm on his forehead. No fever, thank God, just exhaustion.

"It seems you'll live," she said ungraciously.

"Disappointed, *sirena mia*?" Rafael asked without even bothering to open his eyes.

"Supremely," she muttered.

One quick and unexpected move from Rafael, and Sabrina found herself on the bed again. Rafael crushed her, towered over her, stared at her with piercing golden brown eyes. With his right hand he brushed the hair from Sabrina's face. The left remained motionless.

"You're going to hurt yourself," she seethed.

"Most assuredly."

"Get off me."

"I will."

"Now!"

Rafael ignored her order and lowered his lips to her neck. "Did I hurt you?"

"No."

"Did I frighten you?"

"No."

He lifted his mouth from her throat and stared at her with eyes that saw too clearly. "I have told you never to lie to me, and yet you insist on being less than honest. Quite regularly, I might add."

"All right, you scared me. Happy?"

"Why did you come here?"

He lowered his head to her shoulder, rested there, and Sabrina wondered what kind of answer he wanted. "I told you, I was . . ."

"Worried," he interrupted. "Yes, you did say that. You are afraid that I will die and you will be forced to stay on the island. There is no need for you to worry, *sirena mia*. I feel quite strong."

Evidently, Rafael was recovering well. Sabrina could feel the evidence of his arousal pressing against her thigh, swelling as he brushed his lips against her neck and molded his body to hers.

Sabrina knew then that she was completely lost. After all that Rafael had done, this felt so right. His breath at her throat, his body pressed against hers.

"This is impossible," she muttered.

"I am afraid you are correct, *sirena mia*," Rafael said weakly. "A minute ago I felt fine, and now my head is spinning."

Sabrina smiled as she pushed Rafael gently

away. He rolled onto his back. "You lost a lot of blood, didn't you?"

"*Sí.*"

"And now what you've got left is rushing to the one spot on your body where it won't do you a bit of good." She sprung from the bed, turning her back to him before he could see her blush.

"Sabrina," Rafael called softly as she opened the door.

"I'll have Elena bring up a tray," she said. "I know you're hungry."

"If anything happens to me," he said, ignoring her promise, "Pablo will take you to the English colonies. It is arranged."

Sabrina turned in the open doorway. "And when was this arrangement made?"

"Weeks ago," he whispered.

Sabrina closed the door softly. Weeks ago, while Rafael was, as Pablo so succinctly put it, trying to get himself killed. Weeks ago, right after he had left her here to lose their child alone. Weeks ago, when he had deserted her without a word.

She stood in the hallway where she had paced all morning and stared down at the door handle her fingers still gripped. How could she be expected to understand a man like Rafael?

With a burst of energy she swung open the door. Rafael didn't move, but lay on the bed with his right arm over his face. "You're amazing."

"*Gracías,*" he muttered.

"That wasn't a compliment. You're arrogant, and insensitive, and amazingly dense."

"I know."

"*Must* you always agree with me?" Sabrina stepped forward as Rafael dropped the arm that had shielded his eyes. With a sigh, he propped himself up on one elbow. "How dare you go out there and try to get yourself killed?"

"Pablo exaggerates." He was infuriatingly calm.

"I don't think so."

Rafael wasn't going to cooperate. He was going to tell her nothing. This time, when Sabrina left the room, she slammed the door behind her.

There was such beauty here, and Sabrina knew she would miss it when she left. Without Rafael, she wouldn't venture into the water, but she walked along the shore with her shoes in her hand and her skirt hiked up and tucked into her waistband so that the gentle waves lapped over her feet and ankles.

Rafael had awakened much more than her passion, he had awakened her senses. The sun seemed warmer, the water cooler, the night breeze across her skin more welcome. Her entire body had been numb, sleeping, until Rafael had found her on the beach.

When she saw Pablo and Aqualina coming toward her, walking as she was along the edge of the water, her impulse was to turn and run. It wasn't that she was afraid of Pablo, or that she didn't like Aqualina, it was the baby Pablo held in his arms.

It was too late. They had seen her, and Aqualina waved shyly.

The baby had grown so much. She was not so small now that Pablo refused to carry her, though she looked tiny cradled in Pablo's massive arms.

Sabrina tried to smile, but it was such an effort. Why couldn't she just be happy for them? Aqualina certainly deserved a little happiness in her life.

"Good morning," she called as brightly as she could manage.

Aqualina simply smiled, and allowed Pablo to return the greeting. When they met, Sabrina stared down at the baby, giving her the proper amount of attention. God, it shouldn't hurt like this.

"She's beautiful," Sabrina whispered. "What did you name her?"

Pablo translated for Aqualina, and then told her in a gruff voice that the baby was called Olivia. She should have known the name of the baby she had assisted into the world by now, but she and Elena had not discussed it. It was too hard.

"Here," Pablo snapped as Sabrina bent over Olivia. The baby was squirming as Pablo deposited his daughter unceremoniously into Sabrina's arms.

She didn't want this. Didn't want to hold someone else's baby. But a sleepy Olivia accepted her unwilling arms quite easily, molding warmly and solidly to her body.

"She's heavier than she looks," Sabrina said softly, glancing down at a fat cheek and tufts of soft black hair.

Pablo agreed sullenly, and Aqualina launched into rapid Spanish, bright, sharp words Sabrina had no hope of following. When Aqualina was silent, Sabrina looked to Pablo for translation. Instead, Pablo turned a scowl to his wife and shook his head as he refused her.

Aqualina lifted a sharp chin and argued with her husband, a man who surely struck fear into the hearts of men across the world. He was easily twice her size, Sabrina could never remember seeing him smile, and still he stood there and allowed his wife to lambast him.

Finally, he turned to Sabrina and Olivia again. "Aqualina says do not be sad."

"I'm not . . ."

Pablo lifted a large hand to still her protests. "Do not argue with this woman. It is hopeless."

She had tried so hard not to let her sorrow show, but Aqualina had seen it.

"She says you will have other children. Many fine, healthy babies."

That should have made her feel better, but it only made the pain worse. "I hope so," she whispered. Olivia had cuddled against her chest and was once again asleep. The baby felt so warm, so right. "I really hope so."

Of course, they wouldn't be Rafael's children. If Pablo could be a father, why couldn't he? Damn him, how could he do this to her?

Reluctantly, she handed the sleeping Olivia back to her father. Pablo took his daughter carefully, and the child fell smoothly into his embrace. Her breathing didn't change, her eyelids didn't quiver. For Olivia there was only peace, and warmth, and love.

A perfect world.

Sabrina said good-bye and continued her walk down the beach, but the beauty of the morning didn't entrance her as it had just a few minutes earlier.

Rafael slept for the better part of a week, and he did not see Sabrina in all that time. He heard her, in the hallway outside his chamber, on her own balcony, in her own bed. It was Elena who had brought his meals and changed his bandages.

And she did it all so ungraciously, barely speaking to him. While he had been gone, Elena's loyalties had shifted to Sabrina.

He missed her, his gift. Her body, her laugh, her stubbornness. He craved her, more than he should, more than he thought possible. What would it be like when she was gone, and he could no longer even hear her? This island that had been his refuge would become a prison, just as it had once been—and perhaps still was—for Sabrina.

He heard her step onto her balcony, as she did every morning. Sabrina could deny that she found charm on his island, but it was a lie. She looked with great admiration at the sea and the tall palms, at the bright wild flowers, at the unequaled sunsets.

Rafael left his bed, feeling energized for the first time since his homecoming. He stepped quickly into black trousers and a white shirt, and then strolled onto the balcony with a lazy step and a yawn.

He had intended to give Sabrina a feigned surprised, "good morning," but his astonishment was real.

"What the devil are you doing?"

Sabrina sat on and leaned precariously over the rail as she reached for a large red flower that was just beyond her reach.

"I've almost got it," she said, not even bothering to glance his way.

With a Spanish curse, Rafael stepped onto the sturdy railing of his own balcony and took the short leap that landed him just behind Sabrina.

The move startled her, and she had begun to swing back toward the balcony even before he snagged her around the waist and yanked her to safety.

"What are you doing?" Rafael asked darkly as he released Sabrina.

She glanced from his balcony to where he now stood. "What am *I* doing? I'm just trying to pick a flower. You're the one who's pretending to be Zorro. Shouldn't you be in bed?"

Rafael ignored her. Who was this Zorro? He would not ask. Without a word, he placed himself on her perch, reached forward, and plucked the red flower from the vine that had climbed the tree just past her balcony.

"Here," he said, handing it to her impatiently as he returned to his feet. "If you want more, there are a hundred blooms growing around the house. You need not risk yourself for a flower."

Sabrina stared, not at him but at the bloom in her hand. "I wanted this one."

His anger faded quickly, as it usually did where Sabrina was concerned. "And what is so special about this particular flower?"

"They don't last, you know, on the vine. One day, and then they fall and another bloom or two takes its place. I wondered if, maybe, I put it in water and kept it out of the sun, it would last a little longer."

Rafael stepped away from her. He wanted too much to take Sabrina's face in his hands and kiss her. "What difference does it make, if there are always other flowers to fill the emptiness where that one once was?"

He thought it an innocent question, but the expression on Sabrina's face as she lifted it to him was stern. "It's so easy for you, isn't it? Everything can be replaced. Nothing lasts, and that doesn't bother you at all."

Rafael leaned against the railing and crossed his arms over his chest. Sabrina was magnificent, with fire in her eyes and in her cheeks. When the morning sun illuminated her, as it did now, there was fire in her hair as well. "Are we speaking of the bloom you hold in your hand, *sirena mia*, or of something else entirely?"

"It's easier to have a conversation with Elena than it is to talk to you," Sabrina said in a low voice.

"Really? I have always thought that you and I communicated very well."

She blushed, turned almost as red as the flower she held carefully in her hand. When Sabrina allowed her body to speak for her, there were no misunderstandings, no confusion about what she wanted.

She ignored her evident embarrassment. "You look much better. When will we be able to leave?"

Just that easily, she stole the moment of joy in which he had been basking, a joy he found in simply watching her. "As soon as you like, *sirena mia*."

She nodded her head. "Soon. In a few days, I guess. There's no reason to stay here."

"None," he agreed reluctantly.

"It might be best if you rested for a few more days."

"Perhaps."

Sabrina studied the bloom she cradled in her hand. "Do you think I could transplant these tropical plants somewhere where it's a little colder? I could wrap the roots in damp cloth, keep it watered until spring. I've already decided that I don't want to go as far north as Boston. You're right, it will be much too cold there."

She cocked her head to one side, and still she did not look at him. "Surely there's an English settlement in the South. Georgia or the Carolinas. It might not be much, yet, but that's where I want to go."

"Is it?"

She lifted her head then, just a little. "Yes."

"And what will you do there?"

She shrugged her shoulders, and even smiled a little. "I don't know. Open the first fast-food restaurant, I suppose."

Even though she smiled, Rafael's stomach knotted. She had nothing. All she could do was marry, and hope that her husband would care for her and give her fat babies. "You will take the gold and gems I gave you."

"I will not," she said sternly, and her smile died. "You can't buy me off."

"I am not trying to . . . buy you off. I will never spend all the gold I have. I want you . . ."

"No."

"Do not be stubborn, Sabrina."

"I'm not going to take that treasure just to make you feel better. . . ."

"So I am a bad man because I will feel better if I know you are not hungry?" He had not intended to lose his temper, but he interrupted Sabrina angrily. "Because I want you to have a roof above you and warm clothes in the winter? Would you suffer just to spite me?"

Sabrina twirled about and entered her chamber, and Rafael took a single step forward, following her, before he stopped. It was true; she would prefer to endure life-threatening hardships rather than take his gifts. That was no surprise. Had she not told him that she would never forgive him?

He clenched his hands as he turned away and returned to his own balcony with an easy leap.

# Chapter Nineteen

She would not have him. As he sat silently in the great room, Rafael watched Sabrina. She argued nonsensically with Elena, mixing her oddly accented English and truly horrible Spanish. Such a beautiful noise. Those delicate hands of hers gestured broadly, emphasizing every point. Elena was just as emphatic as she raised her shrill voice. The disagreement had something to do with the crabs that would be their dinner.

Rafael paid little heed to Sabrina's actual words. It made no difference what was said. The sound of her voice, even as she haggled, was enchanting. He was content to sit back and watch as she seduced him with her gentle movements, with the toss of her head. There was not another woman in the world like this one.

He had known yesterday, watching her cradle

that fragile flower in her hands, that he still wanted her more than he had ever wanted anything. In the hours since then, he had tried to deny that desire, but it was impossible to ignore the truth.

She would not have him. Oh, perhaps he could seduce her. Sabrina still had passion for him, even after all that had passed. He had seen it in her eyes, had felt it days ago when she had lain so briefly and reluctantly beneath him. A touch, and she would falter. A kiss, and she would be in his arms, in his bed.

But he would not be satisfied simply to have her body again. Once, that had been all he desired, but now he wanted it all. The heart she had given so freely, the soul she had shared.

Heaven help him, he wanted to give her everything she wanted. Love, children . . . a new life.

It would mean leaving everything behind. Piracy. This island. The *Venganza*. Even his vendetta against Falconer. They would have to go somewhere far away, where they would never be found. A life far away from the sea. Was it possible?

But of course, this knowledge that Sabrina meant more to him than he had planned and the musings on a new life came too late. If he had offered Sabrina this chance weeks ago, she would have taken it gladly. What a fool he was. Only in losing Sabrina had he found her.

Sabrina threw up her hands in surrender, and Elena stomped victoriously into the kitchen.

"You have learned to communicate with

Elena quite well," he said as Sabrina passed his chair without a hint of a glance. He wanted to reach out and snatch the swaying brown and gold skirt she wore and pull her onto his lap, but he allowed her to pass untouched. She was headed for the stairway, escaping to her chamber.

"Yeah, I learned to communicate with Elena," she snapped. "I didn't really have much choice, did I?" She stopped at the foot of the curved staircase and spun around to face him defiantly.

He expected her to run from him at any moment, but she remained there with one foot on the bottom step, poised to run but motionless. "I know I should not have left you here," Rafael admitted in a low voice.

"Am I supposed to forgive you because now, when it's too damn late, you admit you were wrong?"

"I knew it then."

She did not respond immediately, and it seemed the large room was filled with a silence that could be seen and touched, it was so heavy. If he turned from her now, if he averted his eyes and ignored what had been said, Sabrina would flee to the safety of her chamber and he would likely never have this opportunity again.

"I knew it," he continued, "as I searched for Falconer. It haunted me even as I attacked the Frenchman Billaud and tried to forget."

"Did Falconer . . ." Sabrina began.

"I did not find him," he interrupted, the anger rising within him just as it had when he had been unsuccessful in locating his old enemy. It was an anger laced heavily with frustration. "If I had found Falconer I would have killed him, no matter how many men he surrounded himself with. If I had finished this years ago, you would not have been hurt. That is another wrong I cannot make right."

Sabrina turned her back on him, began to climb the stairs slowly, as if her feet were heavy. The life had been drained from her, the spark that made her bright doused. By him.

*"Sirena mia?"* he called softly, unsure if she would respond to his voice. For a moment, he thought she would not. She took another step before she turned to face him. Sabrina was not a helpless creature, but at the moment she looked so very fragile. Pale, delicate, frightened. "I am so sorry the child was lost."

They had never spoken of the child, but the loss had been between them, as tangible and impenetrable as a warrior's shield.

"I've never wanted anything so badly in all my life," Sabrina admitted softly, "as I wanted that baby." Even from a distance he saw the tears shining in her eyes. Sabrina, who never cried for herself, but only shed her tears for others. His pain from long ago, the child she had wanted.

He stood and stepped forward, taking long steps, wondering if Sabrina would run from him as he had run from her. He needed to hold her, to comfort her. As he climbed the steps her tears fell, silent streams down her cheeks. He ran the last few steps.

When he touched Sabrina the shield shattered. He gathered her into his arms and she wept, loud, long sobs of mourning. Her tears dampened his shirt, and as he held her gently she tightened her fingers at his sleeve, hanging on as if she would fall without his support.

He spoke to her softly, words she could not understand. They seemed to soothe her, anyway. The sobs grew quiet, and Sabrina melted, falling against him, into him. He held her, knowing that without his embrace she would drop to her knees. This was what she had needed, what he had run from. Comfort. Solace, and a sharing of the knowledge that they had both lost something precious.

Together, they sank to the stairs, and Rafael sat with Sabrina against him, as her rare tears continued to fall silently.

"That baby was a part of you, and a part of me," she whispered. "It was magic and wonder, and I thought that no matter what happened to me, where I went or how I lived, I would always have something of us. Now there's no baby and no *us* and I've never felt so alone."

Rafael brushed a strand of hair away from her dampened cheek. "There will always be us, *vida mia*. No matter how many leagues separate you from me. You are here." He took her hand and placed it against his chest, so she could feel the pounding of his heart. "Always."

She fought modestly against his grip, but he held her gently until she folded her fingers against his chest. Perhaps she could forgive him, even though she had said she would not, even though he himself never would.

278

"Stay with me, *vida mia*." He waited for Sabrina to draw away from him in anger, but she did not. She pressed her face against his chest and hid there. "Let me take you far away from this place, and we can start again. Perhaps you can take me to your world, where there is no Falconer and no injustice."

She shook her head gently but did not draw away from him. For a moment he thought that gentle shake of her head was a refusal of his offer, but then she wrapped her arms around his waist and held on tight.

"I would love to take you there, but it's impossible." She lifted her face to him, bright, shining eyes that were sapphire blue with streaks of green. "I never said there was no injustice where I come from. There's less suffering, but life's not always fair."

"We will find a place."

"You said . . ."

"I said many things, *sirena mia*, and I never lied to you." She stiffened in his arms. "I did not want to love you, but from the moment I found you on the shore you have been a part of me." He pulled her right arm from its tenuous place at his waist, took her hand in his own and brushed his fingers against the engraved ring she wore. "*Autre ne veux*. I wish for no other," he translated. "It is true. You are wearing this on the wrong hand, by the way," he said, slipping it from her finger and drawing her left hand from his back to cradle it as gently as Sabrina had her precious flower.

"Here it is closest to your heart." He slipped the ring onto the proper finger.

"Rafael . . ." There was a hint of protest in her whisper of his name.

"*Vida mia,* let me give you everything you want. I know nothing can replace what was lost." He took Sabrina's face in his hands. He needed to see her eyes. "Let me love you. We will have more babies, as many as your heart desires, and . . ." He hesitated. There was a flash of uncertainty in Sabrina's eyes. Suspicion, perhaps. A lack of faith, certainly. She wanted to believe him, but he had hurt her too badly. "I will never leave you again."

"Rafael . . ."

"Have I ever lied to you?" He interrupted before Sabrina could refuse him. "When I hurt you it was with the truth, never with lies. If I could I would change many things, but we cannot go back. We can only start again."

"Rafael . . ."

"How can I prove to you . . ."

Sabrina silenced him with a single finger against his lips, a gentle pressure that touched his heart and stole the words from his mouth.

"Rafael," she began again, and this time he knew he had to allow her to complete her objection, "you know I love you." She said the words as if they hurt her. "I just don't know if that's enough anymore."

He held Sabrina there on the steps for a long time, unwilling to release her. She cried again for the child she had lost, and as the sun set outside the home he would soon abandon, Rafael found that his own eyes stung with unshed tears.

Sabrina wanted to believe what Rafael promised, but it was in her nature to be cautious. Especially when she'd been burned.

She held on to the fact that he had never lied to her. His failings were colored with brutal honesty, but she still had doubts about this offer to leave everything behind and start again. With her. It was too perfect, too much to ask for.

The morning walks had become a ritual, a stable tradition in an unstable world. In the days after she'd finally left her bed, she'd found peace of a sort on her own in an untamed setting. Here along the beach, or between the shore and Rafael's house, in junglelike growth where it was possible no other human had ever been.

At first she had been wary, especially along the jungle path and beneath the tall palms. She found herself looking this way and that for critters but finally decided that she made enough noise to scare away anything smaller than she was. And it was the small things she was afraid of—snakes, lizards, spiders.

The stretch of beach she had taken to walking in the morning was straight. The water was unfailingly calm, with the contrast of fine white sand against an aquamarine sea. That one time she'd run into Pablo and Aqualina, but every other morning she'd had the beach all to herself. It was a good place to think; the only place, it seemed, that she could think clearly.

In the sunlight the ring on Sabrina's left hand flashed. Rafael had known when he'd placed it in her trunk what the inscription meant, and now that she knew the ring was even more precious to her than it had been before. It was almost too much to wish for, that he could love her as much as she loved him, that he would give up everything he knew for her. That he truly wanted no one else.

She stayed away from the house too long, walking along the sand and pondering the past and the future. By the time she returned the sun was high in the sky, and the heat of the day was strong.

Rafael was waiting for her in the main room, standing before a cold fireplace. He tried to act as if he wasn't actually watching for her, but his head turned toward the door too quickly when she entered.

"I went for a walk," she explained before he could ask her where she'd been.

"I know. Elena said . . ." He stopped, perhaps realizing that he'd given himself away by revealing that he'd already inquired about her. "She said you often roam the island when you wake."

Sabrina nodded her head as she passed Rafael. He was waiting for the answer she'd refused to give him last night, and she wasn't ready to give him one. More than anything, she wanted a life with the man she loved. Rafael, her lover, not Rafael the pirate bent on revenge. She wasn't certain he could leave that part of himself behind.

She ran up the stairs, not sure what she'd do when she got to her room, but knowing that she couldn't face Rafael with this indecision between them. If she looked at him too hard, if he smiled at her, if he touched her, she'd hand herself over without a single misgiving, and any chance of the control she'd thought she might have in this life would be gone.

The door to her room was standing open, and she approached cautiously. She was certain she'd closed it when she'd left early that morning.

With a light push, the door swung open, and Sabrina held her breath. The room was a riot of orange and red and yellow and bright pink. The flowers were everywhere. On the floor, in bowls on her dresser, on the bed.

Covering the bed. Blooms two and three and four deep concealed the spread. The scent of island flowers filled the room, a heady perfume.

"You will not allow me to give you gold and gems, and so I give you this."

Sabrina turned slowly. She hadn't heard Rafael climb the stairs, hadn't known until she'd heard his soft voice that he was with her. "They're beautiful."

"There should be nothing but beauty surrounding you."

Sabrina took the first step, a hesitant move toward Rafael. "You picked all of these for me."

"*Sí.* From the highest limb, from the lowest vine. Everything on this island is yours."

Rafael didn't move as Sabrina reached up to sweep aside a softly curling strand of hair that fell forward and brushed his cheek. Not so long ago, everything Rafael possessed had been claimed with certainty. *My* ship. *My* home. *My* cove. *My* island. *My* mermaid.

"*Vida mia,*" she whispered. "What does it mean?"

He hesitated, no more than the span of a heartbeat. That delay in what should have been a simple translation was telling. "It means darling. I told you that."

"*My* something. You said you'd never lie to me, Rafael." The accusatory tone in her voice was mild but undeniable. "My *what*?"

Rafael sighed, and Sabrina saw something unusual in his eyes. Uncertainty. Vulnerability.

"My *what*?" she repeated, closing what remained of the gap between them.

"My *life*," he whispered.

Sabrina lifted her face, and Rafael bent forward slowly to touch her lips with his tender mouth. Just that easily, her decision was made. She had argued to herself more than once that it made no sense to believe that she had been carried here, to another time, another life, simply to love Rafael, but at the moment it made very perfect sense.

"Where will we go?" she breathed as she drew her lips away from his.

Rafael's answer was a smile, a bright, wicked smile that wiped away the uncertainty she'd seen in his eyes.

"I do not know." He lifted her easily and carried her into the flower-filled room, kicking the door shut behind him. "We will decide later. Now I can think of only one thing."

"And what is that?" Sabrina asked with a smile, as Rafael placed her gently in the center of the bed.

"To make love to you," he whispered, trailing a soft bloom against her cheek and across her neck. "To be inside you, a part of you. Again and again, *vida mia.*"

Rafael undressed her as if they had all the time in the world. He drew soft-petaled flowers over her flesh, lingering at her breasts, teasing her hardened nipples with the brush of a petal. When she thought the gentle stroke would drive her mad, he replaced the teasing flower with the heat of his mouth, the pressure of his tongue.

She ran restless fingers through Rafael's hair, held him tight. Every circling movement of his tongue, every brush of his mouth, every breath against her flesh, brought a new flicker of pleasure.

By the time he moved his mouth to hers, she ached for him, and her hands at his restrictive clothing were not nearly as patient as his had been.

She tore at his shirt, yanking it upward so she could feel his skin against her own. Rafael pulled his mouth from hers just long enough for Sabrina to jerk the shirt over his head.

His breath came faster as she reached between them to untie the drawstring at the waistband of his trousers, and when his shaft was free he pressed against her, into her, filling her with an impatient thrust.

285

He plunged hard and deep to fill her, rocking against her in a primal rhythm to which her body responded instinctively. He kissed her, exacting and luscious, demanding and giving, and when he began to whisper against her mouth it was with soft and rolling Spanish, sweet, familiar words that caressed her as surely as the stroke of his body inside hers.

"In English, Rafael," she whispered, and he opened his eyes. He stared at her relentlessly as he rocked against her, thrust into her and claimed her as his own.

"I adore you," he whispered. "I am nothing without you. I want no one but you, *vida mia*." He kissed her, fixed his mouth softly to hers. She came apart beneath him, shattered so hard and so completely that the world stopped. There was nothing but this.

"I love you," Rafael breathed against her lips as he tensed and filled her completely, driving into her quivering flesh hard and deep. He gave himself over to her, completely and readily, and Sabrina could feel the heat and the power of his fulfillment.

His head was buried against her shoulder and his body was crushed heavily against hers. She didn't feel trapped by the pressure and the weight, not at all. She felt wonderfully free.

Sabrina reached out and lifted a flower that lay beside Rafael's hip. Lazily, she drew the petals up his side, and he groaned against her neck. It was a good groan.

"I've always loved you, you know," Sabrina said softly. "I fell for you the moment I saw you, and I'm not a woman given to hearts and flowers."

"You love flowers," he argued gruffly. "And you have been after my heart from the beginning."

"Guilty."

"And now you have it."

Sabrina smiled and twirled her fingers lazily through Rafael's hair.

He rolled away from her but did not leave her arms or the flower-strewn bed. "We must go far from this place, *sirena mia*."

"Why? I love it here."

Rafael smiled and cupped her cheek, kissed her softly. "I cannot risk your life and the life of our children with the path I have chosen. There is too much *venganza* in this part of the world. Too much danger. It could find us, even here on this island."

Sabrina brushed a battered bloom across Rafael's chest. "I don't care where we go, as long as we stay together."

Lazy fingers trailed down her throat to her chest, and Rafael rocked those dark, strong fingers over sensitive flesh. His eyes followed the path of those fingers.

"I have heard of a place," he said dreamily, "called California."

Sabrina sat up. "There's a California? Of course there is. That would be perfect. We could have cattle and a vineyard and you can build us a house exactly like this one. I want a balcony, and flowers, and you." She brushed the petals lower, across Rafael's navel.

"California," he repeated. "It is a long journey from the Spanish Main to California. Ah, *sirena mia,* you will make a farmer of me yet."

"I think you'll make a wonderful farmer." The flower dipped lower, grazed sensitive skin.

Rafael gripped her wrist and pulled the flower away from his skin. "What are you trying to do to me?"

Sabrina leaned forward, kissed Rafael lightly, and slid her fingers beneath the waistband of trousers that had not yet made it all the way off.

"Let's get rid of these, shall we?" With Rafael's help she slipped the trousers down his legs and tossed them to the floor, where they landed in a profusion of brightly colored flowers.

# *Chapter Twenty*

Rafael ate his morning meal alone, but he did not feel lonely. Not at all. Sabrina slept peacefully in her chamber far above his head, contentment on the angelic face he had watched by morning's light. He would not wake her for all the treasure in the world.

In the day and night that had passed since he had gifted her with flowers and his heart, she had slept very little. He himself had slept even less, but he felt not tired at all.

There was not a single second thought, no nagging doubts about his decision to leave all this behind.

Elena was still angry with him, but then she did not know all that had happened, all that was yet to happen. She had practically thrown his plate of fruit and bread at him, and had blatantly ignored his cheerful *"Buenos dias."* Elena had, in fact, given him a glare that had most certainly been passed from mother to son. That glare looked as fierce on the small woman as it always did on Pablo.

He owed Elena a debt he would never be able to repay. She had cared for Sabrina when he could not, when he would not, and she had tried to protect their child. From him. Elena, in her wisdom, had known what was most precious even when he did not.

He had never faced Elena with the truth that she had lied to him when she had told him Sabrina was not with child. Even when he had returned with an injured Sabrina, Elena had said nothing, but had attended to her patient with the utmost care.

She had known how fragile Sabrina was, and had continued to protect her and the child from him, until it was too late.

It was no wonder she was so angry.

Rafael fingered the heavy jewels in his vest pocket. They were inadequate, certainly, but he knew no other way to express his thanks and to make amends.

Since Elena was unlikely to return while he remained at the table, he would have to go to her. Rafael stood slowly, preparing himself to face her ire as he stepped into the kitchen.

She was not cooking, but scrubbing the surfaces of her beloved kitchen with strength in those thin arms. As he took a few silent steps to close the distance between them, she turned to face him, unsmiling and openly mutinous.

Without a word, he took the ruby choker

from his pocket and offered it to her. Rubies small and large dropped from his fingers, and the fine gold work glittered in the sunlight that poured through the open door.

Elena stared at the offering for only a moment, and then she turned away from him to return to her scrubbing.

For a long moment Rafael stared at her back, and the hand that held the jewels dropped slowly.

"Forgive me," he said softly, "but I do not know how to thank someone for protecting my heart, for taking care of my very soul."

Elena stopped scrubbing, but she did not turn to look at him, and after a long moment he tossed the rubies carelessly onto the closest surface—a damp table where, on most afternoons, Elena sliced fruit and cleaned fish.

"It is yours," he said softly. "To keep, to wear, to fling into the sea. With this bauble comes my gratitude, for taking care of her, for defending her. For protecting the child."

He waited for a response, but his only answer was unbearable silence, so he turned his back on Elena and the peace offering, anxious to return to Sabrina.

"I never thought to have a wife," Rafael mused.

Sabrina leaned into him, naturally, easily. It was good to return to the cove. She'd missed the site and hadn't even allowed herself to realize it. "All our time together, and you've never even

291

mentioned marriage. I had begun to believe you thought me a loose woman."

He glanced down at her as if her teasing words were serious. "You are my wife," he insisted softly. "We have been married from the moment I placed the ring you wear on the correct finger, *vida mia*. Do not doubt it."

Oddly enough, she didn't. There was no need to set a date, to send out invitations and reserve a chapel and choose a dress. They'd said their vows, made their commitment. No two people could be more married.

"I don't suppose you have a preacher or a priest on this island, anyway, unless one of your men has a secret past I haven't heard about," she mused. "What about the others? Did Pablo and Aqualina go to Tortuga to be married?"

They had finished their swim some time ago and had allowed the sun to dry their skin.

"No," Rafael finally answered in a low voice. "Aqualina will not leave here. This island is the only place she feels safe."

"Falconer?" Sabrina whispered.

"*Sí.*"

Rafael brushed her cheek with a lazy finger. "I performed the ceremony for Pablo and Aqualina myself."

"You?"

"It is my island, after all, *sirena mia*. There were ceremonies also for Cristóbal and Maria, and for César and Benita. The others did not wish for a ceremony. If you would like, Pablo can say the words over us." His teasing finger slid down her neck. "If you need a ceremony . . ." He shrugged his shoulders.

No ritual would make her feel more married to Rafael. She had already promised herself to him, and he had claimed her as his wife. It was enough. It was more than enough. "Do you know what I want?" She leaned closer, and with a gentle hand pushed Rafael until he fell backwards, off the blanket and into the sand.

"*Sí.*"

"I want a party."

His wide smile faded. "A party?"

"A celebration, before we leave the island." She leaned over Rafael and propped herself against his chest. "I hardly got to know any of the women here, except for Elena, but I think it would be nice. There could be music and food and dancing."

His smile reappeared. "You will dance for me?"

"I will dance *with* you."

"Then it is done."

Rafael looked so content, but then this cove had always calmed him. He was relaxed here, at home. She'd seen that bit of peace in him, even before he had accepted her love and admitted, in English so she would understand, to his own love. And he was ready to leave it behind for her. For them. Good heavens. Married. Nothing had ever felt so natural, so perfect. Almost perfect.

"There is one little, very minor thing I should probably tell you." She'd been putting this off, wondering if it was really necessary, knowing in her heart that it was very necessary. The tone

LINDA JONES

of her voice had put Rafael on alert. She could
see a hint of caution in his eyes, could feel it in
the tightening of the chest she leaned upon. "We
never discuss where I came from."

He relaxed, and even gave her a small smile.
"It does not matter."

"You should know," Sabrina insisted. "But I
don't think we should tell anyone else." Nervously, she drew away to sit in the sand beside
him. She remained close to the body Rafael
stretched across the warm sand, but she no
longer touched him.

She had his full attention. Rafael rolled up
easily and brushed some of the sand from his
skin. "All right. You will tell me now?"

Sabrina bit her lower lip tentatively.

"You do not have to speak of it," Rafael assured her, "if you wish not to. Whatever distresses you now, it is in the past."

"Not exactly," Sabrina muttered, and Rafael
leaned close. "What I mean is, it's not exactly in
the *past*. Dammit, there's no easy way to say
this. I came from the future," she said quickly.
"I won't even be born for more than three hundred years. Don't ask me to explain how, because I can't. I fell into the water, and when I
opened my eyes I was looking at you." She
waited for laughter, or for anger, or for an incredulous stare. But as she looked into Rafael's
face, she could see that he wasn't even surprised.

"Three hundred years," he repeated softly.

"I know it's hard to accept."

Rafael said nothing, but stared out at the cove

with an almost serene expression on his face. The wind lifted his heavy curls just slightly, and washed over her own body with a balmy hand.

"This answers many questions," Rafael said thoughtfully. "I have always known that you are different from other women, and the strange world you speak of, where women have control and pain and hunger are rare . . . the future." He actually smiled.

"You believe me?"

He stroked her face and her neck with slow fingers. "Of course I believe you. You lie badly."

"Rafael!"

"I needed you, and you needed me. Some force brought you to my feet, and the rest was left to us." He bent down to kiss her softly, and that was when Sabrina realized that her mouth was hanging open. "Why should that be so difficult to understand?"

He accepted so easily, her story as well as his belief that some higher power had brought them together. Of course, Rafael had always embraced each day as it came, never questioning, never analyzing.

"I love you so much," she whispered.

"Do you know it makes my heart hurt when you say that?" His voice was soft in her ear.

"Should I stop?"

"No. It is a good hurt."

Sabrina smiled at that whispered statement. A good hurt. Rafael fell back to the blanket, and Sabrina fell with him, ending up with her head resting on his chest and his hands in her hair.

His fingers stroked lazily, mindless and

soothing caresses. "Do you miss it? The future? Do you wish for all that you had in that world?"

"No." Sabrina circled his flat nipple with her finger. "I was never happy there." She was happy now, with Rafael beside her. They had such plans. California. A ranch or a vineyard, depending on what they found at their destination. Children . . . the children Rafael had once refused her, he now spoke of with a smile.

"And so you came here, to me."

"Yes."

"My life has changed as much as yours, *sirena mia*, though I have traveled not at all."

Sabrina lifted her head. There was wonder in his voice, and she looked for it on his face. Beautiful Rafael, unyielding renegade, brutal pirate, tender lover . . . they were all hers. Love was as much a miracle to Rafael as her impossible journey was to Sabrina.

"I know," she whispered as she brushed her lips against his.

What Sabrina wanted, she would have. Elena had grumbled, but not for long, and now the main room was filled with the flowers Sabrina loved, enough wine to intoxicate the *flota*, and a variety of fruits and meat and bread.

Rafael surveyed the heavy table with a grimace. He had not been truly hungry for a very long time, but he remembered too well what it was like. So much of his life had been filled with hardship and pain, and now everything had changed.

His children would never know hunger, that

he swore. Sabrina would never want for anything, and if it was in his power, she would never know pain again. He would protect her from pain with his very life. Could he do this? Could he leave all that he knew behind and start again?

Yes, and no.

Justice was important to Sabrina. And, Rafael admitted reluctantly, to him as well. Falconer had to be made to pay for his many sins. For Elisa and Aqualina and all the others. He could not start a new life knowing that Falconer lived, that the Englishman would not be punished for his crimes.

He could not walk away from the evil that had shadowed his life, could not forget the purpose that had kept him alive all these years.

There could be no escape from this life until Falconer was dead.

Sabrina would object, of course, but there were some atrocities a man could not forget. Not even when it meant risking his own life and a new beginning. Going after Falconer now, when the Englishman was bound to know that Rafael had been looking for him, would be dangerous. Standing in the bright and bountiful room, Rafael smiled wryly to himself. He had always had the devil's own luck, cheating death at every turn. Would that good fortune continue, now that he had everything to lose?

"You look magnificent."

Rafael turned slowly toward Sabrina's soft voice. She stood near the top of the curved staircase, a vision in the white and gold gown, with pearls at her neck and dangling from her ears.

*"Vida mia."* Rafael stepped forward. "You take away my very breath."

"Don't we make a great mutual admiration society?" Sabrina asked as she continued down the stairs with a wide grin on her face.

· Rafael straightened the jacket of his white suit and waited for Sabrina to come to him. That meant ignoring the urge to run up the stairs to join her and take her in his arms. "I now regret that I extended invitations to the crew and their women," he admitted. "I do not want to share you, even for a short while."

He did not have nearly enough time with Sabrina before the crew and their wives arrived as a boisterous crowd, invading the festive room and immediately attacking the table. Elena was there, and though she gave him not a single glance, she did wear the rubies around her neck. Perhaps she was trying to forgive him.

Wine flowed, and the normally peaceful room was filled with shouts and laughter. Sabrina stayed at his side, quiet but observant and content, and when Cristóbal brought out his guitar, her smile brightened.

They began the first dance alone, but soon the others joined in. None of his men or their women had Sabrina's grace. They danced with enthusiasm, and often with a glass of wine in one hand and a hunk of bread or meat in the other. Rafael longed to fall into Sabrina's strange swaying dance, so he could hold her close and feel the beat of her heart against his.

A dance of a time yet to come.

"We'll leave soon, won't we?" Sabrina asked as he twirled her past the fireplace.

"*Sí*. Very soon, I think." Now was not the time to tell her that he had one more run to make before they headed for California and their new life. He did not want to ruin this evening, this celebration of their pledge, for her.

"I'm so excited."

It showed on her face. In pink cheeks, bright blue-green eyes, and a devastating smile. Sabrina's hair had grown in her time here, and it swung just above her bared shoulders. That sight, the tips of her soft hair teasing her flesh, was suddenly more than he could bear. "We should have had this party just for the two of us," he whispered. "If we were alone, I would have you on the pillows in front of the fire, *vida mia*."

Her smile widened. "Our guests won't be here all night, will they?"

"No."

It would be cruel to ruin the evening with the sharing of his decision. He would wait until this celebration was over to tell Sabrina what he had to do. Perhaps he would wait until after he had made love to her on the pile of soft pillows by the fireplace, until after he had told her again that he loved her. Perhaps he would spend all night showing Sabrina how he adored her, and by the light of the rising sun he would tell her what he had to do before they began a new life. He could not wait much longer that that.

The celebration was interrupted when Esteban crashed through the front door. The music stopped abruptly, the dancing came to an end, and all heads turned toward the door and a waiting Esteban.

"Ship coming in," the small man said breathlessly.

"Flag?" Rafael snapped.

"None."

The crew scattered to assemble their weapons, and the women followed their men closely.

"Who is it?" Sabrina asked as Rafael pulled away to gather his own sword and knife. They were never far away, even now.

"I do not know. Go to your chamber and stay there until I come for you."

"Rafael." Sabrina blocked his path. Surely she would not ask him to stay, to allow his men to endanger themselves while he waited within these walls. "Be careful," she whispered, and then she kissed his mouth quickly, a brief touch of her lips to his.

Sabrina paced in the darkness of her room, heedless of the full skirt that hampered her movements. She fingered the pearls at her throat, as if they were her own, extremely expensive, worry beads. Again she told herself she was probably worrying for nothing. Just because there was a ship approaching the island late at night, that didn't mean there was an attack coming. The men had scattered because they were cautious, not because they were frightened. Rafael wasn't necessarily in danger.

The dagger she had taken from César was grasped in one fist, as much a talisman as the

pearls. The weapon made her feel less vulnerable, though she doubted it would do her a bit
of good against a sword like the ones the English pirates had wielded against Rafael's men.
Still, she held on to the grip tightly, even when
her palm began to sweat.

There was enough cynicism left within her to
make her wonder if this wasn't happening because she and Rafael were so close to everything they wanted.

From her balcony she could see nothing of
the pier. There were no sounds of fighting, no
shouts or screams or explosions, but she wasn't
sure what noise would penetrate the thick foliage that surrounded this house.

Anything could be happening.

Sabrina wanted to rush to the pier and see
for herself what was happening, but Rafael had
asked her—had *ordered* her—to stay in her
room. So she stayed put, even though she
wanted nothing more than to be beside Rafael.
She'd distracted him once, as the English had
attacked the *Venganza*, and she wouldn't do that
again.

So she paced, and fingered the pearls that Rafael had given her, and gripped the dagger in a
sweaty palm.

The knock at her door was soft, but still Sabrina jumped. Rafael wouldn't knock. Ever.

With César's dagger held defensively before
her, Sabrina opened the door. She recognized
the man who stood calmly in the hallway but
couldn't name him. He was one of Rafael's crew
who lived on Tortuga.

He was a husky man who stood no taller than she, and he stared at her with wide, black eyes. "The captain," he said in guttural and unsteady English, "he is much hurt. He asks for you."

Sabrina almost ran him over as she left her room and hurried down the hall, lifting her skirt with both hands as she ran to the bottom of the stairs, only to stop suddenly. She didn't even know where Rafael was. The pirate passed her, brushing lightly by. Vestiges of the party remained in the main room, dying candles and empty tankards, dirty plates and glasses barely touched with wine. The pillows near the fireplace had been scattered, as if someone had walked right through them.

Nothing would happen to Rafael, not now. Life wouldn't be so cruel. Sabrina knew that was a lie, but she repeated the lie as if it were gospel again and again anyway, as she followed the pirate into the night, allowing him to lead the way to Rafael. He was headed quickly along the path to the pier, and Sabrina had to run to keep pace with the broad man who never looked back.

Docked beside the *Venganza* was another ship. Taller, longer, it sat silently in the water.

"What happened?" she asked breathlessly.

"*¿Qué?*" The man slowed as he turned to her.

"Never mind," Sabrina said, shooing him forward with the hand that clutched César's dagger. She would find out soon enough.

She recognized several of the men who stood on the deck of the larger ship, solemn Spaniards who watched her suspiciously. They had all been on board when Rafael had found her on the Florida beach.

"Here." The man who had led her to the ship pointed down, at an opened hatch. Narrow stairs led to a hallway below, and Sabrina struggled with her skirts to descend the steps.

There was a cabin to her right, and a pale light burned inside the small room. Her insides tightened at the uncertainty she faced, but she didn't slow her step. She had to know.

"Rafael." She rushed into the room prepared to face the very worst, only to find it empty. It took a moment for her brain to register that everything was wrong, and when she spun around the pirate who had brought her to this ship was blocking the doorway.

He stepped just inside the cabin and reached out quickly. Sabrina stepped back, but not before the pirate's fat fingers took the dagger from her hand, so damned easily. He not only snatched the dagger away but turned it against her. Moving much too fast for such a stocky man, he reached out and captured her necklace, ripping the pearls from her neck. A few pearls hit at her feet, landing against her full skirt and there on the cabin floor. The pirate who held César's dagger close to her heart grasped the damaged strand of pearls tightly in his deceptively fat hand.

She looked him in the eye. Was it going to end like this?

"So sorry, *Señorita* Sabrina," the pirate said softly as he backed slowly and cautiously away from her and into the narrow hallway to slam the door of the cabin closed. She heard the ominously heavy fall of a bar on the opposite side of the door, but it didn't stop her from attacking it with all her force. Her attempt was useless. The damned door didn't budge.

With a curse she turned away from the door, and for the first time took a good look at her surroundings. This cabin was much larger than Rafael's quarters aboard the *Venganza*, with a fair-sized bed, a table and chair bolted down, and a small empty bookcase. There was a single candle burning softly, and a supply of replacements in a dish nearby.

There was also a large bowl of fruit, a pitcher of water, and a chamber pot. She didn't know what she was doing here or why she had been taken, but whoever was responsible had planned this, and evidently had no intention of releasing her anytime soon.

"Idiot," she muttered under her breath. It had never occurred to her, as she'd blindly followed Rafael's man, that a trap might await her on this ship. All she'd thought of was Rafael.

Rafael. Sabrina's heart sank. She knew, without a doubt, that her only value to these men was as bait for their captain. If they wanted her dead, she would have been dead the moment she'd opened her bedroom door.

And he would come after her, would risk his life to save her. She didn't doubt that for a moment.

It wasn't fair. They'd been so close to everything they wanted. She loved Rafael, and he loved her. They had a lifetime to look forward to . . . and for a few days she'd been gloriously happy. Hell, maybe she wasn't *supposed* to be happy. Maybe it was her fate to fall short at every turn, in any time.

Sabrina knew it wouldn't do any good, but she kicked at the heavy door, and pounded her fists against the solid wood, and screamed shocking obscenities at the pirates who had taken her.

There was no break in her attack until the ship was underway. The movement of the craft changed sickeningly, and she almost lost her balance. The shouted insults resumed, and she screamed at the kidnappers until her voice was rough and her throat burned. There was no response. None.

The ship lurched, and a pearl rolled awkwardly across the floor. Sabrina knelt down and picked up the pearl, and then another one that traveled in a crooked path to land at her feet.

As she gathered the half-dozen pearls that danced across the floor, her anger gave way to fear. Where were they taking her?

# *Chapter Twenty-one*

There had been no attack of his island fortress, no battle to be fought, and Rafael made his way quickly to the house to tell Sabrina that all was well. As he made his way through the quiet night, an easy smile crossed his face. Sabrina waited, and there was a long and pleasant evening stretching before them.

What a surprise it had been to find his own men on the strange ship that bore down on his island in the dark of night. They were discontent with the recent long interludes when they were not at sea and had taken the ship they commanded from a drunken Dutchman. Gold did not last in the hands of these men, and they lusted for more.

It had taken some time to convince them that he was giving up this life, and more time still to explain his decision to the men who lived on this island with him—Pablo, César, Esteban, and the others. They had attempted to change his mind, all but a cheerless Pablo, who accepted his resolution with a deep frown but not a single word of protest.

There would be one more run, of course, and he would have to ask these men to join him on that journey. Once they arrived at Jamaica, though, they would wait at Port Royal while he finished his life's work. There was no mention of this final excursion as they stood around a blazing fire not far from Pablo's cottage. Now was not the time.

In the end his men had accepted his decision, and the Dutchman's ship had sailed with Rafael's blessing.

He entered the house through Elena's quiet kitchen, and his smile widened as he stepped into the main chamber. The fire was dying, flickering softly on the scattered pillows before it. Perhaps he would carry Sabrina down the stairs tonight, and make love to her in front of the fire, as he had promised earlier. Once they left this island, it would be months, perhaps years, before they were surrounded by such luxury.

It was not gold they would lack. He had treasures buried from the coast of Florida to Hispaniola, and they would arrive in California with a fortune to last a lifetime. Ten lifetimes. But it would take time to recover the treasure, to travel that great distance to California, to build a home again.

Rafael ran up the stairs, anxious to see Sabrina and to tell her that there was no danger. He called her name as he pushed her chamber door open, but immediately he knew she was not where she was supposed to be. The room was silent, and cold, and lifeless, and a warning chill traveled down Rafael's spine as he stood in the doorway.

"Sabrina?" Again, he spoke her name, in the hope that he was wrong, that perhaps she waited on the balcony for his return.

Why did she never do as he asked? From the moment he had seen her, she had proven stubborn. Did she search the pier for him? Had she run from this house with nothing but César's puny dagger for defense?

He descended the stairs quickly, angrily, his feet barely touching the steps as he flew. In her chamber she would have been safe, but Sabrina seemed to care nothing for her own safety. He would have to watch over her for the rest of their lives. It seemed that women from the future were much trouble.

Rafael followed the path to the dock, only to find it eerily silent. The *Venganza* sat quietly in the water, and the other ship had been gone for some time. There was no sign that Sabrina had come here searching for him, and yet he was certain . . .

There was no reason to worry, and yet he was troubled. This warning instinct had saved his life many times. The hair stood up on the back of his neck, his hands were cold and damp, and his heart thudded much too hard as he turned back to the house.

Where would she have gone? To Aqualina, who waited with Elena in Pablo's cottage? If that was true, why had he not seen her there? She would not have remained in the cottage once the danger was over. She would have joined him by the bonfire, most certainly. Perhaps she had searched for him and had returned home to await him even now.

The trees and vines grew so thick the moon barely lit his path. He hurried to the house in the shadows, hoping that this time he would find Sabrina there. Knowing, deep in his heart, that he would not. He finally left the heavy shroud of trees to see the moonlight shining fully on the front door, and at the sight before him Rafael froze.

César's dagger, unmistakable with its carved handle, had been impaled in the door, and pearls, Sabrina's broken pearls, were twisted around the blade.

It had been there before, as he had left the house in search of her, and he had not seen it. Had not known that the warning waited on the other side of the door through which he had stormed in his search for Sabrina. He took another step forward before he saw the note the dagger pierced.

Impatiently, Rafael tore the note from the door. He wanted to be wrong, prayed to be wrong, but he knew who was behind this. The note confirmed his fear.

Falconer.

Rafael burst into the house. Elena had begun to clear the plates and glasses that littered the table and even the floor, and when she looked up at him, when she saw the expression on his face, she dropped a glass so that it shattered at her feet.

"I need Pablo," he snapped. "And the others. He has taken her." Elena stared at him, and he realized he had spoken the order in English. He repeated the words in Spanish.

Elena ignored the broken glass on the floor, uttering a curse as she ran from the house to find her son.

Rafael climbed the stairs, the short note clutched in his hand. *You know where to find her.* The note had been signed with a large and lavish *F*.

From a trunk in his room, Rafael gathered his weapons. A pistol, a sword, his curved knife. He filled a leather bag with gold and at the last moment added Sabrina's emerald necklace. God only knew how—*if*—they would escape Falconer. If she had the emeralds, Sabrina would be able to start again. With or without him.

He jerked off the white jacket he had worn to dance with Sabrina and tossed it onto the bed, and with a thousand whispered curses he strapped the weapons at his waist. Every fear, every nightmare, was coming true. He had been right to refuse Sabrina all that she wanted, wrong to allow his love for her to weaken his resolve.

His men were waiting silently in the room below, and Rafael stopped on the top step. All eyes were on him, and the faces turned up to him were grim. He did not trust easily, never had, but these were the men to whom he had entrusted his life on more than one occasion. Now it was not only his own life he was forced to trust in their hands, but Sabrina's life as well.

"This time he has gone too far," Rafael said in a low voice that was surprisingly calm. "Falconer. He has taken her, my Sabrina, my wife. I cannot order you to come with me to save her. To risk your lives for this old *venganza*. It will be very dangerous, and I cannot promise you that any treasure waits on Falconer's plantation."

He waited for them—some or all—to move away, to throw up their hands in refusal, but no one left. No one even moved.

"I cannot order you, but I will implore you to accompany me. I need you all. Falconer will be waiting, and he will not be alone." Rafael leaned on his sword, used the sturdy blade to steady himself. "We may be forced to fight against men we have fought alongside in the past, the men who took her for Falconer. I do not know what awaits us, but I offer you this." For a moment it had seemed his strength was fading, but it was returning now, rapid and sure. "This house, this island, the treasure that is buried beneath the double palms near my cove."

For a long moment no one spoke. "I for one need no compensation for such a task," Pablo finally seethed to break the silence. "Falconer's blood is the only enticement I require."

"Still, it will all be yours." Rafael locked his eyes on his second in command. "I am not coming back. No matter what the outcome of this venture may be, I will never return to this island."

Pablo nodded his head slowly.

"Who is with me?" Rafael asked, stepping quickly down the stairs. "There is no time to waste."

It was soon clear that all his men were in agreement. Without question. Without reserve. They left to collect their weapons for the second time that night, and to ready the *Venganza* to sail.

Rafael stood near the fireplace and sharpened the knives he would carry with him. They were already razor sharp, but he could not stand still. The rasp of steel against stone calmed him, reminded him of what he had yet to do. Pablo was the first to return to the house, and he carried with him enough steel to arm the *flota*.

"This is for you, Captain," he said, offering a two-handed sword with a double-edged blade nearly four feet long.

Rafael took the weapon reverently. "This is your Toledo, your greatest prize."

Pablo turned away as if the gift were nothing. "Use it well, Captain. For all of us."

Sabrina sat on the edge of the bed and rolled a perfect pearl in the palm of her hand. She hadn't been able to sleep, hadn't really even tried.

It was only an estimate, since she saw no daylight and no meals were brought to her, but it seemed not much more than a full day had passed. She had no idea how long this journey might be, but if they planned to leave her completely on her own for the duration of the voyage, it wouldn't last much longer. The fruit, water, and candles seemed sufficient for a couple of days, three if she were very frugal. No more than that.

Was this Falconer's work? He was Rafael's greatest enemy, but considering Rafael's profession there were certainly others. The Frenchman Billaud he had battled, his own countrymen—the sailors of the fleet, other pirates, men from all over the world, from whom Rafael and his men had taken stolen treasure.

She didn't doubt for a moment that Rafael would come after her, any more than she doubted that that was exactly what her captors intended. She hated to admit it, but Rafael had been right all along . . . falling in love could end up costing him his life.

Her own life was far from secure, and had been from the moment she'd dropped from that pier and Patrick to land in Rafael's time. She was beginning to understand just how violent and uncertain this era was. A long and safe life was not assured. Hell, it wasn't expected by even the most careful person, much less by someone who lived a life of piracy. Like it or not, she was forced to accept the fact that once Rafael came for her, she was worth nothing to her captors.

Her only comfort was the certain knowledge that if anyone could do it . . . if anyone could save her and himself . . . it was Rafael.

By the time the pirate who had taken Sabrina came for her, she was as calm as Rafael's cove. She knew, logically, that hysteria would only hurt her chances for survival. Rafael would come, and she would be ready for whatever happened after that. Her serenity surprised the short and stocky pirate, and he watched her suspiciously as he led her from the cabin.

Sabrina still held one of the pearls she had picked up off the floor. She rolled it against her palm, and somehow it calmed her. It became a secret worry stone, a *thing* to focus on to keep her concentration from slipping. To keep her from falling apart.

It was night, a dark night but for the light of a sliver of a moon, and the dock across which they walked was deserted. All was ominously quiet, and the weathered boards beneath her feet gave the impression that this was an old and abandoned pier. There would be no one to call to for help, no one who was not in on the kidnapping, at least.

Alone, the man who had taken her from Rafael's island led her from the ship.

"I thought you were Rafael's man. Maybe even his friend," she said accusingly.

He was apparently not insulted. His only response was to lift broad shoulders. "Since you come he is changed. We do not sail the seas the way we once did, and I am poor again. When you are gone the captain will return to us and our days will once again be rich."

"You can't find another pirate to sail with?" Losing her temper wasn't going to help, but, dammit, this was so incredibly stupid. "The *Venganza* is not the only ship in the water."

He shrugged again as he led her carefully away from the ship.

"We are Spaniards," he argued. "The French and the English, they do not like the Spanish, and I refuse to sail with the *flota*."

"What's wrong with the ship you sailed from Rafael's island to this place? It's much larger and much better than the *Venganza*."

The dunce didn't get it. "We need our captain."

Sabrina shook her head. "You idiot. Whoever had you take me only wants to kill Rafael. You're leading him right into a trap."

The dimwit shook his head. "No. The Englishman, he only wants you."

The Englishman. It had to be Falconer. "Well, we'll see about that," Sabrina said easily. Once he realized she wasn't going to run, the nasty little pirate relaxed his grip on her arm.

There was no transportation awaiting them at the small, deserted dock, so they walked down a well-worn path that was rutted with wheel tracks. Dense growth lined the path, and Sabrina wondered with more than a twinge of misgiving what waited there. Critters, no doubt. Tiny and long reptilian monsters. Spiders. Insects of every kind.

The path was almost pleasant compared with the dark jungle that lined it. She'd never been brave. Not once in her entire life. Telling Rafael that she loved him had been the bravest thing she'd ever done, and look where that had gotten them.

One thought kept running though her mind. Without her, they'd have nothing to use against Rafael.

She broke away so quickly the pirate was surprised. He cursed loudly, but Sabrina was almost immediately lost in darkness. She plunged forward, not looking down, not even glancing to the side, but staring straight ahead into the jungle growth that threatened to restrain her, pushing past and jumping over anything and everything that got in her way.

She heard the surprised pirate following, and recognized a few of the curses he muttered, but he was clumsy and slow, and his size no doubt hampered him. After a few, very long minutes, he gave up. She heard him retreating, going to gather a search party, she assumed. Her pace didn't slow, not for a second.

What would she do when the sun rose? How long before the darkness that was her shield was gone? It would be difficult to hide, even here. The white-and-gold dress she wore would stand out like a beacon among the dark green. A touch of sun against the fabric and she'd be visible from yards away.

If she moved deeper into the jungle, stayed where the growth was dense, perhaps the sun wouldn't touch her at all.

There were no more thoughts of critters. She couldn't afford them. She forged straight ahead, ignoring the darkness, ignoring the exotic plants that blocked her way. More than once, she cursed her beautiful white gown and the full skirt that slowed her progress.

She ran until she was so tired her legs threatened to buckle beneath her. Too late, she realized that she should have gotten some sleep on board the ship that had brought her here. Two days had passed since she'd awakened to prepare for the celebration, and it was all catching up with her. Her body and her mind were shutting down.

Sabrina muttered beneath her breath, cursing herself as surely as the pirate she'd escaped had cursed her. She was so incredibly foolish. This was all her fault. None of this would be happening if she'd made Rafael leave the island days ago, when they'd first decided to go to California.

When she stumbled into the small clearing she couldn't resist sitting on the jungle floor and resting her back against a gnarled tree. Her legs shook and her heart was pounding, and she needed a few minutes . . . just a few minutes. She even closed her eyes, but only for a moment. Just one moment.

She could hide here, and maybe Rafael would be safe. There were bananas and other fruits she was beginning to recognize, and with a little care she could evade Falconer and his men. At least for a while.

A smile crossed her face as she saw Rafael's comforting face behind her closed eyes. It was as if he watched over her, even now.

\* \* \*

He should be sleeping, to rest and to prepare himself for what was to come, but Rafael stood at the rail and watched the sea dance in the break of dawn.

How could he sleep without Sabrina beside him? If he could not save her, how would he ever sleep again?

Pablo joined him but said nothing. There was nothing to be said, nothing that could change what was to come.

When the sun hit the ocean the world came alive, woke to another day that was like every other—and unlike any that had come before.

"Elena will be allowed to live in the big house as long as she pleases," he said softly.

"As you wish," Pablo answered without turning his gaze from the ocean before them.

"There is a small treasure buried along the path. Twenty paces from the front door and ten paces to the left. It is marked with a stone."

Pablo finally rotated his head slowly.

"Also for Elena," Rafael finished.

Pablo's answer was a low grunt.

"Under the carpet in the main room, there is a loose board." Rafael lifted his face to the sun. "Beneath there is a small sack of gold coins."

"Also for Elena?" Pablo asked brusquely.

"No," Rafael answered sharply. "For your daughter, when she is older."

The *Venganza* cut quickly through the water, taking him to his destiny.

"It is true," Pablo whispered. "You will leave it all behind."

Gladly, gratefully, if he was very lucky. "Have you ever thought of farming, Pablo?"

*One moment Rafael was there and everything was fine, and the next she was drowning, just as in all the nightmares that had come before. This time she wasn't alone. Rafael was still with her, and for once she wasn't cold. She was warm, even as she fought to find the surface and a badly needed breath of air. The light was different, too, she realized. In the past, this nightmare had always been dark. It was a part of the fear, that fear of drowning all alone in the dark and the cold.*

*But here there was light. It broke through the water in bright shafts that made everything beautiful, and still she fought to get to the surface.*

*It was impossible. She forgot the surface and reached for Rafael, but no matter how hard she swam, how desperately she tried, she couldn't get to him.*

*And then he smiled. Beneath the water, his hair floating around his head, the shafts of light encircling him, he was content. He didn't struggle to reach the surface, but beckoned to her.*

*She quit struggling and reached for Rafael again, and he was there. His hand was in hers, and then his warm arms wound around her body, and then his mouth found hers.*

When she opened her eyes, there was light. Not a lot, but a hint of dawn lit the small clearing. Sabrina realized with mounting dismay that not only had she slept, she'd slept quite soundly for hours.

She heard a faint crashing sound in the jungle

and realized that was what had awakened her. Men approached, hacked their way through the growth and toward her. They were close.

Sabrina stood and ran away from the approaching noise, but she hadn't gone far before her legs gave way beneath her and she fell to the ground. An excited shout rose in the jungle, not so very far away, and she knew she'd been seen. Damn white dress.

She jumped to her feet and ran, but before she'd gone far there was a hand on her arm that yanked her roughly back so that she was forced to spin and face the man who had stopped her. Pale fingers dug into her flesh, and she lifted her head to look up into the ashen and deceptively innocent face of Rafael's enemy.

Deep lines bracketed his mouth and reached from the corners of his eyes, and the ruffle at his throat couldn't completely hide the wrinkles there. This Falconer was no young man.

"Ahhh," he said, and he smiled as he tightened his grip on her arm. It was a smile that made her insides churn. "Rafael's whore." He said the ugly word gently, as if it were a caress. "I did have plans for our night together, you know, and you ruined them by running so obstinately. We could have had great fun." His eyes hardened. She had heard the term *heartless* all her life, and now she knew what it meant. "That was very thoughtless of you, dear. So many wasted hours. Rafael will be here soon, and now I must prepare."

"Damn you," she seethed, trying to pull away from him. "What do you want?"

He smiled, a soulless and cold smile that might have appeared attractive to someone who didn't know the man and what he was capable of. "What do I want? Very simple. I want Rafael dead, but first I want him to suffer. He has been a thorn in my side for years." He spoke as if Rafael were a pesky fly to be swatted away.

Sabrina tried to pull free, but Falconer held tight. "After what you did to him . . ."

"Oh, yes, the girl . . ." Falconer said absently as he threw Sabrina into the arms of a waiting pirate, one of a contingent of three. The man who held her gripped her arm even more tightly than Falconer had. She ignored the lackey who held her and watched as Falconer brushed a spot of dirt from his jacket.

"What girl?" Falconer ignored her and turned his back to her. He led the way, back through the jungle, and the pirate who held Sabrina propelled her forward. "What girl!" she repeated angrily.

Falconer glanced over his shoulder and gave Sabrina a wicked grin that chilled her, and she knew then that the vendetta that had ruled Rafael's life had nothing to do with the scars on his back.

"An entertaining story," Falconer said as he turned away from her. "Perhaps I'll share it with you as we ready ourselves for Rafael's arrival. There's not much time to waste, but perhaps as we make our way back to the house, I can recount the tale of how this all began."

Falconer pushed past dense growth, much of which had already been broken by her run last night and his progress as he and his men had searched for her. They had made a path of sorts, though it was almost impossible to see.

"Her name was . . ." He paused, as if trying to remember some insignificant detail. "Elisa, I believe. Yes, that was it. She was a pretty chit, but hardly worth all this trouble."

Falconer gave her an unemotional account of that time, years past, when Rafael had been an indentured servant, fourteen years old and smitten with a young girl who had come to live on his plantation. He told her, as casually as if he shared a recipe, how he had bought the girl from her father, and what he had done to her. Falconer spared her no detail, and as they stepped from the jungle and onto the path, Sabrina's stomach turned, so that she thought she would retch all over the pirate who held her.

He was unaffected by the telling of the tale. "I thought Rafael was dead, for several months, actually. And then," he said with a bit of animation, "that damned Spaniard came here, to my very own home, and tried to kill me." He spun around, and with a jerk lifted his shirt to reveal a small puckered scar on his side. "He stabbed me," he said, as if he still couldn't believe what had happened. "I really did think I was going to die."

Now he showed some enthusiasm. Some life. He'd shown none as he'd told her what had happened to Elisa.

"That's nothing like the scars on Rafael's back." Or on his soul. She didn't say that, wouldn't give Falconer the pleasure. And for a sick man like him, it would be a pleasure.

Falconer raised a fine eyebrow as he straightened his shirt and tucked the tail into his buff trousers. "He was a servant, no better than a slave. Rafael was mine to do with as I wished, as was the girl."

In spite of the nausea that still plagued her, Sabrina smiled. Her grin surprised Falconer. His pale eyes narrowed to slits, and that oh-so-pleased expression on his handsome face faded.

"You're going to die ugly," Sabrina whispered, leaning forward and pulling against the man who held her. "I can't wait to see it."

# Chapter Twenty-two

Falconer's place looked, to Sabrina, somewhat like a Southern plantation house. It was large and square and formal, beautiful and at the same time forbidding, even by the soft light of morning. Its austere sterility suited him, just as Rafael's enchanting and lavish home reflected his personality.

Her own condo, in the old life, had been clean and efficient. That two-bedroom home had been small, but not too small. There was, after all, no one else living there. In her well-ordered space there were no knick-knacks to dust, no clutter to distract from the classic lines of the gray furniture her decorator had chosen. Things would be different now, if she survived this.

She wanted to be surrounded by fat pillows and a room full of scented candles. Shocking red silk and ocean breezes. Bright flowers and deep green plants. She wanted color in her life.

The room to which Falconer escorted her was, as she expected, white and beige and formal. Heavy curtains hung over the tall windows of the second-story bedroom, and the bed that dominated the room was high and long. It was lovely and very, very cold.

A gown had been placed neatly across the bed, an ice blue monstrosity that was heavy with lace and sewn-on pearls. It was as pale and gaudy and arrogant as the house in which she was being held captive.

Sabrina didn't see the girl in the corner until the child stood slowly. It appeared she had been waiting, quietly, patiently, perhaps all night. Her dark eyes were wide and sleepy and, as she fastened her gaze on Falconer, afraid.

"This is Amelie," Falconer said as he placed the flat of his hand against Sabrina's spine and pushed her into the room. "She will help you prepare."

"Prepare for what?" Sabrina snapped as she spun around to face the gloating man.

"For Rafael's coming. It won't be long now. You are to wear the gown I chose for you, and Amelie will . . ." He waved his delicate hand over her head. "She will try to do something with your hair."

Sabrina glanced down at the stained and torn gown she wore, the white and gold Rafael had chosen for her, and then she placed a steady hand over her tangled hair. When she lifted her eyes to Falconer again, she managed a small smile. "No, thank you."

"I insist." His pale eyes were as icy as the gown he had provided for her.

"I prefer to wear what I have on, until Rafael arrives," she said calmly and steadily. She wanted nothing of this man but for him to leave her alone. "Actually, you have a lot more to worry about than what I'm wearing."

Falconer smiled, a sparkle in his disconcerting eyes. That sparkle chilled her, because it told her plainly that he wasn't worried at all. "Amelie," he called, lifting an inviting hand to the child as he stared boldly at Sabrina. "Come here, my dear."

Amelie took small, hesitant steps, staring at the floor as she obeyed the order. She was a thin little girl, with delicate wrists and hands, and her bowed head barely reached Sabrina's shoulder.

"Hurry along," Falconer prodded, and Amelie practically ran to the door.

Sabrina expected Falconer to take the child with him and leave her alone in the vast bedroom. Already she was thinking that there had to be a way to escape from this place. The window was a possibility. Her only possibility at the moment. When Falconer was gone and she could think more clearly, she'd come up with something.

Falconer placed his hand beneath Amelie's chin and forced the child to look up at him. He smiled, widely and completely, but Amelie was clearly terrified.

The blow Falconer delivered to the child's face was unexpected . . . at least to Sabrina. Amelie must have known it was coming, because she didn't make a sound. Not a whimper or a gasp of surprise.

Falconer turned cold eyes to Sabrina. "I don't want to hurt you," he said as if he were talking to a naughty child. His voice was calm, almost soothing. "At least, not yet. I want you to be in one piece, unmarked and dressed in that lovely gown I personally selected for you, when Rafael arrives. So, my dear, when you disobey me, I will punish Amelie instead."

"You son-of-a . . ." Sabrina stopped when Falconer very calmly lifted his hand. "Don't," she said softly. "I'll wear the dress, if that's what you want. I'll let Amelie fix my hair. Just don't . . . don't hit her again. She's just a child."

The hand Falconer had raised dropped slowly, to stroke Amelie's hair. His gaze raked over the child slowly, from head to toe. "Amelie will soon be a woman, isn't that right, my dear?"

"Yes, my lord," Amelie whispered. Her English was good, with just a trace of a French accent.

Sabrina took Amelie's thin wrist in her hand and pulled the child gently away from Falconer. "Get out," she said in a low voice when Amelie was safely behind her. If Falconer wanted to smack the child again, he was going to have to come through her. She didn't think he wanted to do that. At least, *not yet.*

He smiled at her, a cool grin that told her he viewed this encounter as an easy victory.

"Let me look at that," Sabrina said when the door was closed and the sound of a key turning in the lock reverberated through the room. A drop of blood beaded at the corner of Amelie's mouth, and Sabrina gently wiped it away with the edge of a dampened cloth she was no doubt supposed to bathe with. There was no tub, but a good-sized basin of water sat on the dresser, along with a short stack of neatly folded linen towels.

"It is all right," Amelie whispered impatiently. "We must hurry. If he comes back and you are not ready, he will be angry."

"I'm sorry he hit you. I didn't know . . ."

"Hurry," Amelie prodded.

The girl's hands were fast, and the torn and stained white gown was soon discarded. Sabrina was able to convince Amelie that she could bathe herself, but the girl waited impatiently, wringing her hands and pacing at the foot of the bed.

"Would you like to leave this place?" The question obviously surprised Amelie. Her eyes grew wide and her mouth dropped open.

"I am pledged for four more years."

Did Amelie know what Falconer had planned for her? Did she have any idea what the next four years could be like? Perhaps she did. The girl had paled when he'd mentioned that she'd soon be a woman. "I know, but . . ."

"My mother is here," Amelie interrupted, resuming her restless pacing, "and my little sister. If I were to run away, they would suffer." Sabrina scrubbed her skin, scrubbed away the dirt

328

and the scent of the jungle, the feel of Falconer's hand on her arm. "You know what he is like." Amelie's voice was a soft whisper, as if she suspected Falconer might be listening at the door. "He rarely punishes those who oppose him. Instead, he punishes the loved ones of his enemies. He says it is more . . . more effective and satisfying."

Everything fell into place as she listened to Amelie's words, clicking together as surely as the last pieces of a puzzle. Rafael's objection to love, his adamant refusal to have a child, all stemmed from his short time here on Falconer's plantation. He was afraid of having what he loved taken away.

And perhaps he had been right all along. Falconer was prepared and calm. He enjoyed the game. Rafael would be angry, hotheaded as he rushed headlong into Falconer's deadly trap.

"Someone's coming for me," Sabrina said, her voice a conspiratorial whisper to match Amelie's. "My husband, Rafael. If you change your mind . . ."

"Rafael? He is the Spaniard?" Amelie's question was whispered in awe.

"Yes." Sabrina dropped the linen towel into the basin of water, stunned by Amelie's sudden bright smile.

"I have heard such stories of a Spaniard, but I did not think they were true." Her smile faded. "I have only been here a few months, and sometimes I do not know what to believe. Who to listen to. Even if the stories are true, perhaps it is not the same man."

"What did you hear?"

Amelie was not content to stand idly and talk, but motioned for Sabrina to sit in a fat, white chair. As she brushed the tangles from Sabrina's hair, she spoke. "He comes in the night and without making a sound to whisk away those *he* has hurt."

Sabrina didn't think it was an accident that Amelie never referred to Falconer by name.

"The Spaniard comes like the wind, silent, without warning, and he rescues us. Some of us. Sometimes he sets a fire as he leaves, in the fields. Once, I hear, he set a ship afire, and it burned for a full day in the dock." Amelie sighed. "I think he would burn this house, but there are often others here. Not just *him*."

"You mean . . . children?"

"Yes."

Sabrina closed her eyes. Rafael, who claimed to have no nobility and love nothing, was a warrior. As brave as any soldier, as valiant as any knight.

"He'll be here soon," Sabrina whispered. "And this time I think he'll come more like a hurricane than a soft night breeze."

Rafael paced the deck, the Toledo sword gripped in his right hand as he readied himself to face Falconer. He waited, even though his instincts screamed at him to attack without delay. To run to that damned plantation and take Sabrina from Falconer.

Sabrina was not hurt. In order for this to work, he could not allow himself to believe that

Falconer had harmed her. Whatever the Englishman had planned for Sabrina, whatever his revenge, he would want Rafael to see it all. He would want Rafael to watch his wife die.

Surely Falconer was expecting an assault, a full and forceful offensive attack. He would have many men waiting for that attack, well-armed and battle-ready soldiers to fight off Rafael and his humble crew. The idea of storming Falconer's fine house with all his crew and a fierce battle cry appealed to Rafael's anger, but he dismissed the possibility.

Sabrina would have dismissed such a plan as being very impractical.

They waited in a small inlet that was shielded by heavy growth. Their route had taken them south of the island, and they had approached this boundary from a route that would not be visible from Falconer's dock. It had taken hours longer than necessary, hours in which Rafael had agonized over the plan.

What if he was wrong? What if every minute he delayed was a minute of torture for Sabrina? Right now, as he paced the deck of the *Venganza*, she was in Falconer's hands. The thought enraged him, and he hefted the Toledo to study the sharp blade in the moonlight.

He could not allow his emotions to guide him, not now. If he stormed the house as Falconer surely expected, he and Sabrina would both be dead.

This agony was his punishment for not killing Falconer years ago. After the first failed attempt, and Falconer's subsequent heavy guard, close access became difficult, and Rafael had convinced himself that punishing Falconer by taking his servants and burning his fields was enough.

It had never been enough.

If he had been successful in killing Falconer the first time, Aqualina would not have suffered. If he had sacrificed his own life in order to take Falconer's, others would not have suffered. Sabrina would be safe.

This time, Falconer would not survive. This time, Rafael would make certain the evil man was dead.

"Esteban," Pablo whispered, and Rafael turned to watch the spry little man clamber over the side.

"It is as you said it would be," Esteban revealed with a smile. "The docks are well guarded. There is an army of men waiting there. The house is surrounded as well."

"Did you see her?" Rafael asked gruffly, not caring how much his voice revealed.

"*Sí.*" Esteban's smile faded. "She is unhurt."

"She is in the house?"

Esteban nodded.

"Were you seen?" Pablo asked impatiently.

"No." It was clear Esteban found the question insulting. "I touched the house, peeked into several windows, and I saw the *señora* pacing in a large room that was filled with books."

"Did you speak to her?" Rafael snapped.

"No," Esteban said, and his arrogance faded. "There was no opportunity to tell her that tonight she will be free. She was not alone."

"Falconer?"

Esteban shook his head. "A child, a little girl."

Rafael lifted the sword in his hand and pointed toward the dense growth. "He is expecting an army, not one man. Alone, I can make it."

"No," Pablo protested. "We stay with your original plan. Through the hills."

The frustration was proving too much for him. Sabrina was so near, and there was still so much that could go wrong. "It will take too long. . . ."

"No," Pablo snapped, proving his own impatience was as close to the surface as Rafael's. "We take out the sentries one at a time, get the woman, and return to the ship the way we came."

"Falconer dies." Rafael eyed the sharp-edged blade of the Toledo. He could take Falconer's head off with this sword, and then he could leave the plantation knowing there would be no miraculous recovery.

"If he is near, and there is time. . . ."

Rafael turned to Pablo, and his first mate became silent at the stare he was given. "Falconer dies. If it becomes necessary, you will leave me behind and bring Sabrina here, to the *Venganza*. You will sail the moment all of you are on board, and if I am not here you do not hesitate. You do not wait. I want my wife off this cursed island."

Pablo remained maddeningly calm. "We will wait."

"I order you . . ."

Pablo was not listening. His mind was on the mission ahead, not on the argument with Rafael. His attention was riveted on the overgrown shore, his mind on the details of the plan they had formulated as they sailed to Jamaica. Finally, he returned his attention to Rafael.

"This is not the *flota*, Captain," Pablo said softly, "and you are no admiral. We will wait."

"Sit down," Falconer ordered in a petty voice that was just slightly too high-pitched.

Sabrina glanced over her shoulder. Falconer sat in a delicate chair in the library where she'd spent the last several hours, either in Amelie's company or with this despicable man. The outfit he wore for the evening was cream and tan, lace and satin as resplendent as her own elegant and ostentatious gown. He had been calm and assured all day, but now even his patience was wearing thin.

Taking a deep breath, afraid to defy Falconer even in this, Sabrina took a seat similar to his own, settling herself in a chair that looked much too fragile to sit in. She didn't want to see Amelie punished again.

Amelie had been dismissed some time ago, leaving Sabrina alone with Falconer.

"Perhaps he does not care for you as much as I had thought," Falconer said absently.

"Perhaps." Sabrina tugged at the high collar of the gown he had insisted she wear. The lace scratched her throat and tried to choke her. Her only relief came when she slipped a finger beneath the lace to give herself some breathing room. If that wasn't bad enough, Amelie had pinned her hair so tightly atop her head that she was suffering from a pounding headache that made her want to rip the pins from her head and the lace from her throat.

"Uncomfortable? Don't worry, I'll have you out of that gown before you know it." He gave her a cocky grin, a smile that wrinkled his face and narrowed his eyes to unreadable slits. "I am simply waiting for Rafael. Somehow, I thought he might like to watch."

Sabrina was careful not to allow her fear to show. Like the bogeyman in a horror story, this man *fed* on fear. Hers, Amelie's, Rafael's. And how many others? "Really," she said calmly. "I didn't think I was your type."

"You're not," he said quickly.

"I didn't think so." It was the greatest effort she'd ever made, but she smiled softly. "If it makes you feel any better, you're not exactly my type either. You're a gutless coward, a wuss who hides behind women and little girls."

He studied her as if he were watching a bug and trying to decide if he should step on it or set it afire. "You don't appeal to me at all," he whispered hoarsely. "Taking you will be a sacrifice I make in order to punish Rafael. Killing you will be a pleasure." He said the words so slowly and surely, Sabrina didn't doubt that they were true. "I don't know if I'll have the patience to do it slowly, as I should. We'll just have to wait and see."

"The thought of you touching me makes me sick," Sabrina snapped. She wanted to be calm,

# LINDA JONES

to beat Falconer at his own game, but his smug expression was driving her to distraction. "Why don't you do me a favor and kill me first?"

"I don't think so." He flicked absently at the lace that fell over his hand. "I have this planned to the last detail, you see, and I do so hate for my plans to be upset. My men have strict orders not to kill Rafael. They will bring him here, to me, and they will hold him while I force myself to ravish you."

"You won't touch me," Sabrina said softly. Falconer surely heard her, but he continued as if he hadn't.

"I will kill you with my bare hands," he promised with a smile. "My face will be your last sight in this life, and when you're dead Rafael gets what he deserves. I'll have him lashed to the very tree where he was disciplined all those years ago, flog him 'til I tire of the sport, and then, to be certain he won't come back this time, I'll eviscerate him and leave his entrails for the wild dogs."

Sabrina leaned back casually, forcing a calmness she didn't feel. "You get off on this, don't you? Scaring me. Telling me what you think you'll have a chance to do to me and to Rafael. Dream on, you sadistic creep."

Falconer was apparently unmoved. "You talk boldly for a woman who, it seems, has been forgotten. As I said, I do hate to change my plans, but if I must I'll send you back to Rafael." His eyes twinkled, and delicate fingers twitched in excitement. "One piece at a time."

Sabrina held her temper, stifled the urge to

jump from the chair and physically attack Falconer. The pleasure would be rewarding but fleeting, and definitely not worth the consequences. If he didn't hurt her with the sword at his side, he would take his revenge on Amelie.

Nothing she said seemed to touch him. He didn't react to her insults, and in fact apparently enjoyed their dangerous conversation. He was, right now, more amused than bothered.

"You pervert," she finally said. The lace at her throat was driving her crazy, and she tugged hard. She could barely breathe with the lace collar pressing against her throat. It would rip away with one good jerk, and still leave a decent neckline.

"Did Amelie do a poor job of dressing you?" Falconer asked with mock concern. "Must I punish her again for doing an inadequate task?"

Sabrina allowed her hand to drop into her lap. "No. It's fine. Really."

Falconer smiled at her discomfort. "You and Rafael make quite a pair. You're a great deal like him."

"Thank you."

"It wasn't a compliment, my dear," he said liltingly. "I was just making the observation that you two have the same failing. The same tragic sense of honor that will be the death of you both."

"You wouldn't recognize honor if it bit you on the ass."

He laughed out loud, and the echoes of his laughter sounded throughout the library. Such a sound of cheer was out of place in this house.

"You are so refreshingly candid," he said as his laughter died. "It will almost be a shame to kill you. Almost."

Where was he? Dammit, she'd expected Rafael long before now. It had been dark for hours, and she didn't want to spend a single night in this man's house.

Of course, Falconer had expected Rafael hours ago as well. He was getting antsy, though he was good at hiding his frustration. Sabrina knew Rafael was too smart to walk right into Falconer's trap. Did the Englishman know that, or did he think Rafael was simple-minded?

Doubts. If only she could plant a few doubts in Falconer's mind, Rafael still might have a chance. "I'm afraid you may have to kill me without the added pleasure of having Rafael watch."

Falconer lifted a fine, straight eyebrow. "And why is that?"

"He's not coming. I thought he might . . . even though we had that argument just a couple of days ago." She did her best to look forlorn. "He'd be here by now if he was coming. If he loved me, he wouldn't allow me to stay here for all this time." Her voice broke, just a little, and she realized that perhaps, deep down, she harbored her own doubts. "Rafael knows you too well, Falconer. He knows what you're capable of."

"What kind of argument?" Falconer asked softly.

Sabrina shrugged her shoulders. Rafael had always said she was a lousy liar. What if Falconer saw through her lies now? Best to stick as close as possible to the truth. "I'm afraid Rafael doesn't always appreciate my candor as much as you do."

It was nothing more than a flicker, there in Falconer's eyes. A flicker of doubt.

"I called him a pig," she explained. "Several times, actually. He didn't seem to mind that as much as when I told him that being a pirate was no better than being a common thief."

Falconer reached down and touched the hilt of his sword, his long fingers playing with the delicate scrollwork at the guard.

"If you must know," she continued softly, and with just a touch of melancholy in her voice, "we were lovers, but for Rafael there was never anything more than that." The words came so easily, because Sabrina remembered all that Rafael had said to her when he had offered her pleasure and nothing more. "I can be easily replaced," she whispered.

"I don't think so," Falconer said softly, but he faltered slightly.

Sabrina turned her face to the window and the blackness beyond. "If Rafael was going to rescue me, he would have done it already."

Falconer had no response to that whispered assurance.

# Chapter Twenty-three

Torches burned brightly at each corner of the house, lighting the grounds but leaving fragments of complete darkness where no firelight touched. Rafael crouched in the shadows. César was a short distance away and to his left, and had already dispatched the guard at that post. Esteban was to the right, and Rafael awaited his signal. A silent Pablo waited at his side.

Nervously, he fingered the knives that he had attached to his belt. They were ready. *He* was ready. The waiting was torture.

There were men, his men, at the front of the house, and Rafael could only hope that they had found the same success as César and Esteban. So far all was well, the silence assured him. There were no shouts of alarm, though he waited for that cry to break the night's stillness.

When their jobs were done and the house was

secure he would enter with no one but Pablo to assist him while the rest of his crew, surrounding the house in place of Falconer's men, kept watch. Once Sabrina was out of the house they would all abandon their posts and escort her to the *Venganza*. He had commanded it.

At last the signal came from Esteban, a raised hand at the edge of the lighted ground, and Pablo left Rafael's side. He would circle around the house, see that all was secure, and only then would Rafael move forward.

It was by far the most difficult maneuver he had ever participated in. Sitting and taking no action at all while Sabrina waited for him to save her, holding back while he waited for the others to do their part . . . it was truly torture. He held to the plan only because it was safest for Sabrina.

Rafael took a deep, calming breath. He could not afford this anxiety, and so he looked ahead to a moment when the waiting was over. When Sabrina was safe and in Pablo's hands, Falconer would pay. Leaving Jamaica without assurance that Falconer was done with this life was impossible to comprehend.

Not for the first time during this long day, Rafael wondered if it was possible that Sabrina carried his child again. For so long he had fought her, denied her as he had denied himself, but now he admitted that he wanted it to be true.

If he died here, then Sabrina would have something of him. Such a powerful and undeniable truth, and she had whispered that truth against his chest as she had cried for the child that was lost. A babe would be a bit of both of them, proof that they had found love and perhaps even a force more powerful than love. Rafael wanted to leave Sabrina with a remembrance besides the gold Pablo was instructed to give her should he not survive.

Why did he, even now, envision with such yearning a child of his own? He had refused Sabrina for this very reason. *Venganza.* He had lived his life so carefully, and still his worst fears had come true. The one person on this earth he loved was in danger because she was his. There was no other reason for the peril she was in now.

And yet he knew he would not trade the months that had passed since he had found her. Not for treasure, not for revenge, not even for his own life. Heaven above, he would not sacrifice those months even for Sabrina's safety now.

He had stopped believing in many things long ago. God. Justice. Honor. Love. Still, he could not believe that Sabrina had come to him from such a distance only to be used against him by his enemy. And as he waited he found that he wanted to believe in everything he had lost. . . . He wanted everything Falconer had taken from him.

"It is secure," Pablo whispered. The big man had approached so silently—or else Rafael had been so lost in thought—that he had not heard him coming. "She is in the southwest corner room, and he is with her."

342

Rafael tested the weight of Pablo's Toledo sword in his hand. "Then it is time," he said calmly.

He left the shadows and walked boldly to the rear entrance of Falconer's house, with Pablo directly behind him, and without hesitation entered the hell that still occasionally visited his nightmares.

Without slowing his stride, Rafael kicked open the library door. He gave Sabrina a quick glance, just enough to assure himself that she was unhurt, and then he turned his stare to Falconer.

Rafael lifted the Toledo and pointed the tip at Falconer's heart as the Englishman stood.

He had waited a long time for this moment. For justice. For *venganza*. "Surprised?" he asked, twisting the tip of the blade that had not yet pierced Falconer's fine cream jacket. "You appear to be somewhat bewildered. Did you think I would come with an army, shouting and screaming as we attacked? Did you think rage would carry me to you again?" The tip of the Toledo disappeared beneath cream satin. Just the tip. "I am not a child any longer."

Falconer wore a sword with a fine, thin blade but had not touched the scrolled grip. Rafael took a step forward, and Falconer backed away so the steel of the Toledo would not pierce his heart. The almost simultaneous movement was repeated three times, very quickly, until Falconer's back was against the wall.

"*Sirena mia*, did he hurt you?" He did not take his eyes from Falconer's face, could not. If he looked at Sabrina now his control would be gone.

"No." Her answer was soft, and he realized that she had not left her chair.

"Then perhaps I will kill him quickly."

In a panic, Falconer made an attempt to draw his sword. Rafael saw it coming in the pale eyes, in the twitch of effeminate fingers, and before the sword could be raised the Toledo swung down and to the side, slicing through the satin of Falconer's sleeve and deeply into the flesh. The thin-bladed sword clattered to the floor, and once again the blade of the Toledo touched Falconer's heart.

He had waited a lifetime for this, had waited half his days to stand before this man with a sword between them. This was his right, Sabrina's justice, Falconer's due, but Rafael suddenly did not want Sabrina to watch. She had seen enough. Behind him, her gown rustled softly as she stood.

"Come with me," Pablo said softly from the doorway.

"No. We wait for Rafael." Her voice shook, though she tried to hide it. She tried to be so strong, always.

"*Sirena mia,*" Rafael began, twisting the blade slightly. "*Vida mia.* Go with Pablo, and do as he says as if his words are mine."

"I'm not going to leave you here," she insisted, her voice an indignant whisper.

Rafael glanced over his shoulder for a quick look at Sabrina. One too-quick glimpse of her face and the love he always saw there; that was all he could allow himself. Watching her was a luxury he could not afford, and he immediately returned his gaze to Falconer's colorless face.

"Go with Pablo, now," he insisted. "This will not take long. I will soon be with you." In the distance, a shout went up, and Falconer smiled crookedly.

"You'll never leave Jamaica. You might kill me, but my men will slaughter you and leave your body for the wild dogs."

Rafael ignored the promise. "Do not wait for me," he ordered in a low voice. "If you reach the *Venganza* and I am not behind you, sail."

"No," Sabrina said softly.

"Sabrina . . ."

"No!" He could hear her moving forward, quick steps that would soon bring her to him.

"Pablo," Rafael said softly. "Get my wife away from this place. Now."

The sounds of Sabrina's protest were soft and brief. Surely she knew this was for the best, and perhaps she even realized that he could not finish what he had to do with her eyes on his back.

"Your wife," Falconer whispered, more to himself, it seemed, than to Rafael. "Now *that's* a surprise."

Pablo's heavy footsteps and the rustle of Sabrina's gown finally faded away to nothing.

"Well," Falconer said casually when they were alone, "this is hardly fair."

"Fair?" Rafael repeated incredulously. "You want what is fair?"

"I am unarmed. If you kill me now, it's murder." What a sensible and calm argument he offered. "Cold-blooded, unjust murder."

Rafael stood close to Falconer, with the Toledo angled upward and still touching the fine satin jacket.

"What do you know of justice? Nothing. You murdered Elisa, and how many others?" In a flash of uncontrollable anger, Rafael drew, left-handed, one of the knives from his belt and swung the blade upwards to cut Falconer's cheek from his chin to just beneath one wide eye. It was not a deep cut, but blood welled up quickly and dripped to his once pristine collar.

Rafael used the knife to pin Falconer's right arm to the wall. The blade pierced lace and cream satin, there at a finely crafted cuff, but no flesh. Falconer flinched just the same.

"You use children for pain and for your sick pleasures, destroying their lives."

"They are nothing," Falconer said softly, raising his left hand slowly to his cheek to touch a rivulet of blood that marred his ashen skin. "Men like us," he said calmly, "we're different. We take what we want and say to hell with the rest of the world."

Rafael did not like being compared to a man such as Falconer. "I want you dead," he seethed, gripping the sword with both hands.

Falconer stood helpless against the wall, his face and arm bleeding, and Rafael tightened his hands on the Toledo's grip.

"Wait." The single word was a plea. "At least make it a fair fight. Let me have my sword."

The word *fair* coming from Falconer's mouth was blasphemy. Before another word could be said, Rafael had pinned Falconer's left arm to the wall with another of his knives. Again, no flesh was pierced.

"Did you make it a fair fight when you killed Elisa?" Rafael breathed. He had never been so close to Falconer, and he saw now that this monster was just a man. An evil man, who did not deserve to live. "When you took Aqualina to your bed and hurt her so that she did not speak for more than a year, was that *fair*?" His voice did not—could not—rise above a whisper.

"When you whipped me to the point of death, were there any thoughts of what was *fair* in your heart?" Beyond all reason, he wanted to hear Falconer admit that he was wrong, wanted to see the man grovel before him. But Falconer did not grovel, and there was no more time for this. Men were approaching—Falconer's men.

"What do you want?" Falconer asked. His voice was calm, but Rafael could finally see the fear in his eyes. "This plantation? My treasure? A dozen ships? Name it, and it's yours. I'll retire to England, and this time I'll remain there."

Rafael shook his head.

Falconer opened his mouth to argue, perhaps to offer more, but never got the chance. Rafael put all of his strength into the thrust that pierced Falconer's cold heart. He screamed as he attacked with such force that the broad and glittering blade of Pablo's Toledo sword exited at Falconer's back and pinned him to the wall of his luxurious library.

Blood stained Falconer's jacket, bright red on cream satin, and Rafael released the sword and backed away, watching for a long moment until he was sure the Englishman was truly dead.

Men were in the house, and coarse English shouts confirmed Rafael's suspicions that it was Falconer's army who approached. He swept the lightweight sword from the floor, in case there came a need for it, and left by way of the window, leaving Falconer pinned to the wall for his men to find.

"We're not sailing without Rafael," Sabrina insisted when she saw the *Venganza*. Pablo was beside her, and the others—César, Esteban, the guitar player Cristóbal, and three more, were directly behind. They shielded her quite effectively from any attack that might come from the direction of the plantation.

They'd surrounded her protectively over hills and through a dense forest that was nothing like the jungle in which she'd spent the night, and now they had almost reached their destination. Rafael still had not caught up.

"The captain, he gave his order," Pablo said gruffly.

Sabrina stepped into the calm waters of the inlet and to the rope ladder, climbing swiftly, all the while watching the path they'd followed for Rafael. Where the hell was he?

Any moment, she thought as she paced the deck. Rafael would come bursting through the forest and onto the beach at any moment. A wind rose, and clouds blocked the moon. With a concerned murmur, Pablo lifted his head to the changing skies.

Impatiently, Sabrina ripped the pins from her hair and tossed them over the side. The lace that scratched her throat followed, torn from ice-blue silk with a violent wrenching of her trembling hand.

"Come on," she whispered, her words a plea as she watched the beach.

The crew was readying the ship to sail, and every second that ticked past brought them closer to deserting Rafael. She wouldn't let that happen.

Pablo was watching the beach just as intently as she was, and it was surprisingly simple to slip beside him, grab the knife from his belt, and point the sharp blade at his massive belly. He looked down, without so much as a hint of surprise on his surly face, and then turned black eyes to her face.

"We wait," she ordered softly, and Pablo lifted a hand to still the crew.

Perhaps it was only minutes that passed, but it seemed like hours. The *Venganza* was ready to sail. The crew waited expectantly, and Pablo effectively ignored the knife Sabrina held against him, steady and threatening. Everything was still, the air, the sea, until at last Rafael emerged from the darkness surrounding the growth of trees. She held her breath, waiting for the army that might be following, but behind him all was silent and still.

Pablo took the knife from her so quickly and easily, she didn't know what was happening until the weapon had been taken from her hand and returned to Pablo's belt. He didn't even bother to look at her or at the knife as he accomplished this easy task.

When he did finally look at her he actually smiled, and she realized that he could have taken the knife from her at any time. She didn't doubt it.

Sabrina forgot Pablo and their little game, and when Rafael scrambled over the side she was there, grabbing an arm so she could touch him, so she could assure herself that they were really together. She touched a spot of blood that marred the perfect whiteness of his shirt, realized with blinding relief that none of it was his, and pulled her hand slowly away.

"They are coming?" Pablo asked, and he turned his attention to the shore.

"No." With an impatient swing of his arm Rafael tossed the sword he carried into the ocean. The bloodstained shirt followed, sailing through the night and into the sea, and then he gathered Sabrina into his arms.

"Did he hurt you?" he asked for the second time.

"No," she assured him.

"I did not want to leave you there for so long, but it was the only way."

She could hear regret in his voice, and sorrow, and helplessness.

"It never crossed my mind that you might not come for me," she said, "but I never expected you to come breezing into the room with a smile on your face, as if you were dropping in for tea."

Sabrina lifted her head to look at him, and a

stiff breeze pushed his hair away from his face, so that even in the dark she could see the features she loved, the eyes that soothed her with a glance.

He kissed her, a light brush of his lips against hers that became many little kisses.

They sailed away from the cove, and Sabrina turned her head to find that Pablo watched them from no more than two feet away.

Rafael gathered her against his chest. "Pablo, I am afraid I left your Toledo behind."

Pablo lifted his big shoulders in an unconcerned shrug. "You put it to good use?"

"*Sí.*" A brief explanation that apparently satisfied Pablo followed, but it was in rapid Spanish that Sabrina had no hope of following.

She waited until Pablo had moved away before she spoke. "He's dead?"

"He is dead," Rafael confirmed.

It was such a relief, to know that that evil man was gone. That he wouldn't hurt anyone else again, that Amelie would be safe. "Good," she whispered.

"I thought I would know satisfaction when I finally killed Falconer, but there was none," he revealed softly. "He had to die, he had to be stopped, but there is no comfort in revenge."

Sabrina slipped her arms around Rafael's waist and held on tight.

They were not far away from Jamaica's shore when the waters began to dance wildly. Rafael kept his arms around her, and they watched the sea silently. Wind whipped against them and around them, but they didn't move from the rail.

"Where are we going?" Sabrina asked softly.

"Cuba."

"What's in Cuba?"

Rafael looked down at her and smiled. "A bit of treasure for a new ship. Then we will sail to a small island not far north of there to recover a chest I buried some years ago."

"And then to California?"

"*Sí*. Well, perhaps we will take one or two more quick trips to recover a *bit* of gold."

"A bit?" She wasn't certain what a pirate thought of as a *bit* of gold.

"Enough for a lifetime."

The wind picked up, fast and bitterly cold, and Sabrina shivered.

"*Vida mia,*" Rafael whispered into her ear. "I need you."

They slipped into the cabin without another word, and in the darkness Rafael came to her. He kissed her, held her tightly against his body so that she could feel the beating of his heart and the insistent press of his arousal against her belly. His lips claimed her, as insistently and surely as he had always claimed her as his own. His gift, his mermaid, his life.

Rafael's hands left her only long enough to loosen his belt and drop it to the floor, where it landed with a loud thud that reminded Sabrina briefly of the weapons he always wore there, and then his body was pressed tightly against hers again.

With a low groan, he raised her skirt impatiently, lifted her in his arms, and stepped forward so that her back was pressed against the wall. Without hesitation, without a single word, he thrust inside her quickly and fully, satisfying the shared need to be joined, to be one. Sabrina wrapped her arms around his neck and threaded her fingers through his soft curls. With his touch he wiped away everything ugly that had come before.

He took her hard and fast, surrendering to a demand that was primal and comforting and savage. In moments the completion shattered her, and Rafael came with her, over the edge, into their own world.

Rafael became still, so very still, and he held her there with his arms cushioning her and his head against her shoulder. Finally he whispered, soft and beautiful words she was beginning to understand.

For a while longer he stood there, his head resting warmly against her, his breath in her hair, and then he carried her to the narrow cot.

"I knew the moment I saw you in the sand, with the ocean washing over your body, that you were mine," he said as he began to work the ties of her gown. "I knew that you would change my life, that you would possess me as no one ever had. But I did not know that you would become a part of me, that I would never have enough of you. That I could not live or think or even breathe without you."

He removed the gown slowly, kissing the flesh he bared to the night air.

"Do you know how much I love you?" Sabrina

# LINDA JONES

asked as he came to her. This time, there was nothing between them. He pressed his bare chest against hers, rubbed a leg against her thigh.

"*Sí,*" he whispered. "That is the most amazing gift of all. The most wondrous of all these wonders you have brought to me, is that you love me."

He made love to her again, slowly, luxuriously, and as the squall surrounding the *Venganza* increased, they made a storm of their own.

354

# Chapter Twenty-four

The storm that tossed the *Venganza* did not lessen as the night passed, but intensified, so that the ship rocked violently. Rafael left Sabrina sleeping peacefully, with a whispered promise to return soon.

He had nothing to wear but the white trousers that had been splattered with Falconer's blood. The spots of dried blood were not as many as those that had stained the shirt he had tossed into the sea, but they were a reminder of the night that had passed.

With Falconer dead, there was nothing to keep him from a new life with Sabrina. California. A vineyard, she said, or beeves. She called them . . . cattle. He found that he smiled down at her. His father had been right, all those years ago. A farmer. A house full of children. It was just as well. Piracy had begun to bore him, anyway.

He would never be bored with Sabrina.

With an absentminded touch, he fingered the full leather sack that hung at his belt, a heavy pouch that hung there beside the remaining knives he wore. His fingers fluttered from the leather pouch to the knives. Pablo's perfect weapons.

He himself preferred the perfectly deadly weapon of a woman's body. Sabrina's body, coming without pause to his with all the heart and soul she possessed. Taking him in, loving him, and changing every truth he had always accepted without question.

One by one he removed the sharp knives from their sheaths and placed them, point down, into the floor, there in the corner where they were lost in shadows. From all that he could remember, farmers did not carry such weapons.

With a final glance at a sleeping Sabrina, Rafael climbed from the cabin.

It was morning, but the sky was ominously dark. The *Venganza* was surrounded by black clouds and angry waves that crashed over the deck, as if the devil himself attacked.

Sabrina opened her eyes knowing Rafael was not in the cabin. The bed was cold and empty without him, and there was no sound but the roar of the storm that refused to relent. Her stomach lurched with each roll of the little ship, and she gripped the edge of the cot tightly—as if that would do her any good if the *Venganza* capsized.

Getting dressed was difficult. If there had been any other option, she would not have worn the ice blue silk Falconer had chosen for her. It had not been made for one who had to dress without assistance, and there was too much fabric to battle with as the cabin rocked and rolled. The laces were in the back, of course. Contorting herself, she managed to tighten the laces from her waist to halfway up her back—enough to keep the gown from falling completely off.

She stayed in the cabin, waiting impatiently for the storm to abate. It should have blown over long ago, but it was as strong as ever. Perhaps it was even growing stronger. She was certain that was true when the ship's lurch intensified, tossing her about, and water poured through the opening in the ceiling.

Without a second thought she scrambled up and out, away from the threat of drowning in the small cabin. What awaited her on deck was just as frightening.

The crew battled the storm, and they were losing. Sails were ripped, and waves crashed over the side of the ship, threatening to wash them all away. Hard rain pounded the deck and the pirates, and the wind . . . the wind was brutal and violently forceful.

No storm should last this long or be this powerful, unless they had sailed right into a hurricane.

Rafael was at the center of the ship, working

with César and Franco as they attempted to lower the damaged sail. Rain beat against his face and his body, a rain that fell so hard it was as if a cloud of gray separated him from her, made him less real.

The shelter of the aft bridge provided no relief at all from the rain and the wind that assaulted the *Venganza*. The wind whipped her skirt so hard, she felt it might pull her into the sea, and the rain pelted her until she was soon soaked to the skin just as Rafael and the rest of the crew were. She stayed near to the cabin's entrance, reached out and grabbed the nearest rigging to latch herself onto the sturdy rope. Without it, she was certain a gust would carry her away.

The roar of the wind was deafening. A hurricane, a storm like this, was a force to be frightened of. Her lifelong irrational fear of water had nothing to do with the fright that grabbed her now.

There was no land in sight, though they could have been right upon an island and wouldn't have known it. The slanting rain cut her field of vision dramatically, so that there was nothing in this world but the *Venganza*, her crew, and the storm.

When he had the ripped sail down, Rafael came to her. His pants were soaked and clinging to his legs, his hair was plastered to his head, and his body dripped with water, rain, and the waves that continued to crash over the sides of the *Venganza*.

"Where are we?" She screamed into his ear so he could hear her. "Are we close to Cuba?" It was a stupid question, and she realized it as soon as the words were out of her mouth. There was no radar to guide them, no radio to call for help, and the crew surely felt, at this moment, as isolated and lost as she did.

"We were blown off course last night," he yelled, and still she could barely hear him. "North. I am not sure exactly where we are." Rafael placed a wet hand against her cheek. "Wait below."

Sabrina shook her head. "No. I stay with you. Besides, I'm just as likely to drown down there as I am up here." She didn't want to argue with Rafael, not now, but the idea of being trapped in that cabin as it filled with water was too much to face.

He kissed her quickly, and left her to cling to the rigging. When all the sails were down and had been deposited in the hold, the crew did as she already had . . . they each found something to hold on to.

She didn't know which was more brutal, the wind or the sea that pounded them. Rafael made his way to her, battling the wind and the waves to reach her. When he was with her he grabbed onto the rigging and placed his body between her and the worst of the wind.

Impossibly, the winds intensified, until Sabrina was certain the ship would be lifted from the waves and carried into the sky. Waves rose high, far above the sides of the ship, and crashed down with unbearable force. Sabrina watched as one pirate, the normally quiet Franco, was lifted and tossed into the sea. His mouth was opened wide, but his screams were lost in the roar of the wind and the crash of the waves.

Rafael tried to protect her, as he had from the moment she'd come to his time. He held on to her as tightly as he held the rigging that kept them from flying into the ocean, wrapped his arms around her head so that her face was buried against his shoulder. Even with that protection Sabrina felt as if she would sail away at any moment.

Destiny. From the start, Rafael had tried to convince her that destiny had brought them together. That fate had deposited her at his feet. But it seemed to her that something had been trying just as hard to pull them apart.

They could fight their own failings, they could fight the Falconers of the world . . . but how could they fight a force of nature like this?

When the wave came it crashed over them both, drenching their bodies and making it impossible to breathe. When the wave receded, withdrawing with a power that was impossible to comprehend, it lifted Rafael as if he weighed nothing, ripped him with a violent jerk from her and the rigging.

She reached for Rafael as his arms were pulled from her, and even managed a fleeting touch to his hand before he was whisked away from her. He was there, and then, in a heartbeat, he was gone.

Sabrina loosed her hold on the rigging and looked squarely at the storm. Rafael was gone, torn from her hands by the sea and the wind.

Her heart stopped, her hands trembled, and when the next wave came and washed her away she wasn't even surprised. Her last sight was of Pablo, who still managed to hold on. He watched her with a stunned and pained expression on his face, as she was carried into the turbulent ocean.

It was too much like her nightmare. The light, the darkness, the agitated sea around her. She was drawn downward, even when she fought and kicked and pushed against the sea as she tried to find the surface.

The soaked skirts of her gown pulled her down, down into the murky waters. Her effort was useless, and still she fought. Somewhere, perhaps just beyond her reach, Rafael shared her struggle. He fought the same waves, the same storm. Dammit, if they had to die like this they should at least be together.

She couldn't even see the surface anymore. . . . Her lungs burned, and her chest ached, and the world went black.

"She's probably drunk. Don't get too close," a voice hissed. The speaker was close by, but not too close, and Sabrina opened her eyes to the sun and the sand and two girls who stared down at her curiously. They wore teeny bikinis, but then, they were just kids, teenagers who could still get away with wearing something like that.

They backed away as Sabrina sat up.

"Rafael?" She rose to her feet, eyes on the calm ocean before her. The girls ran, glancing over their shoulders as they made their escape.

Sabrina ignored them. If she'd made it, maybe
. . . She shook her head, knowing it was impossible, but she shouted again, calling his name,
searching the beachfront frantically.

She walked through the waves that crashed
gently over her feet and the soaked silk skirt,
and in spite of the impossibility of her hopes,
she searched the shore for a sign. A body, a
scrap of three-hundred-year-old wood, a few
pieces of eight scattered in the sand. People on
the beach, the snowbirds and the tourists, drew
away from her, pulled their children from her
path protectively.

Whispers followed her. *Drunk. Crazy.*

Was she crazy? Had it all been a dream? A
glance down proved that her journey had been
real enough. She still wore the damned gown
Falconer had forced her to wear, though it had
been torn and soaked by the storm and whatever power had brought her here. Whatever had
happened, it hadn't been a hallucination or a
dream.

Her wedding ring glinted brightly in the sunlight, and she lifted that hand slowly. *Autre ne
veux.* It had all been real.

"Rafael!" She stepped into the ocean. The
skirt floated around her legs, dancing in the
calm waves as she moved unerringly forward
and into the sea.

He wasn't here. He'd lived more than three
hundred years ago, and against all reason she
had found him, and loved him, and been ripped
from him before they'd had a chance for a safe
and long life together.

362

She'd never expected life to be fair, but this was so unfair it made her angry, and, dammit, it hurt. There was a pain, a real ache deep in her chest. If anyone on this earth deserved a little justice, a little happiness, it was Rafael.

Directly before her, yards away, the water broke. With a splash and a great intake of air, Rafael rose from the sea. His eyes were on her as he swam toward the shore, and he stood as he neared her to walk through the gentle surf and unerringly into her arms.

She'd never seen or touched anything more beautiful, more wonderful than a dripping wet and wondrously warm Rafael.

He held her tight. "Your world?" he asked, amazement in his soft voice at her ear.

"Yes."

"I thought it was over, that we would not have a chance, and then the sea calmed and I came to the surface and I saw you, splashing about in the waves as if you have no fear."

She wouldn't let him go. Couldn't. "We made it," she whispered, the wonder of that statement almost lost in the roar of the waves. "We made it."

They sat side by side in the sand, and Sabrina's knees quaked, still. Rafael had led her from the ocean, an arm around her waist and his eyes on the changed skyline, quite some time ago. She didn't know how long they'd been sitting here. An hour? Maybe no more than fifteen minutes.

"At least I am not naked, as you were when I

found you," Rafael said thoughtfully.

Sabrina lifted her hand to his face, so he could see her wedding band. "And I have this. I think because it already existed. We brought the past with us."

Rafael reached out and brushed a few grains of sand from her face, and Sabrina smiled.

"I can't go back to the way things were before," she whispered. "I don't want to. I'll sell the business, and with the profit we'll buy an island in the Caribbean." Her smile faded. "Well, I'm not likely to get that much for it, but maybe we could get a condo somewhere."

"A condo?" He closed one eye skeptically, and Sabrina motioned to the buildings over her shoulder, a balcony at every identical unit.

Rafael grimaced and slipped his arm around her waist. "I know how you like to make plans, *sirena mia,* but perhaps this one time you will allow me to make a contribution to your strategy."

"What kind of contribution?" The water lapped not far from their feet, with a comforting splash and a gentle ripple.

"To start," Rafael said casually, "keep your business or sell it. It matters not." He disengaged a leather pouch from his waistband and dropped it unceremoniously in her lap.

Sabrina peeked inside, and sunlight sparkled on emeralds that were nestled on a bed of gold coins. It was that awful, ugly necklace he had thought she'd love. "Rafael, do you have any idea what this is worth here?"

"No."

"Hundreds of thousands, I'm sure." She closed the bag tightly, before anyone else could get a glimpse. "With this we could . . ."

"With these jewels you detest so, we can buy a ship, something small, I think. I will teach you to sail, and you will have your island and anything else you wish for." He leaned close and kissed her neck. "Anything."

She couldn't bear to tell him that those hundreds of thousands wouldn't be near enough to buy a boat and an island and everything else they would ever need. "You're all I ever wanted."

He grinned, that brilliant grin that made her heart skip a beat, and kissed her lightly. "You will have your island, if you wish it, or your vineyard, if it pleases you. But first, I think, we will set sail and search for the treasures I buried. Most are not so very far from the Spanish Main."

"After three hundred years do you really think you'll find anything?"

Rafael shrugged his shoulders. "Maybe. Maybe not. But it will be exciting to search for treasure with you, *sirena mia*."

The girls who had been whispering as she'd awakened walked by, staring with bold admiration at Rafael. They didn't hiss in disgust this time, but smiled flirtatiously and giggled with their heads together after they'd passed.

Rafael watched their progress, eyebrows lifted in surprise.

"Eyes front," Sabrina said softly.

"Do you have one of those . . ." He waved a hand after the giggling teenagers.

"Bathing suits?"

"Ahhh," he said, pulling Sabrina into the sand. "Of course."

Sabrina flicked a grain of sand from Rafael's arm. "Let's do it."

He listed toward her and glanced warily at the sunbathers and romping children on the beach. "Excuse me?"

"Let's look for that treasure of yours. We may not find anything at all. . . ."

"Or we may unearth a fortune in gold and silver and gems."

Sabrina placed her hands against Rafael's cheeks, stared into dancing pale brown eyes. "I'll take whatever fate hands us, as long as I have you."

"*Sí, vida mía,*" Rafael whispered. "*Sí.*"

# *Epilogue*

It had taken just over a year to find the right
buyer, settle on the right price, and get to this
table. A few more minutes, and she would no
longer own Steele Corporation.

The business didn't feel like hers anymore,
anyway. Patrick had been running the company, and doing a good job. The new restaurants had opened on time, and the company
was making a nice profit.

Of course, after several months of keeping the
company going on his own, Patrick had been
rather shocked to find that Sabrina was alive,
and even more surprised that she had returned
with a husband.

"I understand you've bought a vineyard in
California."

Sabrina smiled at Hank Littlefield, the man
who was taking over the corporation and would

soon own every Annalina's restaurant. He reminded her a little of her father, but he smiled more often.

"Yes." She felt a little guilty for being so anxious to rid herself of her father's life's work, but that was exactly how she felt. Anxious. The cranberry suit she wore was uncomfortable. The shoes were too tight. The panty hose were ridiculous. Earlier, her hair had been pulled up into something resembling a sensible bun, but Rafael hadn't liked that at all, and it now fell naturally around her shoulders and down her back.

She looked over her shoulder to Rafael. He stood directly behind her, arms crossed over his chest, hair pulled back in a ponytail, diamond studs sparkling in his ears. Even in an expensive black suit, he looked like a pirate.

They'd sailed for months, and had found one of Rafael's buried treasures on a small island in the Caribbean. Everything else was gone, or else the landscape had changed so much he couldn't be sure they were digging in the right place. It didn't matter. They could live very well for a hundred years on what they'd unearthed.

It had been a year of adjustment for them both. Rafael was becoming accustomed to a world where everything had changed, and he had quickly developed intense likes and dislikes. Actually, he liked almost everything, but he hated Atlanta traffic (who didn't?) jeans that were too tight (but he looked damn good in them) and television (which was too loud and too *busy*).

In the past several months, Rafael had made a few necessary changes in his wardrobe and in his speech, but he still had that accent she loved, and he always looked like a pirate, no matter where they were or what he wore.

The diamond studs he wore in his ears, replacements for his gold loops, were a concession not to fashion, but to Tony's grasping fingers.

"Where is Antoñio?" Rafael leaned forward and whispered hoarsely in her ear as she signed the last of the necessary papers.

"Mary has him, and he's fine," she answered just as softly. "She's showing him off to all the employees, that's all."

She lifted her eyes and saw that Patrick had fastened his eyes on Rafael once again. Poor Patrick; he was terrified.

Sabrina passed the last of the papers to Littlefield, and he passed her a generous check.

"On to California," he said with a smile.

"Yes," she said.

"No," Rafael answered just a beat behind her.

Since he had barely said a word since the proceeding had begun, all eyes turned to him.

"Not yet," he qualified.

Before anyone could ask questions, Mary came in with Tony in her arms. He was a good baby, most of the time, but he was squirming and fussing, and Mary was ready to hand him over to his mother. She didn't get the chance. Rafael intercepted her and took the baby. Tony immediately quieted down, as he always did when Rafael held him and whispered to him in Spanish.

Sabrina turned a bright smile to Patrick, and then to Hank Littlefield. "Mr. Littlefield, do you have children?"

He returned her smile. "Yes. I have four daughters."

She glanced at Patrick again, to see that he had paled considerably.

"Are any of them interested in joining you in the business?"

He told her, briefly, about each of his four daughters. The eldest, who was married to an engineer and living in north Alabama. The youngest, a five-year-old who was many years younger than her sisters. And the twins, who were majoring in business at the University of Alabama, at the moment.

Sabrina glanced at Patrick briefly. He had kept the restaurants afloat without her for more than a year, but she couldn't forget what he'd done to her. What he'd tried to do.

"We've implemented a strict policy that does not allow dating among the employees," Patrick said quickly. "It's worked well, and I do hope you approve. It's been effective in stopping problems before they start."

The statement was for her benefit, she knew. A promise, a plea not to tell all at this point.

Rafael stepped quietly from behind her and circled around the table so that he stood behind Hank Littlefield. Tony was cradled easily in his arms, content, almost but not quite asleep. After a quick glance at the baby, Rafael stared across the table to Patrick.

"A man's children are his most precious treasure," he said.

Littlefield craned his neck to look up at Rafael. "That's very true."

"As one father to another," Rafael said seriously, "I would suggest that you keep your daughters away from this man." He nodded almost imperceptibly, and Patrick squirmed.

*"Sirena mia,"* he said with a smile as he turned his attention to her, "are you finished here?"

With that Rafael led her from the office, and into a deserted hallway.

"What's Littlefield going to think?" she whispered.

"They will work it out," he said nonchalantly, handing Tony to her without breaking his stride. "I might have stayed longer, to explain that I would have cut your Patrick's heart out months ago if you had allowed it, but I am too eager to get away from this place. There are too many people and too many buildings and too many cars in Atlanta."

Tony cuddled against her chest, opened and closed a small fist, and was immediately fast asleep. "Where are we going, by the way, if we're not going to California? The vineyard's just sitting there waiting for us."

He shrugged, as if it didn't matter at all.

"In a few months, it will still be sitting there waiting for us," he said calmly.

371

"Rafael!" she stopped suddenly, and he turned to face her with a smile.

"Scuba diving," he said softly. "I saw this program on television . . ."

"You hate television," she interrupted.

"*Sí.* But it helps Antoñio sleep at three in the morning," he explained.

Sabrina had to smile. How many new mothers had a husband who not only helped with the baby, but insisted on sitting up in those early morning hours?

"All right," she conceded as Rafael backed her against the wall. He kissed her lightly, and Tony was cushioned between their bodies. "Scuba diving."

"In 1659," he whispered, "there was a storm almost as strong as the one that carried us here. Three ships were lost, three vessels of the *flota* that were returning to Spain heavy with gold."

"And you want to look for them?"

"Yes," he whispered, adding another soft kiss.

"It's been over three hundred years," she protested lightly. "The ships might have been recovered already, and surely they've shifted. The odds . . ."

He silenced her with another kiss, and she forgot all her other arguments.

Who was she to talk of odds and impossibilities?

"All right," she whispered against Rafael's lips. "I guess California and our vineyard will be waiting when we've finished searching for treasure."

If they ever finished. Rafael grinned, and she couldn't help but return his smile. He might someday be a farmer, but he would always be a pirate at heart.

**Read on for a preview**

**of Linda Jones's newest**

**Faerie Tale Romance,**

**coming in October 1998**

**from Love Spell!**

# Cinderfella

by
Linda Jones

# Prologue

*Kansas, 1895*

It wasn't just a ranch; it was an empire. It wasn't just land; it was his kingdom.

Stuart Haley shoved his hands in his pockets and squinted against the golden radiance that poured through the window. The setting sun shone on this fine house, lit the study that was his domain in this, his castle.

What would come of his empire when he was gone? Felicity, the eldest and most practical of his three daughters, was firmly settled in Boston with that physician husband of hers and a little girl of her own. Jeanette, who had been flighty all her life, was now content to make a home in Philadelphia with her husband, a lawyer for God's sake. They had their own lives, families of their own. Neither of his older

377

daughters had any concern for their childhood home.

He never should've allowed them to go East. Maureen had been so insistent on seeing her daughters properly educated, and one after another his girls had left home for a so-called better life. Hogwash! He should've insisted that *one* of them stay here and marry a local boy who would become the son he'd never had, but he'd never had the heart to deny Maureen anything.

Charmaine was his only hope. If he was to see this kingdom passed on to his own blood, it would be through her. His youngest daughter was his *last chance* to save this empire.

"Where are your thoughts, Stuart?"

Maureen's soft question wiped the frown from his face, and when he turned to see her standing in the doorway of his study, his heart beat a little faster. She was nearly forty-five years old; he was just past forty-eight. They'd been married twenty seven years—and the sight of her still took his breath away.

"I was just thinking about Charmaine. She'll be here in three days."

Maureen's smile was brilliant. If anything, she was more beautiful today than she'd been at seventeen, when he'd met her and fallen instantly in love. Her hair was no longer a pale blond, but a light brown streaked with touches of gray. Her body had matured, with the birth of three children and the passing years, but she was slender and graceful as ever. "I'm excited, too."

He'd never uttered a word of displeasure to

378

Maureen about not having sons. He'd rather have her than a dozen sons to follow in his footsteps. The girls had come not much more than a year apart, each more beautiful than the last, and then—nothing. Not because they hadn't tried. The doctor had no answers, and Maureen had finally accepted her inability to have more children as the will of God. It had rarely been mentioned in the past fifteen years.

"Maybe she'll decide to stay," he said hopefully.

Maureen crossed the room, sliding gracefully across the thick carpet and stepping past his polished walnut desk until she stood beside him. She slipped a slender arm around his waist and leaned against his side. "She might not, you know," she said softly. "This is just a visit, and she only agreed because your letters have been so insistent. She'd just as soon wait to see us when we can make the trip to Boston."

"She does like the city, doesn't she?"

Maureen nodded. "Remember her last letter? It was three pages long and exclusively about that masked ball she attended. Felicity and Howard evidently thought it much too foolhardy, but Charmaine had a grand time."

Charmaine was his only hope. Somehow he had to convince her that there was nothing in Boston that she couldn't have in Salley Creek. "We could throw a masked ball right here."

Maureen laughed lightly. "Here? Why, there's never been such a thing in Salley Creek."

"There's got to be a first time for everything." He would show Charmaine that Salley Creek

379

could be just as exciting as Boston. There would be music, food, people from miles around. Men, lots of good, solid Kansans who would be happy to marry into the Haley family.

"I don't know . . ."

"Let's do it." It was the perfect solution, and his mind was made up. "Why, Charmaine might even meet a man who can convince her to stay here where she belongs."

"Stuart!" Maureen stepped away from him and stared up with shock into those big blue eyes of hers. "You're not thinking . . ."

He couldn't stop the grin that spread across his face.

"You *are*!"

"And why not?" He pulled her back into his embrace.

"If I put out the word that I'm looking for a husband for Charmaine, every eligible man for a hundred miles will be here. There's bound to be *one*—"

"Stuart!"

"—one man who can convince Charmaine to stay here where she belongs." It was a chance he had to take. "Dammit, Maureen, what have I worked for all my life, if not for my family? What's going to become of this place when we're gone?"

Her blue eyes softened. "I should have given you a son."

He placed a finger over Maureen's lips to gently silence her. "You know I wouldn't trade any one of my girls for a son. I have no regrets about my life, and goodness knows there's nothing

380

like having four beautiful women in the house to keep a man on his toes."

His finger slid away, and he bent to kiss her. Her lips were welcoming, tender and anxious. She pulled her mouth away from his, but continued to hold on tight.

"Don't get your hopes up about Charmaine staying. She's been away eight years, and not once in her letters or during our visits east has she expressed a desire to come back to Kansas to live. She's building a new life for herself in Boston, with the help of Felicity and Howard."

"You don't know," he began, turning with Maureen in his arms and heading for the door, "that there's nothing and no one who can convince her to stay. We'll have that masked ball, and just see what happens."

"But Stuart," Maureen protested weakly.

"We'll talk about it later," he said, propelling her toward the stairs to their bedroom.

# Chapter One

Odd, this flutter in her chest could only be called excitement. She hadn't expected it at all, but the closer the train came to Salley Creek the more decidedly eager Charmaine felt.

"Isn't it beautiful?" she breathed, turning from the window to her traveling companion.

Ruth looked less than impressed, but the poor girl had been sour since their departure from Boston, even though Felicity had promised a nice bonus for this service that was above and beyond that of ladies' maid. Charmaine would have been quite content to travel alone, but Howard would have none of that, so Charmaine found herself saddled with this young and inexperienced woman who evidently didn't like her job *or* traveling.

Ruth glanced beyond Charmaine's shoulder, as if perhaps she'd missed something in her earlier perusal of the landscape. "It's lovely, in its own simple way," she said tactfully.

Lovely. Charmaine ignored the hint of doubt in Ruth's voice. Green, rolling hills as far as she could see, the tall grasses swaying in the wind. Sunshine touching it all with a gentle golden light. Sky so wide and so bright a blue it nearly hurt her eyes to look at it. It was lovely, and she hadn't missed it until this very moment.

Her homecoming was spoiled by the certainty of her father's plans. Yes, she knew exactly what he wanted, what he *expected* of her. He tried to be subtle, the poor dear, but it simply wasn't in his nature. A few loudly mumbled sentences on his last visit to Boston, terse lines scribbled at the bottom of her mother's letters—his intentions were quite clear. He wanted her to come home and stay, marry a man who would follow in his footsteps, and have a baby every year until the Haley land—all 720 acres—was bursting with them.

How could she make her father see that she was a modern woman, with ideas and plans of her own? She would forever be the baby in his eyes, she feared, and he would never approve of her plan to live in Boston and assist Howard by giving lectures and distributing manuals to educate women. Charmaine was certain she was meant for greater things than domesticity, and working with Howard gave her such a sense of purpose. Still, Stuart Haley would never understand why one of his daughters might choose never to marry.

They were almost there. She could see the

buildings at the edge of Salley Creek. Goodness, it had grown in eight years, but it was still such a small town. The buildings were rough and low, with only one rising above two stories. The entire tiny town was dusty and crude, in a charming way, and utterly isolated. How could she convince her father that she could never be happy here, except for the occasional visit?

Charmaine nervously smoothed the skirt of her blue serge traveling suit. Why, she just wouldn't mention it. When he brought up the subject she would be vague and pretend not to understand. She could do that, couldn't she? Pretend not to understand and keep her opinions to herself. Keeping her opinions to herself had never been her strong suit, but in this case she would make the effort. And when her father gave up, as he surely would, she would visit and rest, spend time with her mother, and see old friends.

In spite of her nervousness, she smiled widely. Eula was still in Salley Creek, married to the owner of the mercantile and the mother of two. Delia was teaching school now, unmarried and living with her brother, since their folks had given up the farm and moved back to St. Louis. Those were the only two she was sure of. So many of her old chums had moved on, searching, as she was herself, for a better life.

Ash Coleman was still there, she was sure, even though her mother never mentioned him in her letters. Maureen Haley had never approved of her youngest daughter's childish infatuation with the son of the farmer whose land

384

adjoined theirs to the west, and Charmaine remembered still that the very idea had made her father livid.

He was firmly planted in her mind, an indelible part of her memories, but in the past few years the clarity of his features had faded from her. Sometimes, for a fleeting moment, he would be there so clearly, and then he was gone. Ash had been beautiful at seventeen, when she'd last seen him, and all her life the sight of him had made her heart beat a little faster. She'd even declared—to Felicity and Jeanette more than once and on one mortifying occasion to Ash himself—that one day she was going to marry him.

Goodness, why was she wasting her thoughts on such childish memories? Ash Coleman was probably already married and raising a brood on his father's farm. After all, he was twenty-five years old.

They were slowing down, approaching the station at last. Charmaine fluffed the oversized bow at her throat and checked her fashionably small felt hat to see that it was seated properly. She couldn't believe that she was so excited about a two-week visit in a town where nothing ever happened. There would be no seminars, no heated discussions of the latest manuals over coffee and cake, no theater, no concerts. Why, if she were to discuss the latest thoughts on women's rights she would likely shock all of Salley Creek. If she were to discuss the latest findings on the more intimate aspects of marital relations she'd likely be run out of town on a rail. This was, after all, a sleepy town where nothing ever happened and time stood still while the rest of the world marched forward.

Oh well, in her heart it would always be home. And it was, after all, just for two weeks.

She saw her father's head towering above the rest as she stepped down to the platform. He was wearing a great smile, a grin that deepened the wrinkles on his weathered face. Less than a minute later she was lifted from her feet for a great bear hug.

"I can't believe you're finally home," he said as he set Charmaine on her feet.

It sounded so permanent, *finally home,* but she wouldn't argue with him now and ruin this homecoming. Her mother's hug was gentler, but no less loving.

After introducing Ruth and making arrangements for the luggage to be delivered, they all walked from the depot to the house. Charmaine was positioned comfortably and closely between her parents.

"You're too durn skinny," her father said as he slipped his arm over her shoulder.

"She is not," her mother said with a despairing sigh. "She's perfectly lovely and looks very grown up."

Charmaine didn't correct her father with the admission that she was far from skinny, nor did she tell her mother that at twenty-one she *was* grown-up. She was too busy looking past her parents to the bustling town that was familiar and at the same time very unfamiliar. There were two mercantiles *and* a feed store, and with customers coming and going they all seemed to flourish. The bank had doubled in size, and there was a restaurant right next door. The post office now had its own building, leaving the funeral parlor the lone occupant of the building they had once shared.

The boarding house, the single three-story building in town, had expanded and was freshly painted. Right next door to the boarding house was a small pharmacy, and there was a sign in the window advertising ice cream. At the end of the street stood the newly built stone schoolhouse, which had recently replaced the log cabin where the children of Salley Creek had attended school for thirty years.

There were lots of people out and about, most of them strangers to Charmaine. Some of the faces that turned her way were vaguely familiar, but names eluded her. Eight years hadn't seemed like such a long time until this very moment.

Ruth was evidently unimpressed. She kept her eyes on the boardwalk and followed silently.

Memories flooded Charmaine as she walked down the boardwalk, sandwiched between her parents, who were chattering happily: The move from the original ranch cabin to the big house at the edge of town, when she was six years old. That crotchety old schoolmaster Mr. Warren. Her first heartbreak at the age of ten, when Zachary Middleton had told her he didn't play with girls. She could almost taste the lemon drops her father had always bought for her when he purchased his tobacco from the mercantile.

She remembered Ash Coleman laughing at her when she declared she was going to marry him one day, and how well she remembered watching him ride away with his father, laughing still, a man at sixteen while she was still a puny and unformed twelve.

He'd called her Runt, then, after hearing Jeanette use that dreaded nickname once as they left church. It had always been the bane of Charmaine's existence that she wasn't tall and willowy like her sisters. She'd always been short, and though she'd been a late bloomer her breasts and hips had rounded quickly. Even now, she wished for a leaner and taller frame, a more austere silhouette. There were some people who simply refused to take you seriously if you were short and rounded in the wrong places.

A squeal that was uncannily familiar after all these years made Charmaine stop in her tracks. She whirled around in time to catch the woman who hurled herself forward.

"I can't believe you're really here!" Eula said as she squeezed once and then stepped back, her hands resting comfortably on Charmaine's arms.

The voice hadn't changed, but Charmaine was sure she wouldn't have recognized Eula if she'd passed her on a Boston street. Not only was the dark-haired woman considerably taller than she'd been at thirteen, she'd put on several pounds with each of the two children she'd given birth to, a fact she'd complained about in her frequent letters. Charmaine, to her dismay, had barely grown an inch in height since leaving Salley Creek. She stood a mere five feet, one inch tall, if she stood as straight as possible. She had to look up into Eula's face.

"Neither can I. Can you come home with me now? Talk to me while I settle in? We have so much to catch up on." A visit with Eula would also postpone the inevitable confrontation with her father.

Eula shook her head quickly. "I can't. This is a busy time of the day for us. The only reason Winston allowed me to run out here and greet you is so I can give a message to Mrs. Haley."

Eula straighted her spine and turned to face Charmaine's mother. "Winston is certain he can have those supplies for you in two weeks, and Mrs. O'Neal is going to help me with the masks."

"Two weeks?" Maureen Haley repeated, obviously disappointed.

"Masks?" Charmaine looked to her mother for an answer.

"Two weeks, ma'am, and that's paying extra freight costs for the materials that are coming in from San Francisco."

Maureen Haley had always been unfailingly practical, and she was calm now. "That doesn't leave us much time for preparation, does it? Oh well, we'll just have the party in three weeks."

"Party?"

Eula turned her smiling face back to Charmaine. "Why, everyone's so excited they're about to bust. Just think of it, a masked ball right here in Salley Creek. I've already started working on my gown."

"I'm supposed to return to Boston in two weeks." Charmaine directed this statement to her mother, who continued to smile serenely.

"Another week or two won't make all that much difference, now will it?" she replied.

"Not a bit," Stuart Haley thundered.

Charmaine rolled her eyes at her father's hearty and much too jolly interruption. Fortunately, no one saw but Eula, and her only reaction was a slight lifting of dark eyebrows.

"There's nothing in Boston," he declared with finality, "that won't still be there in a month or two."

Charmaine sighed. Her two weeks had already turned to a month or two?

Eula hurried back to the mercantile and her husband, Winston, and Charmaine was physically turned about with her father's big hands on her shoulders.

The air that drifted through the open window was cool, almost cold, but Ash didn't make a move to close it. Fall was a busy time of the year for him, but he always enjoyed it while it lasted. Winter was close behind, and that meant bouts of snow and ice, and wind that was truly cold.

In the moonlight, the farm was peaceful. The barnyard was quiet, the fields beyond perfection in the soft light of the moon. In the house all was quiet as well. No one stirred but him. He was the restless one, the one who roamed the house or stood at an open window long after dark.

He heard it, a soft peal that carried on the wind. Midnight struck on the Salley Creek clock that old Randall Salley had erected before his death. It was his gift to the town, he'd said, a monster of a clock that sounded each hour of the day. Ash couldn't always hear the chimes, but when the air and the wind were right the sound carried to his window like a soft and plaintive cry in the night.

The peal of midnight reminded him that another day had begun, another day that promised to be just like the one that had passed.

He closed the window softly.

She'd been home five days, and already she was beginning to feel like the child her parents treated her as. They refused to accept that she was no longer thirteen, that she had thoughts and plans of her own.

There wasn't a single ally in this house, not even the one person who shared her predicament. Ruth was quite unhappy with the change of plans. An extended visit to Salley Creek, Kansas, was not on her agenda, but like Charmaine she saw no way out of the predicament. Instead of joining forces and commiserating, Ruth preferred to take her frustration out on Charmaine.

The evening meals were becoming a tedious routine. Her father went on and on about how wonderfully the ranch was doing, and how great some man or another was, and how splendid it was to have his baby home.

After the first three nights, she'd quit trying to tell him that she was *not* his baby anymore.

She wanted to go home. Home to Boston. It wasn't just her father who had her distressed. Eula, her oldest and dearest friend, was so changed. She had become everything Charmaine had preached against in the past two years. How could poor Eula be truly happy? She was a virtual slave to her husband's whims, working in his store, keeping his house, bearing and raising his children. And yet she seemed to be happy, poor thing.

Charmaine had at first had such hope for Delia. She was a schoolteacher, a dedicated professional, an independent woman . . . but a brief visit had quickly revealed that Delia had but one desire in life: to find a man, get married, and settle down into the same drudgery Eula groveled in.

It had been Eula who'd shared the news about Ash Coleman, remembering that Charmaine had once been smitten. John Coleman, Ash's father, had passed on last year, and Ash was sharing the ranch with his stepmother—a woman Charmaine had never met or heard about—and two stepbrothers.

It occurred to Charmaine, then and now, that she really should stop by the Coleman farm to pay her respects to Ash and perhaps meet the rest of the family. That would be, certainly, the civilized and proper thing to do.

Her father was going on again, as he speared a large chunk of beef, about the plans for the masked ball. He really seemed to think that if he threw a party she would stay. Goodness, he didn't understand her at all.

"Stuart, you should see the dress we're making for Charmaine," her mother said between delicate bites of beef. "It's the most gorgeous creation, snow white with just a touch of peach in the bodice and skirt ornamentation. Seed pearls are sewn into the neckline and into a floral motif on the full skirt."

Her father winked at her and smiled widely. "Sounds like a wedding dress to me."

Charmaine took her napkin from her lap and placed it, slowly and gently, on the table by her plate. She couldn't go on this way, not for another two weeks. Her father had to understand who she was and what she wanted. Now was as good a time as any to get this over with.

"I've made a very important decision recently." Charmaine's voice was low and composed, but the calm was all an act. Her heart pounded, and her palms began to sweat. "I do hope you'll understand and support me." She straightened her spine and took a deep breath before continuing. "I'll probably never marry."

"What?" her father leaned forward, head tilted to bring one ear closer to this unthinkable statement.

If she explained, surely he would understand. "Women are meant for more than breeding and submission to a man's pleasure, and what other reasons—"

"Charmaine Haley!" Her father shot to his feet, and his face turned an alarming shade of red.

"Now, now." Maureen Haley patted the hand her husband had placed on the table and now leaned against. "I'm sure Charmaine didn't mean what she said." A censuring look that was surely meant to convey an order to agree shot between Charmaine and her mother.

"I *did* mean what I said," Charmaine insisted gently. "There's an entire world outside Salley Creek, and it's growing and changing every day. There's more to life for an educated woman than a sorry existence of emotional servitude and physical subservience."

Stuart Haley narrowed his eyes as if he couldn't believe this was his daughter he was looking at. "Howard filled your head with this nonsense, didn't he, that puny little pompous ass."

"Now, Stuart—"

Charmaine interrupted her mother. "Howard is an intelligent and well-respected physician, your son-in-law and the father of your grand-daughter. I think it's inappropriate for you to call him a pompous ass."

"What has he done to you?" With a sigh, her father took his seat.

If only she could make him see that what she was doing was important, necessary, and *right*, she could enjoy her visit here and then return home to Boston with a clear conscience. And perhaps in the future they could avoid these awkward moments. "I've assisted him in several seminars, distributed educational manuals, and spoken with those women who were uncomfortable discussing personal matters with a man, even one who is a physician."

"Personal matters?" he asked, as if he didn't really want to know. "Personal matters such as what?"

"Marital continence, for one." She tried not to blush, but this was, after all, her father. "Contraception, if the more desirable self-restraint is impossible. The unhealthy influence of the bicycle and romantic novels on young women, for another. Then there's the physical detriment from the corset, and the—"

"Marital continence?" he repeated in a monotone. "Does that mean what I think it means?"

"Of course. Healthy marriages don't depend on a physical relationship." She forgot, for a moment, that these were her parents. "Once a married couple has all the children they desire, abstinence is the healthiest course of action for everyone involved. The myth that the marital embrace is necessary—"

"Maureen, make her stop."

Charmaine bit her lower lip as she studied her father's unnaturally pale face. "I didn't mean to embarrass you, Daddy."

His shock gave way to anger. She could see it, as the color came back to his face all at once and his jaw hardened and his gray eyes glinted like steel. She could see it, as the hands that had been flat on the tablecloth slowly balled into fists.

"Boston!" he spat. "I never should have sent you there, and you're not going back!"

"Daddy!" Charmaine shot to her feet as her

395

father did. They stood at opposite ends of the long table, facing one another defiantly. "You can't—"

"This discussion is over," he said as he turned away. "I think I'll skip desert tonight, Maureen. I've lost my appetite."

After her father stormed from the room, Charmaine slowly and gracefully took her seat. He'd change his mind, in a day or two. After all, she was twenty-one years old, and he couldn't force her to stay here. He couldn't keep her prisoner.

"Well, Charmaine." The slightly edgy voice reminded Charmaine that she was not alone. Of course, her mother would understand. Her mother wouldn't force her stay here when the time came to leave. "That was a scene I could have done without."

It *had* turned rather ugly, there at the end. Charmaine hadn't meant to embarrass her father, not really; she'd just said what was on her mind as she usually did. If he would simply accept the fact that she was a grown woman and treat her as such, they wouldn't have a problem at all.

"I did think Daddy was more open-minded than this," she declared sensibly.

"And whatever gave you that idea?"

There was a sharpness Charmaine had never heard in Maureen Haley's voice, and she realized again that she had not a single ally in this house. Not even her own mother.

# NO ANGEL'S GRACE

## LINDA WINSTEAD

From the moment Dillon feasts his eyes on the raven-haired beauty, Grace Cavanaugh, he knows she is trouble. Sharp-tongued and stubborn, with a flawless complexion and a priceless wardrobe, Grace certainly doesn't belong on a Western ranch. But that's what Dillon calls home, and as long as the lovely orphan is his charge, that's where they'll stay.

But Grace Cavanaugh has learned the hard way that men can't be trusted. Not for all the diamonds and rubies in England will she give herself to any man. But when Dillon walks into her life he changes all the rules. Suddenly the unapproachable ice princess finds herself melting at his simplest touch, and wondering what she'll have to do to convince him that their love is the most precious gem of all.

_4223-1                                              $5.50 US/$6.50 CAN

Dorchester Publishing Co., Inc.
P.O. Box 6640
Wayne, PA 19087-8640

Please add $1.75 for shipping and handling for the first book and $.50 for each book thereafter. NY, NYC, and PA residents, please add appropriate sales tax. No cash, stamps, or C.O.D.s. All orders shipped within 6 weeks via postal service book rate. Canadian orders require $2.00 extra postage and must be paid in U.S. dollars through a U.S. banking facility.

Name_____
Address_____
City_____ State_____ Zip_____
I have enclosed $_____ in payment for the checked book(s).
Payment **must** accompany all orders. ☐ Please send a free catalog.

Someone's Been Sleeping In My Bed

A Faerie Tale Romance

Linda Jones

**WHO'S BEEN EATING FROM MY BOWL?
IS SHE A BEAUTY IN BOTH HEART AND
    SOUL?
WHO'S BEEN SITTING IN MY CHAIR?
IS SHE PRETTY OF FACE AND FAIR OF
    HAIR?
WHO'S BEEN SLEEPING IN MY BED?
IS SHE THE DAMSEL I WILL WED?**

The golden-haired woman barely escapes from a
stagecoach robbery before she gets lost in the Wyoming
mountains. Hungry, harried, and out of hope, she stumbles
on a rude cabin, the home of three brothers, great bears of
men who nearly frighten her out of her wits. But Maddalyn
Kelly is no Goldilocks; she is a feisty beauty who can fend
for herself. Still, how can she ever guess that the Barrett
boys will bare their souls to her—or that one of them will share
with her an ecstasy so exquisite it is almost unbearable?

\_52094-X                    $5.99 US/$6.99 CAN

Dorchester Publishing Co., Inc.
P.O. Box 6640
Wayne, PA 19087-8640

Please add $1.75 for shipping and handling for the first book and
$.50 for each book thereafter. NY, NYC, and PA residents,
please add appropriate sales tax. No cash, stamps, or C.O.D.s. All
orders shipped within 6 weeks via postal service book rate.
Canadian orders require $2.00 extra postage and must be paid in
U.S. dollars through a U.S. banking facility.

Name_____
Address_____
City_____State_____Zip_____
I have enclosed $_____ in payment for the checked book(s).
Payment <u>must</u> accompany all orders. ❑ Please send a free catalog.

## *Christmas Spirit*

### ELAINE FOX
### LEIGH GREENWOOD
### LINDA WINSTEAD

## *Three Heartwarming Tales of Romance and Holiday Cheer*

*Bah Humbug!* by Leigh Greenwood. Nate wants to go somewhere hot, but when his neighbor offers holiday cheer, their passion makes the tropics look like the arctic.

*Christmas Present* by Elaine Fox. When Susannah returns home, a late-night savior teaches her the secret to happiness. But is this fate, or something more wonderful?

*Blue Christmas* by Linda Winstead. Jess doesn't date musicians, especially handsome, up-and-coming ones. But she has a ghost of a chance to realize that Jimmy Blue is a heavenly gift.

___4320-3                    $5.50 US/$6.50 CAN

**Dorchester Publishing Co., Inc.**
**P.O. Box 6640**
**Wayne, PA 19087-8640**

Please add $1.75 for shipping and handling for the first book and $.50 for each book thereafter. NY, NYC, and PA residents, please add appropriate sales tax. No cash, stamps, or C.O.D.s. All orders shipped within 6 weeks via postal service book rate. Canadian orders require $2.00 extra postage and must be paid in U.S. dollars through a U.S. banking facility.

Name_____
Address_____
City_____ State_____ Zip_____
I have enclosed $_____ in payment for the checked book(s).
Payment <u>must</u> accompany all orders. ❏ Please send a free catalog.

# ATTENTION ROMANCE CUSTOMERS!

## SPECIAL TOLL-FREE NUMBER
### 1-800-481-9191

*Call Monday through Friday*
*12 noon to 10 p.m.*
**Eastern Time**
*Get a free catalogue,*
*join the Romance Book Club,*
*and order books using your*
*Visa, MasterCard,*
*or Discover®*

Leisure
Books